Cowboy Passion

Bakersville Saga Five and Six

Helen Hardt

Cowboy Passion
Second Edition
This book is an original publication of Helen Hardt

This is a work of fiction. Names, characters, places, and incidents either are the product of the author's imagination or are used fictitiously, and any resemblance to actual persons, living or dead, business establishments, events, or locales is entirely coincidental. The publisher does not assume any responsibility for third-party websites or their content.
First edition published by Musa Publishing, 2015
Copyright © 2015 Helen Hardt, LLC
Cover Design by Kelly Shorten
kmdwebdesigns.com

All Rights Reserved
No part of this book may be reproduced, scanned, or distributed in any printed or electronic format without permission. Please do not participate in or encourage piracy of copyrighted materials in violation of the author's rights. Purchase only authorized editions.

Paperback ISBN:9780990746157
PRINTED IN THE UNITED STATES OF AMERICA

Warning

This e-book contains adult language and scenes. This story is meant only for adults as defined by the laws of the country where you made your purchase. Store your e-books carefully where they cannot be accessed by younger readers.

Praise for *Cowboy Passion*

Yeeeehaw! Helen brings it, AGAIN! Two great stories wrapped in one great book. Helen brings love, passion and the element of danger to each of her stories. There is a depth to each story that makes you want to keep turning the pages and dig deeper into these characters.
~*Delightfully Dirty Reads*

I love this installment of the Cowboy series. Helen is a wonderful writer, and I read all six parts with bated breath, waiting to see what was happening next each time. You should ride this roller coaster with tissues. Trust me.
~*Brenda's Book Beat*

Praise for Helen Hardt

Flawlessly written and in my opinion a work of art...
~*Girly Girl Book Reviews*

Is it hot in here? I mean it's July, the sun is blazing, but I'm sitting in an air conditioned house sweating bullets. Congratulations Ms. Hardt, you dropped me into the middle of a scorching hot story and let me burn.
~*Seriously Reviewed*

Ms. Hardt has a way of writing that makes me forget I'm reading a book. It's more like slipping into a world she created and getting lost for a while.
~*Whipped Cream Reviews*

I loved this book. The characters were wonderful. They each showed their vulnerable sides as well as their strengths. They are real people and have real problems but also some very loving solutions...
~*Night Owl Reviews*

Ms. Hardt creates magic...
~*The Romance Studio*

Helen Hardt writes as smooth as a hot knife cutting through butter. Her words take you away and you feel like you are watching the story play out right in front of you.
~*Delightfully Dirty Reads*

Treasuring Amber

Bakersville Saga Five

by

Helen Hardt

In memory of my grandmother, Theresa Zeuch Freitag

Chapter One

"You want me to come to a baby shower? Are you kiddin' me?" Harper Bay paced the length of his father's—now *his*—office in his mother's—now *his*—ranch house.

His little sister's sigh cut right through the phone. "Couples showers are the new thing now, Harp. Amber says—"

"Sheesh, Catie." Harper Bay rolled his eyes, thankful his sister couldn't see him through the phone. He was damn sick of hearing what Amber Cross had to say. That bleached blond manicurist who had become Catie's new soul sister spouted off all kinds of newfangled ideas, and he didn't like a one of them. "Dallas and Annie just had the twins a month ago, and none of us guys had to go to a shower. And you forget one important little detail."

"What's that?"

"Last time I checked, I'm not a 'couple.'"

"Co-ed shower, then. We're talking semantics here." Catie's tone softened. "Don't you want to welcome little Violet?"

How in hell does she do that? Her petal-soft voice never failed to make him wilt. He was a sucker for his baby sister, and he'd be just as much of a sucker for his new niece. Violet was a beauty even at a week old, with a mop of black hair and eyes the darkest sapphire blue. They'd probably turn big and brown like Catie's. She'd be a heartbreaker for sure.

But a baby shower? He was a man, for God's sake. A damned cowboy. Cowboys did not go to baby showers. That had to be in a rulebook somewhere.

He shook his head. "What's Chad think of this nonsense?"

"Chad says 'whatever makes me happy.'"

Christ.

Whipped.

Harper had known Chad McCray most of his life. A bigger womanizer hadn't existed on the planet…until Catie reeled him in. Now Chad was the epitome of whipped. His face was probably next to "whipped" in the damned dictionary. Harper couldn't prevent a chuckle.

"What are you laughing at?" Catie demanded.

Why not be honest? "Just your whipped hubby, that's all."

"For your information, Chad is *not* whipped."

"Give me a break, Catie-bug. You have the cowboy wrapped around your little finger, and it won't be long till that pretty little daughter of yours has him twisted around hers, too."

Catie's soft laugh gave her away. She knew her husband was whipped. Heck, she was whipped, too. Those two were crazy about each other. Crazy in a way his and Catie's parents had never been. Crazy in a way Harper had never been and probably never would be. He had a ranch to run now. When his father passed away several months ago, Harper had become sole owner of Cha Cha Ranch outside of Bakersville, Colorado. His mother, who'd inherited the ranch when Harper was a boy and transferred it to her husband, still lived in the big ranch house and would for as long as she wished. His uncle, Jefferson Bay, also lived there. Jeff had been estranged from the family for the last three decades, and they were slowly—very slowly—rebuilding their relationship.

Nope, no "whipped" for Harper. He had too much to do. Too many responsibilities. He wasn't sure when he'd last had a date.

How long had it been since he'd had sex? Too damn long. Had they changed it?

"Harp?"

Reality. Catie. Sometimes the magnitude of owning a whole beef ranch overwhelmed him. "Sorry, just thinking." He sat down in his father's—*his*—chair. "I really think I'll pass on the shower thing, Sis."

"Please? Rafe is coming with Angie. They're coming in from the western slope just to attend."

"They haven't seen Violet yet. They're coming to see her, not for the shower."

"So they'll kill two birds with one stone."

"I suppose they will. I, however, have already seen my beautiful niece, and I plan to see her a lot. Just not during some girly shower."

"It's not going to be a girly shower."

"Oh yeah? You getting a stripper?"

Another sigh from Catie. "Geez, Harp."

"Sorry." Though he wouldn't mind seeing Amber Cross strut her stuff naked. Damn, she had the body of a stripper. Lithe long legs curled around a silver pole, platinum locks falling over rosy-skinned shoulders...pink nipples peeking through...

His groin tightened.

Christ. His body betrayed him. Amber was so not his type. Though she was a Texas native and the reigning Bakersville Rodeo Queen, she was about as far from the girls Harper had grown up with as Maine was from California. Cute Colorado farm girl? *Hell, no.* Nearly white tresses, long red fingernails, leather miniskirts, and sequined tube tops...

Damn, the woman was hot.

Hot, and a major pain in the ass with her couples shower. She'd had Catie doing all kinds of weird crap in the last year. Thursday night happy hour at The Bullfrog had become a tradition for his baby sister. She never missed it, even when she'd been big as a house with Violet. Virgin drinks, yes, but still out on the dance floor shakin' her booty with her new BFF.

He couldn't believe Chad allowed it. Heck, of course he did. The man was so whipped.

"So are you coming or not?"

"You know I love you and I love Violet." He sighed. "But no. I'm sorry."

"Have it your way, then. Everybody else in town will be here."

"Tell everybody else I said hi."

"Fine." Her voice cracked. "Goodbye." Catie's phone clicked.

He didn't want to hurt her, but a baby shower? Sorry, this cowboy wasn't turning in his man card.

* * * *

"Hey, Tom, give me a Fat Tire."

"Comin' up." Tom Grayhawk, the bartender, smiled. "What's eatin' at you tonight?"

"Nothin'." Harper turned and looked toward the door. "Oh crap."

"Now what?"

"Here comes that damn Amber."

Tom chuckled. "Damn Amber? She's a luscious thing in my book."

"Hot as hell," Harper agreed, "but not my type."

"Hot as hell isn't your type?" Tom slid a bottle of beer across the wooden counter.

"This particular girl is definitely not my type. Do you know she wants me to—"

"Harper Bay."

Amber's voice was low and sultry, like the smoky aroma of aged bourbon. She slid onto the bar stool next to Harper and crossed her long tan legs. The woman was always a light bronze, even now, in springtime. Had to be fake. Her denim miniskirt hardly covered her thighs as she sat. Harper tried not to stare.

"What'll it be, beautiful?" Tom asked.

"Like you have to ask?" Her long brown eyelashes batted at Tom.

Harper's jeans seemed tight. He wiggled uneasily on his stool.

"One cosmo comin' up," Tom said.

"So," Amber said.

Harper cleared his throat. "So what?"

"You've got your little sister in a dither over this shower thing. She can't stand the thought of you not being there."

He let out a huff. "She'll get used to it. Men don't belong at baby showers. Why didn't she have the shower months ago, anyway? Before Violet was born?"

"'Cause she and Chad didn't want to know the sex. They wanted to be surprised in the delivery room. So I advised—"

"You advised? Another one of your cockamamie ideas?"

She shook her head and rolled her eyes. Totally blowing him off. Why did that irk him so much?

"I advised her to wait till the baby was born so people could bring gender appropriate gifts. It made perfect sense to Catie. Who wants a bunch of yellow and green baby clothes?"

"Yellow and green?"

"Yes, yellow and green. No one buys blue or pink when they don't know the sex. Everyone knows that."

He smirked. "Pardon me. I missed the lecture on baby shower purchasing etiquette."

Amber pursed her lips. "Was that supposed to be funny?"

"Hardly. None of this is funny from where I'm standin'. I am not going to a baby shower. Case closed."

Tom set the cosmo in front of Amber. "Simmer down, Harp. I'm going. It'll be a great party."

"Am I truly the only guy left in this town who thinks this is an atrocity?"

"I didn't say that, but the baby is your niece. She's my brother's niece. So I'm going to pay my respects. Besides, Chad McCray throws a great party."

"See?" Amber said. "Tom knows what he's talking about. You've really upset Catie. Besides, couples showers aren't anything new. They're all the rage in Texas."

"Well, we certainly want to do everything the way they do in Texas." Harper shook his head. "But last time I checked, I'm not a couple."

"Neither am I," Tom said, "but I'm going. I'm tagging along with my dad and Lilia."

"I'm not a couple either," Amber said. "So what?"

Tom curved his lips upward in a lopsided smile.

Shit. He's up to no good.

"Why don't you two go together?"

Good God in heaven.

Amber would say something, surely. She'd shoot that idea down. The two of them had less in common than Jesus and the devil. Harper waited, tense.

Come on, Amber. Speak. Tell him you'd rather be hung out by your toenails than be my date at some couples shower.

"I'm free if you are," she said coyly.

Christ.

"Well, then, you all have a date." Tom smiled and raised one eyebrow.

Damn it, Grayhawk, I owe you one. "I can't be her date since I'm not going."

There. Still a save.

"No, no, no," Tom said. "This lovely lady needs an escort. And you don't want to disappoint your pretty little sister."

Hitting him right where it hurt. And now he had to take Amber to the party on top of everything else. Either that or reject her right here. Even though they had no interest in each other, he was too much of a gentleman to do that.

He gritted his teeth. "Fine."

Amber winked at Tom and sipped her cosmo. "Perfect. I'll look forward to seeing you. Pick me up at the beauty shop on Saturday at two."

Tom winked back.

Harper downed the last of his beer and plunked the bottle on the bar. *Damn it all.*

He'd just been played like a fiddle.

Chapter Two

"Well, hey there, Harper." Judy Williamson, the owner of the salon where Amber worked, looked up from the head she was blowing dry.

"Hi there."

"I hear you're taking Amber to the party this afternoon. I'm closing up early when I'm done with Lisa, here. We're all heading over."

"Great." Could he be less enthused?

Amber sat in the back of the salon, cleaning up her...was it a desk? What did one sit at to do nails, anyway?

"Hey there," she called. "I'll be with you in a sec."

"No hurry." He sat down and thumbed through a hair styling magazine.

"When are you going to let me play with that gorgeous mane of yours, Harp?" Judy asked as she clicked the blow dryer off.

"Uh...well, I still see Ron over at the barber shop, you know."

"Not often enough. You'll be touching your shoulders in a few more days."

"Works for me."

"You've got a gorgeous head of hair, just like both your sisters and your mom. I love doing all their hair."

I'm sure you do. "Amber, you coming?"

Was the whole world bound and determined to turn him into a woman this week? First a shower, now Judy wanted to do his hair?

Amber got up from her table and grabbed a bag. "Yes, I'm ready."

Did she have to wear miniskirts all the damn time? The woman had one fine pair of legs, and her curvy little ass stuck out just right. Her platinum hair was pulled into a high ponytail today. She had one sexy neck. Truth be told, she had one sexy everything.

He'd said it before. Amber Cross was hot.

If only she weren't such a gigantic pain in his ass. She and her Texas ways. If Texas was so great, why the hell was she here?

Couples showers. Christ.

"I'm ready, Harper."

Eyes so light brown they were almost gold stared up at him. How had he never noticed her eyes before? They were amber. Amber like her name.

"Yes?" she said.

He blinked. "What?" He inhaled a whiff of lavender. She even smelled good.

"You're looking at me funny."

"Oh, sorry." He eyed a pink gift bag dangling from her wrist. "What's that?"

"My present for the baby, of course. What are you bringing?"

His eyebrows shot up. A present? "Um...I guess I didn't think about it."

"It's a shower, Harper. You *shower* the baby with gifts."

"I'll get her whatever she wants. She's my first niece after all."

"You can't go to this party empty-handed. Come on." She grabbed his hand—he tried to ignore the tingle—and dragged him across the street. "Let's see. What can we find on short notice?"

"I don't need to bring anything. Catie knows I'm good for it."

"Yeah, yeah, yeah. Let's try here." She led him into Terry's gift shop. A froufrou place. Harper had never set foot in there.

"Here." Amber handed him a pink teddy bear the size of a small car. "This'll work."

"Just what every kid needs," Harper said under his breath.

"I heard that. Pick something yourself, then. But we're not leaving here till you buy something for your niece."

Harper chose a stuffed brown horse, chocolate brown just like Catie's favorite mare, Ladybird. Teddy bears were overdone anyway, and Catie would appreciate this more.

"Will this do?"

Amber nodded. "Perfect for any child of Catie's. Now go pay."

Harper paid and shoved the receipt in his pocket. "You're not going to make me wrap this, are you?"

"Nope. We'll just take it as is. Let's get moving. We're late now. Where'd you park?"

"Behind the salon."

The drive to Catie's ranch house took over a half hour, but Harper didn't have to worry about making conversation. Amber chattered on about all kinds of things, some of which Harper found interesting, to his surprise. Amber wanted to learn barrel racing. Looking at her fake nails and platinum hair, he'd never have guessed racing would interest her. Though she had performed well enough on horseback to win first runner-up at the rodeo queen competition last summer. When Catie married and had to step down, Amber stepped up. She was now the reigning Bakersville rodeo queen. She had moved from Texas just a few months before last year's pageant, and she beat all the local girls except Catie. The McCray brothers had judged, and Harper knew how tough they were. Amber had earned the crown, no doubt.

"Do you ride much, Harper?"

"I run a ranch. I ride all the time."

"Do you compete?"

"I didn't last year. But I have in the past. I bust broncs and ride the occasional bull."

"Really? Bull riding? That's so dangerous."

"Not if you know what you're doing. I once saw Dusty McCray stay on a scary ass bull for six seconds. Course she gave herself a concussion afterward."

"Yes, I know. I heard about her and that bull of hers, El Diablo. They're still offering that half-mil purse, aren't they?"

"Every January at the stock show in Denver, and every summer at the rodeo here in town." He chuckled. "You're not thinking about taking up bull ridin', are you?"

"Heavens, no. I'll stick to horseback, thank you. I do admire a woman with those kinds of balls though, if you'll pardon the expression."

"Dusty McCray has balls and then some. That little girl's been through more than most."

"Yeah, Catie told me about her cancer, and about how she probably won't have any more children. I feel bad for her."

"It's a shame, no doubt. But she has quite a brood of nieces and nephews to dote on now, including Catie's Violet."

"She has a brother, doesn't she?"

"Yeah. Sam. He hasn't been around in a while. He lives up in Montana. They have a small ranch up there. I think he's planning to come for the rodeo in a few months though. He's a bronc buster like me."

"Hmm. Can you beat him?"

Harper let out a laugh. "He's damn good. But so am I."

Amber smiled, parting her cherry lips to reveal perfect white teeth. The skin around those gorgeous golden eyes crinkled. *Good God, the woman is hot.*

"I wouldn't mind learning bronc busting myself," she said, "though I think I'll stick to barrel racing for now. Maybe I'll ask Dusty McCray to teach me."

"She hasn't raced in years. Not since she had Sean."

"Yeah, true. I'm sure there's someone else around who can give me some pointers. Catie mentioned this guy who used to work for Chad a while back. He's back in town. His name's Blake something or other, and she says he knows the sport pretty well. He worked with his sister who's a champ."

Harper pursed his lips. He knew exactly who Amber was talking about. "Blake Buchanan, yeah." Blake Buchanan was also a champion coward and loser. He'd left town three years ago after impregnating the mayor's daughter. She'd had a miscarriage, but still. Course the man did know barrel racing.

"I was thinking I might check with him. I've heard he's a great coach."

Sweat beaded above Harper's lip. Why would he care if Amber worked with some loser who seduced an innocent young woman? Amber hardly looked innocent anyway. No one that hot could be innocent.

None of his business anyway.

Thank God. They arrived at Catie's, and the conversation ended.

The place was already crowded as a stampede. Surely no one would have noticed if he hadn't shown up.

Nope. Catie would notice. He sucked in a breath, and with Amber clinging to his arm, walked inside.

"Amber!" Catie waded through the throng of people dragging a tall black-haired cowboy with her. "I'm so glad you're here. This is the man I've been telling you about. Blake Buchanan. This is Amber Cross, and you remember my brother, Harper."

Amber's golden eyes blazed as Blake approached.

On instinct, Harper wrapped his arm around Amber's waist and pulled her into his side. Warmth coursed through him.

"Hello there, darlin'," Blake said. "I hear you want to learn to race."

Harper's esophagus threatened to reverse. Here he stood, one arm around a stuffed horse, the other around a woman he wasn't interested in.

Was he?

Of course not. So totally not his type. But damned if he'd let her be bait for Blake Buchanan's snare.

"Where's my niece?" he said to Catie. Nothing like changing the subject.

"Chad's got her. They're out back. Come on out. Angie and Rafe arrived a while ago. We've got food and drink out there. It's such a gorgeous day. I'm so glad it's warm this spring."

Leave Amber here with this guy? No way. He handed the stuffed horse to Catie. "For Violet. Come on, Amber. Let's go get a drink."

"Oh. Okay." She touched Blake's arm. *Damn her.* "We'll talk later, okay?"

"Sure enough. I'm gonna use the little boys' room and then I'll be right out with you."

Harper followed Amber out to the pool deck. The pool was covered. They'd fill it next month most likely. Late April was too early here in Colorado.

Everybody and his brother had shown up here. Caterers made their way through the crowds carrying platters of food. Several bars were set up. He led Amber to the closest.

"What'll you have?"

"Cosmo."

"Of course." What she saw in the froufrou drink was beyond him.

He ordered a beer for himself and looked around. Dallas and Annie McCray were here with their brood. Zach and Dusty and Sean. Joe Bradley, the mechanic. Doug Cartright, the sheriff. Judy had made it. His big sister, Angie, and her husband, Rafe Grayhawk, were talking to some people Harper didn't recognize. His mother and Uncle Jeff were making their rounds.

His father had been gone for over six months, but Harper still had a hard time accepting it. He owned Cha Cha Ranch now. He knew the ranching business. That part was no problem. But Uncle Jeff, Dad's brother, had surfaced after his death, claiming to own half of their western slope ranch, Bay Crossing. But that wasn't the biggest surprise. Turned out he was Angie's biological father. To top it all off, Mom had invited Uncle Jeff to live at the main ranch house at Cha Cha. So instead of moving in there, in the house he now owned, Harper stayed in his modest ranch house on the other side of the property. Not that he minded. He loved his house.

Harper had always known his parents had married because Mom had been pregnant with Angie. What he hadn't known was that Dad's younger brother, Jefferson Bay, had been in love with his mother. When Jeff went to prison for a crime he didn't commit, Mom had married Dad and convinced him the baby was his.

The thoughts choked in his throat. Harper still had a hard time with that one. He and Catie were Dad's kids, but not Angie. And his mother had tricked his father. Funny thing was, Angie was no longer holding a grudge. She had forgiven Mom and was working on a relationship with Uncle Jeff. If Angie wasn't upset, why should he be? After all, his father was still *his* father.

Course maybe Angie found it easier to accept because she was in love and newly married. She oozed happiness.

Harper had never been in love. He'd never understood what the fuss was about. He'd been interested in women, sure. Had dated quite a bit, a couple seriously, even. But fireworks had never gone off. He doubted that kind of love existed.

At least not for him. He had too much going on anyway. Heck, he had a ranch to run. His own ranch. He didn't need kids running around. If he wanted kids, he'd come see beautiful little Violet. And all the kids Angie and Rafe would have. They were already talking about starting a family. Course they lived at Bay Crossing on the western slope, but they'd come visit.

"Quit looking so sullen, Harper. Let's mingle." Amber grabbed his elbow and started toward Rafe and Angie.

"Hey, you two!"

Angie gathered them both in a hug. Amber's body crushed against his, and tingles shot up his spine. What the heck was going on?

"It's so good to see you guys."

"You just saw us at your wedding two weeks ago," Harper said dryly.

Angie swatted him on the arm. "What crawled up yours, Harp?"

"He's pissy because I made him come to this baby shower," Amber said. "He thinks showers are supposed to be for women."

"I think you're right," Rafe said.

"Yeah? Then why are you here?"

"Ang and I hadn't seen the baby yet till today. I wanted to see her."

Harper melted a little. "She's beautiful, isn't she?"

"Without a doubt." Rafe's black eyes softened as he looked at his wife. "I hope we have some good news soon."

"You're certainly putting a good amount of effort into it," Angie teased.

Harper tensed. He didn't need to think about his big sister having sex. Or his little sister for that matter. Though baby Violet was a wonderful result.

"Whose idea was this couples shower, anyway?" Rafe asked.

"Mine," Amber piped in. "It's really just an excuse for a big party, and Catie sure has the spread for it. Plus we all get to welcome Violet and pay our respects."

"It doesn't sound so bad when you put it that way," Rafe said with a chuckle. "I'm always up for a good party."

"Me too," Angie agreed. "Amber, we'll be here a few days. Can you get me in on Monday for a mani-pedi?"

"Absolutely." Amber took the last sip of her cosmo and looked up at Harper. "I see yours is nearly empty too. Can I get you another?"

"I'll get them." He took her glass, glad to be gone from the conversation. When his sister started talking mani-pedis, nothing interesting could possibly come of it.

* * * *

Harper Bay was one fine-looking man. The second most eligible bachelor in Bakersville, behind mechanic Joe Bradley. At least that's what the local gossip columnist touted. Joe was handsome, no doubt, but Harper had a tousled sexiness—that mane of walnut hair that was always in disarray made Amber's heart patter. Judy talked all the time about how she'd love to get her fingers in it.

Amber'd love to get her fingers in it too. She eased away from Rafe and Angie and watched as Harper stood at the bar getting their drinks. She wasn't looking for a relationship. Nope, keep it simple—that was her motto. That's why she'd come to this small town, and she wasn't about to complicate her life with a man. Still, she couldn't ignore the sizzle that raced over her skin whenever Harper Bay was near.

"There you are, darlin'."

She turned to see Blake Buchanan. Also good-looking, but more refined with slicked back black hair and gentle brown eyes. A refined cowboy. That was a hoot.

"Hey, nice to see you again," she said.

"You know, I can't shake the notion that we've met before. Have we?"

Amber shook her head. "No. I'd definitely remember you. Besides, I've only lived here for a little over a year."

"Yeah? Where'd you move from?"

"San Antonio."

"Hmm. I spent some time there off and on. Is it possible we could have made each other's acquaintance at a party?"

"I wasn't the partying type." She didn't want to think about the life she'd left behind. Not when she'd found such a nice new one here in Bakersville. She was rodeo queen for goodness' sake.

He smiled. "I never forget a face. I'll definitely figure this out. We've met."

Amber's nerves skittered under her skin. What did he mean?

"So about your interest in barrel racing," he continued. "What are you looking for?"

Icy black fingers gripped the back of her neck. *Stay away*, her inner voice warned. *This guy will hurt you.* Her inner voice rarely surfaced, but when it did, she'd learned to trust it.

She cleared her throat. "I'll let you know on that. I haven't decided yet if I really want to get into racing."

"But Catie said you were chompin' at the bit."

Amber let out a nervous giggle. "She must have been exaggerating. Don't worry, I'll call you if I'm interested."

"How about a drink later, then? I'll take you to the Bullfrog."

She shook her head. "That's kind of you, but I'm already on a date today."

"With Catie's brother, I know. But I got the impression that was just a 'friends' thing."

"Not at all. It's a new relationship, but one I definitely want to explore."

God, I hope Harper can't hear any of this. He sauntered toward them holding her cosmo and another beer.

"Thank you, honey," she said, taking the drink from him.

His eyebrows arched. "You're welcome...sweetheart."

"Well, I can tell three's a crowd here," Blake said. "I'll see you all later." He walked away and then stopped dead in his tracks. He turned around and came back toward them.

"Miss Amber, I do believe I remember how I know you after all."

Chapter Three

What in God's name was up with Blake Buchanan? And why in hell was he at Catie's party? Sure, he'd worked for Chad in the past, but he'd been gone three years. He'd left town amidst gossip, after disgracing Evie Luke, the mayor's daughter who was now the town librarian. Catie had still been in high school when he left. She hadn't known him at all. Why was she all of a sudden his champion?

A cold anvil landed in Harper's gut, and a truth settled in his mind. He must keep both Catie and Amber away from Blake Buchanan. The man was a jerk and up to no good. Harper felt it in the very marrow of his bones. It ached.

"Oh?" Amber fidgeted, her knuckles white as she grasped her martini glass.

"Yeah, back in San Antonio there's a place called Rachel's."

"Never heard of it," Amber said.

"Really? I'd swear I've seen you there. I'd never forget those legs."

"You're mistaken." She latched onto Harper's arm. "Let's go find Chad. I want to hold Violet."

Sounded good to Harper. Besides, he had a few questions for Miss Amber Cross himself. Every cowboy west of the Mississippi knew about Rachel's in San Antonio.

It was a strip club.

* * * *

As she breathed in the fresh scent of baby powder, Amber's uterus skipped a beat. She silenced her reproductive organs and handed Violet back to Catie. "She sure is precious."

"Thank you." Catie beamed up at Chad. "We sure think so."

"Now you know I'll babysit anytime."

"Of course. Violet will love having her Auntie Amber come to sit. Won't you?" Catie cooed to the baby.

"I need to talk to you when you have a minute," Amber said.

"Oh, sure." Catie kissed the top of Violet's head. "She'll be ready to go down for a nap in about twenty minutes. I'll come find you."

"Perfect, thanks."

Chad handed the cosmo he'd been holding back to Amber, and he and Catie left to show Violet off to more people. Harper pulled Amber aside.

"Before you talk to Catie, you need to talk to me."

"What about?"

"About San Antonio."

Amber gulped.

"About Rachel's."

"What about it? I've never heard of it."

"You expect me to believe you lived in San Antonio and never heard of Rachel's? Sorry, not buyin' it."

Amber gulped again. She glanced down at her drink. Damn. Still half full. Couldn't use the old "could you get me another drink?" eye batting thing.

"Okay, okay. It's a gentlemen's club downtown."

"On the outskirts of town, and it's not a gentlemen's club. It's a strip club. And the strippers are known to take certain liberties. For money."

Amber's heart thudded. "Just how would you know all of this?"

"Easy." His lips curved into a sardonic smile. "I've been there."

"Oh?" She arched her eyebrows.

"Now don't go lookin' at me like that. Every cowboy goes to Rachel's at one time in his life. It's kind of a requirement I think. A rite of passage."

"And I suppose you paid for liberties?"

"Me? Hell no. I look but don't touch. I kind of feel sorry for those girls."

Amber tried to hide her surprise. "Sorry? Why? They make great money."

"So you *are* familiar with the place then."

Amber inhaled. Why wouldn't her insides stop quivering? Maybe she'd said too much. "Not really. I just know strippers usually make good money."

"Not all strippers. But at a place like Rachel's I'm sure the money can be great. Course it's been a long time since I've been there."

"Oh?"

"Yeah. Chad McCray—don't tell Catie—dragged me there when I turned twenty-one. He was twenty-three or twenty-four at the time. We were in San Antonio on an overnight for a rodeo."

"How old are you now?"

"Thirty."

Amber exhaled the breath she'd been holding. The flip-flops in her tummy slowed down a bit. He wouldn't recognize her.

"I can't believe you and Chad would go into that place."

"So you do know it."

"I've heard of it."

"Now I wonder…why in the world would Blake Buchanan think he had seen you there?"

"I'm sure I haven't the slightest idea." *God, how can I stop this conversation?*

"I'm thinking you're hiding something, Amber, and I aim to find out—"

Her drink fell out of her hand and hit the grass with a soft clump. She threw her arms around Harper's neck and smashed her lips to his.

Anything to shut him up. To end this conversation.

She hadn't expected the kiss to be so powerful.

Harper's lips were full, and oh, so soft. He parted them gently, and his tongue swept into her mouth, bitter and malty from his beer. Amber wasn't fond of beer, but on Harper it tasted like nectar. She let her tongue entwine with his. His response overwhelmed her. He wanted to kiss her. Heck, he was enjoying it.

So was she.

The kiss became more hurried, frantic. Their lips slid against each other's, searching and learning. Amber glided her fingers through Harper's tousled hair, soft as suede.

"Mmm."

His soft groan was more of a vibration against her lips than a sound. His arms tightened around her. One hand caressed the side of her neck. The other glided down her side, over the curve of her hips, and squeezed.

A delicate sigh left her throat, muffled by the kiss. His lips became her world. A soft, lush, romantic world, a world full of arousal and promise, a world where her nipples tightened, threatened to poke holes in her bra. A world where her sex heated. Lord, it had been a long time.

Had it ever been better?

She'd kissed a few men in her day. It had never been like this.

She jerked when a harsh sound cut into her dream.

Harper ripped his lips away from hers. Chad McCray stood next to them.

He cleared his throat again. That had been the harsh sound. A silly smile curved over his lips. "Hey there, Harp, Amber. Anything you all want to share with the rest of us?"

Harper's turn to clear his throat. "We were just—"

"Yeah, yeah. I see what you're doing. It's great, really. But this here's Catie's party for Violet. I don't want you two stealing her thunder."

"Oh, of course not." Amber's cheeks warmed. She was no doubt turning about thirty shades of scarlet. "We'd... I mean I'd...never do anything to spoil Catie's party."

"Me either," Harper said. "This was nothin', Chad. Just...we've had a little bit to drink and all..."

"Yeah." Blame it on the alcohol. That would work. No need to let everyone know she'd kissed him to make him forget about Rachel's. Evidently it had worked.

Now if she could only calm down the throbbing between her thighs.

Harper's lips were red and swollen. Were hers? She touched her fingers to them. They felt hot.

Catie ambled up, sans Violet. "Mary put the baby down for a bit," she said to Chad, and then turned to Amber. "You wanted to talk to me?"

"Yeah, yeah I did. Would you two excuse us for a few?"

"Sure thing. Go on and have your girl talk," Chad said. "I'll take care of Harp. I have a few questions for him myself."

I'm sure you do. Sheesh. What would Harper tell Chad about their kiss? Did guys even talk about things like that? Hell if she knew. She really knew very little about men.

She and Catie wandered away from the crowd. Catie led her to a charming little bench behind the pool house. "So what's up?"

Amber plunked her behind down on the wooden bench. Where to start?

"What do you know about Blake Buchanan?" she asked.

"Not too much, really," Catie said. "He worked here for Chad a while back. Chad said he was a great worker. He knows tons about horses, I guess."

"Why'd he leave?"

"He left town because Evelyn Luke—you know, the librarian?—got pregnant. Blake was allegedly the father. At the time, Evie's dad was mayor of Bakersville. It's a small town. Pretty soon everybody knew."

"So what? Lots of women get pregnant out of wedlock. That's hardly a reason to chase a guy out of town."

"It is when the father of the girl tries to shoot the guy."

Amber perked up. "What?"

"Yeah. Mayor Luke went all crazy and ended up coming over here to Chad's, where Blake was living at the time, and holding him at gunpoint."

"What happened?"

"Well, he said Blake would marry his daughter or else. Blake said no way, and I swear to God, Chad said he heard the gun cock."

Amber's muscles froze. One of her greatest fears was to be held at gunpoint. "Chad was there?"

"Yeah, they were in one of the stables."

"So did the guy shoot Blake?"

"Nope. Another guy walked in on them and ended up tackling Mayor Luke to the ground. I can't recall who it was. Chad could tell you. He's no longer here. Anyway, they called the sheriff and the mayor got carted off to jail."

"And Blake?"

"Left town running. Can't say I blame him. Evie ended up losing the baby. She still says it was Blake's. He denies it. So who knows? But I'm not going to persecute a guy for having sex. Heck, I got pregnant out of wedlock after sex with Chad, and I was a completely willing participant."

"Yeah, I know." Amber smiled. "That's what led to me being rodeo queen."

"And you're a much better one than I ever would have been."

Nausea gripped Amber's throat. If Catie only knew… Turns out she wasn't the perfect rodeo queen after all. She shook her head. She'd actually thought she could escape her past, start again somewhere new. A small town, where no one had heard of Rachel's. Where no one had ever heard of Ambrosia Love.

Why hadn't she dyed her hair? She'd thought to do it when she came to Bakersville. But she loved her ultra-light blond hair. It was natural, inherited from her Swedish mother. Judy could attest to its authenticity. She hadn't touched Amber's hair since she moved here.

Of course it wasn't her hair Blake had recognized. Nope, damn those long legs. She couldn't change them, that was for sure. And truth be told, she didn't want to change them any more than she wanted to change her hair. They were part of her. She'd learned to like herself again. Why did Blake Buchanan have to come to town and threaten to spoil everything that was going right?

"Whatcha thinking?" Catie asked.

Amber shook her head again. "Just wondering, is all. You know, why Blake Buchanan would come back here after all the gossip."

"I hear he needs work. That's why I thought of him when you said you wanted to take up racing."

"Why doesn't Chad hire him at the ranch?"

"We don't really need anyone right now, and neither do Zach or Dallas. You know, I should ask Harper if he could use him at Cha Cha."

God, would this ever end? "I got the feeling Harper doesn't think too highly of him."

"Really?"

"Yeah." It wasn't actually a lie. Tension clearly existed between the two men.

"Well, I'll just have to have a talk with Harp then. Blake's a good guy who's had some tough breaks. He deserves a chance. I mean, look at my mama, giving my Uncle Jeff another chance."

"He's the father of her oldest child. There's a little bit of a difference there."

"I suppose. But still… Here comes Harp now."

The handsome cowboy ambled toward them, his lips pursed and forehead wrinkled.

Amber's tummy sank. He did not look happy.

Chapter Four

"Catie, why in the hell are you hanging out with Blake Buchanan?"

Amber exhaled, relieved. Harper was angry with Catie, not with her. Blake hadn't gotten to him, though Harper had no doubt already guessed her secret.

"He's a friend of Chad's."

"I just spoke with Chad. They aren't friends. Blake used to work here. Chad thinks he's okay, but they aren't friends."

"I just thought, since Amber wanted to learn to race and all, and Blake knows more about racing than anyone else in this town, except maybe Dusty—"

"You weren't thinking at all, little bit. The man's no good. I want both you and Amber to stay away from him."

Fine with me, Amber thought. Not that she took orders from men, not even a man with kissing skills like Harper Bay. This edict, however, she'd be happy to obey. In fact, if Harper decided to chase Mr. Buchanan right out of this town, she'd be okay with that.

"Chad says he's okay," Catie said.

"Chad says he was a good worker. That's what he told me. He also said he's not hiring him back right now, and he asked both his brothers not to either."

"Right. Because none of them need anyone."

"True enough. But also because Blake doesn't have the best reputation. He got chased out of Bakersville three years ago and he maintains his innocence. No one knows for sure who fathered Evie's miscarried baby except Evie herself. Hell, I don't care if it *was* Blake. They were both consenting adults at the time, and it's ancient history. So he runs off to San Antonio and now he's back. Why now?"

"I don't know," Catie said. "Maybe he missed it here."

"Could be." Harper stroked his chin. "But there's more to why Blake left San Antonio than you know."

"What might that be?" Amber asked. She couldn't help herself. Curiosity got the best of her.

"I can't tell you. I got the information in confidence from a friend."

"What friend?"

"Let's just say I made a quick phone call while Chad and I were talking."

"A phone call to whom?"

"I can't say. I'm sorry. Just stay away from Buchanan, both of you."

"Come on. You have to tell us," Catie said. "You must have told Chad."

"No, I didn't tell Chad, and I don't have to tell you. And I'm not going to. I will tell you that Blake no longer has contact with his parents, sister, and little brother. They wrote him off a couple years ago."

"So we're supposed to just do what you say because you say it? Without any information?" Catie whipped her hands to her hips.

Harper chuckled. "You look just like Angie when you do that."

"You're avoiding my question."

"That's right. I'm done talking about this." He turned to Amber. "Another cosmo?"

Amber shook her head. "Nope. I always stop at two."

Catie let out a laugh. "Yup, she always stops at two. When are you going to tell me why that is, Amber?"

"I just know my limit, that's all."

"If you say so." Catie smiled and shook her head. "Since both of you are determined to keep secrets from me, I'm going to go check on Violet. You two try to stay out of trouble."

"She's got a belly full of fire worked up now," Harper said.

"Can you blame her?"

"I suppose not. You, on the other hand, didn't put up too much of a fight about Blake Buchanan."

Amber sighed. Did this man forget nothing? She might have to kiss him again. The thought pleased her. "Why should I? I hardly know him."

"That's not what he seems to think."

"Harper—"

"Look, I don't know why he thinks he knows you from Rachel's. And I don't give a damn if you used to take your clothes off for a living."

"I didn't—"

He put two fingers on her lips. A jolt shot through her.

"Let me finish. Please."

She nodded.

"I never thought you were my type at all, Amber. You're beautiful, no doubt, but different as all hell from the girls I'm used to. I hadn't given a thought to you in…that way. Until you kissed me, that is."

Amber's cheeks warmed. Was he attracted to her? What was he after? "I'm not sure what you're saying."

"I'm saying…aw, hell. I've never been any good at this. You want to go get a bite to eat after this shindig's over? Maybe talk a little?"

She smiled. "Harper Bay, are you asking me out?"

"I'm trying. You're not makin' it easy."

Amber's heart pounded. The kiss had been ecstasy for her. She hadn't thought it possible that he'd enjoyed it just as much. Yet she didn't want to complicate her life with a man right now. She was enjoying her alone time in this small town. Life was good.

Course Harper Bay just might make it better. Heck, it was only dinner, right?

She smiled. "I'd love to have dinner with you, Harper."

His lips curved upward in a smile that lit his whole face. He grabbed her hand, and electricity rushed up her forearm.

"I'm glad to hear that. How long do you think we have to stay at this shower you dragged me to?"

Amber laughed and entwined her fingers through his. "I guess we've stayed long enough."

* * * *

Blake Buchanan drove back from Chad McCray's ranch to his hotel in downtown Bakersville. If he didn't find work soon, he'd be shit out of luck. He had debts that wouldn't wait much longer.

His cell phone vibrated in his pocket. His pal Bernie calling him back.

"Hey, Bern."

"Blake, sorry I missed your call. What's happening up north?"

"Same old same old. Lookin' for work. I need some help with a situation."

"What can I do you fer?"

"Remember when we used to hang out at Rachel's?"

"Don't remind me. I still have the scars from my run in with that big ass bouncer."

Blake chuckled. Bernie sure knew how to get his ass in trouble. "You remember that sweet blond number with the legs?"

"Myrna?"

"No, blonder. She could wrap around a pole like nobody's business."

"Yeah, yeah. She left about a year or two ago, didn't she? What was her name? Andrea or something?"

Blake took a drink from the bottle of beer he held. "Ambrosia. She called herself Ambrosia Love."

"How could I forget? She was fine."

"She was. Still is." He lay down on his bed and set the beer on the night table. "You're not going to believe this, but she's right here in Bakersville, Colorado, working as a manicurist."

"No way."

"I'm not kidding. She's still hot as hell. Goes by Amber Cross."

"Wow. You gonna hook up with her?"

Blake's skin prickled. "I'd love it, but I have bigger fish to fry at the moment. Donetto isn't going to wait forever for me to pay him back. He already knows where I am."

"Well, of course he knows. You went back to a town you used to live in for God's sake."

"I came back here because I thought I could find work." He grabbed the beer and took another drink. "I was a damn good ranch hand at one time. I never should have gone to San Antonio."

"Wrong. San Antonio was fine. You never should have gotten involved with Donetto. Period. I tried to warn you."

"I know, Bernie, I know. But listen, I need a favor."

"What's that?"

"I need the password to your brother's web site, the one that costs an arm and a leg?"

"I can't give you that."

"Look, I can't afford to pay the fee to log in myself. Please. I might be able to pay Donetto back if I can find the lovely Ambrosia on the site."

"Blake—"

"Please, Bernie. I'll owe you big."

Silence on the other end of the line. Blake's heart pounded.

Then, "Shit. All right. I guess it can't hurt. Log in as DickRobbins, password sw34789."

"Thanks, you're a pal."

"Just don't let Lance find out you're using his site for free. He'll fuckin' kill me."

"Understood."

They said goodbye and hung up.

Amber seemed like a nice enough girl, and Blake didn't want to hurt her, but better her than him at this point. She was tight with Catie Bay McCray, and that meant she had access to cash.

Blake needed cash.

He also needed his legs walking and his heart beating. If he didn't come up with cash soon, he'd lose all of that. Paul Donetto's goons would see to it.

He fired up his laptop. Damn thing was so freaking slow. Of course it was, it was five years old now. Rachel's in San Antonio. Hardly the classiest place in town, but one of the biggest money-makers. He and his cronies had hung out there a lot. He fed in the URL to Lance's web site and started looking around.

Candy Hart. Eliza Bends. Taryn Apart. All ladies he recognized. He crept through page after page, discovering some new faces, enjoying some old ones.

Bingo.

Ambrosia Love.

Otherwise known as Amber Cross, best friend of Caitlyn McCray.

He didn't relish hurting such a beautiful young woman, but hey, times were tough. Surely young Amber would pay handsomely to keep the good folks of Bakersville from finding out about her past.

Chapter Five

"When you asked me to dinner, I figured you meant we'd go out." Amber smiled as Harper pulled his truck into the driveway of his ranch home on the Cha Cha Ranch grounds.

"Why? I love to cook. And I've got the best beef right here."

Amber let out a laugh. "Chad McCray always says he's got the best beef."

"He's dreamin'. He's got the third best. I raise the best here at Cha Cha, and a close second comes from Bay Crossing, our place on the western slope."

"Right, Angie's ranch."

"Angie's and Catie's, technically. But Catie lets Angie and Rafe run it. She's busy at Chad's ranch."

"Yeah, I know." Since when was her voice so wistful? "Catie sure is a lucky girl. She's got everything her heart desires."

"True that, especially since she's desired Chad McCray since she was five years old."

"I've heard the story." Amber grinned. "She stole Chad right out from under my nose when she got home from Europe last spring."

"Were you really interested in Chad McCray?"

Was that a twinge of jealousy in his voice? She wasn't sure. "No, not really. He's great looking and a lot of fun, but it was never more than a little fling. It didn't go anywhere anyway."

"You mean you didn't sleep with him?"

"Not that it's any of your business, but no, I didn't. I haven't slept with anyone since I moved here. I've hardly dated. It hasn't been a priority."

Oops. Had she said too much? She didn't want him to think she wasn't interested. She definitely *was* interested in him. Which surprised the heck out of her. He was a stud, for sure, but not really her type. A little too stiff. Why all the fuss about a co-ed shower? Sheesh. And too lawyerly. Course he was a lawyer, if only a non-practicing one. The real reason was she just wanted to be free of men for a while. Dancing naked in front of them for two years did that to a woman.

"Maybe we can change that."

"Are you saying you want to date me?"

His dark gaze seared her. "I think we're dating right now, aren't we?"

"I would have bet everything I had that I wasn't your type at all, cowboy."

"I didn't think you were either, but that kiss changed my mind."

Amber agreed. Her cheeks warmed. "It was something, that's for sure."

"So why did you kiss me anyway?"

"I think you already figured it out. I wanted you to stop talking about Rachel's."

"So...anything you want to tell me about that?"

"Not really."

"I won't judge you."

"I never said you would. It's a time in my life I prefer not to think about. A girl has to make a living, you know."

"True enough. And for what it's worth, I won't hold that against you. Not that I'd want to see either of my sisters doing it."

"I wouldn't want to see either of your sisters doing it either. I care about them too much. It's not the noblest of callings. Little girls dream of being ballerinas or cowgirls or doctors or astronauts. I doubt any get a child-size pole and pretend to be a stripper."

Harper let out a laugh. "You're probably right."

"Geez, I sure hope so." *Change the subject, Amber.* "So what are you making me for dinner?"

"Like I said, I got the best beef right here, so...steak on the grill?"

"Sounds great."

"You're not one of those vegetarians?"

"Do I look like a vegetarian to you?"

He laughed. "Well, you're built great. But no, you look like a girl who likes a juicy steak."

"Yup. Rare. Better yet, blue."

"Blue? Seriously? I love 'em blue. Blue it is."

"What can I do to help?"

"Nothing."

"Come on. I love to cook."

"Okay," he laughed. "Grab some stuff out of the fridge and throw a salad together. And you can toss a few potatoes in the microwave. That ought to be a good dinner." He started toward the door and then turned. "And pick us out a bottle of wine from my rack."

"Cowboy, I know nothing about wine."

"Hmm. Okay, I'll pick the wine then." He ambled to his well-stocked rack and bent down.

Nice view. The man had one fine ass.

"Here's a nice Carmenére. You'll like it I think." He took it into the kitchen and Amber followed.

"Wow!" She couldn't help the awe in her voice. "This kitchen rocks. We could have some fun in here."

"I'm sure we could. And we could do some great cooking."

Amber giggled. "I meant cooking. Though this stainless steel surface looks extremely sanitary."

Harper opened the bottle of wine and poured two glasses. He handed one to Amber. "Let me know how it is."

She took a sip. "Like I said, I know nothing about wine, but this is good. Kind of spicy."

"There you go. Take another sip and let it float on your tongue for a minute and then ooze down your throat. Can you get the berries, the green pepper?"

"Green pepper?" She took a sip and followed his instructions. The wine was soft on her tongue. She swallowed. "I'll be damned. I do taste green pepper."

"Told you." He smiled. "I'm going to throw these steaks on the grill. Be back in a minute."

Instead of waiting, Amber followed him out to the patio and watched as he lit his gas grill.

He turned to her, his brown eyes blazing like the flames on the grill. "Amber?"

"Yes?"

"May I be frank?"

"I thought you were Harper." Bad joke. *Really, Amber? Did you really say that?*

He smiled that lopsided smile. "I'm serious."

"Okay, sorry. Sure. What?"

"Would you come to bed with me?"

"Huh?" Talk about spur of the moment. No talking? No kissing? No heavy petting? No seduction attempt whatsoever?

"Here's the thing. I haven't been able to think straight since you kissed me at Catie's. All I can think about is you in my bed. I'm not sure I've ever wanted a woman this badly."

He advanced toward her. "You're so beautiful. And those lips…so full and red." He traced them with his fingers.

Her skin heated. Little jolts lit up where his skin touched hers. One finger trailed over her cheek, down her neck, and over the swell of her breast.

"I bet these are perfect like the rest of you."

Her nipple tightened.

His eyebrows arched. He'd noticed.

"I see you're not immune."

Immune? Who could be immune to him and his tousled charm? He was yummy. "Of course I'm not immune. Why do you think I agreed to have dinner with you? But I didn't agree to hop in the sack with you."

"No, you didn't. That's why I'm asking nicely."

"Have you ever seduced a woman, Harper? Because if you have, I hope you did a better job than you're doing right now."

He laughed. "I've had a few in my day. Though less than you probably think."

She smiled.

"I just don't see any reason to beat around the bush. I want you in my bed. I want to kiss those lips of yours until they're raw, I want to suck on those hard nipples until they're crimson from my whisker burn."

Amber heated. Her sex throbbed. How was he doing this?

"I bet you're sweet as a candy apple between your legs."

Harper Bay? How had she always thought he was some kind of Goody-Two-shoes? He was the second most eligible bachelor in Bakersville for a reason. She hadn't known he could talk so dirty. And she hadn't known it would make her crazy with desire.

"The steaks'll burn."

"We can save the steaks for later." He moved toward her so their bodies were touching. His hardness pressed into her belly.

Dear God. How could she want him so much? This was hardly her idea of a seduction, but if he pressed much harder she'd fall into his bed in a minute.

Yet he wasn't kissing her. He was simply gazing at her, with beautiful brown eyes so intent and so full of fire she thought they both might burst into flames at any moment. He traced the outline of her lips again, and she darted her tongue out and touched the tip of his finger.

He smiled. "You are so very sexy, Amber."

She let out a nervous giggle. "So are you."

Finally, he lowered his head and touched his lips to hers. Just a soft peck, barely a whisper. Passion shot to her core. From a little tiny kiss.

Seemingly of its own accord, her hand rose, cupped his cheek, his stubble prickly against her palm. She brushed his shoulder length hair back behind his ear. Soft as silk.

"Mmm, that feels nice." His voice was barely above a whisper.

"You have beautiful hair."

"So do you." He brushed his lips lightly against her cheek.

She shivered, her eyes closing. "It's natural, you know."

He stepped back. "Really?"

She opened her eyes. Why had she said that? "Yes, really. You didn't think it was?"

"I assumed it wasn't. It's still beautiful."

"Everyone thinks it's dyed. But it's natural. My mom was Swedish."

"Was? Is she gone?"

Amber's stomach knotted. "I...I don't know. I haven't seen her since I was sixteen."

"Oh?"

"She kicked me out of the house."

Harper grabbed her hand. "I had no idea. What happened?"

"It's a long story."

He led her to the living and room. "Let's sit down."

"Okay."

"You want to tell me?"

"It's no big deal. I stayed with a friend and went to the vocational high school. That's where I learned to do nails. I got my license and my high school diploma. With honors even. But I had to leave my friend's house once I was out of school. Her mother kicked us both out. I had a hard time finding a job right out of beauty school, and long story short, she and I ended up at Rachel's when we were barely eighteen."

"Wow."

"I couldn't serve alcohol. Couldn't *drink* alcohol. Not legally anyway. But I could take my clothes off. Something doesn't seem right about that."

"I agree."

She sighed. "It was a living. A pretty good one, truth be told. I made enough to take some riding lessons. I had done a little when I was younger and my mother kept house for a rancher. I was pretty good too."

"I know you were. You are, I mean. I saw you ride at the rodeo queen competition, remember?"

She smiled. "That's right. Judy let me use her horse. She was a beauty. But anyway, the money was good. I can't lie."

"Yes, I'm sure it was."

She shifted her shoulders, hoping he'd believe what she was going to say. "But I swear, Harper, I never did any of that other stuff. I only stripped."

"I believe you." He took her hand and caressed her palm. "What happened with your mom? Why did she kick you out?"

"She was a drunk. She couldn't afford both me and her booze. The booze won."

"And your father?"

"Never knew him. He's supposedly a bronc buster named Morgan Cross. His name's on my birth certificate, but I've never met him. He wasn't part of my life. I'm not sure my mother ever told him about me. In fact, I've wondered on more than one occasion if she just made the name up."

Harper's eyes widened. "I don't think she made up that name."

"Why do you say that?" A warm ray of hope shot through her veins. "Do you know him? I never could find anything on the net about him."

"Not by that name, you wouldn't. But I assure you he does exist. He goes by the name Thunder Morgan. He retired a few years ago."

"Well, he must have brown eyes then. My mother's are ice blue. She's got the typical Scandinavian coloring. So do I, except for these darn eyes."

"I think he has brown eyes, but I never really paid much attention. His hair's a sandy blond. He and my father were friends. He'd come by the ranch every so often, usually during the rodeo. He hasn't been around for a few years, but he showed up at my father's memorial service."

"*I* was at your father's service!"

"I know. Freaky, huh? He was only at the church though. He didn't come back to the house. He's a good man, Amber. I doubt he knew he had a daughter. If he had, he would have been a part of your life."

"Is he married?"

"Nope. Never married that I know of. He was on the rodeo circuit forever. Not much of a life for a family."

"A better life than living with a drunk, I'd bet."

"Yeah, maybe. Hey, that's why you never drink more than two drinks, isn't it?"

"Yeah, pretty much. I've had a few bad experiences with alcohol, so now I keep to my limit. I figure alcoholism is in my genes. I'm not giving it any help."

He smiled and twirled one finger through a lock of her hair. "That's smart."

"Even when I was at Rachel's, I never did the booze or drugs like the other girls did."

"You're very strong."

She squirmed, embarrassed by his near reverence. She was so not worthy of it. "Don't put any halos on me. It's not like I never got drunk before. I did. Twice to be exact. The first time I blacked out and lost several hours. Scared the hell out of me. You'd think it would have scared me enough never to do it again, but I was young and stupid."

"We all are, baby. There's not a one of us who doesn't do something stupid when we're eighteen."

She smiled. What a nice guy he was. "The second time I ended up in bed with a stranger. Thank goodness he turned out to be a nice guy. That's when I got scared straight and decided not to tempt fate. No more than two drinks at a time. Like I said, alcoholism is probably in my genes."

"I still say you're strong."

"Not strong enough. If I were, I'd never have ended up at Rachel's."

Tears filmed over her eyes. Why in hell was she talking to Harper Bay about this stuff? And how did he know her father? Crazy. Just crazy.

"I'm sure you did the best you could. Stripping may not be the classiest job out there, but it's an honest living. As long as there are men in the world, there will be a market for beautiful women to take their clothes off."

"You're not extolling the virtues of your gender, cowboy."

"Baby, men are rarely virtuous. We all think with our dicks half the time."

Amber couldn't help but laugh. "You got that right."

"You have a beautiful smile, baby, and a great laugh." He wiped a stray tear from her cheek. "Let's get those steaks ready."

Amber shook her head. "The steaks can wait. I want to take you up on your previous offer. I'd like to go to bed."

Chapter Six

A crackle of energy passed through the air—hot, raw, and carnal. Amber's skin sizzled. Did Harper feel it too? A deep sexual hunger stirred to life in her gut.

Harper turned out to be a gentle lover. He removed her clothes with care, slowly and deliberately, to the point where she wished he'd hurry up a little. The spiral of need burst out of her belly and flowed like molten honey through her veins. Her arousal—unlike anything she'd ever known—sent sparks over her whole body.

Every touch tingled as though she were holding a blow torch. She looked down at his crotch, at the arousal apparent beneath his jeans. She gulped and dragged her gaze back up to his face. His dark eyes consumed her with raw need. Sensations of ice and fire raced up her spine. Her hunger for him gnawed at her, and the tickle between her legs intensified.

He'd discarded her shirt already, and he stroked up her ribs, to the edge of her bra. She leaned toward him, as though a magnet drew her. His finger reached underneath her bra and stroked the sensitive skin of her breast.

Her breath caught. Her nipples tightened against the satin of her bra. Slowly, slowly he caressed, until the need to shout at him to take the damn bra off almost overwhelmed her.

As though he read her mind, he deftly unhooked the offending garment and tossed it to the floor. Her ample breasts fell gently against her chest. The air hit her nipples and they tightened even further. He leaned down, and his firm wet mouth closed over one peak.

Such sweet suction, such gentleness. He drew on the nipple, sucking, tonguing, teasing. The ache between her legs heightened. With his other hand he cupped her other breast, and she leaned into him, letting his palm rub against her, hold her. Fingers clamped around the nipple and she sucked in a breath. Just a touch of pain, the right amount. It spiraled downward and intensified her need.

"Mmm. Beautiful." His breath caressed her skin. "Gorgeous breasts, baby."

Thank you, she said in her mind. It came out as a soft sigh, the air blowing wisps of his silky hair into further disarray.

His other hand wandered to her crotch. Through her jeans, he rubbed her most intimate place. "Are you getting wet, baby? Wet for me?"

Another sigh was her answer.

"I'm hard for you, Amber. So hard. God, I want you."

Amber wasn't sure she'd ever wanted a man this much, this intensely. How could this be happening? With Harper Bay? Brother to her best friend? They didn't have chemistry did they? Couldn't possibly.

Yet her body responded to his touch like it had to no other man's. Not that she was overly experienced. In fact, she hadn't ever had a serious relationship. A couple dates here and there, two one-night stands, one of which had been a drunken mistake. What did it feel like to have real chemistry? To fall in love?

She foisted the thought from her mind. This was not love. Harper certainly wasn't in love with her. So he knew a few things about her past now and he didn't hold them against her. That didn't mean he was in love with her. To the contrary, it only meant he was a nice guy.

Was it too soon to fall in bed with him?

Yeah, it really was. She pulled away.

"Baby? You all right?"

"Yeah, yeah. I'm fine. I'm just not sure this is the right thing to do after all."

"Oh?"

"I mean, we hardly know each other."

He pushed a stray curl behind her ear. "I know I'm attracted to you. I know I'm hard for you. I want you. And I know you want me. If I reached into your panties right now I'd find you wet. I can tell by looking at you. Your cheeks are ruddy, your eyes smoky, your lips swollen and trembling. You want this, Amber."

She couldn't deny it. "It's not a question of what I want. It's a question of what is right."

"We're attracted to each other. We want each other. What's not right about that?"

How could she tell him when she didn't know herself? All she knew is that Harper was someone special. Someone she could actually imagine a future with. And she didn't have time for a man right now.

Well, that wasn't exactly true. She'd just decided against men for the time being. She wanted to finally be her own person and not be subject to the whims of men like she'd been during those years at Rachel's.

But Harper? Yes, Harper was a decent guy. A guy she could fall for. So the last thing she wanted was a one-night stand with him. If she slept with him now, she'd destroy any chance for a relationship.

Was he even looking for a relationship? Probably not. Still, sleeping with him now felt both very right and very wrong.

Very right because she was wet and horny and extremely attracted to him.

Very wrong because he was the type of guy she wanted in her future, and she might destroy that possibility if she fell into bed with him on the first date.

"I'm sorry. I know I said I wanted this." She scooted away from him. Had to be away from him to get her body under control. Still she shuddered. It wasn't working. "I was feeling close to you. I told you things I haven't told anyone, and I'm not really sure why. But I don't sleep around. I don't want you to get the wrong idea about me."

He cocked his head. "You worked at Rachel's."

A sword of anger lanced through her. How dare he assume— "As a dancer, damn it. Not as a prostitute!"

"You're right. I'm sorry. I don't know why I said that." He stood. "I'm a big boy. It's been a long time since I've slept with anyone, and the truth is, I'm horny as hell for you. But I'm also a gentleman. I understand a lady can change her mind."

"Thank you." She smiled, and her anxiety eased a bit. "I assure you I'm not in the habit of being a tease. If you want me to go, I will. We don't need to have dinner."

His dark eyes danced as he grinned. "Of course we do. I've got the steaks all ready to go. I hope you'll stay."

Thank God he wasn't angry. "I'd love to stay. Thank you."

"But if you expect me to have dinner with you and not jump your bones right here and now, you have to do something for me."

"Of course. What's that?"

An adorable dimple cut into his left cheek. "Put your shirt back on, baby. Right now you look good enough to eat."

Amber warmed as she donned her bra and shirt. "Better?"

"Not really," he teased, "but it'll do for now. There's one thing we need to get clear though."

"Yeah? What's that?"

"I like you, Miss Amber, and I'm not done tryin' to get you into my bed."

She laughed. "That's fine by me. If we continue to go out and we like each other, that's where we'll end up. I'm looking forward to it."

His dark eyes gleamed. "So am I." He stood. "Now about those steaks."

"I'll get our salad ready."

She went to the kitchen to start work as Harper went outside to the patio to put the steaks on the grill. He came back in with a serious look on his face.

"One thing I want to know."

"Sure. What?"

"How did no one know till now that Thunder Morgan is your dad?"

"I never told anyone his name till you." She shook her head. "Funny. I told you a lot of things tonight that I never talk about. My mother, for example. Rachel's. I've never told Catie or Angie any of that stuff."

"Still, you knew his name."

"You got a cutting board?" Amber rinsed off a tomato. "I knew it was Morgan Cross, not Thunder Morgan."

Harper grabbed the board out of a cupboard and handed it to her. "True. I guess most people wouldn't know his real name. I only know it because he was friends with my dad."

"Can you tell me a little about him?" She sliced into the tomato's red flesh.

"Careful, I've nearly de-fingered myself with that knife." He winked. "He's a good guy. Retired now."

"How old is he?"

"I haven't a clue. Probably in his late fifties or early sixties. He knew my dad from his days on the western slope. He worked as a ranch hand for my great-grandpa when he was just starting out. Once he took a few good-size rodeo purses, he left the ranch and went out on the circuit. Never married, never had kids. Or rather, I never knew he had kids. My guess is he doesn't know either."

"I seriously thought my mother made up the name to put on the birth certificate." She dumped the tomato into the salad bowl and began chopping a few scallions.

"He's a real person, and she told you he was a bronc buster, right?"

"Yeah. They must have met when he was in Texas doing a rodeo or something. She never told me more than his name and the fact he busted broncs. I stopped asking after a while. Then she kicked me out."

"Why? Why did she kick you out?"

Amber sighed and tossed some bagged lettuce into the bowl. "Who knows? She was a drunk, Harper. I have no clue why she did half the things she did. I wasn't much of an expense to her. I did all the cooking and cleaning. If I didn't the place was a sty."

"Did she work?"

"At the post office, yeah."

"At least she held down a job."

"As far as I know. Once I left I never looked back. I have no idea what she's doing now."

"You mean you haven't seen her?"

"Heck no." Amber tossed the salad to keep her hands busy while past emotion crept into her. She held it at bay. "Why would I want to see the woman who kicked me out of her house when I was only sixteen? If it weren't for my friend Laura taking me in, I'd have been on the streets."

"I guess I can't blame you." Harper's arms slipped around her waist from the back. "I'm sorry life was so tough for you. It's hard to imagine a mother not wanting her child. My mother loves her children so much."

"You don't know how lucky you are."

"I was mad as hell when I found out she'd duped my dad about Angie's paternity. It wasn't fair to him or to Jeff, my uncle."

"Angie's real father, yeah I know." Amber leaned back into Harper's hard chest. Instantly her agitation lessened. Ahhh. What a remedy for the anxiety produced by the subject of her mother.

"But I'm beginning to understand why she did it." Harper's breath was warm against her scalp. "She did it for Angie. To give her a good life. She married a man she didn't love so her child would have a great life. There's a lot of selflessness in that."

"There's a ton of selflessness in that, Harper. Don't hold a grudge forever."

"You should take your own advice, baby." He turned her around to face him. "Do you ever think about seeing your mother? Working things out?"

Her tummy churned. Here came the agitation again. "There's a huge difference. My mother never did anything out of selflessness. Who in hell kicks out a sixteen-year-old girl? That's plain selfish."

"True enough." Harper trailed one finger over her outer ear. "Maybe she had her reasons though."

"Yeah. She couldn't afford me plus the booze. Typical Karen Hedstrom priorities."

"That's her name? Karen Hedstrom?"

"Yup."

"And you never knew your father at all?"

"Nope. She never saw him again after that night."

Harper's brow furrowed. "Interesting."

"Why?"

"Why she'd put his name on your birth certificate. Give you his last name."

Amber shrugged. "Doesn't seem so weird to me."

"Maybe not. You're twenty-two right?"

"That's right."

"Twenty-two years ago Thunder Morgan was already pretty well-known. If you are truly his daughter, why wouldn't your mother have tried to contact him to get child support?"

"Don't ask me. I have no idea how Karen's mind works. She was probably too inebriated to think of it."

"Hmm. Doesn't seem to make sense."

"It's too late now. I'm way too old to get child support. He wasn't there when it counted."

Amber tried to turn around and grab the salad bowl, but Harper stopped her. "If you'd known your father was famous, would you have tried to contact him?"

"I don't know." She shook her head. "Why the third degree, Harper? Maybe he's not even my father. I really don't care. I've made it on my own for the last six years. I don't plan to start taking help from anyone now."

"I'm not saying you need his help. But wouldn't you like to know him?"

"What good would it do now? He didn't want me before."

"Baby, that's not fair." His strong hands gripped her shoulders. "He didn't *know* about you before."

She sighed. "Look. You now know more about me than pretty much anyone in the world. Could we just eat our steaks?"

"Crap, the steaks!"

He ran outside. A few minutes later he returned. "Well, they won't be blue, but they'll be medium rare. That okay with you?"

She laughed. "That's just fine. I'll put the salad on the table. And when we sit down to eat, could we please talk about something besides my genetic makeup?"

"Absolutely." He brushed his lips over hers.

Chapter Seven

Harper had a perpetual hard on thanks to Amber Cross. And he had a sneaking suspicion that she *was* his type after all. He'd have loved to screw her brains out the previous evening. In fact, he'd brought it up because he'd assumed she'd hop in the sack with him. She'd worked as a stripper, right? Course that didn't mean she was easy, and he berated himself for being so prejudiced. Even so, she'd almost gone through with it. When she changed her mind he thought he'd explode. But now, having had the night to ponder it, he was glad they hadn't done the deed.

Amber Cross was special. Maybe even the one. He'd never in a million years imagined it would be her. But clearly they had chemistry, both physical and emotional.

She wasn't a quick fuck.

The girl'd had one hard life. For the life of him, he couldn't figure out why her mother wouldn't have gone after Thunder Morgan for child support. Unless Thunder Morgan wasn't Amber's father after all. But then why would Karen have named him on her birth certificate?

Amber was holding something back. Harper wasn't sure what it was, but he was sure of one thing.

He was going to find out.

* * * *

Amber had Sunday off. She relaxed in her studio apartment above the beauty salon. It was tiny but cheap, and it worked for her. She had finally saved up enough money to buy a tablet, and she fired it up after she'd downed her first cup of coffee.

Her Google search? None other than sweet Daddy himself, Thunder Morgan.

He had his own web site, of course.

Her heart nearly stopped. There on the web page were her light brown eyes.

She'd always been a dead ringer for Karen Hedstrom, except for the eyes.

He was handsome—sandy gold hair graying at the temples. An older man now, but she flipped through his gallery and caught sight of him in his younger years. Wow. Buff and beefy, just the way Karen liked her men.

Why on earth would he have been interested in bedding a worn-out drunk like her mother?

And why, why, *why* hadn't her mother gone after him for child support?

Harper was right. Something was up with this story. Amber scanned each page of the web site. Nowhere was the name Morgan Cross mentioned. She did a Google search cross referencing the two names. Nothing.

Either Thunder Morgan was not Morgan Cross, or he had left that name behind for some reason.

Two things niggled at her.

First, Harper would not lie. He was Catie's brother, and he was a good man. He wasn't a liar. If he knew Morgan Cross was the birth name of bronc buster Thunder Morgan, that was how it was.

Second. She couldn't overlook it or deny it. The man stared at her from her computer screen with her own eyes.

"I'll be damned," she said aloud.

She had questions. Tons of questions. She should go to Karen. But she hadn't spoken to the woman since she'd been kicked out of her house. What would she do? Go to San Antonio and show up on her doorstep?

Hi, I'm the daughter you threw out with the trash. Uh, how come you neglected to tell me my father was Thunder Morgan? And how come you neglected to tell him he had a kid?

She couldn't do any of those things. She didn't have two nickels to rub together. How would she get to San Antonio? On her looks? Hardly.

Her cell phone interrupted her thoughts.

She smiled. It was Harper. They'd exchanged numbers last night.

"Good morning, beautiful," he said. "Feel like some coffee?"

"I'm on my second cup already." She laughed.

"How about I come get you and we'll head to Rena's for some more. And maybe a croissant or two?"

"A croissant? You mean a cowboy like you doesn't want a hearty bacon and egg breakfast?"

His chuckle warmed her ears. "Well, that does sound good."

"Come on over to my place then. I'll make you breakfast. And my coffee's better than Rena's."

"Better than Rena's? Them's fightin' words."

"She brews a good pot, for sure. But mine's better. Strong, thick, and black, like my men."

"Huh?"

She giggled into the phone. "Just a joke, cowboy. From a movie I saw once."

"I won't turn that down. I'll be over in half an hour or so."

She took a quick shower and let her hair hang in wet waves around her face and shoulders. Then she tidied up the place, which didn't take long given its size, and started a fresh pot of coffee. She looked in her small fridge. Plenty of eggs and bacon, good. Also a few apples and a few cartons of yogurt. That was about it. Time to do some shopping. She'd get to that later today.

She started the bacon, and by the time a knock sounded on her door, the tiny place was alive with the aroma of smoky pork.

"Come in," she called.

"Hi there." Harper entered carrying a bouquet of wild flowers. He handed them to her.

"Thank you. That's so sweet." She grabbed a jar out of a cupboard and put the flowers in water.

"I've never been up here before," he said.

"It's small but comfy. It's actually really convenient to have everything in one room."

He sat down on the edge of the bed. "A double, huh? Not a lot of room."

"Don't need a lot of room just for me." She gave him what she hoped was a teasing smile and served up a plate of bacon and eggs. "Here you go."

"Smells great."

"Just sit down at my little table there." She pointed. "Dig in."

"You've fixed this little place up real nice."

"It worked well since this is about all I had to bring with me. I roomed with my friend Laura and another girl in San Antonio. Most of the furniture belonged to the other girl. I was thrilled when Judy showed me this place. I knew I wouldn't have to go out and buy a lot of stuff I couldn't afford."

"Makes sense." He took a bite of eggs. "Mmm. Good. So, I've been thinking."

"About what?"

"About your situation."

She gulped down a sip of coffee, her nerves on edge. Was he going to bring up Rachel's again? "What situation might that be?"

"About your dad, Thunder Morgan."

Oh, that was all. She breathed easier. "Funny you should mention him. I was just doing some research this morning."

"And?"

"And he was already a pretty big name by the time he hooked up with my mother. So I'm confused why she didn't tell him about me."

"Maybe she didn't know how to get in touch with him. The world wide web wasn't as worldwide twenty-two years ago."

"That's true, but he was a pretty big name, especially in rodeo country."

Harper swallowed his mouthful. "Well, there's one way to find all this out."

"And that is?"

"You could ask her."

Amber nodded. She'd thought of that, but... "Yeah, I suppose. But I literally haven't seen her or spoken to her since she kicked me out."

"So?"

Clearly Harper wasn't getting it. Of course not. He'd had a model childhood. "It's a little awkward."

"She's your mother, and you deserve some answers."

"I deserve a lot of answers. Doesn't mean I'm going to get any."

"Can't hurt to try."

She sighed and pushed her plate to the side. "The thing is, Harper, it *can* hurt. I don't want to go back to San Antonio. I left for a reason. I got the hell out of Rachel's. I don't want to go back there."

"Even to find out more about who you are?"

"Can't I find out from here? I mean, you said you know Thunder Morgan. You could contact him."

"Yes, I could do that, I suppose."

"Would you?"

"For you?" He leaned forward—the table was so small—and brushed his lips against hers. "Anything."

Her skin erupted in tiny bumps. Just a small peck, and here she was ready to hop into the sack with him again. And with her bed only twenty feet away—in plain view, still rumpled—it'd be darn easy.

Nope. Not going there. Not tumbling into bed with Harper just because he was tousled and sexy and oh so sweet to her.

She stood. "More coffee?"

He shook his head. "I'm doing fine. What are you doing the rest of the day?"

"No plans. I need to hit the grocery store. Pretty much all I had left was eggs and bacon. You got lucky this morning."

"Not as lucky as I'd like to." His voice was soft, husky, so very masculine.

She swooned just a little bit.

"I've been thinkin'," he said, his voice huskier than seconds before.

"About what?"

"About us."

"There's an us?"

"There could be, I think. I'm not lookin' for anything serious. Not just yet, anyway."

"Neither am I," she said and meant it, but her heart sank just a little.

"But I know one thing. I really want to kiss you right now."

He stood and took the coffee pot from her hands. Amber's breath caught as his finger trailed over her lower lip.

"You have such a gorgeous red mouth, baby." He cupped both of her cheeks and touched his lips to hers. The kiss was light and teasing, just enough to still her resistance.

Not that she had any resistance. What a crock.

He tasted of the robust coffee, the smoky bacon, with just a hint of minty outdoorsiness, an unexpected taste of wildness. He brushed his firm full sexy lips back and forth over hers.

Her eyelids fluttered closed, and she gave herself to the kiss, to the passion and desire that flowed between them. How difficult it would be not to fall in bed with this man! The moist heat of his mouth against hers tormented her, made her want more. Made her want all of him.

The kiss became stronger, more possessive, every bit as raw and unapologetic as it was tender and sweet.

Perfect.

The perfect kiss.

She sighed into his mouth, let her tongue entwine with his. She thrust her hands into his silky hair, let it flow through her fingers. So soft, like silk fringe—and beautiful, tousled, and sexy like the rest of him.

His groan vibrated against her lips and gums. The pressure of his lips increased, and he kissed her as though he wanted to devour her right then and there.

Without thinking, she stepped backward, backward, until the back of her legs hit the side of her bed. She sat, pulling him with her, until they were lying, him on top, still kissing with the frantic desire of new lovers.

His lips left her mouth and crept over her cheek to her ear. "I want to give you pleasure, Amber. I want to show you how good I can make you feel."

Yes, yes, yes, she said in her mind. Her sex pulsed between her legs. Her nipples tightened into buds so hard she was sure they'd freeze and fall off. They ached for his lips, his teeth, his tongue. She wanted to rip off her clothes and climb on top of him.

His strong hands roamed over her shoulders, across the swell of her breasts still covered by clothing. Fingers fumbled at the waistband of her jeans, and soon he was tugging them over her hips.

"Is this okay?" he whispered.

She nodded.

"Naughty girl. No panties."

She let out a soft laugh. "I was in a hurry."

He tossed her jeans on the floor. She lay, her body taut and full of tension, tight as a bowstring, her breasts and shoulders still covered, but naked from the waist down.

He touched her clit, and she nearly shattered right there. He rubbed her softly, moved downward into her folds.

"Mmm. So wet for me, baby."

Her body thrummed to the point she was sure he could hear the low purr. She thrashed her head from side to side on her rumpled comforter.

His fingers picked up speed, just a little, and he eased one inside of her while his thumb circled her clit.

She sighed.

"You like that, baby? Do I make you feel good?"

She closed her eyes, basked in the warmth covering her body, the desire flowing through her veins. "Yes, yes. Just like that, Harper."

"Mmm. You're beautiful. I need to taste you."

When his lips replaced his thumb on her clit, she soared to the ceiling. It had been a long time since anyone had made her feel this good. She wasn't sure anyone ever had, truth be told.

Sensation after sensation bombarded her body.

"God, baby, you're so sweet," he said against her folds, his breath a soft caress.

He continued to stroke the inside of her with his finger, and he added another as his tongue worked the rest of her flesh. She tangled her fingers in his hair, moving her hips against him, guiding his mouth in the right rhythm.

The spasms started in her clit, rocked through her wet channel, and spread up into her torso and then outward to her arms and legs until even her toes tingled. She flew, she danced, she soared, all without leaving the bed.

"That's right, baby, come for me." Harper thrust his fingers in and out of her in a racing rhythm matching her breaths.

"God, oh God," she heard herself scream. "Good. So good!"

When she finally floated downward, encased in pure nirvana, she opened her eyes. His head was still between her legs, his lips and chin glistening with her cream. She couldn't speak. Could barely move her head.

He smiled, his brown eyes glowing. "Again," he said, and he went back to work.

Chapter Eight

Going down on Amber was pure pleasure. Though he loved pleasing a woman, Harper had never enjoyed this part of sex more than he did at this moment. She tasted of citrus and honey and warm musky woman. Her beautiful pink flesh tantalized him. He couldn't get enough of her. His dick pulsed inside his jeans.

He aimed to keep it there. She didn't want to rush into anything, and truthfully, neither did he. This was for her. Just about her.

It might kill him, but so be it.

He brought her to a second orgasm, and then to a third. He started going for a fourth, but she begged him to stop.

"Please, Harper. You're going to kill me."

He grinned at her. "But what a way to go."

She fisted her hands in his hair and pulled him toward her. Their mouths mashed together, and he let her taste herself on his tongue. Mmm, did she enjoy that flavor as much as he did? From the moans and sighs coming from her, she did.

They kissed with passion, with fire, with unbridled lust. He ground his erection against her firm supple thigh. God, those legs. Wrapped around and over his shoulders they'd been heaven.

A vision popped into his head, of Amber's amazing legs wrapped around a silver pole at a strip club. At Rachel's.

He broke the kiss.

Why'd he have to think of that? Yes, he'd once thought she had the body of a stripper…

She looked up at him, her golden eyes wide. "Is something wrong?"

He shook his head. Nothing was wrong. He just didn't like thinking of her that way. He didn't judge her. At least he didn't think he did. She hadn't had much choice after her mother kicked her out. At least she'd finished school first.

"No. I'm fine."

She smiled. Oh, she could kill a man with that knockout smile.

"Good. Now I think it's your turn."

He shook his head. "Nuh-uh. That was for you, baby. Only for you."

"Surely you don't expect me to be so selfish."

"I certainly do." He cracked his wiseass grin. "And don't call me Shirley."

She burst into laughter. "The same movie! I love those corny lines."

"Me too," he said, laughing.

He got up. Still hard as a rock.

Oh well. It was Sunday. Ranches didn't stop on Sunday. "I have to get going. A million things to do at home."

"Are you sure you don't want—"

He shushed her with two fingers on her beautiful swollen lips. "I wanted to please you. And I want you to know I'm not just in this for sex. I like you."

"Wow."

"And just so you don't think my actions were completely altruistic"—he kissed the top of her forehead—"I enjoyed the hell out of that."

"That makes two of us." She stood. "I *will* pay you back though."

He kissed her rosy cheek. "I certainly hope so. But on your own time. When you're ready."

"What if I'm ready right now?"

Good God! He wasn't made of stone. "Baby, I'm tryin' to make a point here."

"That you're a gentleman. I know."

"That I want you, but that I'm willing to wait."

"What if I'm not?"

He pressed his lips to her forehead. "Good. The sooner the better in my book. But not today. I've gotta run. I'll call you later, okay?"

Her smile turned into a little pout. Man, even frowning she was beautiful. "Okay," she said.

"Thanks for breakfast."

"You're very welcome. Anytime."

"I'm counting on it." He gave her big wet kiss.

The weakening in his knees surprised him. This woman had a huge effect on him. And he liked it. He liked it very much.

He grabbed his Stetson, winked, and left.

* * * *

Amber was arranging groceries in her tiny fridge after a quick trip to the store when a knock on the door interrupted her thoughts.

Harper! Her heart did a flip-flop. He'd come back. She couldn't wait to see him. They'd make love now. She wouldn't make him wait any longer. She opened the door with a huge smile on her face.

That turned into shock. And a little bit of horror.

Blake Buchanan. Blake Buchanan holding a laptop.

"Hello, Amber."

"Mr. Buchanan. What can I do for you?"

"Now that's a right good question. May I come in?"

"What for?"

"I have something I want to show you, and after that, I think you'll agree we have tons to talk about."

She gripped the doorknob with her sweaty palm. "If you want to talk, call me on the phone."

"Then I wouldn't be able to show you what I want to show you."

"I'm sure I could not care less."

"I think you're wrong about that…Ms. Love."

Amber's stomach churned. Ms. Love. Ambrosia Love. He did remember her.

Play dumb. He can't have anything. You didn't do anything wrong.

She cocked her head. "Excuse me?"

His brown eyes shot darts. Had she really thought them gentle when she first met him?

"Ms. Love. Ambrosia Love. That was your stage name at Rachel's, wasn't it?"

She loosened her grip on the doorknob, tried to relax. "I can't see what business that is of yours."

"I think you might disagree once you see what I have to show you. May I come in?"

"No."

"Well then, I'll have to send this stuff over the Internet, and security being what it is these days, I can't be held responsible for who might see this information."

She swallowed and hoped he didn't notice. "What information do you think you have, Mr. Buchanan?"

"Information that I don't think you'd want anyone in the good town of Bakersville to see."

Had someone seized the back of her neck? Her airway seemed compromised. Couldn't get enough oxygen. She counted to ten, willed herself to calm down. What the hell was he talking about?

She'd danced at Rachel's, that was all. An admirer talked her into a lap dance once. She'd taken his two hundred and sworn never to do it again. Wasn't worth it. She'd spent the whole time trying to keep his paws off her. She'd hardly danced at all. But she had a rule. No one touched the goods. She wasn't *that* desperate.

She steeled herself. "Look, it's no secret that I danced at Rachel's."

One side of his mouth rose and a huff of air escaped. "Danced? That's quite a euphemism, isn't it?"

"Danced." She gritted her teeth. "It wasn't the classiest job in the universe, but it paid the bills, and I saved up enough to start a new life. Anything wrong with that?"

"Nothing at all."

"Then why exactly are you here?"

"Because you did more than dance, Ambrosia. And I have proof."

She gulped. What the hell was he talking about?

"Ready to let me come in?"

"Absolutely not." She pushed him out the door.

"Fine. Give me about an hour to circulate these photos on the net."

Her throat constricted again. *Breathe, Amber, breathe.*

"What photos? I didn't do anything!"

"I've got photographic proof otherwise."

Curiosity got the best of her. Chad and Catie knew this guy. She felt sure she wasn't in any physical danger. Heck, if she didn't find out what was going on, she was liable to pass out from hyperventilation.

"Fine. Come in then. Let's see what you think you have."

He entered. "Nice place."

She scanned the room for a paper bag. There, on the table, holding lemons from the store. She dumped the lemons on the table and crunched the bag in her fist. "It's cozy. Now enough with the small talk. What do you want?"

"Look, I understand why you worked at Rachel's."

"For the money," she said, "pure and simple."

"I know that, and I understand. We all do what we have to do sometimes for the money."

"Do you have a point?"

"As a matter of fact, I do." He set his laptop on the table and sat down. "I want to show you a web site."

Her nerves skittered. Doctored photos, maybe? She hadn't the foggiest. Whatever it was, he wasn't going to get away with this.

"Shall we?" He pulled the other chair close beside him. "Have a seat so you can see."

She was too curious not to. He typed in some letters and a password, and photos of nude women popped onto the screen.

Truly, she told herself, *you have nothing to worry about. You didn't do anything wrong. You never posed for photos. The one lap dance you did was out in the open, not back in the private rooms. Nothing to worry about, Amber. Nothing.*

Until the first photo emerged.

Her bowels clenched and nausea gripped her throat. The blond girl with the slim muscular legs…legs famous for her pole dancing. That girl lay on a red satin sheet, her legs spread wide, another woman's head—Laura's head!—between them.

"It's enhanced," she whispered. "It can't be me."

"It is." Blake clicked on the screen. "And so is this."

This time she was on a man's lap, naked, her nipple between his lips. Her back arched and her eyes shut—clearly enjoying the stimulation.

She swallowed hard. "I'm going to throw up."

"I don't doubt it. Here's another."

This time she was giving a guy a blow job. Bitterness coated her tongue. She swallowed a heave.

"Seen enough?"

"It can't be. I never…posed for these. I don't understand."

"How many drugs did you do in your Rachel's days, Amber?"

"Damn it!" Tears welled in her eyes. "I didn't do any drugs! I hardly drank. It can't be me. It just can't be."

"This one will tell the tale I think."

A black-and-white photo appeared. Her ass was in the air, and a triangle shaped birthmark was apparent on her right butt cheek.

As if of its own accord, her right hand wandered to her hips, over the spot where her own birthmark marred her skin.

How could this be?

"How many more pictures are there?"

"There are twenty-four altogether. Six are girl/girl, two solo, the rest with men."

"Am I…having sex in any of them?"

"Alas, no. But you're doing pretty much everything else."

Her stomach threatened to empty. She covered her lips with her hand. "I don't understand."

"Neither do I. You seem like a nice girl."

"I really don't remember."

He powered down the laptop and flipped it closed. "I'm sure you don't. But unfortunately, that gets filed under the heading of 'not my problem.'"

"What do you mean?"

"What I mean is, I owe a bad man a lot of money. If I don't pay him soon, he's going to break my legs or worse."

God. He wanted money. Money to keep these photos out of the public eye. They were already on a web site. How many people had already seen them? Would it matter at this point?

"What web site are these on?"

"It's a private web site. Men pay top dollar to visit it."

"Where in hell did they get the pictures?"

"I haven't a clue. And I don't care. Like I said, I just need money."

She sighed. "And if you don't get it?"

"The good folks of Bakersville will get some brand new impressions of their reigning rodeo queen."

She clasped both sides of her head. To think she'd actually thought she could be happy here. That she could make a new start.

No such luck for Amber Cross. She was that lush Karen Hedstrom's trashy daughter. She always would be. Some things couldn't be escaped.

"How much do you need?" As if it mattered. She didn't have two dimes to spare.

"Twenty grand."

Icy fingers gripped her neck. "Twenty grand? You think I have twenty grand? This is where I live, for God's sake, in this oversize closet!"

"Ambrosia—"

"*Don't* call me that!"

"I'm a reasonable man. I'll give you some time to get the money. You're a good friend of Catie McCray, and I happen to know she's loaded."

Catie? Seriously? She couldn't tell Catie about this.

"Your new boyfriend Harper's pretty well-off too."

She *really* couldn't tell Harper about this.

"Even Judy Williamson has managed to put away some money over the years."

Her boss? Was he kidding? She couldn't tell any of these people. She'd be run right out of town.

Where had those photos come from? She'd never done drugs, hardly ever drunk alcohol.

Except that one night when she blacked out.

Oh God.

She'd been at Rachel's for a few months, had gotten pretty popular, when two of the more experienced dancers invited her and Laura out after work one night. They went to their apartment. The bed had red satin sheets…

Oh my fucking God.

What was the woman's name? Megan? Martha? Something with an M. Were there photos of Laura too? Of course there were. She'd seen Laura's head between her own legs. She grabbed the laptop.

"Hey!" Blake said.

"Shut up, you creep. Let me see this. Get that web site back."

Surprisingly, he fired up the computer and brought it back up. She grabbed it away from him, clicked on the home page, and found the index of the girls' names. Sure enough, Laura Lee. Laura still worked at Rachel's and probably had no idea she was all over this web site.

She shook her head. She felt for her friend, but right now Laura was the least of her worries.

"I don't have that kind of money."

"Like I said, I'm a reasonable man."

"What is this web site?"

"I told you. It's a paid site. Patrons of Rachel's can see the girls in action. Indulge their fantasies."

"How do you know about it?"

"I know people."

"Who?"

"Not your concern."

"I'd say it's very much my concern. What happens if I *do* pay you off? Then no one in Bakersville finds out about this. But I'm still plastered all over the net and anyone who pays for the privilege can see me in photos I had no idea I posed for."

"Again, not my problem."

She gulped and mustered all her strength. "It just might be, after all. Extortion happens to be a crime, you know."

"You think anyone will believe you? Look at your background, Amber. You were a stripper. You posed for photos."

She clenched both fists. "I did *not* pose for photos!"

"You can say that till the cows come home, but we have the physical evidence right here. Trust me, no one in Bakersville will know where these photos came from. They won't know they came from me. You can blab it all over town that Blake Buchanan tried to coerce you into paying him to keep the photos secret. Still, the photos speak for themselves. Do you think people will care whether I tried to get money out of you? Do you think they'll even believe it? Hell, no. They'll be too busy gossiping and sneaking looks at the goods. You'll be ruined in this town."

She shook her drooping head. He'd beaten her. "And every other town I try to escape to, I assume, unless you get your money."

"Now we're speaking the same language."

Tears rolled down her cheeks. "Why are you doing this?"

"Because I can. Because I need the money."

"I told you, I don't have it."

"You have a week." He turned off the laptop, closed it, stood, and walked to the door. "I'll be in touch."

Amber slammed the door, ran to the bathroom, and emptied her stomach.

Chapter Nine

Amber had been crying on her bed for an hour when her cell phone rang.

"Hey, baby, it's me."

Harper. She sniffed. "Hi there."

"Listen, I know this is short notice, but can you come to my place for dinner tonight?"

She was a mess and a half. She had to turn him down. "I'm sorry. I can't, Harper."

"Do you have other plans? If so, change them. This is worth your while, I promise."

An evening with Harper could do wonders for her, but it would only be a temporary fix. It pained her to turn him down. "I said I can't."

"Baby, what's wrong? You sound all nasal."

"I'm fine. It's just…allergies. Terrible hay fever."

What a stupid lie. But maybe he'd buy it.

"Take an antihistamine then. And get yourself all prettied up and come to my place for dinner."

Can't he take a hint? "Harper, if you want sex, I don't think—"

He laughed. "Of course I want sex, Amber. You're hot, and I like you. But that's not what this is about. Just say you'll come. Please?"

"I really can't."

"You won't regret it, I promise."

Of course she wouldn't regret it. She'd never regret spending time with him. But she was screwed up right now. Her eyes were swollen and her nose red. She glanced at the clock beside her bed. Two.

"What time?"

"How does six sound?"

Four hours. Could she get herself together in that amount of time? God knew she needed something to get her mind off the mess she was in. She couldn't accomplish anything toward her goal of twenty grand on a Sunday evening. Why not spend it with Harper?

"Okay, I'll be there."

"Great! I can't wait to see you. Bye now."

"Bye."

She turned her head back into her pillow and cried some more.

* * * *

An hour later she steeled herself and rose from the bed. A quick look in her bathroom mirror and she considered calling Harper to cancel. She looked like death, to put it bluntly. Not death warmed over.

Just death.

Her eyes were red and puffy, her cheeks and hair matted with tears and snot, her skin pasty and gray, her nose so red she could double as Rudolph.

Like an idiot, she'd neglected to get the web site information and password from Blake Buchanan, so she couldn't do any research on her little problem. He hadn't left a number, just said he'd be in touch.

Asshole.

She turned on the shower and cranked the water as hot as it would go. She needed heat, and then she'd splash her face with cold when she got out. Hopefully that would avert some of the swelling.

She washed her hair twice and conditioned it with a hot oil treatment. When she dried off and looked at her face, she was pleasantly surprised. She splashed several handfuls of cold water over it, and she looked almost normal. Eye drops got rid of the red eyes. Her eyelids were still slightly swollen, but probably not noticeable to anyone who didn't know to look for it. Now if she could just keep from crying until after she got home from Harper's.

That's all it took—just that one thought and tears started to flow. She gulped them away. Nope. Had to stay strong at least for tonight. Heck, for tomorrow too. She had to go into work. She needed all the money she could make right now.

She dried her hair and pulled it into a high ponytail. The stretch would make her face look less cried out. Well, it was a thought anyway. She put on just a touch of makeup and lipstick.

She dressed in a denim miniskirt and silk blouse. She slid on navy mules and pronounced herself fit—as well as could be expected—for human eyes.

She had an hour before she needed to leave, so she got her tablet out and Googled Rachel's. Time to find out what might be going on.

Marta. That was the woman's name. She was European—German, or Austrian. Amber never knew which one. She went only by Marta. She wasn't stuck with a stupid stage name like Ambrosia Love.

Maybe she didn't need one.

She wore leather and furs and diamonds, all gifts from the men she serviced, Amber had assumed at the time. Now she wasn't so sure. Perhaps she made her own money...by luring unsuspecting new young strippers to her place to get drunk and have their photos taken.

Amber shook her head. Surely alcohol couldn't have been responsible for this. She and Laura must have been drugged. But with what?

Tears threatened again, and she clicked off her tablet. No use crying over spilled milk, or alcohol, or whatever they'd given her.

Damn it, I want a nice evening with Harper. And she would have it. She could lose it tomorrow.

She had no doubt she would.

Her body remained tense during the half-hour drive to Harper's ranch house. She tried breathing in through her mouth, out through her nose, and finally gave up. Relaxation wasn't to be.

Tonight she might forego her two drink minimum. Some alcohol might be just what she needed.

Course she really didn't want to go there. Not with the genes she carried inside her. And certainly not with what she'd just learned had happened one of the two times she'd allowed herself to get drunk.

She'd have a nice glass of wine. Harper liked wine and he seemed to know a little bit about it. She'd had half a glass with him last night, after all. And that was after she'd had two cosmos at the party.

Course it was a lot later that she had the wine, so she hadn't really violated her own rule.

One glass of wine. Hopefully it would relax her.

Maybe with a valium chaser?

Sheesh.

She drove onto the Cha Cha ranch property and followed the directions Harper had given her. Soon his ranch house came into view. She liked his house. It wasn't huge and sprawling like his mother's a few miles away, or Catie's that she shared with Chad.

Modest was nice. More her style.

She parked, walked to the door, and knocked.

Harper opened it, looking just as tousled and sexy as he always did. How did his hair always look so charmingly disheveled? It just begged her to run her fingers through it. His muscular rancher's body looked heavenly in jeans and a black western shirt.

McCray boys be damned. Harper Bay was the most handsome man in Bakersville.

"Hey, baby. It's great to see you." He pulled her close and gave her a smoldering kiss.

The familiar jolts coursed through her. God, this man affected her like no one else.

"So what's the big surprise?" she asked.

"What makes you think there's a surprise? Maybe I just wanted to have dinner with you."

His eyes gleamed. Mischief. He was up to no good.

"Stop kidding around, Harp. I've had a day and a half."

"You have? What's wrong, baby?"

Aw hell, what'd I go and say that for? She sure didn't want to get into that with him. Not tonight. "Oh, just my allergies and all."

"I didn't know you had allergies."

That was because she didn't. "Just some hay fever. It acts up now and then."

He took her hand. "So what did you do today?"

"Other than sneeze my ass off? Just went to the grocery store." *And got blackmailed. Nothing much.*

"Would you like a drink? I learned how to make a cosmo just for you."

"Did you?" *God, he's sweet.*

"Yup. Got one all ready for you. I even tasted it, and you know what? It's not half bad."

"Of course not. Do you think I'd drink something bad?"

He furrowed his brow. "It's pink, Amber."

She let out a laugh. "That's the splash of cranberry, genius."

"Yes, I know that. It's just, I never thought a pink drink would taste good. But it's pretty good."

"It's basically a vodka martini with some triple sec and a splash of cranberry juice, Harp. It's not all that girly of a drink."

"Yeah, but it's pink."

She shook her head, smiling. "So you've mentioned."

He handed her the drink. "Aren't you having one?"

"I don't do pink drinks." He grinned.

"What are you having then?"

"A vodka martini."

She laughed again. "You're too funny. So are you going to tell me what my surprise is?"

"It'll be here soon."

"Oh." She perked up. Granted, she'd had a shit day, but she was like a little girl when it came to surprises. She loved getting presents. Always had. She'd gotten darn few in her lifetime. She took a sip of her drink. "Not bad, cowboy, for your first time."

"Thank you." He waggled his eyebrows at her.

Damn, he was good-looking. Shudders ran down her spine and settled between her legs. She hadn't thought it possible to get turned on tonight, after the day she'd had. But Harper Bay could do it to her.

"Go on out to the deck and have a seat," he said. "I thought we'd eat outside. It's such a warm night for the end of April."

"Sounds good." Actually it sounded great. Amber loved the outdoors, and Colorado was such a beautiful state.

"I'll be out in a minute. I want to take care of a few things."

"Okay." She went outside and stood on the deck, inhaling the fresh evening air. The peaks of the Rockies glowed violet and indigo against the azure sky spotted with fluffy clouds. The sun was an orange ball sitting atop the snowcapped mountains. She inhaled again, ignoring the aroma of cow that crept by.

She took a seat at his patio table. It was set for three.

Three?

So her surprise was a person?

Who could it be?

Before she had time to think, the French doors opened with a squeak behind her. She stood and turned to see Harper and a nice-looking older man with dirty blond hair and golden eyes.

Harper's dark eyes sparkled. "Amber, I'd like you to meet Thunder Morgan."

Chapter Ten

Amber's pulse pounded inside her head. *What the fuck has he done?* She was in no condition to meet her birth father. She'd just been blackmailed, for God's sake. To be fair, Harper didn't know that, but still, he was interfering in something that wasn't his business. Who did he think he was, anyway?

"Harper"—she forced a smile—"may I see you inside for a moment?"

"What's up?"

She steadied her breathing, afraid she might lose control. "Just something I need to get your opinion on in the kitchen. You don't mind, do you, Mr. Morgan?"

"Not at all."

She clenched her teeth. Could this day get any worse? "We'll only be a minute."

She dragged Harper through the kitchen and out into the living room where she could be sure Thunder Morgan wouldn't hear them.

"What in God's name were you thinking?"

"Relax." He pushed a strand of hair behind her ear. "I didn't tell him anything. I just gave him a call when I got back home this morning and found out he was in Denver for a few weeks. So I invited him up for dinner. He's a great guy. I want you to get to know him."

Amber stared at him. He was actually serious. "And exactly what do you propose I say to him? 'Hi, I'm the daughter you never knew you had?'"

"Of course not. As far as he knows, at least for tonight, you're my friend. My date. Whatever you want to be."

"What I want to be is not here."

"Amber, come on. I didn't tell him your last name, so no worries. I thought you'd be happy to meet him."

"You caught me off guard, Harper. Jesus! Don't you think I might have liked a little time to prepare for this?"

"If I had given you time to prepare for it you would have freaked out."

"Uh…yeah. Kind of like I'm doing now?"

"I mean you would have freaked yourself out into a frenzy before he ever go here. Now you can just go with the flow."

She paced around his Berber carpet, sure she was wearing tracks in it. "Does this look like a person who's going with the flow?"

"Calm down, baby. You're going to get along great."

"So I'm just supposed to—what?—talk about *what* exactly? What do I have to say to a bronc buster?"

"You're the rodeo queen. You have a lot in common. You represent the rodeo."

Yeah, the rodeo queen. If Blake Buchanan had anything to say about it, she'd be dethroned in a week's time.

"And a few days ago you talked about learning barrel racing."

She rubbed her temples. Her interest in barrel racing seemed like a lifetime ago. Yet he was right. It had only been a few days ago. Why, oh why, had she ever wanted to race? If she hadn't, Catie wouldn't have introduced her to Blake Buchanan, and he wouldn't have recognized her from Rachel's and started snooping around on the Internet.

What if, what if, what if?

What if her mother hadn't kicked her out? What if she'd been able to get work doing nails and had never gone to Rachel's?

She sighed. Life was full of "what ifs."

"Amber"—Harper traced her lower lip with his finger—"I'm sorry if this isn't a surprise you particularly wanted. I thought you'd be happy. I wouldn't do anything to make you unhappy."

"I know that."

"But I invited him here. He's a friend of my family. And right now we're being rude."

She nodded. "You're right, of course. I'm sorry. I just wish I knew what to say."

"You're good with people. I'll start him talking, and then you just pop into the conversation when you're ready, okay?"

"Sure, I can do that." She let out a breath. "I guess it's now or never then."

"Come on." He took her hand. "You'll be great."

* * * *

Thunder Morgan had led an interesting life, traveling the rodeo circuit. He'd even done German rodeos for a while. He had a wonderful sense of humor, and soon Amber was laughing until tears formed in her eyes.

Her eyes.

They were almost identical to his.

Did he notice?

"Did you ever regret not settling down?" she asked.

"Well, not overly," he said. "Sure, it would have been nice to have a wife to come home to and kids to carry on the name, but would it have been fair to them? Would it be fair to a wife to never be home, to never help her with the kids? Would it be fair to the kids to have to grow up without a father?"

A lump formed in Amber's throat. "I see what you mean."

"I was a traveler. For a while I didn't keep a permanent residence at all. I just hit circuit after circuit, winning purse after purse, putting away what I could for a rainy day. When you're in the rodeo, you know you can't do it forever. It's kind of like pro football. Your body eventually says no more."

"Seems you had quite a good run," Harper said.

"Yup, a sight better than most."

"Do you keep a permanent residence now?" Amber asked.

"Sure do. On the western slope. Not too far from Harper's ranch out there."

"I told you that Thunder used to work at Bay Crossing, didn't I?" Harper said.

"Yes, of course," Amber said. "That's how you know him."

"Nothing like the western slope," Thunder said. "I love it here, don't get me wrong. And I've seen some wonderful places during my travels, but I always knew when it came time to retire, I'd be back on the slope with the peaches and apple orchards and vineyards. I'm looking into winemaking now."

Harper raised his eyebrows. "Really? I didn't know that."

"Gotta do something to keep busy," Thunder said. "It drives me crazy to sit around doing nothing."

"Me too," Amber said. "I'm always finding something to do on my time off."

"What do you do, pretty lady?"

"I'm a manicurist."

"You don't say? My mother was a manicurist. Small world."

Not that small. Manicurists were a dime a dozen, but Amber didn't say that. Instead, she found herself feeling closer to him, wondering if her interest in doing nails came from his mother.

She let out a huff of air and hoped neither of them noticed. She was grasping at straws. She'd decided to learn nails because the vocational high school offered it, and she'd have a skill with which to make a living. She didn't have some huge dream to be a manicurist. She was good at it, true, but was it her life's work? No.

If she could do whatever she wanted, she'd ride horses. That was what she loved.

And maybe *that* was from her father. She smiled.

"You look happy," Harper said.

Happy? Meeting her real father, finding out her love of horses might have come from him? It sure hadn't come from her mother. Karen wouldn't know a horse from a cat. Yes, happy was a nice word. A glowing warmth caressed her skin. For a moment she'd forgotten about her ill-fated meeting with Blake Buchanan earlier.

Damn. Had to think about that.

"I'm doing all right," she said. She turned back to Thunder Morgan. "Tell me about your place on the slope."

"It's a ranch house on about a hundred acres. I don't need a lot of space for just me and a couple horses and a couple dogs. I have neighbors who care for the animals while I'm away."

"When do you plan to start making wine?"

"I have to find a vineyard first. There are a couple small ones for sale. I'm looking into it. I have a little nest egg. Bronc bustin' paid the bills. It didn't make me rich, that's for sure, but I can afford a small operation."

"What kind of wine do you want to make?"

"Red, definitely. I'm partial to Rhone blends. You know—syrah, grenache, mourvedre."

Amber shook her head. "You'll have to excuse me. I was telling Harper just yesterday ay that I know absolutely nothing about wine. I like the taste of most of it, though. Especially reds."

"I have a great little Rhone blend we can try tonight with our steaks," Harper said, rising. "I'll get it. And Amber baby, you'll get your steak blue tonight."

"You like your steak blue?" Thunder smiled. "A girl who likes her meat still mooing is a girl after my own heart."

* * * *

"I can't believe you did that," Amber said after Thunder left, "but I'm glad you did. He's amazing."

"And he's your dad."

She shook her head. "I wouldn't have believed it, except for the eyes. I'm a dead ringer for Karen otherwise. But those eyes of his. It was like staring into my own."

"So, baby, when are you going to tell him?"

"Tell him what? That he's my dad?" She scoffed. "I think around the fifth of never."

"You can't be serious."

"Of course I am. He's got a life, Harper. A life that doesn't include a twenty-two-year-old daughter he never knew he had. He'll probably think I'm lying. I doubt he even remembers my mother."

"You said so yourself. The eyes tell all."

"Yes, but other than the eyes I don't look a thing like him."

"There's DNA testing."

"I couldn't ask him to do that."

"Why not? If he doesn't believe you, that's the one way to know for sure. For both of you."

"He's such a nice guy. I don't want to screw up his life."

"Who says you'll screw it up? He never married. He's retired now. He's all alone. He might welcome the idea of family."

Would he? Amber's heart did a flip-flop. It was possible. She sure loved the idea herself. She hadn't spoken to Karen in over six years. While she finished school, Laura had been her family. Laura's mother hadn't been around all that much, and once they'd both graduated, she very nicely told them to get the hell out. At Rachel's the girls were her family, with Marta as a mother figure.

Marta.

Some mother figure, drugging girls and exploiting them.

Blake Buchanan and those horrible Internet images catapulted into her mind. Her tummy—full of blue rib eye, tomato-and-mozzarella salad, loaded baked potato, and green beans—threatened to betray her.

Escape. She longed for escape. And there sat Harper, his dark eyes smoking, his hair tousled and sexy as usual, smiling with those full pink lips surrounding nearly perfect white teeth. One of his front teeth slightly overlapped the other. A tiny imperfection that made him even sexier. Her heart melted.

He'd done something so wonderful for her tonight. He'd found her father and brought him to her.

So a man wasn't in her immediate future. At least that's what she'd thought. Maybe she'd rethink her stance.

He wanted her. Even now, just sitting on the couch, electricity sizzled between them. His finger brushing her forearm sent tiny flames igniting over her whole body.

Her need was more than physical, though. She liked him. Liked how he treated her, liked his openness, his forthrightness, how he'd told her in no uncertain terms he wanted to take her to bed. It was a statement of pure honesty. Who couldn't respect a man who valued honesty above all else?

She liked his family, liked his place, liked pretty much everything about him. Loved that he'd offered to bring her breakfast this morning.

Loved that he'd brought her father to her.

Loved.

She was falling for Harper Bay.

Damn it.

His arms would be paradise—a whimsical escape from Blake Buchanan and his threats.

How she longed for escape. Escape only Harper could give her.

His deep voice interrupted her racing thoughts. "Don't you think?"

"Think what?"

"That Thunder might welcome the idea of family at this point in his life?"

His beautiful eyes, crinkling in the corners, ensnared her. "I suppose he might."

She melted into his arms.

When their lips met, all doubts rinsed from her mind. Her body took over. She wanted to make love with Harper. She would not stop like she had last night.

He traced the outside of her lips with his soft probing tongue. A butterfly kiss. Laura had taught her about that back in high school, after Karen had kicked her out. She'd never experienced one until now.

The kiss warmed her, heated her, turned her into a blistering inferno. Had she not known better she'd have been convinced her skin was glowing red with passion. Harper replaced the tip of his tongue with his teeth, and he nibbled gently over her upper lip, her lower, and sucked the lower lip into his mouth.

Amber sighed. Goosebumps erupted over her flesh. How was it possible to feel so hot yet so cold at one time? A soft moan met her ears.

It took a moment to realize it had come from her own throat.

"I love kissing you, baby," Harper whispered against her mouth. "You're so soft and sweet, so responsive." He parted the seam of her lips with his tongue and eased it inside.

If she'd had any shred of resistance left, his tongue erased it. She bathed herself in the kiss, let it consume her. Her tongue met his with passion so powerful she thought she might explode with desire and lust.

They ravaged each other's mouths. Amber touched Harper's cheek, and his stubble scraped against her fingers and palm. So masculine, so right. He was so handsome, beautifully sculpted, and she wanted him so much. Her heart beat against her sternum so hard and fast she felt sure he could feel it in his own chest.

And still they kissed. His hands wandered over her shoulders, her arms, until they found her breasts. Her nipples tightened and budded against the fabric of her bra. They ached for his mouth, his tongue.

"Please, Harper, make love to me."

Had those words come from her mouth? Yes they had, and she meant them with all her soul.

"Oh, baby." The deep timbre of his voice vibrated over her. "I want you so much."

He rose and took her hand, led her upstairs to a large master bedroom. A four poster king-size bed draped in a mahogany comforter sat against one wall.

He turned to her, his eyes smoldering. "Are you sure this time?"

Her clit throbbed with each beat of her heart. "I'm sure, Harper. Take me to bed."

He gently led her to the bed and eased her down upon the silky covers. "You're so beautiful, Amber."

Her skin warmed. His words touched her heart, her soul. She knew she was attractive. Those years at Rachel's had proved that. But to hear it from Harper's full lips that had already given her so much pleasure was nirvana.

He slowly undressed her, discarded her blouse and her bra, and feasted on her nipples.

Sweet ecstasy. His mouth felt so good on her breasts, so good and so right. Her areolas wrinkled, pushing her nipples out farther, sending tingles to her core.

She'd had some experience—not a lot, but some—but never had she known a man who could drive her as crazy as this one.

"Your breasts are delicious," he said.

He moved downward and deftly removed her skirt and panties. She started to kick off her mules, but he stopped her.

"Leave them on. You look amazing."

She wanted to please him, truly she did, but leaving them on reminded her too much of her days at Rachel's. She didn't want anything to taint this night. She kicked them off anyway, hoping he wouldn't notice.

He looked down, frowned slightly, but said nothing.

And into her mind came a single thought. *He understood.* She knew he did.

He spread her legs and smiled. "I can't wait to taste you again."

She tried to stop him, or she at least thought about it. He'd given her so much pleasure this morning that she wanted to please him first.

But when his tongue touched her hard bud, she was lost. He feasted on her folds, her clit, all of her, his stubble grazing over her and making her hotter. She shuddered. Had anything in the world ever felt as good as this?

Her hips rose, thrust against his mouth, urging him to delve deeper into her wetness. Her naked body tingled against his fully clothed one.

"You're wearing too many clothes, cowboy."

"Shh," he said against her, his voice a soft vibration against her slick folds. "I'm busy."

Far be it from her to bother a busy man. She reached forward, grabbed two fistfuls of his silky hair, and pulled him farther into her heat.

"God, that feels amazing." When had her voice lowered an octave?

He held her at bay for what seemed like an eternity, until she couldn't help but shout at him. "Please, you've got to let me come!"

He thrust two fingers inside her, and she shattered. Up she flew to the highest peaks of the Rockies. Her entire body throbbed along with her sex, and when she floated downward, his fingers still moved in and out of her, gently now, softly.

So good. So very good.

He lowered his head, but she stopped him. "Oh no, not this time."

"You didn't like?" His devilish smile told her he knew otherwise.

"Are you kidding? You're the most talented man in the world at that."

"High praise."

"Indeed. But it's my turn. There are a few things I'm pretty good at too."

She pulled him down on the bed and maneuvered on top of him. His erection pulsed against her naked wet sex. How she wanted him. She was ready to yank down his pants and mount him then and there.

But no. She wanted to please him first, as he'd pleased her. She unbuttoned his shirt slowly, all the while trailing light kisses over his neck and chest. His copper coin nipples stuck out through chestnut chest hair. They were turgid, begging to be sucked. She obliged.

"Oh, baby, you have no idea how good that feels."

She chuckled against his warm flesh. "I think I have a vague concept."

"I know... I just...my nipples are really sensitive. More so than most guys, I think. At least that's what women say."

She let his nipple tumble from her lips and looked up. "You've had a lot of women, huh?"

His eyes were heavy, half-lidded. "Not a lot. A few. They've all been amazed at how my nipples react."

"I see." She placed a soft kiss on one nipple. "They're delicious, actually."

"I'm glad, baby, because you can keep doing that forever and I won't complain."

"With pleasure." She sucked and tugged, moving from nipple to nipple and loving every second of it.

Harper squirmed beneath her, his jean-clad erection pushing against her.

She wanted to see him naked. In all his tousled sexy glory. She let his nipple go and rained tiny kisses down his chest, his belly, pausing to lick his belly button. With precision, she unsnapped and unzipped his jeans.

Lord. No underwear.

"Commando? Expecting to get lucky tonight?"

"Just hoping, baby, that's all."

His erection sprang free from a nest of brown curls. He was magnificent, large and golden, with a drop of fluid glistening on the head of his cock. She licked it off.

He shuddered beneath her.

"You like that?"

"God, baby, yes. Suck me. Please."

"Since you said please." She twirled her tongue around the swollen head and savored the salty masculine flavor. He groaned in pleasure. She warmed, and her own sex throbbed.

Pleasing him pleased her. More than it had with any other man she'd been with.

She continued her assault, trailing her tongue along his length to his base and back up again, teasing and teasing, until she finally lowered her mouth and took all of him to the back of her throat.

"Ah, God, baby," he groaned. "Yes, take it all."

She could do this for hours, suck his beautiful cock. She wanted this as much as he did.

Surprising. She'd never enjoyed this aspect of sex much.

Until now.

Until now when she was with a man she truly cared about.

When had she started caring this much? When had she fallen in love?

Don't go there, Amber.

She resumed her task, loving every delicious moment of it.

"Baby, baby..."

She lifted her head. "Yeah?"

"Nightstand drawer. Condom."

God, yes. Condom. She wanted him inside her. She grappled in the drawer and retrieved a foil packet. Quickly she ripped it open, sheathed him, climbed atop him, and sank herself onto his hardness.

Had she ever felt so full? So complete?

Slowly she moved up and down, finding his rhythm, letting his own pistoning hips guide her.

"Yeah, baby. God, yeah." His voice was deep, and his tone seemed to be hugging her, urging her to make love to him. "Fuck me. That's it."

Not a word she liked. But he said it so sweetly that it turned her on even more. She wanted to fuck him. She wanted to fuck his brains out. Her whole body felt like a rocket ready to launch.

She moved faster. Her clit rubbed against him as she pumped, and oh, oh...*yes*. The orgasm hit her with more force than she was prepared for, and she nearly fell off the bed.

His strong hands steadied her. "That's right, baby. Come for me. Come."

The climaxes kept coming and coming. His hips gyrated harder up into her.

"Harper, so many, God...God, yes!"

"Yeah, baby. I'm going to come." He thrust up into her faster. "Yes, yes, baby."

As he spilled into her, her orgasms slowed. She fell forward onto his chest, their perspiration mingling into a scent of musky completion. She inhaled against his neck. Mmm. Their own special aroma. Perfect.

"Oh, baby," he growled. "That was amazing."

She nodded against his neck. Couldn't bring herself to speak yet.

"Amber."

She drew all her strength and sent it to her vocal cords. "Hmm?"

"Stay with me. Spend the night."

She snuggled against him, already half-asleep.

Chapter Eleven

"Rise and shine." Harper's voice cut through Amber's dream of lovemaking.

She opened her eyes. "Hey. What time is it?"

"Six. I gotta get moving. Ranches don't run themselves."

"Yeah. I'm working today too. My first client's at eight, so I need to go."

"Time for breakfast?"

"I wish I could. I have to get home and shower and change."

He grinned. "You could shower here."

She could...

Images of Harper's manly body covered in droplets of warm water enticed her, but... "Ha. Then I'd never leave. But I'll take a rain check on the shower."

"I'll hold you to that. Do you have time for a quick cup of coffee?"

"Only if it's to go. Sorry."

"Okay. I'll get you one." He leaned down and gave her a light kiss on the lips. "Last night was wonderful, baby. Thank you."

Thank you? No man had ever thanked her for sex before. Should she thank him back?

"Um...you're welcome?"

He chuckled. "You are priceless, Amber. I never would have thought you were my type, but damn, I love being with you."

Not his type? Was that an insult? "What do you mean by that?"

"Just...you're not like the country girls I grew up with. You're more sophisticated. You look different. You act different. I mean, I always thought you were beautiful. I just had no idea I'd like you so much."

He hadn't hedged for words, thank God. "So that was a compliment then?"

He laughed again. "Of course it was."

"Good. 'Cause I like you too. And last night was amazing for me as well." She got up and started collecting her clothes.

"I'll get your coffee, baby. Meet me down in the kitchen."

* * * *

"Angie, when are you and Rafe going back to the slope?"

"Tomorrow. Why?"

Amber sighed as she clipped the cuticles on Angie's right hand. "I need to talk to someone."

"I've got all day today. I want to go see Violet this afternoon, but other than that I'm free."

"I've got a full schedule today," Amber said. "Can we have dinner?"

"Sure. Why don't Rafe and I meet you at the Blue Bird?"

She exhaled a long breath. "Well...I was kind of hoping we could talk alone. Nothing against Rafe but—"

"Girl talk?"

She had no idea. "Yeah, something like that."

"How about lunch?"

"I can't take lunch. I'm booked through. Please? It's important."

"Of course. Rafe'll understand. The Blue Bird?"

"My place, actually. I need privacy."

Angie's hand stiffened under Amber's ministrations. "Amber? What on earth is going on?"

Amber looked down, unable to meet her friend's gaze. Would Angie believe her? Would she understand? Angie had her own skeletons, so she was Amber's safest bet. Catie was busy with the new baby, and Judy was her boss, for goodness' sake. She wasn't that close to anyone else yet, at least not enough to trust with this. "I'll tell you tonight. God, I really need to talk to someone."

"Okay. Tonight at your place. You're obviously distraught. I'll get take out from the Blue Bird and bring it over. Say six?"

"Six thirty."

* * * *

"No offense, Amber, but you look like hell."

Amber held her door open and Angie walked in, carrying a takeout bag from the Blue Bird and a bottle of wine. "Good to see you too, Ang."

Angie made herself at home in Amber's small abode, setting food on the table and grabbing two plates out of the cupboard. "Come on and sit. There's obviously something you need to spill. Where's your corkscrew?"

"Top drawer." Amber plunked down at the table and thunked her head on the hard surface. "God, where to start?"

A soft pop met her ears—the wine cork.

"I can't hear you when you're talking into the table, hon."

She lifted her head and sighed.

"So does this have to do with my brother?" Angie poured two glasses of wine.

Harper? He was the least of her worries, except he'd want nothing to do with her when he found out the other issues she was dealing with. Amber shook her head. "No. I mean, not really."

"Seems you two are getting along pretty well."

"We are. I'm surprised, to be honest."

Angie laughed. "So is he. Never in a million years did he think you were his type."

So she'd heard. "Have you talked to him about us?"

"Not really. He just said he likes you a lot and he's looking forward to seeing where it goes."

She nodded. She felt the same. He knew more about her than she'd let on to anyone so far in Bakersville, and he wasn't judging her. Course the relationship wouldn't go much further if she couldn't keep Blake Buchanan at bay.

Stripping at Rachel's was one thing. Pornographic photos on the net were something else entirely.

"I like him too." She sighed. "A lot." Big understatement.

Angie took a sip of wine and began to take the cartons out of the Blue Bird sack. "So what's the problem then?"

"With Harper? There is none." At least not yet.

"Okay. What else is going on? There's a new guy in your life. You should be shining like the sun. Instead you look like you've been reincarnated as a rag."

She couldn't crack a smile. "Damn, Angie. You cut right to the chase, don't you?"

"I try."

Amber let out a controlled breath. *Here goes nothing.* "I haven't told you much about my life in San Antonio."

"No, you haven't. Every time I've asked you've changed the subject."

"You're right, and I'm sorry. It's not a time in my life I like to talk about. Or even think about for that matter."

"Well, you did tell me about your two one-night stands." She winked.

True, she had. About seven months ago, before Angie and Rafe had hooked up. Angie had said she needed some sex, and Amber had suggested a one-night stand. Who would've thought two one-night stands would turn out to be the tamest things she'd done in San Antonio?

Amber picked up her wine glass and took a long sip. "I guess it's best to start at the beginning."

For the next hour, she poured out her whole sordid story, beginning with being kicked out of Karen's house to leaving San Antonio.

Angie listened with rapt attention, her green eyes wide. "And Harp knows all of this?"

"All of what I've told you so far."

Angie smiled and patted Amber's forearm. "My brother's a good man."

Her friend's touch soothed her...but only a little. "That he is."

"If he's okay with all of this, why are you so upset?"

Those same icy fingers gripped the back of her neck. "Because I haven't told you everything yet. I've only told what...what I remember."

"Sorry, babe. Not following here."

"Oh God." She pushed her wine glass ahead of her. "Is there any more?"

"Yeah." Angie poured another glass. "I've never seen you drink more than two drinks."

"This is only my second."

"I know. I'm just saying."

Amber took a sip. It was a nice red, kind of spicy. She'd hoped to learn more about wine from Harper. She'd hoped for so much...

"You know that guy who used to work for Chad? Blake Buchanan?"

"Yeah."

"You've lived here most of your life. You already know the story about him and the librarian."

Angie nodded. "Heck, that's old news. Evie's over it. I thought the whole town was."

"Maybe they are. I don't know."

"He seems like a nice enough guy to me."

Amber widened her eyes. Seriously? Angie couldn't see through the jerk? She was as blind as Catie. "He's not a nice guy, Ang."

"Oh? Why do you say that?"

Amber swallowed the lump in her throat. "He's blackmailing me."

Angie nearly spat wine across the table. "Say what?"

"Did I stutter? He's blackmailing me."

"How?"

"Turns out he was in San Antonio for a while, and he remembers me from Rachel's."

"So what? If Harper knows, and I know, and we're fine with that, what makes you think everyone else won't be fine with it?"

"I'm rodeo queen, for one thing. Hardly a job for a stripper." She clutched the stem of her goblet. "But that's not the issue."

"What is, then?"

Amber gulped down the last of her wine. *Damn.* She'd met her two drink max. She could use another.

She swallowed, her tummy fluttering. Angie was her friend. She would understand. Wouldn't she?

She cleared her throat. "Blake Buchanan came by yesterday with some photos on the Internet."

"Photos of you?"

She nodded. "They were definitely me. Thing is, I have no memory of posing for them at all. I found my roommate Laura on the web site too, and I know she'd never pose either."

"Nude photos?"

She had no idea. "Yeah. More than just nude photos. I'm doing things in them."

Angie's eyes widened. "You're doing…*it?*"

"Not *it*, in the literal sense, but pretty much everything but."

Angie paused. A long pause. Then, "But how? If you don't remember… I don't understand, Amber."

"Neither did I at first, but I'm pretty sure I was drugged. I seriously have no memory of the whole thing."

"What web site is it?"

"It's an expensive paid web site for Rachel's patrons, as far as I can tell."

"Do you have the URL?"

"No. He didn't give it to me, and I didn't think to ask for it." Why hadn't she gotten the damn URL? "I wasn't thinking at all. This came at me from left field."

"I understand. Do you have any idea how this happened?"

"I have a hunch. There was a woman at Rachel's—her name was Marta. She was kind of our mother hen. One night she invited Laura and me to her place. We got to drinking…and I blacked out. I've only been drunk twice in my life. The other was when I had the first one-night stand that I told you about. Anyway, I recognized the bed at her place from the photos."

"You think you were drugged?"

"I can't see any other explanation. I was obviously awake in the pictures. Something had to make me forget. I assumed I was drunk and I blacked out. Now I'm not so sure."

"Something to induce amnesia—"

"Exactly."

"Like the date rape drug, maybe?"

"Maybe. I have no idea. Do I look like I have a clue about drugs? I never did any of them. Hell, even if I'd wanted to, I couldn't afford them."

Angie squeezed her forearm. "Honey, I know. I'm not accusing you of doing drugs."

"I know. I'm sorry."

"No need to apologize."

Amber choked out a sob. "Blake wants twenty grand in a week or he goes public with the photos."

Angie raised her eyebrows. "Twenty grand?"

"Yes. I told him there's no way I can get it, but he says that's not his problem."

"Well, there's no problem." Angie patted her arm. "I'll give you the money."

Amber sighed. What a wonderful friend. "Angie, that's not why I wanted to talk to you."

"I know that, honey. I know that. But you need help, and I have the means to help you."

"But don't you see? If we give him the money, he'll just keep holding the photos over my head. When he needs more money, guess where he'll go? And in the meantime my photos are on the Internet! Without my permission. Hell, without my knowledge!"

Angie scooted her chair closer and wrapped her arms around Amber in a tight hug. "We'll figure this out, I promise."

"I hope you're right."

"I want you to listen to me. There's someone who can help you."

"Who?"

Angie let out an exhale. "You won't like it."

"I'll try anything at this point."

"Harper. You have to tell Harper."

Chapter Twelve

"Are you crazy?" No way was she telling Harper. He'd never forgive her.

"He's a lawyer, Amber. He can help."

"Things are going well with us. I don't want to risk that."

"Don't you see? Harper cares about you. He won't let anyone hurt you. And he can help. These photos are up without your permission. That's not legal."

She gulped. "I know that. But what can I do?"

Angie grasped her hand. "You can tell Harper, and we can go from there."

Amber's head jarred at the ring of her cell phone. She didn't recognize the number.

"Hello?"

"Hello, darlin'. It's Blake."

Blake Buchanan. Her body stiffened. "It's him," she mouthed to Angie.

"What do you want?"

"Just checkin' in. Seeing how things are going. I know you're dining with your friend Angelina Bay Grayhawk. And I know she's loaded. Did you get my money yet?"

Nausea seized her. He was out there. Watching her. How dare he violate her that way?

She nearly laughed out loud. He'd clearly already thrown caution to the wind by blackmailing her. There wasn't much he wouldn't do, was there?

"Don't call me again."

"Hey, I'm just looking out for both of us. The sooner I get my money, the sooner I'm outta your hair, and you can go on with your life."

Anger boiled in her belly. "Don't you dare patronize me. Say you get your money. What then? You haven't given me the web site URL. For all I know the photos will still be there and you'll come back to me the next time you find yourself strapped for cash."

"Hey, the deal was you get me twenty grand and I don't divulge this information to the sainted town of Bakersville. There was nothing more than that."

"So my photos stay on the web site then? You want me to pay twenty grand for that?"

"That's your only choice for now. I have no power to get the photos down."

"Then what good are you?" She clicked the phone off.

"You're just going to piss him off," Angie said.

Tears streamed down her cheeks. "I don't give a damn!"

But she did. That was a lie. She didn't want to be ruined in Bakersville. She loved it here. She'd finally found a place that felt like home. She'd found friends. She'd even found a man. A man who felt like home.

Maybe he'd understand. Angie thought so.

Angie took both her hands. "Go to the bathroom and get cleaned up. We're going to go see my brother."

* * * *

"Harper, you're not being fair."

Harper paced up and down. "Fair?" He glared at his sister. "None of this is fair."

"You're absolutely right," Angie said. "But it's the most unfair to Amber."

He looked over at the woman—the beautiful woman he'd begun to think of as his—and his heart broke. He could handle that she'd been a stripper, that she'd been kicked out of her house by a drunken mother and she had to find a way to earn a living. That was admirable. Noble even.

But the photos?

True, she claimed to have no knowledge of their existence prior to yesterday. Could he believe her? He wanted to, but evidence pointed against her. By her own admission, she was awake and fully active in the photos.

And after supposedly finding all this out, she'd come to his home, slept in his bed, in his arms, as if nothing had happened.

What the hell am I supposed to think?

He didn't know her at all.

"You're not the woman I thought you were."

"Harper, please." She walked toward him, reached out to him.

His heart hurt. How he wanted to take her hand. He ached to pull her into his arms and hold her, to promise her he'd do anything, anything at all to make sure that look of sadness and horror never marred her beautiful face again.

But no. He'd be strong. He'd always thought she wasn't his type. Turns out his first hunch had been right.

He pulled away from her. "I'm sorry, Amber."

"Harper," Angie said, "please."

"I'll help you," he said. "I'll do what I can to get rid of Buchanan's threat. I have some information I got in confidence from a friend. It should work to hold him off, at least until you relinquish your rodeo queen crown in a few months. That'll keep the scandal at bay. After that, you can"—he gulped—"leave town if you want."

Angie whipped her hands to her hips. "Damn it, Harp! How can you be so cruel?"

"Cruel?" He thumped his fist on his father's—*his*—desk. "How do you think all this makes me feel? I thought I had finally found someone special."

"You did! Amber's special."

He looked at her, slumped in a chair, her pretty features distraught and anxious. Her face ruddy, eyes swollen, nose red and glistening. Again his heart hopped in his chest. He wanted to run to her, soothe her, tell her he'd take care of her.

"I'll take care of Buchanan. That's all I can promise for now."

"Harp—" Angie started.

Amber stood and interrupted. "It's okay, Angie. We tried."

"I'll help you, I said." Harper raked his fingers through his hair.

"You'll get Buchanan off her back," Angie said.

"Yes."

"That's not helping."

"It's all I can do right now."

Amber shook her head. "Stop it, Ang. I want to go home now."

Angie helped Amber to the door, and the two walked away.

Amber walked out of his life.

He sat at his desk with his head in his hands. How had it come to this? They'd shared such a special time last night, and all the while she'd known about this stuff in the back of her mind. Dishonesty, that's what it was. He could forgive a lot, but not dishonesty.

And did he really believe she'd had no knowledge of the photos?

He wanted to believe her. Truly he did. But it just didn't make any sense.

Drugged? Photos of her with others? Posed? Her eyes wide open?

Couldn't be.

And true or not, she should have told him last night. She'd slept with him under false pretenses.

Sadness laced his heart. He'd thought he was falling for her.

He really hadn't been her type all along.

He sat and stared into space for a few minutes and then picked up his cell phone.

"Yeah, Buchanan."

"Blake Buchanan?"

"Yeah that's right. Who's this?"

"Harper Bay."

"Bay? How's it going?"

"This isn't a social call, Buchanan."

"What's up? Don't tell me—your girlfriend's been telling you lies about me."

"First, she's not my girlfriend, and second, I'm pretty damn sure she's not lying."

"What's she saying?"

"That you're blackmailing her."

"See what I mean? That's a total lie."

God, what a piece of filth. Harper wanted to blast through the phone and beat the shit out of him. "Buchanan, I was not born yesterday. I happen to know why you need money."

"I don't know what you're talking about."

"Stop singing that tune, Buchanan. It is so old and tired, and so am I."

"Where'd you get your so-called information?"

"I have friends in high places. That's all I'm saying. I can guarantee the accuracy of my information. Does the name Paul Donetto ring a bell?"

Nothing but static on the line.

"You still there?"

A pause. Then, "Yes. What do you want?"

"Me? Nothin' at all. But Amber, she wants to be left alone to live her life. That's not asking too much, is it?"

"Man, I need money."

"I'm sure you do. But you've obviously mistaken me for someone who gives a damn about your sorry ass."

"You want to give me the money then?"

Harper laughed into the phone. "You have balls, I'll give you that."

"Let's just say I don't give a rat's ass who gives me the money, but if I don't get it, Miss Cross's photos will be common knowledge to every person in Bakersville."

Red rage poured through Harper's veins. "You do know I could have you arrested for extortion, don't you?"

"Where's your proof?"

"You've admitted it to me. And to Amber."

"Have me arrested, and the result will be the same. Lovely Amber is exposed. Literally."

"You really have no idea who you're dealing with, do you? Do you think I was born yesterday?"

"You're a farm boy, Bay."

"A farm boy who's also a licensed attorney. A licensed attorney who has no qualms about kicking your ass."

No response.

Harper continued, "So let's get something straight. You give the lady any more grief, and I'll personally see to it that Paul Donetto gets a first class ticket to Bakersville. But you don't have to worry about him breaking your legs."

"Oh? Why's that?"

"'Cause I'll have beat him to it."

* * * *

Amber had hated to do it, but she borrowed a couple grand from Angie. She had to get out of town. Paying off Blake Buchanan wouldn't solve her problem. It was a pain reliever, not a cure. She needed to go to the source.

It was most likely a lost cause, but she had to try.

"This is it," she said to the cab driver.

He stopped in front of the cracker box house with chipped gray paint. The lawn was dead, and a chain link fence surrounded the front yard. Trash littered the dead grass. A trike sat on the sidewalk outside the house.

Amber counted out some bills and handed them to the driver. "Thanks," she said.

"Much obliged." He got out of the cab and pulled her suitcase out of the trunk. "There you are, miss."

Amber nodded, took her bag, and walked to the front door. She took a deep breath and knocked.

Knocked again. And a third time.

Finally the door opened. A woman in a housecoat stood before her, cigarette dangling from the fingers of her left hand. Her lips were cracked and painted red, and her light blond hair was in disarray around a face that might have been pretty if it hadn't been so hard. Heavy-lidded blue eyes gazed at her.

Amber exhaled. "Hello, Mama."

Chapter Thirteen

"What do you want?"

Amber gritted her teeth. "Nice to see you, too. May I come in?"

"Don't see anyone stoppin' you."

Karen Hedstrom looked old. Old and worn-out and tired of life. In the last six years, she'd aged twenty.

Amber walked through the open door.

"Scat," Karen said, and a cat jumped off the couch. Karen shoved some newspapers onto the floor. "Sit on down if you want."

"Thanks." Amber sat, wondering if she should have brought some penicillin with her. At least a can of Lysol. Amazing her mother hadn't died in this dump. "How've you been, Mama?"

"How've I been? You're gone six years and that's what you ask? I been here. You wanted to know how I'm doin', you coulda stopped by before now."

Seriously? Amber shook her head. "I think you're forgetting the circumstances. You threw me out, remember?"

"That's right. I couldn't afford to keep you any longer. Be glad I didn't sell you off to one of those white slavers. I coulda gotten good money for a pretty girl like you."

White slavers? She is crazy. Or… "You're drunk."

"Well, now, there's a fuckin' surprise, huh? Your old mama's drunk."

"Let's get you sobered up. I need to talk to you. It's important."

"I haven't been sober in years, darlin'."

"Yeah, I believe that." Amber rose and went to the small kitchen. The acrid aroma of trash and cat pee met her nose. Her eyes watered. "I need a place to stay for a few days. And a car. You got one?"

"Do I look like I can afford a car? I hardly leave the house."

"What about work?"

"Got laid off two years ago. Collected unemployment, now I'm on welfare. Can barely pay the rent on this place and keep myself fed."

"But I see you have money for booze." She shook her head. "That was always the way, wasn't it?"

"Necessities come first." Karen cackled.

"Well, I can't live like this." She puttered around in the kitchen and found some coffee. Thank God Karen still had a coffee maker. Amber started a pot, grabbed a rag, and began to wipe down the counters. "You'll make yourself sick if you don't clean this place up."

"No one asked you."

"I'm staying here for a few days. I'll sleep in my old room."

"Sold your bed years ago."

"Then I'll sleep on the couch." She remembered the cat and changed her mind. "Maybe I'll find a cheap motel."

"Suits me."

Unfortunately, she couldn't afford to stay at a motel, even a cheap one, and she couldn't ask Angie for more money. She had overstepped the bounds of friendship as it was. She had no idea when she'd be able to pay her friend back.

"I'll sleep in your bed then. You can have the couch."

"Just a minute—"

"I'll earn my keep, don't worry. I'm going to bleach this place from top to bottom. I can't stand the thought of you living in this filth."

"Ain't you sweet."

"Sweet? Hell no. I can't stand the sight of you, but you're still my mama. And I have some questions only you can answer."

The coffee finished brewing, and Amber poured two cups. "Here, sober up."

She took a sip of her own cup and then went to the bedroom and stripped the bed. God only knew when her mother had last changed the sheets. She started the sheets in the rickety washing machine and went back to the kitchen. Under the sink she found some cleanser and dishwashing liquid. She washed the dishes in the sink, put them away, and then started on the hard part.

"What you doin' here anyway?" Karen asked.

"Like I said, I have some questions for you. And I have some other business in town."

"Yeah? Like what?"

"Not your concern."

"Then what are the questions you have for me?"

"You sobered up yet?"

"Hell, no."

"Have some more coffee. And no more vodka. I just washed ten glasses. Tell me something. If you're laid off, why the heck do you let the house get like this?"

"Just don't care, I guess."

Amber shook her head. Her mother was a mess she'd have to deal with at some point, but she had to fix her own life first.

Amber kept one eye on Karen as she cleaned the kitchen until it shone. She went on to the living room and cleaned and vacuumed. Cleaned the cat's litter box and disinfected all the bathrooms.

After she put the sheets in the dryer, she started another load of Karen's dirty clothes.

By that time, Karen had passed out, her head plunked on the kitchen table.

Good. She'd be sober when she woke.

Amber continued cleaning. When she'd made a decent dent, she looked at her watch. Nearly five. Dinner time was approaching and she wasn't the least bit hungry. She hadn't been hungry since she'd eaten with Harper and her father.

Her father.

She had a lot of questions for Karen.

She pawed through the cupboards and found a can of noodle soup. She heated it on the stove and then woke her mother.

"Mama, I've got soup for you. And a glass of cold water."

Karen swayed her head upward. "What're you doin' here?"

"I came to town. I'm staying here a few days. Remember?"

"Yeah, yeah. You got any aspirin?"

"Sure." Amber fished in her purse and pulled out a bottle of ibuprofen. "Take these."

Karen took the pills.

"Now eat some soup."

"Need a drink."

"No drinks for now. We need to talk."

Karen sighed. "What about?"

"I want you to tell me about my father."

Her light blue eyes widened. "Your father? Shit, I haven't thought of him in years."

"I'm sure you haven't."

"His name was Morgan."

"Morgan Cross, I know. He was a bronc buster."

"Yeah. A champion bronc buster. Man, he was gorgeous."

Amber had no doubt. He was handsome now, as an older gentleman. And she'd seen photos of when he was young. She could only imagine how good he'd looked to Karen.

"You have his eyes." Karen smiled.

Had she ever seen her mother smile?

"I was workin' as a cocktail waitress at a little place downtown. I was barely twenty-one. Thunder Morgan was in town for some publicity thing, and he came in. I'll never forget what he ordered. A margarita with a shot of Cuervo on the side." Karen smiled again. "As if the shot manned up the margarita. Can you imagine? Thunder Morgan drank sugary margaritas!"

Didn't surprise Amber all that much. Angie's husband, Rafe, drank Tequila sunrises, and he was as manly as they came. "Some men like sweet drinks. So what?"

"Hey, I didn't bust his chops about it. Just thought it was cute. Hell, I ended up in the sack with him, didn't I?"

"Did you?"

"If you met him and saw his eyes, you'd know the truth of that."

I have met him. I have seen his eyes.

"So what happened?"

"A classic one-night stand is all. He left town the next day. I never saw him again."

"Why didn't you tell me he was Thunder Morgan?"

Karen huffed. "I didn't want you trailin' after him, tryin' to find him. Hopin' your famous daddy would fix your life. You were born to be trash, just like I was."

An anvil settled in Amber's gut. Why did Karen still get to her? Amber knew better, but still, this was her mother. No matter how old she got, how far away she went, she still wanted this woman's approval.

Time to face facts. She'd never get it.

"He could have made your life a lot easier, Mama. He could have paid child support."

"Nope. I couldn't do that."

"Why not? You were entitled to it. *We* were entitled to it."

"It's a long story, and I can't get into it right now. I need a drink."

"Damn it!" Amber pounded her fist onto the table.

"Ouch. That hurts my ears."

"I don't give a flying fuck, Mama! I've got problems of my own I need to work out, and that's why I'm here. My first problem is you. Why didn't you tell me my father was Thunder Morgan? And why didn't you tell *him* he had a daughter?"

"Damn it, Amber! You don't understand what you're talkin' about."

"I understand that I had a father, a father who never knew about me. A father who could have made both our lives easier. Now you owe me an explanation. Why didn't you go to him?"

"Because he would have killed us both!"

Chapter Fourteen

"Oh, it's you."

Harper grabbed Blake Buchanan's collar. "Where is Amber, damn it?"

"How the fuck should I know? You're crazy, man. Let me go."

He clenched his teeth, the anger for Blake and the fear for Amber settling in his gut. "You're still blackmailing her, aren't you, you piece of filth?"

"I backed off, just like I told you I would. I haven't talked to her in a few days, not since the day you called me."

"Judy says she left town. Took a leave of absence. Now where the hell is she?" Harper pushed Blake into the hotel room and down onto the bed.

"You caught me off guard, but I'll warn you, we're pretty evenly matched," Blake said, massaging his neck.

"Not as mad as I am, we aren't. Where the hell is she?"

"I told you, I haven't got a clue. What do you care anyway? You told me yourself she wasn't your girlfriend."

"She's not, but that doesn't mean I'm not concerned." Concerned? He was downright worried. Sick to his stomach worried.

I miss her.

Damned inner voice. No, he didn't miss her. He was worried. That was all.

"I can have Paul Donetto here in a couple hours. All I have to do is say the word."

"You're bluffing," Blake said.

"You wanna take that chance?"

"Bay, I may not have a choice. I really don't know where she is. Ask your sisters. They seem pretty thick with her."

Harper shook his head. "You really are a moron, aren't you? They're the first two I asked. Either they don't know or they're not saying."

"Look, I know you're upset. I really didn't want to hurt the poor girl. I was desperate."

"Not half as desperate as you're gonna be."

"Calm down." Blake rubbed his temples. "She can't be that hard to find. If you were able to trace me to Donetto, you can easily find Amber Cross."

Harper let out a sigh. The man had a point. He'd just been so damned angry. She could have gone to San Antonio. Or she could have gone to Thunder Morgan. She might have gone to see her mother. Blake was right. She'd be easy to track.

Chad McCray knew a good PI, Larry something or other. He had no more use for Blake Buchanan. He left without another word.

Within an hour, Larry had located Amber in San Antonio.

Harper tried calling her cell. No answer. He called Catie. She hadn't heard anything from her. Not wanting to worry the new mother, he didn't elaborate.

Angie was next.

First his older sister refused to say anything. When he told her he knew she was in San Antonio though, Angie sang like a canary.

"I loaned her some money. She practically begged me. She was so distraught I couldn't say no. But I'm scared, Harp. God knows what kind of people we're dealing with here."

He sat, silent, his heart thumping and his mind reeling. Amber.

Damn, Amber, what have you done?

"Are you there?" Angie asked.

He cleared his throat. "I'm here."

"Please help her. I have a terrible feeling about all of this."

So did he. Like someone had knifed him in the gut. "I don't know who we're dealing with either, Ang. But I know someone who does."

Blake Buchanan.

"Please, Harp. If you can't help her, find someone who can."

He nodded into the phone, knowing full well Angie couldn't see it. "I will help her, Ang. I promise."

He hung up and dialed the Bakersville Hotel. When he was connected to Blake's room, he said, "Don't talk, just listen."

"What is it now?" Blake said. "I told you I don't know where she is."

"I do. She's in San Antonio. She's obviously going to try to deal with this problem herself. I have a proposition for you."

"I'm not interested."

"I think you will be. How much are you into Donetto for?"

"Twenty grand."

Twenty grand. Pennies to Harper, but millions to someone like Amber. And Blake Buchanan.

"You come to San Antonio with me and help me get Amber out of this mess, and I'll pay off Donetto for you."

"I want that in writing."

Harper rolled his eyes at the phone. "No, you don't."

"Uh...yeah, I think I do."

"Trust me, you don't. Donetto's a criminal, you moron. Do you really want your name associated with his in writing?"

"I hadn't thought of that."

"You don't think. That's always been your problem, Buchanan. Now do we have a deal or not?"

* * * *

Killed? Her mother had obviously gone crazy. That nice man she'd met at Harper's wouldn't kill anyone.

"What on earth are you talking about?"

"I'm serious. I tried to find him after you were born. When I finally got hold of him, some woman told me he wanted nothing to do with me or my bastard baby, that a baby didn't fit into his plans, and if I tried to contact him again he'd have us both killed."

Amber's skin crawled with invisible insects. Surely her mother was mistaken. Thunder Morgan? The man with her eyes? The man Harper knew and respected? The man she shared dinner with, who'd called her pretty lady?

Couldn't be.

"Did you try again?"

"Hell no! I couldn't put us in danger. Though there've been plenty of times since then that I've thought I'd be better off dead."

For an instant Amber's heart softened toward her mother. Then she remembered how the woman had kicked her out when she was barely sixteen. Thank God for Laura.

"I know you don't believe this, Amber, but I honestly did the best I could."

Amber's jaw dropped. "Seriously, Mama? You expect me to buy that?"

"I don't expect anything." Karen sniffed. "You were better off without me, and we both know it. I did you a favor by making you leave."

Amber let out a huff. "Please. Don't say that again. You may not have been the best mother in town, but I was sheltered and fed, never physically abused. Lots of kids have it worse. You were just tired of the responsibility."

"I won't deny I was tired. Seems there hasn't been a day in my life that I haven't been exhausted. But trust me, you were better off. I wasn't lying about selling you to the white slavers."

"You're making that up."

Karen sniffed again. "Get me a tissue, will you?"

Amber grabbed a box from the counter and slid it in from of Karen.

"I swear I'm not making it up," Karen continued. "I had offers, and I knew what those folks were capable of. I had to get you out of my house. Out of danger."

Amber shook her head. "You're paranoid."

Clearly her mother needed some medical help. She wasn't functioning with a full deck. Had she ever? She was making things up. When she was younger, Amber had suspected Karen might be a little off her rocker, but she'd always had too much else on her mind in those days—like making sure they were both clean and fed. Looking back, her mother had sometimes suffered paranoid delusions. The thing about Thunder Morgan killing them both was probably no different.

It all made sense now. Her mother was not only an alcoholic. She was mentally ill. Amber hadn't understood before because she'd been too young.

In a way, she'd failed Karen.

No sense going there. She'd only been a kid. She hadn't failed Karen. And there hadn't been anyone else in their lives who could have failed her. They'd been alone.

If Karen was on welfare, she was no doubt eligible for Medicaid. Amber would see she got a physical and mental work up before she left town.

If she left town.

Bakersville held nothing for her now. Angie no longer lived there, Catie was busy with her new baby. Judy could easily replace her at the shop. And Harper? Well, he'd made it clear where he stood.

Yet staying here in San Antonio didn't feel right either. Too many memories—none of them good—haunted her.

"Come on, Mama." She stood and took her mother's arm. "Let's put you to bed." She led her to the bedroom.

"I thought you were sleeping in here."

"The couch won't kill me. I didn't see any evidence of fleas or anything."

"The bed is big. You can sleep in here too."

"It's not that big. The couch is fine. I washed all the sheets in the house earlier."

She helped her mother lie down and pulled a coverlet over her body. On a whim, she leaned down and kissed her forehead.

"'Night, Mama."

* * * *

His stomach hurt like he'd been punched. A vile taste threatened in his throat.

The photos. They were like a train wreck. He didn't want to look, but he couldn't stop clicking on Blake's stupid laptop until he'd gone through all twenty-six of them.

Amber masturbating. Amber with a woman. Amber with a man's cock in her mouth.

How could he have been so wrong about this woman?

He'd wanted to believe her—believe that she'd had no knowledge of the photos ever been taken.

But no. Clearly she was an active participant in the photos. An active participant in possibly contracting a sexually transmitted disease. Granted, she wasn't actually having sex in any of the photos, but still...

How much had she been paid? A lot, obviously. Or maybe not a lot. Maybe she liked posing.

He had no idea.

No fucking idea at all.

And damn, that bothered him. This was a woman he had some major chemistry with. A woman he liked a lot. Thought he might be able to love.

Dear Lord, I slept with her. Thank God for condoms.

He'd been right all along. She was definitely not his type.

He handed the laptop back to Blake. "That's her all right."

"Told you. You still want to go after her?"

He nodded. He'd promised Angie, after all. And as much as he didn't want to, he couldn't stand the thought of anyone involved in this getting their hands on his Amber.

Amber. Not *his* Amber.

"Pack some stuff. Our flight leaves in four hours. We have to get to Denver."

* * * *

Ugh. Had a herd of wildebeests stampeded over her back during the night? Amber stretched. And groaned. Maybe she should have slept in with her mother after all.

Though she had a hunch that bed wouldn't have been any better.

Besides, sleeping on this damn couch was nothing compared to what awaited her today.

Rachel's.

Marta.

She had nothing to bargain with, nothing to say. She still didn't even know the web site URL. She'd tried calling Blake to get it before she left town, but he hadn't picked up his phone.

She steeled herself. She had to try. She couldn't allow herself to be exploited any longer. What they were doing was illegal. She'd thought of calling the cops, but then it'd be splashed all over the news.

And the rodeo queen would fall.

To think, when she'd become rodeo queen, she thought she'd truly left her past behind her.

Think again, Amber.

Karen had no car. Amber whipped out her tablet and hoped like heck she could piggyback onto someone's Wi-Fi.

Eureka. There was an unsecured network in the area. She searched the bus schedules. Nothing convenient. She sighed. She'd have to use some of her cash to rent a car. It'd be cheaper than taking cabs everywhere. She should have done it yesterday when her flight got in, but she'd thought Karen would have a car she could use.

So much for trying to save money. Now she was out yesterday's cab fare, and she had to get to the airport to rent a damn car. The bus would be good for that at least. She could catch one in an hour.

Karen was still passed out. Amber brewed some coffee—mental note, stop at grocery store and get some decent coffee—and ate a granola bar she'd packed in her bag. Mental note—also get decent food in the house. She'd get some money from Karen later—if she had any.

Amber took a quick shower and dressed. Still Karen had not budged. She scrawled a quick note and left it on the kitchen table where she hoped Karen would see it. Then she walked to the bus stop.

In less than two hours, she'd rented an economy car and was on her way to Rachel's.

With a giant lump in her stomach.

The hour wasn't quite noon. Would anyone even be there? Marta might. Her heart thudded. What would she say to Marta? What was the name of the other girl who had been there that night? Marta's roommate? She hadn't seen her again after that night.

But Marta—Marta was always there.

Amber knew she'd still be there, at Rachel's, feigning motherliness and making extra cash by drugging innocent girls.

Disgust—for Marta, and yes, for herself—clutched at her as she drove behind Rachel's and parked her car. If it were possible, this block on the edge of downtown looked even seedier than she remembered.

She'd dressed modestly in jeans and a high-necked blouse. Not the best idea. Texas heat sweltered in late April. Texas heat always sweltered.

What had she been thinking?

She swallowed and gathered all the courage she possessed deep in her gut. She sure as hell would need it.

She left the car, locked it, and steamed forward.

The back door was open, as usual. It was always open for the merchants who delivered food and drink.

The back hallway was dark and windowless, much like the dancers' dressing room. She walked through quickly, trying hard to gain bravery as she went.

Guess she'd have to fake it.

Two male figures emerged in the darkness. Not tall enough to be Oscar, the bouncer. Oscar would still be there. He was an institution at Rachel's. He'd been there for nearly twenty years.

Definitely male. They were talking to another man and a woman.

She slowed her walk, her heart pounding.

The images became clear.

Dear God.

Blake Buchanan. Holding the laptop containing the damning photos.

And Harper.

Chapter Fifteen

"Hi, Amber," Harper said.

"What are you doing here?" she demanded, her skin tightening. Had she been shrink-wrapped? "And why the hell did you bring him?"

"I'm here as your attorney. To help you. And he has information we need."

Amber stomped her foot. "You're not my attorney. I can't afford an attorney."

"Consider it pro bono. You need me. I can't believe you were going to come in here yourself and try to deal with this. You're in way over your head."

She couldn't argue. He was no doubt right. But she had to try. She had nothing to lose at this point. What the hell did he care? He'd already told her they were over.

She let out a breath. "I can't believe Angie betrayed my trust."

"Angie did no such thing. I hired Chad's PI friend to track you down. He found you in less than an hour."

"Must be nice to have a gargantuan bank account and hire a PI whenever you please." Yes, her tone was sardonic. She didn't care.

"Can the crap, Amber. You need both of us."

"I sure as hell don't need *him*." She pointed at Blake. "How did you convince him to come down here with you?"

"That's between him and me," Harper said. "It's not your concern."

"I'd say it most definitely *is* my concern."

"How sweet of you to be concerned about me, darlin'." Blake lifted his lips in a saccharine smile. "But you don't need to be. I'm being very well compensated for my time."

Money again. Harper Bay and his clan could buy whatever the hell they wanted.

"You can both go home." Her voice shook a little. She steadied it. "I'll take care of myself."

"Can't. I promised Angie I'd do what I can."

"I thought you said Angie didn't betray my trust."

"She didn't. But after the PI, found you, I confronted her. She started bawlin'. Was out of her head scared for you. Said she'd loaned you some money but wished she hadn't. She begged me to come down and help you get out of whatever mess you were bound and determined to get yourself into."

Amber said nothing. What could she say? She was in way over her head, and they both knew it.

"My sister really cares about you. She considers you one of her best friends."

Amber gulped. Angie *was* a good friend. Especially in the last six months. She'd put aside her spoiled ways and become a true, caring friend.

The thought warmed her, but another thought iced the first one. Harper *didn't* care. He hadn't come on his own. He'd come for Angie.

He'd meant what he'd said earlier. He truly didn't think she was the woman he'd thought she was. They were over.

She wanted to smack herself, beat herself up for not telling him about Blake in the first place. She'd been so scared of how he would react.

For good reason. He'd reacted exactly that way.

"You've had ample time for hellos and stuff. Now you all just tell us why you're here."

Amber recognized the voice of Leon, the general manager of Rachel's. She moved forward out of the darkness.

"Hello, Amber," Leon said.

He looked the same. Tall, with dark skin and hair, dressed to the nines. Next to Leon stood none other than Marta. Also tall, but light skinned. And of course, dressed to the nines.

Amber's hands clenched into fists and her nerves skittered on end. If she were bigger and stronger, she'd take that bitch down right now.

Harper cleared his throat. "I'm an attorney from Colorado, and I represent Miss Cross. This is my...er...investigator, Blake Buchanan. We have reason to believe that someone at this establishment has been taking photos of your girls and posting them on the Internet without their knowledge or permission."

"I assure you I have no idea what you're talking about," Leon said.

"I figured as much," Harper said. "Blake?"

Blake handed Harper his laptop.

"This, I believe, is one of your girls. A Miss Laura Lee." He clicked. "Taryn Apart." He clicked again. His face visibly whitened. "And this is Ambrosia Love, otherwise known as Amber Cross."

Leon's forehead wrinkled. "I'm not aware of that web site. But the girls are of course free to pose for any photographers they want when they're not on duty here. A lot of our girls moonlight. There's good money in it."

"Amber and the other girls claim they had no knowledge of these photos ever being taken," Harper said, "and they certainly never gave permission for them to be posted."

"Like I said, this web site has no affiliation with this establishment. I've never heard of it."

Harper turned to Marta. "How about you, ma'am? Do you know anything about this?"

"Of course not." Her deep and accented voice melted over the words. "I trust you haven't found any photos of me on the site?"

"That is correct."

Amber seethed inside. Marta wouldn't sully herself, of course. She'd just sully the other girls and pocket the money.

"I'll admit to doing some posing during my time off," Marta continued, "but only for reputable agencies and sites."

The self-righteous tone nauseated Amber.

Harper let out a sigh. "You're both answering just as I suspected. Thank you for your time. I'll be in touch. Come on, you two."

Seriously? "I'm not going anywhere with you," Amber said. "And especially not with him."

"On second thought...you're right. We need to meet with some men who aren't so nice. You won't be safe." Harper handed a business card to Leon. "We'll be in touch."

He and Blake walked out the front door. Amber followed, her fists clenched, her nails digging into her palms.

"You can't control me, Harper Bay. This has everything to do with me. Neither of you give a damn about it. I'm the one emotionally invested here."

In more ways than one, but he'd never know that. Harper Bay would never know she'd been stupid enough to let herself fall in love with him. For that was what she'd done.

But that was yesterday's news. Today's news was she wasn't the woman he thought she was. Well, news for him—he wasn't the man she'd thought he was either. That man would never give up on a woman because of her past—because of photos she hadn't even known about. And because she'd wanted to have one beautiful evening with her father and one beautiful night with her man before she faced the reality of her bleak situation.

Reality hit her like a freight train. He might never believe her about the photos.

Nope, Harper Bay was not the man she'd thought he was.

Too bad her heart couldn't accept that yet.

"Let her come along, Bay," Blake said. "She's right. It's her fight."

Harper's brow creased. "It's too dangerous."

"Damn right it's dangerous," Blake agreed. "It's dangerous for the two of us. But we're going."

"You said this guy's your friend," Harper said.

"Correction. This guy's *brother* is my friend. Lance hardly knows me and vice versa. I'd prefer to keep it that way."

"Then we'll see your friend first."

"Bernie can't help us."

"I think you're wrong about that. You got the URL and password from him. So that's where we're starting."

Amber cut in. How dare they stand there ignoring her? "Do you want to drive, or shall I?"

"Fine," Harper said. "You can come along to see Blake's friend. But once we get the web site guy's information, you can't come, Amber. I'm sorry. It's too dangerous for a woman."

"Bullshit. Like you care anyway." It was a cheap shot, but she couldn't help herself.

"Of course I care. I'm here, aren't I?"

She didn't argue. She didn't really want to talk to him anyway. At least she was going.

"I'll drive," he continued. "Amber, we need to move your car to a better neighborhood, and then we'll be on our way."

Chapter Sixteen

"Hey, Bern," Blake said.

"What're you doin' back in town?"

"Got some business to take care of." Blake shoved his way through the apartment door.

Harper was pleased. At least the asshole wasn't going to roll over and play dead. Yet, anyway.

"Meet some friends of mine. Harper, Amber, this is Bernie."

Bernie was square. Stocky and nearly as wide as he was tall. Even Amber towered over him. His apartment was a typical bachelor pad. Small and a mess.

Bernie stuck out his meaty hand. "Pleased to meet you."

Harper took his hand. Sweaty palm. "Same here."

"So what's goin' on?" Bernie asked.

"We need some information about Lance's site."

"I don't have any information, other than what I've given you—the URL and the password."

"Then we need to talk to Lance," Harper said. "He's been posting photos of models without their consent."

Bernie eyed Amber. The hair on the back of Harper's neck stood at attention. He moved between Bernie and Amber, blocking the other man's view.

"You look a little familiar, honey," Bernie said.

Was that saliva oozing in the corners of his fat mouth? Harper tensed. He seized Bernie by the collar. "You don't speak to her, you hear me? She's not your concern."

"Hold on, Bay," Blake interjected. "This doesn't need to get violent. Not at this stage."

The asshole was right. Though it pained him, Harper let Bernie go. "Where's your brother?"

"How in hell should I know?"

"Because he's your brother, you idiot."

"I have his address. That's all I can give you."

"How about his number?"

"Well, of course I have that."

"Call him. Get him over here."

"Right now? What for?"

"So we can all have a goddamned tea party. Christ!" Harper lunged for the man again, but Blake pulled him back.

"Just call him, Bern," Blake said. "This guy's a hothead."

"What is he? Some kind of enforcer?"

"Worse. He's a lawyer."

Harper eased off Bernie and turned to look at Amber. Her lips were trembling.

"Just get him over here," Harper said. "Tell him it's some kind of emergency. You need to see him."

"What for?"

"I don't know. Make something up. Tell him your mother's in the hospital."

"My mother's dead."

"Your father then. I don't give a flying fuck. Just get the bastard over here."

"I have a better chance of getting him over here for a beer than for either one of our parents."

"A beer then. Jesus Christ, just get him here."

Bernie shook his head and picked up his cell phone. "Hey, Lance." Pause. "Can you come over? I'm havin' some trouble with my hard drive. I'll treat you to dinner." Pause. "As soon as you can. I have a deadline on a project." Pause. "Great. See you in a few."

He clicked the phone off. "About half an hour. So what now?"

Harper sat down on a couch covered in newspapers. "We wait."

A half hour later, a man even stockier and greasier than Bernie arrived. He oozed sleaziness, with slicked-back black hair and a short goatee. His beer belly flopped over too-tight jeans. If Harper had kids, he sure as hell wouldn't leave them alone with the likes of this guy.

"I didn't know it was a party," Lance said, looking around the room.

"It's not," Bernie said.

"So what's going on with your hard drive, bro?"

"Well, uh...these guys have some questions about the Rachel's site."

Lance frowned. "Who the hell are these people?"

Harper stood. "I'm an attorney from Colorado. It's come to my attention that you're posting photos of women without their permission."

"Bernie, I'll fuckin' kill you." With fists clenched, the creep turned to Harper. "I run a legitimate operation. I have model releases on file for all the photos I post."

"Yeah? Then why'd you just tell your brother you're gonna kill him?"

"Because he's an idiot. He knows that web site is nobody's business." He eyed Bernie. "Last time I give you any passwords for your own pleasure."

"So you're legit, huh?" Harper had his doubts. "Then you won't mind if we see these model releases."

"See them? You want to see them, call a cop. Get a warrant."

"How about I get Paul Donetto over here to break your legs instead?" Harper stalked forward. "We're leaving the cops out of it to protect the ladies. But hey, you want to play hard ball? It can be arranged."

Lance's square body visibly stiffened. "You know Donetto?"

"He's a personal friend." Well, not quite, but he knew the man.

Lance's eyebrows shot up.

"I also know all the cops on his payroll." That part was a bluff.

Lance's pasty complexion turned greenish-gray. He looked like he was about to lose his lunch. He turned to his brother. "Bern?"

Bernie shook his head, his face the same gray hue. "Hey, I didn't know he was a friend of Donetto's, I swear. I thought he was just worried about the web site."

"Fine. You can come and see all the model releases." Lance paced the floor of the small room. "Then will you leave me the fuck alone?"

"Sure." Harper hated lying. He was an honest man. But Lance was scum. He'd stay on his back until this was resolved.

They piled into the car and followed Lance to his place. His *nice* place. Posting porn on the web obviously paid very well.

"I work out of my home," he said, as they walked to the door.

"Damn," Blake said. "This is one nice setup."

"It's home," Lance said.

"How come you let your brother live in that shithole apartment?"

"When he brings in some dough, he can live wherever he wants. I made the cash for this place. The only person who lives here is me."

"Whatever," Harper said. He was tired of this. "Let's see the files, please."

"Right this way."

They entered the house and Lance led them to a fully finished full basement that had been turned into an office. "I keep all important documents in these filing cabinets." He gestured to the oak cabinets.

Harper could hardly believe his eyes. This was some classy set up for a guy who made a living in Internet porn. It clearly did more than just pay the bills.

"Let's have a look," he said.

Lance opened a drawer and starting leafing through files. "Here's the file on the Rachel's girls. What name are you looking for?"

Amber stepped forward. "Cross. Look for Amber Cross."

Lance sat down at his huge oak desk and starting going through the papers. "A, B, C, here we go. Amber Lynn Cross, is that the one?"

Harper glanced at Amber. Her face had whitened, and her knuckles gripped the chair in front of her. He took the paper from Lance. It was a standard model release for pornographic material. Harper shook his head. Like he'd ever seen a standard model release for pornographic material. But it looked legitimate. "There's a signature here. Is it yours?"

Amber grabbed the paper from him. Her complexion turned from white to ashen. "It looks a lot like my signature, but I swear to God, Harper, I never signed this."

Sure you didn't.

Harper growled. Who made him angrier, Amber or Lance? At the moment he wasn't sure. "Let me see that file," he said to Lance.

"I don't know. These are confidential papers—"

Harper stepped forward and grabbed the file from Lance's desk. He was sick to death of the sight of this creep.

"Do you know any of the other girls' real names?" he asked Amber.

"Only Laura Lee, my roommate. Her name is Laura Ferguson."

Harper leafed through the papers and handed one to Amber. "This her signature?"

Amber's lips trembled. "I don't know. I'm not sure I ever saw her signature. We each paid our own bills."

"Never saw a rent check or anything?"

"I...I can't remember. I'm sorry."

"See, man?" Lance rubbed his slimy goatee. "I told you I run a clean operation here."

"Were you present when any of the girls signed these?" Harper asked.

"Nope. I get the photos and the releases sent to me, and I put them up on the site."

Was it possible the creep was actually innocent? Harper shook his head. His mother'd always said, "don't judge a book by its cover."

"Get up," he said. "I need to use your computer."

"Now just wait a minute—"

Harper stalked behind the desk, seized Lance by the collar, and yanked him out of the chair. "I said get the fuck up."

Harper sat down and pulled up Microsoft Word. He typed in some standard language and hit print. When the paper came out of the printer, he glanced at it and then handed it to Amber. "Sign this. It's a revocation of the model release. Once you sign it, he has to take your photos down."

"Gladly," Amber said.

"I'll need to see the lady's identification," Lance said. "I'm runnin' a business here, after all."

Harper's ears grew warm. He was about to lose it. "For Christ's sake."

"It's okay, Harper," Amber said. "I'll show him my ID. Anything to get those pictures down." She fumbled in her purse, took out a wallet, and extracted a driver's license. "Here."

Lance looked at it and nodded.

"Satisfied?" Harper rose from the chair, took the release from Amber, and handed it to Lance. "Make two copies of this. One for me and one for the lady."

"I'll do it, bro." Bernie took the release and ambled to the copy machine across the room.

"Now get those fucking photos off the site," Harper said, "and delete every one of them from your hard drive. I also want any copies you have destroyed. Is that clear? As far as anyone's concerned those photos never existed."

"Fine, fine." Lance sat down at the computer. "This'll take a little time."

"You have ten minutes."

"Ten minutes? I'm gonna need a couple hours."

"Then I guess we wait. Have a seat, you two," he said to Blake and Amber.

Amber sat down, her body visibly shaking. "Harper?"

"What?"

"If he destroys the photos, we don't have any evidence."

Evidence? Why would she be concerned about evidence? Was it possible she'd been telling the truth about the photos all along? Harper's heart pounded. "You want to press charges?"

"Not against Lance. I think he's actually innocent. But the fact remains that I did not sign that paper, and I did not pose for those pictures. Yet the pictures are definitely of me, and that looks a lot like my signature. There's only one explanation. I was drugged by Marta and her friend. And so were the other girls."

Either she was convinced she spoke the truth, or she was one damn stubborn liar. He wasn't sure which yet, though her concern for the other girls was admirable.

"Look," Harper said, "we got you taken care of here. If we want to press this further, we have to bring in the cops, and then the whole thing goes public. Is that what you want?"

"Yes. No. Damn it, I don't know." Tears welled in Amber's eyes. "We've taken care of me, but how can I just waltz out of here knowing that other girls have been violated too? And they'll keep doing it. It's not right, Harper."

Harper's heart ached. He wanted to take her in his arms, tell her everything would be okay. But no...she was not the woman for him. Probably not, anyway. Still, she had a conscience, and she was right. Leaving the other girls, who might not know they were on the web site, was wrong.

"What do you want to do?"

"I just don't know. I want to go home. But I'm not sure I have a home anymore. I guess I need to go to my mama's. Her house is a shambles and I want to fix it up for her."

"This is the same woman who kicked you out, right?"

"Yes, I know. But she...she needs me right now. I don't think she's right in the head, Harper."

"If we take you there, will you take the rest of the day to think this through? Figure out what you want to do? Because if this woman is drugging girls, we'll need to bring in some big guns to investigate. I've got a good PI, but if he finds what he's probably going to find, we have to call the cops."

She nodded. "I understand. And I know I'll be dethroned as rodeo queen and I'll have to leave town."

Harper hoped she wasn't right. Bakersville was a nice town, but it was also a small town, and not immune to gossip and innuendo.

"Hey, look, I'm a businessman. I can't have cops sniffing around here," Lance said. "It wouldn't look good."

"Tough shit," Harper said. "In your line of work, you're bound to come across some lowlifes. This can't be news to you. You cooperate with whomever I send your way or I'll have Paul Donetto in here so fast you won't know what hit you. And you'll wish you'd chosen the cops."

Lance's greasy face whitened. Paul Donetto struck fear in him, just as he did in Blake. Harper wouldn't be surprised if Donetto already had a hand in this fiasco, though he imagined this was small potatoes next to smuggling drugs and women.

"Fine, fine. Let's just get this over with as soon as possible, okay? I got a business to run."

"I'm going to need your URLs so I can make sure the photos are taken down. They're not on any other site are they?"

"If they are, I didn't put them there. This site is for Rachel's girls only, and they serve a very elite clientele. Clients pay top dollar for access, and the site claims the photos are exclusive. Whether they actually are? I have no idea."

"Seems we can assume they are for now," Harper said.

"So do you want them destroyed or not?" Lance said.

Harper looked at Amber. "Your call."

Her golden eyes were troubled. "I... Whoever took the photos has copies, I'm sure. Yes." Her eyes went from troubled to blazing. "Destroy the damn things."

"Good enough." Lance sat down at his computer. "They'll be history in a few hours."

"Fine," Harper said. "I'll take you at your word for now. I want to get Amber out of here. She's had enough for one day. I'll be back tomorrow for those URLs. Bernie, can you take Blake back to our hotel?"

"Sure."

"Good. I'll take our rental. Come on." He took Amber's arm and helped her up. "Let's get out of here."

Chapter Seventeen

After picking up her car, Amber drove sullenly, Harper following her, to Karen's house. Amber had long gotten over embarrassment in front of Harper. For him to see the cracker box she'd grown up in was nothing compared to those awful photos.

So this was what her life had come to.

A father she didn't know because he wanted her mother and her dead. She still couldn't wrap her mind around that one. She'd met the man.

Photos taken of her without her knowledge or consent, and a paper with her signature on it giving permission for the horrible things to be posted.

And Harper. Harper, who'd come to her rescue, but only out of loyalty to his sister. Not out of love for her. She still wasn't the woman he'd thought she was.

"This is it," she said as he got out of his car.

His dark eyes were sunken and sad. Was he feeling sorry for her? Well, she didn't need his pity.

"You really grew up here?"

"We did okay."

"Till she kicked you out?"

Amber didn't respond. She didn't want to think about that. Right now she wanted to go inside and have a cup of tea and figure out what to do. But inside was still a shambles.

"Is your mother home?" he asked.

"Probably. She's not working. Most likely passed out somewhere."

"Let's go in and make sure she's okay."

"All right." She was no longer embarrassed by her mother either. "In fact, there's something I want to ask you about."

"What?"

"It's about my father."

"All right."

They went in and found Karen at the kitchen table. She'd actually gotten dressed in jeans and a T-shirt, and she almost looked like she'd showered.

"Hey," she said.

"Hello, Mama. This is Harper Bay."

"Nice to meet you. He your boyfriend?"

Amber's cheeks warmed. She inhaled. "Just a friend." She strode to the counter and put a pot of water on for tea. "Sit down, Harp. You want a cup?"

"Sure. Nice to meet you…"

"Karen. Nice to meet you too."

Amber put three mugs and tea bags on the table and sat down. "Harper knows Thunder Morgan."

"You do, huh?"

"Yes, ma'am. He was a friend of my father's. A good man."

Karen simply nodded.

"Don't you have anything to say, Mama?"

"About what?"

"About my father? About Thunder Morgan?"

"Why would I have anything to say about him?"

Amber pounded her fist on the table. "Because yesterday you told me he threatened to kill us both!"

Harper straightened in his chair.

Karen fidgeted with a hangnail. "Did I say that?"

"Yes, and *after* you'd sobered up."

Harper's eyebrows rose. "Thunder Morgan wouldn't hurt a flea."

"That's what I thought. I've met him. He's a nice man. Why do you think he wanted to kill us?"

Karen pushed a blond tendril of hair behind one ear. "He made it clear to me that night that this was a onetime thing. He wasn't gettin' tied down to anyone, and if I didn't want to go through with it I could back out, no hard feelins'."

"That's a nice guy, Mama, not a killer."

"Yes, he was a nice guy, or so I thought."

"Didn't he use a condom?"

"I don't remember. It was a long time ago, Amber."

"Well, whether he did or not really doesn't matter. I'm here."

Karen nodded.

"Ms. Cross?"

"Hedstrom. Cross is my daddy's name, remember?" Amber said.

"Right, I'm sorry. Ms. Hedstrom, did he make any kind of threat to you and the child at all?"

"Once Amber was born, I tried to contact him. I just wanted him to know he had a little girl. I wasn't gonna ask him for anything."

"Yeah?" Amber said. "So what happened?"

"I tracked down his number and called, and a woman answered."

"And?" Harper said. "She wasn't his wife. He never married."

"I don't know who she was. I assumed she was his wife. Coulda been a maid. A girlfriend. All I know is she asked who I was, and when I told her my name, she said if I ever called there again both me and the little brat would end up dead."

"So whoever she was, she knew you'd had Amber and knew it was from a night with Thunder," Harper said.

"Seemed that way."

"I can't say for sure," Harper said, "but my guess is that Thunder Morgan had nothing to do with any of this. If he didn't make the threat personally, it's possible he doesn't even know you made that call."

"But she knew about the baby."

"You put his name on Amber's birth certificate. That's easy enough to track."

"Why did you put his name on the certificate, Mama?"

"'Cause he's your daddy. You deserved to know where you came from."

"But you never talked about him. Never mentioned him to me."

"I was scared to! I thought you might go out and try to find him and end up dead."

Amber reached out and touched her mother's forearm, offering her comfort the way Angie had offered it to her. Odd, but she wanted to comfort her mother. "I've met him. He didn't make that threat. I'm almost sure of it."

Harper smiled. "I can vouch for him too, ma'am. In fact, I could call him up and get him out here if you want. I think he'd be right glad to know Amber's his."

"I don't want him to see this mess," Karen said.

"Harper, no," Amber agreed. "I want to get to know him, truly I do, but not until this other…er…stuff is taken care of."

No way was she telling Karen about the photos.

"I understand," Harper said. "At any rate, Ms. Hedstrom, I'm sure we can clear this all up with Thunder Morgan."

"Well, he owes me eighteen years of back child support."

"Sixteen. You kicked me out, remember?"

"I'm afraid he doesn't owe you anything, ma'am. Unless a court ordered him to pay support and he didn't, which is not what happened. In all likelihood he didn't even know Amber existed. If you want to get anything out of him, you'll have to take him to court and get an order for back support. Are you sure he's the father? Because the judge will order a DNA test at this point."

"Harper's a lawyer, Mama."

"Oh, perfect. A lawyer." Karen twirled a piece of her hair between her fingers. "He's the father. I may look like I slept around, but I really didn't. So again, I get nothin'. Story of my life."

"You can take him to court," Harper said.

"With what? My good looks? Look at this place. You think I got a dime in my pocket, much less what you lawyers charge?"

"Mama, we'll figure this stuff out about Thunder Morgan, I promise. But not now. I have other things I need to do first."

She had to keep her heart out of it.

"Ms. Hedstrom"—Harper stood—"thank you for your time. Will you be okay here for the night?"

"Of course."

"Good. I'm taking Amber to a hotel."

"Harper—"

"No argument. You need a decent night's sleep. We have a big day tomorrow."

What a wonderful man! If only he could be hers. *Remember, he's not doing any of this for you. He's doing it for Angie.* She nodded. "Okay."

"Come on, then."

She wanted to resist, really she did. But for once it felt so good to have a man take the lead, to take care of her.

Especially when it was the man she'd fallen hopelessly in love with.

If only he could return her feelings. She sighed. That would never be. She'd have to settle for a man who couldn't resist doing a favor for his big sister.

Still a wonderful man, just not *her* wonderful man.

* * * *

Amber took a long hot bath and wrapped herself in the luxurious fluffy robe provided by the hotel. Harper and Blake both had rooms on the same floor. Harper had told her to order room service, but she wasn't hungry. She was tired—oh, so weary—and numb.

So very numb.

She lay down on her bed, wanting to cry. Wanting to sob her heart out. The tears didn't come.

She got up, left the room, and walked across the hall. She knocked on Harper's door.

Harper answered, looking tousled and sexy in green cotton lounging pants and no shirt. His hair was wet and clung to the sides of his neck, Evening stubble had emerged on his chin.

"Amber. You okay?"

She nodded.

"What do you need?"

"I...I don't want to be alone."

He shook his head. "You can't stay here."

Her heart sank. "I'm not asking to stay here. Can I just come in for a little while? Maybe watch some TV or something? I just need to know there's another body in the room."

"I'm sorry. You have to go back to your own room." He walked through the door and grabbed her arm. "I'll walk you back."

He took the key card from her hand and slid it into her door. He opened it.

"Please, can you come in? Just for a few minutes."

"Damn it, Amber."

"I'm sorry if I'm being so needy. It's been…" *It's been what? A hell of a day? A hell of a few days? A hell of a few days from my nightmares?*

A hell of a life?

"Amber, I'm telling you, I can't come in."

"Why, Harper?"

He raked his fingers through his damp hair. "Damn it!" He pushed her through the door and followed her in, slamming it. Then he grabbed her and crushed his mouth to hers.

He tasted of Irish coffee, of salt, of wild berries. She'd never tasted anything more delicious. Who knew that was exactly what she'd been craving? Now was not the time to be coy. She opened her mouth and welcomed his tongue.

Their tongues slithered together in a kiss of wildness and passion. Of pure unadulterated need.

Need. Amber needed him. Now. So much now. But not just now.

Forever.

She stopped her thoughts. Forever would not happen for them. She knew that.

She'd take *now*.

She deepened the kiss and he followed her lead. With her tongue, she traced his teeth, his gums, the inside of his cheeks. His mouth covered hers hungrily. The kiss sent the pit of her stomach into a wild swirl. His lips were hard and searching. She wondered briefly what he might be searching for, but then could no longer wonder.

She let her body take over, let the kiss sing through her veins like a concerto. When his lips left hers she mourned the loss, but as they trailed over her cheek to her ear, nibbling on her lobe, she nearly swooned.

Oh, the sensation. The heady caress of his lips on her neck set her aflame. His lips continued their searing path across her shoulders, where his hands gently eased the robe from her body.

It fell into a heap on the floor. He cupped both of her breasts as his lips reclaimed her mouth.

She kissed him back with a hunger she'd never known. A desire. A raw need, both pure and impure.

Gently he thumbed her nipples, and they hardened into tight buds.

"Oh, baby," he said against her mouth. "God, I've missed you. I have to suck those beautiful nipples."

His lips left hers again, but instead of mourning this time, she anticipated their touch on her nipple. First he merely teased—a lick here, a tug there. The touch was light and painfully teasing. Her clit throbbed.

Dear Lord, I'll die an untimely death if he doesn't suck a nipple between his gorgeous full lips. "Please, Harper. Please."

He locked his lips around a turgid peak and sucked. Sucked. Sucked.

"Oh," she groaned. "So good."

"You're so beautiful, baby. So enticing." He wrapped his lips around the other nipple and sent her surging again.

He pushed her ever so slightly until they were against the bed. Once there, he laid her gently down. Her nipples were red and erect from his attentions, and they wanted more.

As if he read her mind, he clamped his mouth onto one again and sucked.

She writhed beneath him, her hips moving of their own accord. She was wet, she knew. She could feel the moisture between her legs. If only—

Again, he read her mind. One hand wandered downward, and he inserted a finger into her channel.

"Ah!" Her voice was breathy and husky.

"So wet, baby."

God, yes. Wet for him. For Harper. For the man she adored.

He left her breasts and returned to her mouth for a passionate kiss. Her nipples tingled against the hair of his chest. So, so good. His hard body atop hers, she thrust her hips upward, trying to take more of his finger. More of whatever he would give her this one night.

Their kiss deepened, and he added another finger. Harder and harder he thrust them into her, and wetter and wetter she became. Her sighs and moans grew louder, until…

"Yes!" she cried. The climax pushed her upward, nearly out of her own body. She writhed against his probing fingers, against his rock hard chest.

"That's right, baby," he said against her lips. "Come for me. Make it feel good."

She soared higher, the spasms inhabiting her whole body. Only one thing would complete this feeling of ecstasy.

"Harper, make love to me."

He rose slightly, pushed his lounging pants over his hips and plowed into her.

The hardness against her slick walls made her orgasm begin again. She spasmed around his cock as he pumped.

"That's it. Keep coming, baby. You feel so good." His breath puffed against her neck. Still he pumped, harder and faster, until she came yet again.

"God, baby. You're so hot." He kissed her neck, nibbled her ear lobe. "I'm coming, baby. I'm coming."

"Harper, come for me. Come in me."

"What? In you? Oh my God!"

He thrust hard, and she was so sensitive from her climaxes, she felt every single contraction of his cock.

"Mmm." She sighed and closed her eyes. So good. So good to make *him* feel good.

He pulled out of her quickly. "Goddamn!"

She opened her eyes.

He was standing by the bed, his eyes troubled.

"What is it?"

"Condom. We didn't use a condom."

Was that all? "Don't worry. I've been on the pill forever."

"Well, then, at least I don't have to worry about pregnancy."

"What else would you need—"

His meaning her like a freight train, knocked the wind right out of her lungs. *Disease.* With her past, he was worried about disease. She'd never slept around. She'd had two one-night stands, and she'd gotten a clean bill of health after both of them. She'd never slept with men at the club. Even in those dreaded photos she wasn't having sex.

She stood, anger raging through her. "Get out."

"Amber."

"You have nothing to worry about. I'm clean. If you don't believe me, tough shit. I know I'm clean."

"That's not—"

"You're so transparent. That's *exactly* what you were thinking. Do you think for one minute I'm the kind of person who would have unprotected sex if I knew I was a hazard to anyone? Fuck you, Harper Bay. Now *get out*."

He said nothing more. He pulled on his pants and walked out, shutting the door behind him.

Amber curled up on her bed. All the tears that hadn't materialized earlier came now like a tropical rainstorm.

How had she let this happen? She hadn't gone to him for sex. Just some company to ease her loneliness and pain. He had initiated the sex. She should have been stronger. She shouldn't have let it happen. After all, he could never love her.

That was more apparent now than ever.

A rapping at her door interrupted her misery. She must look like hell from crying, but she put the robe back on and went to the door. If he'd come back to apologize, she'd listen. She loved him, after all.

She covered herself with the fluffy robe, pinched her cheeks, pasted a smile on her face, and opened the door.

In the doorway stood Blake Buchanan.

Chapter Eighteen

Her nerves skittered. Every bone in her body ached to scream for Harper. Would he be able to hear her?

"Can I come in?" Blake asked.

"Absolutely not."

"Fine. I'll talk from here then."

"I can't imagine what you think we have to talk about."

He fidgeted, jamming his hands into his jeans pockets and then taking them out again. "I want to...er...apologize."

"Apologize? For making my life hell?" She shook her head. "I'm very sorry to inform you that your apology is not accepted."

"I'm sorry. Really. I was desperate, that's all."

"That's all?" Seriously? "You ruin my life and that's all?"

"I know it's no excuse. I've really fucked up. Chad and Catie were willing to give me another chance in Bakersville. So were some of the others. I even thought I might be able to work things out with Evie. But I had this debt hanging over my head, and even though I had the promise of work in town, Donetto wouldn't wait till I saved up the cash. When I recognized you—"

"You saw an opportunity, didn't you?"

He nodded, the look on his face sheepish. "Yes. I did."

Amber let out a sigh. She was tired of standing. "Are you done?"

"No. Can we talk for a few minutes?"

Her fear had subsided. What was the harm? The man obviously had no intention of leaving until he'd said his piece. "Fine. Come on in. But the door stays open."

"Works for me."

Amber pulled a chair out from the desk. "Sit down." She plunked down on the edge of the bed.

"I want to tell you something. About all the talk in town about me."

"Why tell me anything?"

"Because I truly feel bad about what I've done to you. I want you to know that I'm not such a bad guy."

She rolled her eyes. "I'm afraid that'll take a bit."

"I know that. You see, all that stuff about Evie being pregnant with my kid, it wasn't true. Evie and I never had sex."

"Look, I didn't know you then. I still don't really know Evie. This is none of my business. And I've got my own problems, thank you."

He nodded. "I know you do. And I'm sorry for my part in them. But for some reason it's important to me that you know the truth about me."

"Fine," Amber relented. "Then why did she say it was your baby?"

He shook his head. "I have no idea. It broke me up that she'd cheated on me. I was sitting around, minding my own business, trying to figure out what to do. I mean, I loved Evie with all my heart. I couldn't just walk away. Then her dad came at me with that gun. I've never been so fuckin' scared in my life. At least, up to that point. You know, before Donetto."

"So you left town."

"Hell, yes. What else could I do?"

"You could have stayed and cleared your name. Her dad went to jail. You weren't in any more danger."

He stood and paced a few steps and sat back down. "There was nothing left for me there. The woman I loved had betrayed me. I was a mess. So I came here to San Antonio, got a job on a ranch—that's where I met Bernie; the ranch was his cousin's—hung out at Rachel's a few nights a month to blow off steam. Everything was fine, till I got mixed up with Paul Donetto."

"And why did you do that?"

"I was greedy. Plain and simple. It seemed like easy money. I was doing okay working at the ranch, but I didn't have much left over for savings. I wanted a big nest egg so I could come back here and try to work things out with Evie. I'd heard through the grapevine that she'd lost the baby and hadn't gotten married. She was working as the librarian. So I thought maybe… Anyway, all I was supposed to do was drive a small pickup and deliver some stuff to a warehouse. I had no idea what was in the truck. It had a tarp over it when I got it. And I was smart enough not to ask any questions."

"And?"

"And…some idiot in a semi blindsided me. Long story short, some of the merchandise was destroyed, and I found myself in debt twenty grand to Donetto."

"What was the merchandise?"

"Tools mostly. And some cocaine."

Drugs. Of course. "How'd you stay away from the cops?"

"I'd been told if anything happened to proceed to the drop-off point as planned as soon as possible. Since the truck was still drivable, that's what I did. Didn't stop to see what might be on the road. I didn't find out it was cocaine till later."

"You're lucky you weren't caught."

"You think I don't know that? I was damn lucky. I was also lucky only a little of the coke was destroyed. Some leaked out of one of the bags."

"Why'd you go back to Bakersville?"

"I couldn't save any money here to pay him off. I figured I'd have a better shot back home where living expenses are less in a small town. I could find work and cheap housing on a ranch and get a payment plan going. But Donetto wanted no part of that. He wanted a lump sum. And he wanted it yesterday."

Amber nodded, her skin prickling. "Enter me."

"Yeah. That pretty much sums it up."

"If Catie hadn't told you I wanted barrel racing lessons, we never would have met. I mean, it's unlikely you'd ever come in for a manicure. Not that I'm blaming Catie. It's just…weird to think of chains of events sometimes, you know?"

"Tell me about it." He stood. "Well, now I've got that off my chest. I really am sorry."

"Have you told Harper all of this?"

"Yeah. After he agreed to pay off my debt, he said he wanted the truth and nothing but the truth. Goddamned lawyers."

Amber tried to hide her smile.

"Anyway, I wanted you to know I'm not such a bad guy. And I'm truly sorry. I really felt I had no choice."

"There's always a choice, Blake."

He closed his eyes and let out a sigh. "That's what my daddy always used to tell me."

"Your daddy was right. I had a choice too. I didn't have to work at Rachel's. I could have scrounged around until I found a job doing nails and then scraped by. But Rachel's offered good money, which was heaven for a girl like me. I grew up with nothing. I made the choice to do something I didn't really want to do for the money. And now I'm in this jam."

"You got greedy."

"Yes, I suppose I did."

"Then we're not so different after all." Blake smiled.

"I wouldn't go that far," Amber said. "I think you need to go now. I need to get some sleep."

"Yeah, me too. But look on the bright side. If I hadn't found those pics and blackmailed you, they'd still be posted without your knowledge. Someone would have recognized you eventually. Every cowpoke west of the Mississippi spends a night at Rachel's. It's kind of our birthright."

He had a point, but she wasn't quite ready to accept it yet. What he had done to her still hurt like hell.

"Good night," she said.

He left quietly.

* * * *

Harper slept fitfully, a certain blonde invading his dreams whenever he drifted off. He woke up each time in a cold sweat with a raging erection.

Why couldn't he shake her?

Her reaction last night had been downright rage. She thought—no, she *knew*—she was clean.

He couldn't ever really *know* the truth. He had to choose to believe her. He had to have faith in his heart that she would not lie about this.

When his alarm went off at seven a.m., he felt like he'd spent the night in a torture chamber—physically and emotionally exhausted and in pain.

He was still lying in bed when his cell phone buzzed at seven thirty on the dot. Larry.

"What's the word, Lar?"

"I don't know a whole lot yet. I won't be able to do any thorough investigation until I come down there, but here's what I was able to uncover overnight. I was able to hack into their mainframe and the first security level. Still don't have access to the real good stuff. I can tell you that Rachel's definitely does some shady business on the side, including the web site you told me about. They've also done some smuggling. Some of their women are illegals who do more than just dance, if you get my drift."

Harper got the drift all right. "Are they in league with Donetto?"

"Not from what I can tell. In fact, it doesn't look like Donetto even knows what they're up to. If he did, he'd want his piece for sure."

Hmm. Good. Harper could use that.

"The manager, Leon, seems to be innocent. I couldn't find him associated with any of the underground dealings. The woman, Marta, is originally from Austria. She's not a U.S. citizen, but she's here legally and has a green card."

"When did she come over?"

"About ten years ago. She married a cowboy but they divorced two years later. Might have been a marriage of convenience, who knows? But it was never questioned. After her marriage failed, she found work at Rachel's."

"Can we tie her to the shady stuff?"

"Not yet. She does pose for other sites, though. I'll e-mail you the URLs."

"Okay. Thanks."

"You want some advice?" Larry asked.

"Sure. What the hell."

"Bring the cops in on this. These people are most likely dangerous."

"You just said Donetto's not involved."

"I said from what I can tell, he's not involved. Paul Donetto's not the only dangerous man in San Antonio."

Harper threw the comforter off and sat up in bed. "Point taken. Thanks, Lar."

"I won't be able to get out there for a few days. I've got stuff going on."

"Yeah, I know. I understand. Keep doing what you're doing. If you find anything new, give me a call."

"Will do."

Harper clicked off his phone, rose, and started the shower.

Amber's image popped into his mind. Amber's platinum hair falling in soft waves over her milky shoulders. Amber's full red lips, swollen from his kisses. Amber's hard nipples, pink and wanting, her skin silky smooth under his tongue.

Amber's wetness on his fingers, sweet and tangy as he brought them to his mouth.

He sighed and turned the faucet to cold.

Chapter Nineteen

Friday night. They hadn't accomplished much during the day, though Amber's mother's house was now spotless. If they could sober the woman up, maybe she'd get on with her life.

Amber didn't hold out much hope for that. She did say she wanted to get her mother some help, though, so Harper had arranged a visit to a mental health and substance abuse facility. Amber was convinced her mother was mentally ill.

Amber was back at the hotel now, while Harper and Blake sat out back of Rachel's in a rental car watching the employees' entrance. Amber claimed the night she'd blacked out had been a Friday. It was a long shot, but maybe Marta and whoever else was involved might try the same thing tonight.

Blake sat in the passenger seat, snoring. Harper checked his watch. Three a.m. The club closed at two thirty. So far, only two girls had emerged from the building.

Blake let out a snort. Harper rolled his eyes. Blake wasn't such a bad guy, but Harper would never forgive him for what he'd done to Amber. He'd turned that poor woman's life upside down. She hadn't deserved that, no matter how many mistakes she'd made.

Course, Blake had made his own mistakes. Blackmailing someone to try to cover his own ass was cowardly. Blake had told him he'd apologized to Amber last night. Oddly, Amber hadn't thrown him out. While she hadn't been exactly forgiving, she did seem to understand how he'd let things get out of hand. She understood about greed sometimes taking over.

Harper shook his head. He'd never wanted for anything in his life. What must it have been like for Amber, growing up with Karen in that rundown neighborhood? Getting kicked out at sixteen?

And Blake? He knew nothing of Blake's childhood.

Sometimes, Harper took it all for granted. He tried not to but couldn't help himself on occasion. What did he know about greed? If he wanted something, he went out and got it. Money was not an issue. If it had been, might he have made some of the choices Blake and Amber had?

The fact that he wasn't sure gnawed at him. One thing, though, had become clear as day. He hadn't been fair to Amber.

The door opened and two women emerged. He punched Blake's arm. "Wake up. A couple are coming out."

Blake opened his eyes and let out a huge yawn. "Yeah? Where?"

"By the door, genius."

Nope. Turned out to be nothing. Marta wasn't there.

"What time is it?" Blake asked.

"Three fifteen."

"They should all be out by now, shouldn't they?"

"You'd think. But"—Harper grabbed the steering wheel—"maybe we can't get them for drugging and photographing the girls. But I bet there's money exchanging hands in there for sex. I'd bet you anything."

"You're probably right, but what exactly can we do about it?"

"We can call the cops."

Blake let out a chuckle. "Are you kiddin'? The cops must know. This has been going on forever. They probably close their eyes to it."

Shit. Blake was no doubt right. If only San Antonio had a young, hot-headed detective with a conscience bigger than himself. Harper would look into that tomorrow.

The two women drove away together. Probably roommates, like Amber and Laura had been.

"This isn't working," Harper said. "I guess we should just go on back to the hotel and attempt to get a little sleep."

"Thank God," Blake said.

Harper turned on the engine. As he prepared to back out, the sliver of light from the doorway caught his eye. Wouldn't hurt to see what was what. He cut the engine.

"Now what?" Blake said.

"Check it out."

Out stepped Marta with three girls. They were laughing and walking arm in arm. They ambled to a black minivan and got in.

"Bingo," Harper said. "Looks like we're back in business."

"What're we gonna do? Follow them?"

"That's exactly what we're going to do."

"Christ, I'm exhausted."

"So am I. Quit your bitching."

"Is all this really worth the twenty grand you paid Donetto?"

Harper shook his head. What was with this guy sometimes? "Think about what you just said."

"Sorry. You're right. I owe you big time."

"That's right. Let's get going. You know the area, so I need you to keep an eye on that van. I need to stay far enough back so they don't know we're following. If we lose sight, you need to figure out which way they went based on your knowledge of the area."

"And what if I'm wrong?"

"Don't be wrong."

Harper pulled out and followed the black van. He kept a safe distance behind it and didn't lose sight.

Half an hour later, they pulled up in the parking lot of some expensive-looking townhomes.

"Damn," Blake said. "Drugging women and taking photos obviously pays pretty well."

"This is the porn industry," Harper said. "You saw Lance's digs. He certainly didn't make that kind of dough doing anything upstanding. That guy's as slimy as they come."

"I gotta admit, he's even creepier than his brother."

"Why do you hang out with him if you think he's a creep?"

"We worked on the same ranch, before he started doing his computer work. All us hands hung out on our nights off. Bernie's a good guy, just creepy looking. He can't help that."

Harper shook his head. "Of course. No such thing as eating right and working out."

He didn't give a damn who Blake Buchanan counted as his friends. All he wanted was to get to the bottom of this mess and get the hell out of Dodge. He'd had about all he could take of this fair city.

The foursome entered number three hundred. About a minute later, a large man appeared out of the shadows and entered as well. He could have been the bouncer—Amber said his name was Oscar—from Rachel's, but Harper wasn't sure in the dark. He didn't use a key, so Marta must have left the door unlocked. Harper hoped the man hadn't turned the deadbolt. If he had, they'd have to find another way in.

He turned to Blake. "You know anything about breaking and entering?"

"Hell, no. I'm not a criminal. You know my story. Got mixed up with some bad people. I've never broken and entered in my life."

"Shit."

"So you want me to be a criminal?"

"If you were, the knowledge would come in handy right about now."

"Sorry I can't oblige."

Harper sighed and pulled out some rubber gloves from the glove compartment.

"Hey, a glove compartment with gloves," Blake said. "Ingenious."

"Ha-ha. Funny." He took two gloves out of the box and handed them to Blake. "Put these on. We sure as hell don't want our fingerprints anywhere around here."

They both donned the disposable gloves. Harper unlatched his car door, his heart pounding. "Let's go."

Blake nodded. They crept stealthily toward the door of the townhome. Harper tried the door. Locked, just as he'd feared.

Well, at least they weren't *stupid* criminals. Would've made their jobs a lot easier though.

"Let's go around to the back," Harper said.

They walked around the row of homes to the back door of the unit in question. Also locked. They looked down the basement window well, but the window was covered.

Damn.

They'd been doing this for so long, Harper had hoped they'd gotten careless. No such luck. Course if they'd gotten careless, chances are they wouldn't still be getting away with it. Amber's photos had been taken almost three years ago according to her, and still they were using the same MO.

"I was just thinking," Blake whispered.

"About what?"

"Bernie's gonna get into a hell of a lot of trouble with his brother for giving me that information about the site. Course he isn't the brightest bulb."

"I'd say he's not," Harper said. "But neither is Lance for giving the stuff to Bernie."

"True enough. Lance may be a whiz with computers, but he's got no sense when it comes to anything else."

"What does this have to do with anything?"

"How long do you think it'll take these thugs to find out Lance took down Amber's photos? They'll go to him, he'll produce that paper you wrote up, and they'll know something's up."

"And?"

"Maybe they'll take the site down themselves."

"Are you crazy? They won't take the site down. They'll off Lance. Maybe Bernie too. And they'll come after us." Harper's pulse raced. His words were true.

Blake let out long sigh. "It was just a thought. Since it doesn't look like we're getting in here tonight."

"I guess we should give it up," Harper agreed. "This place is as secure as Fort Knox." His heart fell. He'd really wanted to get something on these guys. Not for Amber, of course. They'd already gotten her photos taken down. But for all the other innocent girls.

His conscience nagged at him. *For Amber. You know it's for Amber.* She was the one who didn't want to leave the other girls exploited. He'd treated her unfairly. He had a lot to make up for.

Course it didn't matter anyway. They'd accomplished nothing.

Well, not nothing, actually. They knew the address. Likely the girls never remembered exactly where they'd been as well as not remembering what went on.

"You're right. Let's get back to the car," Blake said.

They walked to the car and got in. Harper discarded his gloves and grabbed a notepad and pen from the glove compartment. "This is number three hundred. What's this complex called?"

"We're in Peaceful Pines. It's an expensive upscale retirement community."

Harper jerked his neck around until it hurt. "A retirement community? Seriously? Why didn't you tell me that before?"

"I meant to, but we got off topic talking about how well the porn industry pays. I forgot."

"Nothing like hiding in plain sight. No one would look for a porn ring in a retirement community. They must have soundproofed the place. But how in hell did Marta get into a retirement community?"

"Duh," Blake said. "Through an elderly relative or friend. Or with fake IDs. It'd be pretty easy."

Harper nodded. "Yeah, I suppose so."

He scribbled the name of the community on his pad, shaking his head. A retirement community. Ingenious. He shoved the pad and pen back into the glove compartment and started the ignition.

As he put the car in gear, a knock on the window startled him.

He turned to face the nose of a gun—attached to a giant bear of a man.

* * * *

Amber shot up in bed.

She'd had a horrible nightmare. Harper was in trouble. Huge thugs were chasing him, firing shots from long handled shotguns. He ran, huffing and puffing, sweat pouring from his brow into his eyes.

Damn! Why had he and Blake gone out investigating tonight?

She looked at the clock on her nightstand. Four a.m. Surely they were back by now, right?

She called Harper's cell number. No answer. Blake. Again no answer.

She got out of bed, wrapped herself in a robe, grabbed her key card, and walked across the hall to Harper's room and knocked.

No answer.

Blake's room.

Still no answer.

Goddamn them!

She went back to her room and paced across the floor for several minutes, her heart racing. What to do, what to do? She couldn't go out looking for them. She had no idea where to start.

Oh, yes, she did. Rachel's.

She'd start at Rachel's.

Who knew? Maybe they were still there staking out the place. The place had closed to the public an hour and a half ago, but who knew what else was going on?

She hurriedly dressed in jeans, a T-shirt, and flip-flops, ran a comb through her hair, grabbed her purse, and ran to the elevator.

Adrenaline pumped through her. All cognitive thought ceased except for two words in bold black letters that thumped in her head in time with her heartbeat.

Find Harper.

Chapter Twenty

"Get out of the car now or I'll blow this lock off and drag you out myself," the man said.

Harper's heart lurched, and for a moment he thought he was going to throw up. He took a deep breath and exhaled.

"Shit," Blake said. "What do we do?"

"We get out," Harper said, his hands shaking.

Blake was fumbling with his cell phone.

"I said get the fuck out!" The gun banged on the window again.

Harper left his cell phone in the car—they'd no doubt take it from him anyway—and slowly exited the vehicle. The man frisked them both, took their wallets and Blake's cell phone.

"Move it," the man said. He marched them to the front door of the unit they'd been watching. He produced a key and opened the door. "Get inside."

"I guess we found a way to get in after all," Blake whispered.

"Jesus, shut up!" Harper hissed.

His bowels gurgled and his stomach clenched. Every nerve in his body was on edge. He walked into the townhome. The main floor was dark as midnight. What was going on? Could they have been wrong?

The gunman led them to a door and opened it. Steps to a basement appeared. "Go on down." He nudged Harper with the gun.

Harper nearly lost his footing and tumbled down the staircase. He caught himself in time and shakily walked down the steps. Blake's breath was hot on the back of his neck.

At the bottom of the stairs stood a closed door.

"Open it," the man said.

Harper turned the knob.

Inside was a huge room decorated in early American sleaze. He recognized the red satin bed sheets Amber had been photographed on. That was the vanilla area, obviously. On the other side of the room was a stockade, whips and chains, suspension hangers from the ceiling. Every torture device he could imagine, and some he couldn't have imagined in his worst nightmares.

Three women lay on the red satin bed. Two were playing with each other, their eyes glazed over. The other was out cold. *Drugged. God help me, Amber was telling the truth. Amber. Sweet, beautiful Amber.*

Marta, clad in a black satin robe, covered the unconscious girl with a quilt.

Three cameras stood on tripods at various points throughout the room.

No doubt what was going on here.

"I found some peepers," the big man said. "Saw them nosing around out back and followed them to their car."

A bigger man—Oscar, the bouncer from Rachel's—stalked forward. "Good work, Don. Who the hell are you two?" He studied them. "Wait a minute, weren't you in the club the other day? Jesus Christ, this is that lawyer who's been skulking around asking questions. Holy fuck."

"You've got the wrong guys," Blake said. "We don't know anything about any lawyers."

"Cut the crap," Oscar said. "I don't forget a face. What the fuck do you think you're doin' here?"

Harper gulped. "Trying to stop you from harming any more innocent women."

Oscar let out a boisterous laugh. "Excuse me? We don't hurt anyone. They come here of their own free will."

"Right, and then you drug them and have them pose for pictures and make them sign their rights away. We know all about your operation."

"Jesus," Blake said through clenched teeth, "shut the fuck up, Bay."

"What does it matter now?"

Oscar clapped him on the back so hard he almost fell over. "You're absolutely right. What does it matter now? Because I'm afraid we can't let the two of you live."

"Hey, we don't know anything," Blake said, shaking. "Nothing at all."

Harper said nothing. His stomach threatened to empty. For a moment, he envisioned his brains glopped all over the gold carpeting, but then he realized these were professionals. They wouldn't make a mess of things. One bullet to the back of the head, a clean shot. What would they do with the bodies? What would happen to Amber when he and Blake didn't come back?

Weird, his life wasn't flashing before his eyes. Just his brains on the carpet.

And Amber.

Beautiful Amber.

"Take care of 'em, Don," Oscar said. "You know what to do."

"You got it, boss." He nudged Harper and then Blake with the gun. "Come on."

Harper's guts threatened to explode. He was going to be sick right here, right all over Don's ostrich boots. What would happen to their bodies? The goon had taken their wallets with their IDs. They'd be John and Jim Doe.

If they were ever found…

His bowels convulsed. Was he going to shit right here? Right in front of Blake and the thug?

He didn't give a flying fuck.

His life was over.

"Hold it right there, asshole," a deep voice said. "Take the gun off those boys. I got ten of my men upstairs and all around this place, and if you don't do what I say, I'll set fire to this whole operation."

Harper didn't dare turn around. The sound of Don's gun hitting the floor was operatic to his ears.

The next voice he heard was Oscar's. "Donetto. What are you doin' here?"

"I heard there was a party goin' on and I wasn't invited, you dumb fuck."

"Where the hell did he come from?" Harper whispered to Blake.

"I texted him."

"Are you fucking crazy?"

"Hey, Amber didn't want the cops involved. He's the next best thing."

Harper's heart still beat like a bass drum against his sternum. He was safe. He wasn't going to die. At least not yet. Five minutes felt like a lifetime reprieve.

Oscar strode forward. A head taller than Donetto, he was an imposing presence. "This has nothing to do with you."

"So? When has that stopped me from showing up wherever I want to?" Donetto looked around. "Now what exactly is going on here? Buchanan's text said it would interest me. And I have to say, given the looks of things, I'm definitely interested."

"They're drugging girls and taking X-rated photos," Blake said.

"Shut the fuck up, asshole," Oscar said.

"*You* shut the fuck up," Donetto said. He looked at Blake. "Go on."

"They get them to sign the release form while they're drugged, and when they come out of it they don't remember anything."

"And I care about this because?"

"They're making a hell of a lot of money on the Internet. If you shut them down, you have a new clientele. You can start your own site."

"Small potatoes," Donetto said.

"Not that small," Blake said. "They charge twenty grand a year for access to the site. And they have over two thousand members."

"Forty million a year? Must be some hot babes."

"Just Rachel's girls. The men love them and they all have their favorites. It's a fantasy. If they've got the money, they're willing to pay."

"If the site brings in that kind of cash, why not just pay the girls to pose?"

Blake fidgeted next to Harper. "They won't do it. Most of the dancers are nice girls. They're just trying to make a living."

"And you know all this how?"

"My friend's brother runs the site."

"I see." Donetto cocked his gun, which was aimed at the bouncer. "Tell me why I should let any of you shitheads live."

"We'll cut you in," Oscar said. "Jesus, Donetto. This is business. You of all people ought to understand that."

"True, it's business." He walked closer to Oscar. "I'm a businessman myself. I kind of like Buchanan's idea. I'm gonna shut you shitheads down. You're exploiting innocent babes here."

"Since when do you care about exploitation?" Oscar backed away from Donetto.

"When it's being done without my knowledge or consent. I run this area, asshole. When you didn't deal me in, you made a fatal mistake."

Three more men entered the basement and held guns on Marta, Don, and Harper and Blake.

"Hey!" Blake protested.

Donetto looked over his shoulder. "Those two are harmless. Let 'em go." He turned back to Oscar. "Toss all those cameras over here."

When the three cameras were lined up in front of Donetto, he shot them each with a silencer.

Harper grimaced at each shot.

"Now let's fire up that site of yours," he said to Oscar, "and either it comes down, or your brains will be all over the monitor."

He turned around and looked at Harper and Blake. "Damn it, I told you two to go. Don't make me think twice."

Shit. We can really go?

Harper nearly peed his pants. "Let's get out of here," he said to Blake.

"Our wallets," Blake said.

Damn. Harper had forgotten about their wallets. Obviously Blake had been through this kind of thing before. "Who cares about the wallets? Jesus!"

Donetto turned slightly. "Christ almighty. Give them their goddamned wallets so they can get out of here!"

Don retrieved the wallets. Harper gripped his with white knuckles as he tripped up the stairs behind Blake.

When they were out of the unit and in the parking lot, Blake doubled over and heaved. When he was finished, he looked at the ground. "Sorry about that."

Harper shook his head. "No need to be. I thought I was going to do the same thing all over that thug's boots. I've never been so scared in my whole life."

"Me neither, even when Donetto's goons threatened me. This was some serious shit. But now he owes me one."

"Huh? Why would he owe you one?"

"You paid my debt, so that wiped the slate clean. Now I clued him in on a competitor. In his circles, that's a debt. It's probably why he let us go."

"Wow." Harper shook his head. "There's a lot I don't know about the family business, I guess."

"I don't know a lot more than you, but I know a few things. They hate being indebted to anyone. The thing I know most is I never want to get involved with any of those freaks again."

"Brother, me neither." Harper raked his fingers through his hair. He checked his watch. Five fifteen. "Let's get back to the hotel. Thank goodness Amber'll still be asleep so she won't be worrying about us."

* * * *

"Where the hell have you been?"

Amber had been sitting outside Harper's hotel room door for what seemed like days. When his tall, broad form walked up the hallway toward her, she jumped up and ran into his arms.

"Hold on. I'm tired as all hell. I can hardly stand, Amber."

"Where have you two been? I've been worried sick. I've been out looking for you for the last hour. I just got back."

Harper seized her shoulders. "You went out looking for us? Where? Are you insane?"

How she wanted to melt into his hard body. She held herself back. "I...I just went to Rachel's. It was dark and empty. I drove around a little. I had to do something, Harper. I was worried sick."

"Are you crazy? Jesus, Amber."

Blake let out a yawn. "Sounds like you two have a lot to talk about, so if you'll excuse me, I'm beat." He ambled to his door and let himself in.

"We're fine," he said. "But I'm beat too, Amber. Can we talk in the morning?"

"Harper, it *is* the morning."

"Not for me it ain't." He paused at the door. "I can't talk about all this right now. But come in with me?"

Amber's heart lurched. Did he mean? No, of course not. He looked like death warmed over. He and Blake had obviously been up all night.

But he needed her. He didn't want to be alone right now, and she knew all too well how that felt. All she'd wanted was a little company the other night, even though it had turned into more.

What went down tonight? Harper was not himself. He seemed agitated and exhausted at the same time. His eyes were glassy with a faraway look in them. It was a look of resignation, of thankfulness, laced with a little bit of...fear?

The thought niggled at her. She had been right to be worried. Something bad had gone down.

But that didn't matter right now. Harper was here, safe.

"Sure. Let's get you to bed," she said.

She followed him into the room. He plunked down on his bed, still gazing into space.

"Come on," she said, "let me help."

She pulled off his cowboy boots. Then she unbuttoned his shirt and slid it over his broad golden shoulders. Her fingers tingled as they brushed his skin.

He was so broad and manly, so incredibly handsome.

Her hands shook as she unsnapped and unzipped his jeans. The zing of his zipper rang in her ears. He lifted his hips for her as she maneuvered the jeans over his backside and pulled them off his legs.

Clad only in his boxers, he remained in his sitting position.

No hardness beckoned. He was flaccid. No matter. She wasn't after sex. She wanted only to take care of him, to nurture him. He needed her, and she wanted to be needed right now.

She pulled down the covers on the bed. "Lie down, Harper."

She gently eased him into a supine position. His head hit the pillow and his glazed eyes closed.

"That's it," she said. "Sleep now."

She took off her jeans and put his lounging pants on. They were way too big, but way more comfortable than jeans for sleeping. She unsnapped her bra under her shirt and took it off, leaving the shirt on. Then she climbed in next to Harper and snuggled against his hard body.

"Amber." His deep voice, barely more than a whisper, resonated against the walls of the quiet room. Dawn was breaking, and a sliver of light burst through the line in the curtains.

"I'm here," she whispered against his neck.

His head turned slightly and his lips touched the top of her head. "My baby."

She smiled against his hard body. Within a few minutes, his breathing had steadied, and she knew he'd fallen asleep.

"Sleep, my love," she whispered to him. "Sleep all your cares away." She closed her own eyes. "I love you," she mouthed against his warm skin. "I love you so much."

* * * *

Harper woke with Amber in his arms. Oh no, they hadn't! He sighed with relief. He was in his boxers, and she was fully clothed.

Thank God.

First things first. He fired up his tablet and typed in the URL for the Rachel's site. It was down. Donetto had done it. They sure owed him. Harper wasn't sure he liked being in that position. But Blake knew Donetto better than he did, and he didn't think there was anything to worry about.

Of course, the site could go back up at any time. At least they'd taken care of disposing of Amber's photos. He hoped to God Donetto had made sure the rest of the photos were trashed.

He wished he could be sure. For Amber. It was what she wanted. He regarded her lying on his bed, her platinum hair fanned on the pillow, her hands clasped together as if she were praying.

She looked like an angel.

He nudged her gently. "Wake up, Amber."

She opened her gorgeous gold eyes and yawned. "What time is it?"

Harper checked his watch. "Ten thirty a.m. Crap, I'm late. I have to pick someone up at the airport in an hour."

"Okay." Amber rubbed her eyes. "Who?"

"Your father."

Chapter Twenty-One

During the ride to the airport, Harper told Amber about the previous night.

Amber tensed in the passenger seat. Her hand itched to reach over to Harper's, but she held it back. She couldn't believe Harper and Blake had both put themselves in such danger for her. And she hated the idea of Paul Donetto being involved. What if he came after them?

"Blake doesn't think that'll happen," Harper said when she voiced this concern. "Now that Blake's debt is paid, we're even. Sure, Donetto got us out of the mess with the others, but Blake says that was a payoff—for letting him in on what they were doing. Donetto doesn't like others impinging on what he thinks is under his control."

"What does Blake know about it?"

"I have no idea, but he knows more than I know, that's for sure. Besides, we're all going back to Bakersville. There's no debt hanging over our heads like there was for Blake. We're small potatoes to someone like Paul Donetto."

Amber should have been thrilled that her photos were gone and the web site was down. Truly, she was, but her tummy fluttered and her hands were fidgety.

They were about to pick up Thunder Morgan.

Her father.

What would he say?

Harper hadn't told him why he wanted him to come down, just that it was important. Thunder clearly respected Harper enough to take his word for it and fly in.

Would he think *this* was important?

Would he be angry?

Would he demand a DNA test?

Would he tell Amber to stay out of his life?

Fear and uncertainty gripped her like icy fingers again. Why did Harper feel he had to do this? For her? For Karen? For himself? For Thunder?

She had no idea. He'd made it clear enough that she had no future with him. Yet here he was, taking care of her again. She'd never asked him to take care of her, so why did he do it? Maybe he thought if he got her father to take over, he'd be off the hook.

Thing is, he was never on the hook to begin with. True, she loved him, but he didn't know that. She'd never told him.

And she never would.

* * * *

"Thank you for lunch, Harp," Thunder Morgan said, touching his napkin to his lips. "The small talk's been great, and it was great seeing both of you, but now I've gotta ask why you had me come down here."

Amber stiffened. *Here it comes. Now or nothing.*

Harper cleared his throat. "I'm thinking Amber should tell you."

Amber's chin dropped to the table. Seriously? He might have warned her.

"Well, pretty lady, what's goin' on?" Thunder asked.

"Um...well. I'm not sure where to start."

"Always best to start at the beginning," Thunder said.

"Yeah, I suppose so," she hedged. "Do you remember a woman named Karen Hedstrom?"

Thunder's forehead wrinkled. "Hedstrom? Can't say it rings a bell."

"She was a cocktail waitress here in San Antonio about twenty-three years ago. Very light blond hair, clear blue eyes."

Thunder's amber eyes lit up. "Karen? Ah, yes. Gorgeous thing. I remember meeting her. Never saw her again when I came through here. She must've stopped waitressing."

Amber cleared her throat. "Yeah. She did. She...uh...had a baby."

"Did she? I never knew what happened to her. I'm glad she settled down and got married."

"She didn't actually get married."

"Oh? Well, single motherhood works these days. Lots of women are doin' it."

"Yeah." Amber shrugged and looked at Harper. *Now what?*

"Go ahead," he urged. "Thunder's a good guy."

"Sure I'm a good guy. But what's that have to do with anything?"

"You see..." Amber swallowed and gathered every ounce of courage she possessed. "*I* was that baby Karen had. And you're my father."

Thunder didn't react at first. He simply stared. Second by second passed, until Amber didn't think she could bear one more, when Thunder finally spoke.

"Say what?"

There went that shrink-wrapped feeling again. Her guts would squeeze out of her skin any minute now. "You're my daddy. Your name's on my birth certificate. Morgan Cross."

"That's my name all right, but that don't mean nothin'. Karen coulda put any old name on there."

"She swears I'm yours. We can...do a DNA test if you want."

Thunder stared at her intently. "You're the spittin' image of Karen all right, except for the eyes." He kept staring. "God damn it if those aren't *my* eyes. Funny your mother named you Amber. People always tell me my eyes are amber. Did she name you after your eye color?"

"I honestly have no idea," Amber said. "I never thought about it. Aren't all babies' eyes blue when they're born anyway? They must've turned later."

"If you're truly mine, why didn't your mother contact me?"

Harper raked his fingers through his beautiful brown hair. "That's why we called you, actually," he said. "Karen told us that she tried to contact you after Amber was born, but some woman told her you'd have them both killed if she didn't leave you alone."

Thunder's golden eyes turned to saucers. "What?"

"Mama swears it's true," Amber said. "She swears she wasn't going to ask you for anything. She just wanted to let you know you had a little girl, but whoever took the call scared the hell out of her. She never tried to contact you again."

"I would never have said anything like that."

"I know," Harper said. "And Amber doesn't believe it either, do you?"

"No, of course not. I mean, I had met you. You seemed like such a nice guy."

"How old are you, darlin'?" he asked.

"I'm twenty-two."

"Well, the timing's right." Thunder scratched his head. "I wonder... I was livin' with a woman around that time. She was my assistant and she had a thing for me. We weren't involved, but she wormed herself into everything. One of her jobs was to take phones calls. She...was obsessed with me. I ended up having to get a restraining order."

"She must be the one who took Karen's call," Harper said. "I knew there had to be an explanation."

"That must be what happened. Damn it!" Thunder pounded the table with his fist. "That woman caused me more trouble. And if I missed out on a child... God damn it!"

"It's okay," Amber said. "It wasn't your fault."

Thunder's eyes glazed over. "She was a mighty fine-lookin' woman, your mother. How is she?"

Amber sighed. "She's not good, I'm afraid. She's an alcoholic, and I don't think she's right mentally. It could all be part of the alcoholism. I don't know."

"Well, were you happy? Did you have a good life?"

"My life was fine."

"Tell him the truth, Amber," Harper said. "He deserves to know."

"Yes, darlin', please. The truth."

She sighed. "The truth is I grew up in a poor neighborhood, but Mama kept me clothed and fed. I even got riding lessons from a local breeder who Mama kept house for. I loved riding..." She sighed wistfully. Those were good years. "Once the drinking got out of hand, though, times were tough. She made me leave when I was sixteen."

"Christ," Thunder said. "Go on."

"I was lucky. My friend Laura took me in and I was able to finish high school. I learned how to do nails at the vocational high school, and I graduated with honors. Unfortunately, as soon as we graduated Laura's mom kicked us both out."

"I'm so sorry, darlin'. But you've obviously done well for yourself."

Amber didn't want to get into the whole Rachel's thing right now. She hoped Harper wouldn't bring it up.

"I've done all right. I have a good job now in a nice town."

"I'd like to see Karen," Thunder said. "If this is true, I have a lot to make up for."

"No, you don't," Amber said. "Please, I don't want you to feel that way. I'd love to be a part of your life, but I don't want you feeling guilty for not being there before. It's not fair."

"I'm sorry your life was hard," Thunder said, "but you came out wonderful. Your mama must've done a few things right."

Mama and the school of hard knocks. But Amber wasn't going to say that. "That's very sweet of you to say."

"Still, I feel responsible."

"Please don't. That's not what any of this is about. I didn't even know Harper asked you to come down here till this morning."

"That's true," Harper said. "She didn't."

"Young lady, I don't need a DNA test. Those eyes are mine. I'm sure of it. And I did have relations with your mother. One time, but as we all know, that's all it takes sometimes.

"This is all a lot to digest. One thing I missed by bein' on the road all the time was havin' a family. I especially miss it now that I'm retired. If you choose to be a part of my life, Amber, I would be honored."

Tears welled in Amber's eyes. She rose and went to her father. He embraced her in his arms. Warmth spread over her body. She felt safe. A different kind of safe than she felt in Harper's arms.

"Daddy's here, darlin'. Daddy's here."

Chapter Twenty-Two

Harper and Blake went back to Bakersville the next day, after alerting the police about the situation with Oscar and Donetto. Hopefully they'd have a hard time starting up the operation again. The cops would keep their eyes open.

Amber said goodbye to Harper without tears, though she'd cried herself to sleep that night in her hotel room.

She stayed a few more days to take care of her mother. Thunder stayed with her. Together they got Karen admitted to a Medicaid-approved substance abuse facility where she'd receive weekly therapy for her mental issues as well.

"I'm leaving Bakersville," she told her father. "I need to be close to Mama. She needs me now."

"Leaving Bakersville? But you have friends there. A job."

"I'll have to go back in a few months for the opening ceremonies of the rodeo. I'm rodeo queen, and I have to hand the crown over. But I need to get down here now and secure a job so I can help Mama. Be here if she needs me."

"If you could do anything you wanted…anything at all, would it be manicuring?"

She shook her head. "No. That was something I could learn in high school, and I'm good at it. What I'd really love to do is ride horses."

"Well, your newfound father just happens to own a small ranch on the western slope of Colorado. What say you move there? If you need extra cash you can do nails in the city, and I have horses you can ride."

Joy spread through Amber. Living on her father's ranch and helping him run it would be a dream come true. "But Mama…"

"Once her treatment is complete, she can come to my ranch too."

She hadn't expected that. How could she turn this opportunity down? "Are you sure you have the room?"

"I've got four bedrooms and a small guest house. And I'm all alone there. You do the math."

"But this is your retirement. You don't want to be saddled with two more people."

"Darlin', I'm all alone now. I was never lonely on the road. There were more than enough people around to keep me company. Now, all I've got is a few ranch hands. It'd sure be nice to have your pretty face around."

"But I can't impose. And my mother… She's a handful."

"I'm not rollin' in gold, but I was a champion bronc buster, remember? I'm well enough off to take care of my daughter and her mother. It would please me to do so."

Tears misted in her eyes. Her father had come into her life, and he was everything a girl could want in a dad. Her mother was getting the care she needed, and hopefully she would heal so Amber could heal her relationship with her. She could ride horses. Life was finally coming around. Except for one thing.

She'd never have the man she loved.

* * * *

A few days later, Amber sat in her small apartment packing boxes.

"I'm sure going to miss you," Catie said, holding Violet.

"I'm going to miss you too." Amber wrapped a mug in newspaper and placed it in a box.

"I wish things had worked out with you and Harp."

So do I.

But she didn't say it. "Oh, well, things are for the best. I'm going to get to know my daddy after all these years."

"Yeah, who'd have thought? Thunder Morgan is your daddy. That's something else."

"I know."

Amber had stopped ruminating on how different her life might have been if her father had been there when she was growing up. She had him now. That's what was important.

"I'm so sad that Violet won't grow up knowing her Auntie Amber."

"I'll be back in two months for the rodeo," Amber said. "And I'll be on the western slope. You'll come out to visit. I mean, you'll be out to visit Angie anyway. And I'll be there."

"I know," Catie said, "but it won't be the same. First Angie leaves, now you."

"We're not far away."

But Catie was in the mood to sulk, obviously. Violet got cranky and Catie nursed her. Amber taped up the last box.

"That's it," she said. "Judy's taking me to the airport tonight to catch the red-eye outta here, and the movers are coming tomorrow for my stuff. It should be on the slope in a few days." She grabbed her suitcase. "I'm all set."

"I hope you find what you're looking for on the western slope with your dad," Catie said. "And I hope things work out with your mom."

"Things'll work out one way or another," Amber said. "They always do."

* * * *

Harper paced around Chad McCray's ranch house. He hadn't known where else to turn. He'd come over to see Catie but found out from Chad that she and Violet had gone into town to help Amber finish packing up.

"She's leaving for Grand Junction tonight on the red-eye," Chad told Harper.

"Damn."

"What's goin' on with you?"

"I just…aw hell, I don't know. I don't want her to leave."

Chad shook his head. "I gotta say I'm surprised. I could swear that woman was not your type at all."

"She's not," Harper said. "Thing is, she is. She's gotten under my skin. She's been through some stuff that I can't talk about. I don't know if she's told Catie."

"About Rachel's? Yeah."

But about the web site and the photos? Probably not, and Harper didn't want to break her confidence.

"Yeah, Rachel's."

"Can't fault a girl for makin' a livin'," Chad said.

"And I don't."

"But you're havin' trouble processing the fact that you're in love with a stripper, right?"

"No. Yes. Hell, I don't have a clue. I've treated her badly, Chad. She won't want me now."

"How do you know that? And would you sit your ass down? You're gonna wear holes in my rug."

Harper plunked on the couch. *She's not the woman you thought she was.* The voice echoed in his head.

How often he'd heard that voice. He'd been so wrong. She *was* that woman. She was strong, so strong, to have lived with her alcoholic mother, to finish school when she'd been kicked out of the house, to do what she had to do to make a living. She'd never asked another soul for anything. And she was ethical. She hadn't been satisfied to merely have her photos taken down. She'd wanted to protect the other girls as well.

He was in love. Probably had been since that first night.

"I love her," he said quietly.

Chad sat down across from him in an armchair. "Do you? Or is that you just can't resist another damsel in distress?"

"What do you mean?"

"It's kind of your MO, ain't it?"

Harper cocked his head, confused. "I have no idea what you're talking about, Chad."

"When your father died, you became the man of the family. You and you alone were the one he trusted with news of his illness. He didn't tell Catie or Angie. At that point, you began taking care of your mom and of Angie. You'd always taken care of little Catie. Well, now Catie has me. She doesn't need you looking after her anymore. Angie has Rafe. And even your mother is falling in love again. Or for the first time, near as I can tell, with your Uncle Jeff. And here you are, used to taking care of all the women in your family, with suddenly no one to take care of. Enter Miss Cross. Never mind how sweet, beautiful, and downright hot she is. She's got something else you just can't resist, Harp."

"And that is?"

"She *needs* you."

Harper paused. Could Chad possibly have a clue? He did seem to have a propensity for taking care of women—his sisters, his mother, now Amber.

But he cared for his sisters and his mother. They were special to him. His father had taught him to care for those he loved. To man up when necessary.

It wasn't that they were damsels in distress. His sisters and his mother were all strong women.

And so was Amber.

Yes, he wanted to take care of her, but that wasn't all.

He loved her. He was knee-deep hopelessly in love with Amber Cross.

"I'm aging here," Chad said.

"You're wrong." Harper shook his head. "I'm not trying to rescue Amber. At least not just for the sake of rescuing her." He cleared his throat. "I love her, man."

A wide grin spread across Chad's face. "Then go get her, Harp."

Harper did a double take. "What? You want me to go get her? You believe I love her?"

"Sure I do. It's written all over your lovesick puppy dog face."

"Then what was all the crap about 'are you sure you're not just into her because she's some damsel in distress?'"

"I was playing the devil's advocate, you moron. Didn't they teach you that stuff at that highfalutin law school you went to?"

Harper let out a loud sigh. "I ought to let you have it, McCray."

"But you won't, because if you mess up my pretty face your baby sister'll never speak to you again."

"True that." Harper laughed.

"So what are you standin' here for? Go get her."

Harper was already gone.

* * * *

Catie and Violet left, and Amber decided to walk over to Rena's for some coffee. She'd need caffeine to stay up for her late night flight.

She opened the door and Harper stormed into the small studio.

"You were going to leave me!"

Amber shuddered. His anger filled the room, as though it were a presence rather than an emotion.

"Harper? What's going on?"

"Damn you!" He paced the room, his fists clenched. "How did this happen to me? How did you get...*inside* me like this? How am I supposed to live like this?"

Harper punched his fist into the wall. Dry wall cracked with a thud, and a droplet of scarlet oozed down the white surface. He was bleeding.

Amber ached to run to him. To tell him how much she loved him, how much she wanted to be with him. Instead, she said, "Judy'll make you pay for that."

"Crap. I'm sorry. I just can't bear the thought of you leaving."

"I'm sorry, Harper. I want to get to know my father, but I never *wanted* to leave here."

"Then why are you?" He advanced, like a wolf stalking his prey. His brown eyes were feral, primal.

"It's too painful to stay here. You don't want me. I'm not the woman you thought I was."

"What?"

"You know my past now. All my sordid secrets. That last time we made love, it scared the hell out of you that we'd forgotten the condom. You thought I was"—she swallowed—"dirty." The memory cut through her like a knife.

"I'm sorry about that. I just... I've never had unprotected sex before and... Oh hell, there's no fucking excuse." He thunked his head against the wall. "I was wrong, Amber. So very wrong, and I'm sorry. I should never have doubted you."

Amber warmed. It wasn't a confession of love as she'd hoped, but it *was* an apology, and she believed it was sincere. "Thank you, Harper. I accept your apology. It means more than you know."

"But still you're leaving."

"Yes, I am."

"Why?"

"I want to get to know my father. What better way than living on his ranch?"

He sat down on a large box. "I guess I can't compete with that."

"Compete with my daddy? Why would you want to?"

"Why would I want to?"

He rose again, and she wondered if he would hit another wall. Instead he paced back and forth between boxes.

"Damn it, I ran all over the state of Texas to get you out of a jam. I found your daddy for you. I took care of your mother."

Yes, he had. But not for her. "You did all that for Angie, as a favor."

"Angie? Are you serious?" He raked his fingers through his beautifully disheveled hair that now touched his shoulders. "I love my big sister, but not enough to traipse all over God's creation after one of her friends."

She gulped. Her heart did a flip-flop. "But that's not what you said. I didn't think you wanted me. Not after—"

"Didn't want you? I tried. I tried, Amber. But you've infected me. You're like a virus inside me that my body can't shake."

A virus? Hardly the stuff of love letters. But Amber's heart was pounding. Emotion flooded her.

Run to him. Run to him.

Her feet stayed locked in place.

"I ought to take you right here." He stalked toward her, his eyes smoking. "Right here among all these boxes, on the floor, like animals."

"I—"

"I ought to make love to you so violently that you'd never even consider the idea of leaving me again."

"Harper—"

He silenced her with his kiss. A primal, ferocious kiss. A kiss that marked her. Labeled her as his.

They kissed with abandon, their lips grinding and mashing together, their tongues tangling, until finally Amber broke the suction to take a breath.

"Harper."

"Amber, God damn it, don't leave me."

"Harp—"

"I love you, baby. I love you so damn much."

Warmth flowed through her like sunshine. The blood in her veins turned to boiling honey. "You love me?"

"God, Amber, yes. I love you. You're my greatest treasure. Please don't leave me. Stay here. Stay here with me. Be my wife."

"You want to marry me?"

"Please. Please marry me." His dark eyes pleaded with hers. "I don't know what I'll do if you don't."

Amber smiled. As much as she wanted to live on her father's ranch, Harper was her true dream. She and Thunder would still get to know each other. "I guess I could marry you. I mean, it'll save a lot of walls."

Harper looked over at the drywall he'd damaged. "I'm sorry about that, baby. I'll fix it tomorrow."

"Okay. Just let me know what time you'll be by. I guess I have some unpacking to do."

"No, you don't."

"What do you mean?"

"We'll just move all this stuff over to my house."

"But Harp, I can't marry you just yet."

"Why the hell not?"

"I'm rodeo queen, remember?"

"Oh right." He smiled. "Well, the good folks of Bakersville will just have to deal with their rodeo queen living in sin." He lifted her in his strong arms. "I'm taking you home."

Epilogue

"Ladies and gentleman," Mark, the rodeo emcee, announced. "Welcome to the opening ceremonies of the Bakersville Rodeo! We've got a week full of fun and adventure planned for everyone. Zach and Dusty McCray have brought back their bull, El Diablo, and are still offering that half-mil purse to anyone who can ride him for a full eight seconds. Maybe this is the year. Any of you cowboys up for the challenge?

"Our rodeo queen contest is underway, and we'll have this year's pretty ladies come out and strut their stuff in a minute. First though, please welcome last year's rodeo queen, Amber Cross. Miss Cross is escorted by her father, the one and only Thunder Morgan!"

Deafening applause echoed from the stands of the rodeo arena as Amber took the stage on her father's arm.

"Amber won't be single much longer. Next week, after she crowns our new rodeo queen, she'll become Mrs. Harper Bay!"

More thundering applause.

"Congratulations, Amber," Mark said.

"Thank you so much, Mark. I've enjoyed being your queen for a year, but I'm going to love being Mrs. Bay for the rest of my life."

"Well said, Amber. And Mr. Morgan, it's an honor to have you here at our small-town rodeo. But I understand you've been here before."

"Yup," Thunder said. "Busted broncs here fifteen years ago and won a large purse. Thank you, Bakersville!"

Thundering applause again.

Amber and her father left the stage as Mark introduced the grand marshal of this year's parade, Chad's brother Zach McCray.

Harper was waiting for her in the wings.

"You looked beautiful out there, baby," he said.

"Thank you, kind sir."

"You know, the good people of Bakersville don't know what a favor I've done for them."

"And what might that be?"

"I let them have you for two more months when I should've marched you straight to the justice of the peace and made you mine forever."

"Next week'll be here before you know it," Amber said.

"True. And you know what'll be here even before then?"

"What's that?"

His dark eyes gleamed. "Tonight."

Trusting Sydney

Bakersville Saga Six

by

Helen Hardt

In memory of the real Sydney and Sam

Prologue

Denver, Colorado, Five Years Earlier

"Hey, Sam...Chad."

Sam O'Donovan looked up. His sister was on the arm of Zach McCray.

"Hey, Dust." He turned to his companions. "This is my baby sister, Dusty. Dusty, meet Sydney Buchanan and Linda Rhine."

"And this is my big brother Zach," Chad said. "You all want to sit down?"

"We'd love to," Dusty said.

"Sydney's a barrel racer," Sam said. "I've been telling her all about you."

"Are you competing?" Dusty asked.

"Yeah. Day after tomorrow. You?"

"Day after tomorrow. Good luck to you."

"You too. Though I doubt you'll need it. Sam told me about your best time. Thirteen point nine seconds is awesome."

"Sydney's real good too," Sam said. "Her personal best is fourteen point one."

"That's exceptional," Dusty said. "I see you'll be some real competition."

"You want to dance, darlin'?" Zach asked Dusty. "They're firing up the music."

"Sure."

She and Zach left the table, and Sam focused his gaze on the black-haired beauty next to him. Sydney Buchanan's dark eyes mesmerized him. He'd never been one to pick up a girl he hardly knew, but his old friend Chad was obviously a pro at it. He was charming the pants off Miss Linda Rhine this very minute in the Westminster Room at the Windsor Hotel. The Bay siblings did know how to throw a party.

Course, they had money to burn.

Chad took the last swill of his beer and set the empty bottle on the table. "You all want to get on outta here? Go for dinner somewhere?"

"Sounds great to me," Linda said, shaking her blond curls.

Sam turned to Sydney. "How about it?"

She blinked slowly. "Sure, I suppose it's okay."

Damn, those eyes could hypnotize a grizzly.

"Great." Chad stood. "I know a fantastic little Italian place not too far from here. They always have a table for me."

They walked through the room. Zach and Dusty were sitting at a table, eating appetizers from the huge spread.

"We're heading out," Chad said to them. "We're going for a late supper at Amici's. You all want to come?"

Zach shook his head. "No thanks. We have plans."

"Okay, see you guys later." Sam followed Chad, who was already very cozy with his arm around Linda, out the door of the ballroom.

His own hand itched to touch beautiful Sydney. Her dark hair fell to her bottom. The nearly onyx waves glided as she walked, keeping time with her pace. She walked slightly ahead of Sam, and his gaze never left her. Should he touch her?

How I want to touch her.

He wasn't a ladies' man like Chad. He'd had experience, of course, but getting too friendly on a first date—and this wasn't even a first date—wasn't his style. They'd just met at the Bays' party. Getting too friendly on a first *meeting* was definitely not his style. He prided himself on being a gentleman.

Besides, he hadn't had much time for dating during the past several years. First Dusty's illness, and then their father's death, and then nearly losing the farm—not too many moments left for wooing the ladies.

He was totally out of practice. Hopefully he wouldn't make a complete ass of himself.

Chad was right. Amici's had a great table for them, private and out of the way, with a beautiful view of downtown Denver in lights.

His baked ziti was delicious. He didn't say much, just watched Sydney eat her pasta—how could one woman be so sexy eating pasta?—while Chad and Linda rattled on about one thing and another.

"What about you, Syd?" Linda said.

Sam jerked toward the female voice. She was asking Sydney something, but damned if he knew what. He hadn't been listening.

"I've got a fair shot, I guess," Sydney replied. "But Sam's sister is going to be tough to beat."

Okay. They're talking about the barrel racing. Sam nodded. "Dusty's good, that's for sure."

"Why haven't you all been down here to nationals before?" Chad asked.

Sam hesitated. He didn't like talking about their financial situation, especially not to one of the McCray heirs. Chad could write his own ticket anywhere.

"Just haven't had the time, I guess."

Chad pushed his empty plate away from him. "I don't know about the rest of you, but I'm stuffed."

"Couldn't eat another bite." Linda winked.

They've got somethin' up their sleeves.

"We could go back to my suite," Chad said. "Have a few drinks."

Yep, I know what he has in mind. And three—or four—is a crowd. Sydney's gaze locked onto his, her dark eyes brooding.

Damn!

He couldn't take her back to his room at the Holiday Inn. Not only was it not up to the Windsor Hotel standards, but he shared it with Dusty. Not exactly fare for a romantic evening.

"I don't know," he said. "I've got lots to do tomorrow, and it's getting late."

"Don't be a party pooper, Sam." Chad guffawed. "The girls are stayin' at the Windsor. Let's go on back there. The night's still young."

Sydney reached toward him, and her small hand landed on his forearm. His groin tightened.

She blinked those dark eyes slowly and her lips curved into a shy smile.

"We could go to my room."

Chapter One

Bakersville, Colorado, Present Day

"Ladies and gentleman," Mark, the rodeo emcee announced. "Welcome to the opening ceremonies of the Bakersville Rodeo! We've got a week full of fun and adventure planned for everyone. Zach and Dusty McCray have brought back their bull, El Diablo, and they're still offering that half-mil purse to anyone who can ride him for a full eight seconds. Maybe this is the year. Any of you cowboys up for the challenge?

"Our rodeo queen contest is underway, and we'll have this year's pretty ladies come out and strut their stuff in a minute. First, though, please welcome last year's rodeo queen, Amber Cross. Miss Cross is escorted by her father, the one and only Thunder Morgan!"

Sam stood in the McCray brothers' private box at the rodeo arena, taking care of his nephew, Sean. Deafening applause echoed from the stands. A platinum blond siren took the stage on his idol's arm.

Thunder Morgan. The best bronc buster in history, in Sam's humble opinion. He hadn't always won, but he'd always given the audience a good show. The man had style. Too bad he'd retired a few years back.

"Amber won't be single much longer. Next week, after she crowns our new rodeo queen, she'll become Mrs. Harper Bay!"

More thundering applause.

"Congratulations, Amber," Mark said.

"Thank you so much, Mark. I've enjoyed being your queen for a year, but I'm going to love being Mrs. Bay for the rest of my life."

"Well said, Amber. Mr. Morgan, it's an honor to have you here at our small-town rodeo. But I understand you've been here before."

"Yup," Thunder said. "Busted broncs here fifteen years ago and won a large purse. Thank you, Bakersville!"

Thundering applause again. Amber and her father left the stage as Mark introduced the grand marshal of this year's parade, Sam's brother-in-law, Zach McCray.

Sam stopped listening as Mark and Zach traded jibes. Zach was a good man. He took amazing care of Dusty and their son, Sean. Sam could never repay him for that, and the beauty was that Zach didn't expect repayment. He adored his wife and son.

"Hey, Sam, look who I found."

Zach turned to see his sister and a gorgeous black-haired beauty enter the box.

He gulped.

"You remember Sydney, don't you?"

Sydney Buchanan.

She hadn't changed one bit in five years, except maybe she was more beautiful.

"Of course," he said. "Hello." He held out his hand.

When she took it, sparks sizzled up his arm. Those brooding dark eyes seared into his own.

"It's wonderful to see you again, Sam."

"Isn't this great?" Dusty took Sean's hand. "Thanks for watching him."

"No problem. You know I love the little guy."

"He's adorable." Sydney squatted down. "How old are you, sweetie?"

"I'm almost five," Sean said.

"You're almost a grown-up." Sydney touched the little boy's cheek and stood. "You must feel incredibly lucky."

Dusty smiled. "Only every minute of every day."

Was that a hint of sadness in Sydney's dark eyes? Sam wasn't sure. Did she know about Dusty's cancer, and that little Sean was almost a miracle? It wasn't common knowledge outside Bakersville. At least he didn't think it was.

"Are you competing this year, Sydney?" Dusty asked.

"Sure am. That's why we're here. Are you?"

Dusty shook her head. "Nope. I haven't competed since that ill-fated race against you back in Denver all those years ago. I ended up pregnant with Sean and never went back to racing."

"You gave it all up? Even bull riding?"

Dusty laughed. "*Especially* bull riding. Zach wouldn't hear of it, and I actually agreed with him. We were lucky to get Sean. It's unlikely I'll ever get pregnant again."

"Oh." Sydney looked down. "I'm sorry. I didn't mean to bring up anything...well, you know."

So she wasn't aware of the situation. Then why did she look so sad?

"I know you didn't." Dusty smiled again. "It's okay."

Sam truly admired his baby sister. She was the strongest woman he knew. She'd been to hell and back, yet a genuine smile always graced her pretty face.

"You should have won that race, anyway," Sydney said. "You were magnificent."

Dusty let out a sigh and pulled Sean into her arms. "Things worked out for the best, believe me. Look what I got for my trouble. I'm a lucky woman."

Sydney's red lips curved into a half smile. "Yes, you sure are."

"Sam, I've invited Syd and her family to the house tonight for our little get-together."

Sam's heart lurched. Was he happy or unhappy at the news? What exactly did one say to a woman he'd slept with once and never seen again?

The sex had been good. Freaking amazing, actually. None of his other experiences had come close. He shuddered as the image of her crimson lips wrapped around his cock sprang into his mind. She'd licked and teased him until he thought he'd burst.

He dismissed the thought. *Don't need a boner right now.*

Two days later, Sydney had won the barrel race with a time of 14.9 seconds—not a personal best, but damn good.

But her victory had been bittersweet for Sam. Dusty and her mare had out-performed Sydney until the last second, when they knocked over the third barrel. The five second penalty had cost Dusty the race.

Her last race.

Course as she'd said, things had worked out. She married Zach McCray a few months later and had Sean not long after.

"Sam's psyched," Dusty continued, "because Thunder Morgan will be there. He's the father of one of my sister-in-law's best friends."

Great. Now he looked like a star struck little boy to Sydney.

"Really? That's awesome," Sydney said.

"He's been Sam's idol for years."

Shut up, Dusty!

"Do you still bust broncs, Sam?" Sydney asked.

"Yep. I've got a couple competitions this week. I'm thinking about giving El Diablo a try too."

Dusty's eyebrows shot up. "What?"

"You heard me."

"Wow! I remember that bull," Sydney said. "I didn't know you rode bulls, Sam."

"He doesn't," Dusty said.

"I've ridden a few in my day."

"You don't know Diablo."

"You rode him, didn't you?"

"And damn near killed myself and Zach too, if you recall." Dusty put Sean down. "Go play with your Legos, sweetheart."

Sam berated himself silently. He had no intention of riding that bull. He'd only said it to impress Sydney. At thirty-three, he didn't need to be talking himself up to impress some babe. High school had been a long time ago, for God's sake, yet here he was talking big for a girl.

"You two are both amazing," Sydney said. "I'd never get on a bull."

"You just have to understand them, " Dusty said. "They're really sweet, beautiful animals."

"No offense, but every time I watch bull riding, I think those guys are insane."

Dusty laughed. "Some of them are, that's for sure. I know the whole town thought I was when I got on Diablo."

Sam opened his mouth to agree but shut it quickly. Since he'd opened his trap to say he might ride the damn bull, he couldn't very well agree that his sister had been crazy to attempt it.

And no doubt, she *had* been crazy.

Dusty was actually really good with bulls, with all animals. She had originally planned to study veterinary medicine, but her illness, and then her marriage and birth of her son, had changed that goal long ago. Still, she helped her sister-in-law Annie, who was the town vet, as often as she could.

"You guys are still offering that half-mil purse, huh? No one's won it yet?"

"Not yet," Dusty said. "We have a couple cowpokes try every year. Thankfully no one's been seriously hurt."

"Do you still work with him?"

"I take care of him. I haven't tried to ride him again. Like I said, I gave all that up when I got pregnant."

"Yeah, I understand." Sydney's gaze shot to Sean, who was sitting on the floor with his Legos. "Your little boy is beautiful."

"Thank you. We think so."

"So what time are you starting tonight?" Sydney fidgeted a little and played with her hair.

Did she not want to go to Dusty's shindig? Why on earth not? His baby sister and her hubby threw a party like nobody's business.

"Around six. Come on over any time. We'll have a dinner buffet, but it's a 'serve yourself and eat when you want to' kind of thing."

Sam laughed. "Don't listen to her. The McCrays don't do anything halfway. Their 'serve yourself' buffet will be an open bar and a huge spread topped with a baron of McCray beef."

Sydney blinked again. Clearly, the woman was a bit nervous. Because of him? Couldn't be. Five years had passed since their clandestine liaison. No reason to be nervous.

Course his own belly was doing a series of somersaults.

He excused himself and left the box. He found an empty seat in the rafters and plunked down.

Sydney Buchanan.

She hadn't changed a bit. In fact, if it were possible, she looked even sexier and more beautiful.

They had shared an amazing night all those years ago, still the most passionate night he'd ever spent. Bits and pieces of their crazy lovemaking still haunted him regularly, but a long time had passed since he'd relived the entire night.

Opening ceremonies were still going on, but soon Mark's voice became unintelligible, and a vision appeared in Sam's mind.

* * * *

"We could go to my room."

How had they gotten there? Sam wasn't sure, but sure as day, here he was in Sydney Buchanan's hotel room, kissing those beautiful red lips.

He stiffened as she sighed softly into his mouth. He traced his tongue around her luscious full lips and gently eased it into her sweet mouth.

The soft sigh again—it vibrated sweetly against his inner cheeks. He deepened the kiss.

Her response was immediate. Her soft tongue swept against his own. A girl who liked tongue as much as he did. Heaven on Earth. The kiss became more frantic, more urgent. Their tongues tangled together, and Sydney's soft sighs turned into low moans.

She pressed her full breasts against his chest. More heaven. Sam couldn't remember a time when he'd desired a woman this much. He urged her forward until they hit the wall next to the bathroom. He pushed her against the hard surface and ground his erection against her. He was so hard he thought he might burst.

Still they kissed, fully clothed, moaning into each other's mouths. When she ripped away from him and inhaled, he rained wet kisses over her cheek and her neck, spurred by the frantic need that welled within him.

Her scent intoxicated him. Green apples or pears, fruity and inebriating, mixed with a feminine musk all her own. A deep hunger swelled in his groin, and his thoughts strayed to her hidden core. Would she be wet for him? Would she taste as good as she smelled?

He'd soon find out.

But first, the silky skin of her shoulders and the plump swell of her breasts beckoned him.

A few whispered words escaped her lips in a soft breathy caress against his neck. What had she said? He wasn't sure, but they were a husky sound, a helpless sound. A sound of want and desire.

"Do you want me, Sydney?"

"God, yes."

She wore a little black dress—sexy and classic—and right now he couldn't wait to get it off her.

He slid one spaghetti strap off her milky shoulder and pressed his lips to the smooth skin. Fire blazed through his veins. He inhaled, drinking in her fruity, musky fragrance.

She sighed. "That feels so good."

"Good, honey. I want to make you feel good. I want to take you to the stars."

He moved to the other strap and eased it over her creamy flesh. This time he kept going, until he exposed her rosy bosom.

"My God, you're beautiful." He cupped both breasts.

"Yes. Touch me. Please."

A chuckle left his throat. "Since you asked so nicely."

He thumbed both nipples until they were hard and erect beneath his fingers. He tugged at them until he could resist no longer. Then he lowered his mouth to one peak and licked it lightly.

"Yes," she said again. "Yes, suck my nipple."

A girl who liked to talk during sex. Another plus. He clamped his lips over the hard bud. Her texture was satin against his tongue and oh so sweet. He'd never come across nipples that had a flavor before. Or maybe he just wanted this woman like he'd never wanted another.

Crazy. They'd just met. He wasn't one to screw on the first date—if this was even a date. But damned if it didn't feel like the rightest thing he'd done in years.

She sure wasn't complaining either. To be on the safe side, he lifted his mouth from her nipple and met her dark gaze. "You sure about this, sweetheart?"

She nodded, and her smile lit her face like the lights on a country Christmas tree. "I'm very sure. I want you, Sam."

His cock roared to life. "I want you too. God, I want you."

He lowered his head and took the other nipple between his lips. He licked and nibbled, enjoying her moans as she writhed against him. He slid the dress down her side, over the hills of her hips, over her thighs, until it lay crumpled on the floor in a black puddle. He eased her panties down and she stepped out of them. A triangle of black pointed the way to ecstasy. He reached between her legs and smoothed his fingers through her folds. Slick. Moist. Wet.

So wet.

He groaned. "Wet, sweetheart."

"For you," she said, her voice a breathy whisper.

His erection strained harder against the confines of his black pants. They were a loose fit, but damned if they weren't tight as a bowstring right now.

"Take me to bed, Sam."

No need to ask twice. Naked except for her strappy silver sandals, she stood, ruby lips parted, dark hair cascading over silk skin, looking like a creamy dessert.

Still fully clothed, he lifted her in his arms and carried her to the bed. He laid her on the cool sheets, sat down, and started unbuttoning his shirt.

She sat up. "Let me," she said and took over undressing him. With each button and newly exposed skin, she kissed him.

And with each kiss, his skin tightened, and blood rushed through his veins and settled in his already throbbing erection. He felt *her kisses in every pore of his body, every pulse of his heart. Heat curled inside him, threatening his control.*

When his shirt lay in a heap on the floor, she started on his pants. A drop of fluid darkened a hole-punch-size spot on his boxer briefs. She smiled, and he knew she had noticed.

He didn't care. It was no secret how much he wanted her. His rock-hard cock was evidence enough of that.

She eased the boxers and pants over his legs, and her eyes widened.

"You're so muscular. God, your legs are amazing."

He smiled. "Thank you."

"But this"—she slid her hands up his thighs to his cock—"is truly a work of art." She kissed the head lightly, licking away another drop of fluid.

He jerked. Just one tiny touch from her lips on his cock and he was ready to explode. "God, sweetheart. Damn, that feels good."

"Mmm, then this'll feel even better." She took his length between her lips.

Sweet God in heaven! He couldn't come yet. Had to get inside her. But oh, how her mouth tantalized him. On top of the incredible feeling, the image of her full lips gliding over his cock was a major turn-on.

And he hadn't thought it possible to get more turned on.

Oral sex was good no matter what, but Sydney Buchanan had elevated it to a fine art. She alternated swirling her tongue around the head and thrusting her mouth up and down his length. Every time he thought he'd burst, she eased up and brought him back down.

Good thing, too, because this night wasn't ending before he tasted the treasure between those long, beautiful legs.

Gently he grabbed both her cheeks and pulled her toward him for a long, deep kiss. His own saltiness on her tongue drove him crazy, but before he got too frantic, he turned her over so she lay on her back. He broke the kiss and spread her lovely legs.

Between them, her glistening sex beckoned. He kissed each nipple, trailed his lips down her smooth belly to her vulva, and then to her moist folds.

Like silk beneath his tongue. She tasted of sweet pear, of morning dew. He flicked her hard clit with his tongue and then buried it in her wet channel.

She writhed beneath him. "Yes, just like that. Please."

He continued, adding one finger, and then another, all the while licking her, until she clamped down on his hand.

"Yes! I'm coming."

She didn't have to say it. He knew by the pulsing within her against his fingers and tongue.

And God, he was thrilled.

He had to have her, and he had to have her now.

He gently eased his fingers from her and left the bed for a moment to grab his wallet out of his pants and the condom out of his wallet. He sheathed himself in record time and plowed into her tight depths.

"God!" So good, so very good. He pumped and pumped, her hips rising to meet him. He met her mouth with a sizzling kiss, all the while thrusting harder and faster.

When he'd almost reached the brink, he pulled out, turned her over gently, and entered her from behind.

Doggy style. He loved that position. Loved them all. He wanted her on top next, riding him like she rode her barrel racing mare. Only faster and stronger and never ending.

He thrust again. Her sweet ass cheeks wiggled against his hips—beautiful. Everything about her was beautiful, but Sam was a self-professed ass man.

Well, and a boob man.

Aw, hell, he loved it all.

Even her back was sexy—smooth and creamy and all her.

Sydney.

What a woman.

Finally, he could hold out no longer.

"Now, honey, now," he said, and he reached underneath her and rubbed her swollen clit.

When her orgasm began, he let go. Tiny convulsions started at the base of his cock and spread through his length. As the orgasm erupted, the spasms darted through his body, spreading to his arms and legs. Nirvana. He went rigid and plunged into her as far as he could, letting the climax take him.

Shudders racked his body, and when the contractions finally died down, his legs shook. When he stood to dispose of the condom, they felt like jelly.

They rested a bit, shared a glass of wine.

Then they started again.

* * * *

Sam saw only darkness. He opened his eyes. When had he closed them? His erection pressed against his jeans. Well, wouldn't be getting up from this seat for a while. Good thing the opening ceremonies were still going on. Man, that Mark guy was a windbag. Was it really necessary to introduce the florist? Sheesh.

The memory of that night filled Sam with happiness.

Happiness. How long had happiness been missing from his life?

He wasn't *un*happy. Not at all. Yet life had grown stale. He simply existed from day to day. Even when he went on the road to rodeos, as now, his life held little meaning. No one needed him anymore. Dusty had Zach and their son. His ranch was thriving and his able foreman took care of everything. He had dated a few times in the last several years, but he hadn't found anyone who really brought meaning into his life.

Day to day to day to day—the life of Sam O'Donovan.

But at this moment, he was smiling. Joy coursed through his veins.

Sydney Buchanan.

He'd tried once to look her up after he returned to Montana but hadn't kept looking for very long. He'd had a bankrupt ranch to look after. He could have found her if he'd looked harder.

He'd given up.

No more giving up.

He motioned to a vendor selling beer. Too bad they didn't sell shots of bourbon. He could use a stiff one—to help him get rid of his other stiff one.

Sydney Buchanan.

She'd be at Dusty's party tonight.

And she'd be in Sam's bed come morning.

Chapter Two

"Sammy, it's great to have you back in town!" Chad McCray slapped Sam on the back. "I don't get to see my only blood brother enough."

Sam laughed, though the comment saddened him. He and Chad had become blood brothers the day Sam and his family had left McCray Landing where his father worked as a ranch hand. They went back to Montana to stay with his mother's family when she was dying of leukemia.

Though the disease had taken his mother, it had spared his baby sister, thank God. Dusty had responded well to treatment and was now considered cured. She was the picture of health and country-girl beauty, roaming around the crowd and playing hostess in her red gingham blouse and denim miniskirt.

Chad excused himself, and Sam turned to see Dusty approach an older gentleman. Sam jerked in his boots. *Thunder Morgan.* Dusty grabbed the man's arm and pulled him toward Sam. The rodeo queen and her boyfriend trailed behind.

"Sam," Dusty said, "I know this is someone you've been dying to meet."

Sam stuck out his hand. "Mr. Morgan, it's an honor."

The man chuckled. "It's Thunder or Morgan, take your pick. But never Mr. Morgan. Nice to meet you." He turned toward the other two. "Have you met my daughter, Amber, and her fiancé, Harper Bay?"

Sam nodded. "I know Harper. How are you?"

"Good, good," Harper said.

"And Amber, it's a pleasure. You are one beautiful rodeo queen."

Amber's delicate skin turned rosy, and she shook her platinum waves. "Thank you. It's nice to meet you. Dusty raves about you. We're so glad you'll be able to stay in town for our wedding next week."

"I wouldn't miss it," Sam said.

"I know you have lots of questions for Thunder," Dusty said.

Sam nodded. He did. A million, maybe. But at the moment, his tongue was tied in a knot.

Clad in denim shorts and a white camisole, her dark gaze scanning the party, was none other than Sydney Buchanan.

"Sydney!" Dusty motioned her toward them.

She walked toward them slowly. With a little trepidation maybe? Sam wasn't sure.

"Where are your parents?" Dusty asked.

"They decided to stay at the hotel," Sydney said. "My little brother isn't feeling well tonight."

Little brother? Sam knew Sydney had an older brother, Blake, who lived in Bakersville now. But a younger one? Still a lot he didn't know about this gorgeous woman.

"I'm sorry to hear that," Dusty said. "I really wanted him and Sean to meet. They're almost the same age."

Sydney smiled, her lips trembling ever so slightly. Was she nervous?

"Some other time. I'm sure they'll hit it off."

Dusty made the necessary introductions, and Thunder, Amber, and Harper excused themselves to get a drink.

"That sounds like a good idea," Sam said. "Would you like a drink?"

Sydney shook her head and cleared her throat. "On second thought, yes."

"What'll it be? It's full bar here, like I told you."

She smiled. "How about a dry martini?"

"Sounds great." He walked her over to the bar.

"A dry martini for the lady, and a Fat Tire for me." Sam shoved a few dollar bills into the bartender's tip jar and handed the martini to Sydney.

"Thank you," she said shyly.

Was this a coy routine? She sure hadn't been shy that night five years ago. In fact, *she* had invited him to her room, not the other way around.

Course five years was a long time. People did change. Who knew what had happened to her in half a decade? No matter. Sam planned to learn all he could about Miss Sydney Buchanan this evening.

But before he could ask the first question, she excused herself to make a phone call.

Damn.

* * * *

Calm down, Syd. Jesus.

She'd handled this much better at the rodeo. Still, her heart had thumped so hard against her sternum she'd thought for sure Sam could see it.

Now, in this slinky camisole—which had been a mistake, by the way—it must be completely obvious. She leaned against the counter in the downstairs bathroom and regarded her image in the mirror. What had she been thinking?

He was as handsome as she remembered—sandy brown hair, expressive brown eyes, and that body! He'd been ripped head to toe five years ago, and from what she could see, that hadn't changed. If anything, he looked even better. His dark jeans hugged those slim hips and that perfect butt just right—not too tight, but tight enough to see the gorgeous musculature.

She hadn't seen him bust broncs. She hadn't seen him at all after that one night, even though they'd both been in Denver at the Stock Show for the next few days. He hadn't tried to contact her.

A veil of guilt blanketed her. Nor had she tried to contact him.

She should have called.

Yes, *he* could have called. But she *should* have.

No matter. They were just two ships that had passed during one amazing night. They could never pass again for myriad reasons, none of which she could dwell on at the moment.

Why had she come to this party? She'd known it was a bad idea. Dusty McCray was such a sweetie to invite her. Sydney was amazed Dusty had remembered her after so long.

I suppose you never forget your final barrel race.

Sydney hadn't forgotten that race either. She'd won a sizable purse, and it had been her last race for about a year and a half.

She'd been back for a couple years now. She had done well but hadn't been overly successful. Hopefully this rodeo would be good to her. She needed to win a purse—a big one.

She made a quick phone call to her parents at the hotel to check on Duke, and then took a deep breath and left the security of the bathroom. She could make excuses to Dusty easily enough. She wasn't feeling well, or she had to get up early to work her mare tomorrow, or any number of other things could get her out of this house, away from Sam O'Donovan.

In fact, she was tempted to just leave quietly, but that would be rude. Dusty had been so nice to her, and Sydney was not a rude person. She couldn't just leave.

She inhaled again and let out the air slowly. Find Dusty and get the heck out of Dodge.

Finding Dusty meant going out back again, and going out back again meant the risk of running into Sam. It was a chance she'd have to take. She walked slowly through the kitchen out to the back patio and the spacious yard.

She spied Sam deep in conversation with Thunder Morgan. Good. Dusty had said how much her brother admired the bronc busting legend. Hopefully that would keep him occupied long enough for her to escape.

Where the heck was Dusty? Sydney walked around looking, purposely avoiding Sam, but her hostess was nowhere to be seen. *Crap.* She'd have to leave without saying goodbye. She hated to do it, but she had no other choice.

She walked back into the house, through the kitchen bustling with caterers preparing food and drink, through the long hallway to the front door.

She stopped abruptly.

Where the heck did she think she was going? Her father had dropped her off and taken the rental car back to Bakersville. She was supposed to call him later to come get her.

God! What a brain fart. She needed to get a grip.

She pulled out her cell phone. The drive from town was over a half hour. She'd have to hole up here and wait for her dad.

"Leaving so soon?"

She jerked and turned. Sam, gorgeous Sam, was standing in the front doorway. Why hadn't she walked farther outside?

"Yes, I'm afraid so," she said, trying to keep her voice from shaking. "I have an early morning."

"Don't we all." He came toward her. "At least have something to eat first. McCray beef can't be beat."

He took her arm. She sucked in a breath. The man's touch could ignite a forest.

"Come on. You can eat with me."

"But you were talking to Mr. Morgan."

"I have all night to talk to Thunder. He's not going anywhere. Right now I'd like to have dinner with you. If you don't mind, that is."

Mind? Was he kidding? She'd love to have dinner with him. Love to spend the whole evening with him. But it wasn't a good idea.

"Well, I—"

"A person's gotta eat, right?" He smiled.

Lord, he was handsome. She relented. "Okay. Dinner sounds good."

His smile broadened. The man had perfect teeth.

They each loaded their plates with food and sat down at a table with Dusty, Zach, and Sean.

Conversation centered around the rodeo, for which Sydney was thankful. Rodeo talk was easy, free of conflict. She could talk rodeo all night and never tire of it. She loved the rodeo.

When dinner was over, Sydney stood. "I'm so sorry. I have an early morning tomorrow so I need to get going. Thank you for having me."

"Can't you stay a little longer?" Dusty asked. "We have a great dessert spread coming up."

"I wish I could, but I need to get home."

Sam stood. "I'll see you out."

"Um...okay." She couldn't be rude, after all.

They walked through the house and out the front door. "Where's your car?" Sam asked.

"I...uh...need to call my father. He dropped me off."

"No problem then. I'll drive you home."

A half hour in Sam's presence? Sounded like heaven, but not a good idea. "Please, you don't need to."

"My pleasure. There's no reason to bother your father."

Energy pulsed between them. Sydney's loins blazed. How could she manage a half hour with him? Refusing was suddenly no longer an option. She wanted to spend another half hour with him. Wanted it so bad she could taste it.

Despite her sweaty palms and speeding pulse, Sydney kept the conversation on the rodeo. Sam was planning to bronc bust in several competitions. Sydney planned to secretly watch. Seeing his physique in action would be pure pleasure.

Sam insisted on seeing her up to her room at the Bakersville Hotel. Her parents and Duke were in a different room, thank goodness.

When they stopped at the door, Sydney's heart fluttered.

Sam grabbed one of her hands. "I want you to know something," he said.

"What?"

"That night we spent, all those years ago, meant a lot to me."

Her tummy tugged. "It did?"

"Yes. I'd hoped it meant something to you too."

Oh, it had. More than he'd ever know. "Yes," she mumbled. "It meant a lot to me."

"I tried to find you once I got back to Montana. But then I got preoccupied with my ranch. It was nearly bankrupt. I'm sorry. I should have kept looking."

She swallowed. She'd lain low for a while. "That's okay. I understand."

"Well—" Sam let out a huff of air. "It's been nice seeing you again."

"Thank you for the ride."

"My pleasure." He shoved his hands in the pockets of his jeans. "I guess I'll see you around the rodeo."

"Yes."

He turned to leave, and Sydney's body quaked. Fierce desire surged through her. Images of their lovemaking five years earlier flashed in her mind. His cock in her mouth, in her body. Orgasm after orgasm after orgasm—

"Sam?"

He turned. "Yes?"

She threw her arms around him and pressed her lips to his.

Chapter Three

Sydney had never been one to shy away from what she wanted. After all, she'd invited him to her room that fateful day. In an instant, desire overcame intellect, and all the reasons she should stay away drifted out on the wings of passion.

Sam's kissing abilities hadn't waned. His lips parted eagerly for her tongue, and his own met hers with a tantalizing sizzle. He tasted of coffee, of spice, of male beauty. A frenzied kiss, just as it had been all those years ago.

She moaned into his mouth, craving more, all of him.

He ripped his mouth from hers and breathed in heavily. "Sweetheart, what are you after?"

She shook her head. "I wish I knew. All I know is that right now I want you. Do you want me as much as I want you?"

"Baby, I want you so bad I think I might die an early death if I can't have you."

Thank God. Quickly she slid her key card through the locking device and opened the door to her room.

They were on each other like mad, ripping their clothes off until garments lay crumpled on the floor in disarray. Naked, they fell onto the bed. He spread her legs and launched into eating her.

It had been so long! To think she'd abstained for five years.

Abstained.

Why? Had she waited for Sam to come back to her? No, definitely not that. Why had she waited so long? She'd had plenty of opportunities.

His tongue was as talented as she remembered. He tormented her clit, tugged on her folds, teased the entrance to her moist channel.

"Mmm," he said against her, his voice a fuzzy vibration, "you taste so good, sweetheart."

She writhed, grinding against his face. "That feels so damn good, Sam. God, it's been forever."

Had she said that out loud? No matter. This was heaven. She didn't want to worry about saying the wrong thing. She'd just enjoy it.

He pushed her thighs forward and slid his tongue along the crease between her ass cheeks. No one had ever touched her there. Never. Why? It felt amazing. His tongue was silky against that virgin skin.

"Mmm," he said again. "I'd love to take you here sometime."

Her ass? Why was that thought such a turn-on?

"I...don't know—"

"No, baby, not tonight." He pulled her thighs back and set them on his shoulders. His warm brown gaze settled onto hers. "And never without your okay. It's just a thought." He sighed against her skin. "You're just so beautiful, I want all of you."

God, maybe.

Was she actually considering it? The thought aroused her. Icy pinpricks poked at her skin. Something about Sam O'Donovan made her want to do anything and everything to please him. And that thought scared the hell out of her.

Before she could dwell on the thought further, Sam went back to work between her legs. Soon she was flying high, ensconced in a climax so deep she thought she might implode on the spot.

"That's it, sweetheart." He slid his fingers in and out of her. "Come for me. Come for me all night long."

Oh, I will. As the spasms inside her slowed, he bent down and licked her tight bud, and up she flew again. He brought her to orgasm three times, and then four, and when he began a fifth, she pleaded with him to stop.

"I can't take any more, Sam. God, please."

He smiled between her legs, his chin shining with her juices. "Since you asked so nicely."

Déjà vu. He'd used those words before. He got up and grabbed a condom from his jeans, sheathed himself, and thrust into her wetness.

So full, so perfect. How had she gone so long without this wonderful completion? His mouth took hers, and they kissed frantically, passionately, until she had to rip her lips away to take a much-needed breath.

She'd already had multiple orgasms and didn't expect to come again, so the spasms building within her were a welcome surprise.

"I can't believe this. I'm coming again."

"Yeah, baby. Come again for me."

He increased the tempo of his thrusts. "God, yeah," he said. "Oh, God, yeah."

He plunged a final time, and the convulsions of his cock beat against her walls in time with her own climax.

Together they came.

Together they went limp.

"My God," Sam said against her neck.

She couldn't find her voice. Only nodded.

He rolled off her onto the other side of the bed. "It's been a long time."

"For me too," she said. He had no idea how long.

She turned on her side and regarded his gorgeous masculinity. If possible, he'd become even better looking. His sandy brown hair was in shoulder-length disarray, and his warm cognac eyes were heavy-lidded. He was still in the depth of relaxation from his orgasm. His nose was perfectly formed and those lips…too full and pink for a man. Women would spend a bundle on Botox to have them. She couldn't help herself. She leaned over and pressed her mouth to his in a soft kiss.

"That's nice, Syd." He rolled on top of her, pressing his elbows into the bed to keep from crushing her. His gaze pierced hers. "You are beautiful. You haven't changed a bit in five years."

She'd changed. He had no idea. She smiled in spite of herself. "You have. You're even better looking than I remembered."

His cheeks reddened.

She laughed. "You're blushing."

He smiled. "Am not."

"Are too." She lifted her head slightly and kissed his lips again. "Pretty soon your cheeks are going to be as pink as these beautiful lips of yours."

More red. She smiled. This was fun. She reached upward and entwined her fingers through his soft hair. *Mmm, soft as suede.* She inhaled his oaky scent. Fresh as outdoors, just as she recalled.

"It was a wonderful night, wasn't it?" she said.

"Yes." He winked. "You know what, though?"

"What?"

"I'm betting this one will be even better." He crushed his mouth to hers.

* * * *

Sydney woke to the light of dawn streaming through the curtains of her hotel window. She sighed. Colorado mornings were always so beautiful.

Next to her, Sam snoozed on his back, his erection apparent from the tent of the sheets. She gently removed the sheet to view his magnificent body. The satiny bronze of his skin lightened where the streams of sunlight touched it. His cock could have been carved by a Renaissance artist in marble, so perfect it was.

Her sex pulsed just looking at it. She wanted it in her mouth, touching the back of her throat.

Quietly she leaned over and touched her lips to the salty head. She trailed tiny kisses up and down the shaft, licked around his sac.

"Mmm."

She looked up. His eyes were still closed. A slight smile curved the corners of his beautiful lips.

She smiled and bent back to work. She twirled her tongue over his head, savoring the masculine flavor and his husky moans. She took it all until he grazed the back of her throat. She let up, allowing herself to get used to the sensation. It had been a long, long time since she'd done this.

She caressed the hard muscle of his taut thighs as she continued her assault on his beautiful cock. She took him in again to the back of her throat, his moans fueling her desire to please him.

"Sweetheart."

She looked up. His brown eyes were open and locked upon hers. "Yes?"

"If you don't stop now, I'm going to come."

Worked for her. She wanted him to come. She wanted to take him, swallow for him.

Something she'd never done before.

"It's okay. I want you to."

"Oh, God." He closed his eyes.

She continued, and his hips began thrusting upward in time with her oral strokes. Soon the pulses began low on his shaft, and when his fluid shot into her mouth, she took him, relishing the creamy texture, the salty flavor.

"That was amazing," he said when she lay back down beside him.

Happiness flowed through her. "I'm glad you enjoyed it."

He smiled. "I'd be happy to return the favor."

"I'd love it. But I'm famished."

"You want to get room service?"

"They don't have room service here," she said. "We can run up to Rena's and get some coffee and scones or something."

"Hmmm." He rolled over and gazed at her. "Don't really feel like leaving this bed anytime soon."

She laughed. "Neither do I. I think I have some granola bars in my bag. I can make the little pot of coffee too."

He grinned. "Sounds perfect."

After a quick breakfast, he made good on his promise to return the favor and brought her to orgasm twice. Then he thrust into her until they both came so hard, Sydney thought they'd created a sonic boom.

God, sex is good.

No. Sex with Sam *is good.*

Not that she'd know much difference. A high school classmate had taken her virginity in a clumsy coupling. That was the extent of her experience, save for Sam. Didn't much matter anyway. She couldn't have Sam forever, and she'd never want anyone else.

Now they lay together, their arms and legs intertwined, kissing each other sweetly and softly. If she continued kissing him for the next fifty years, she'd never get enough of those soft full lips. They licked each other, made love with their mouths.

A knock on the door startled her. She jerked beneath Sam.

He raised his head. "You want me to get that?"

She shook her head, "No, I'll take care of it." It was probably her mother or father. She couldn't let them find her here with Sam. How would that look?

Course she was over eighteen. Wasn't really their business. But still, they were her parents. They didn't need to see their daughter enjoying the afterglow of incredible sex.

She rose and retrieved her robe from the bathroom. Before she opened the door, she threw Sam his jeans. "Better put these on."

"Okay." He took the jeans. picked up his shirt, and traipsed to the bathroom.

The knocking pounded again. "I'm coming."

When she opened the door, her heart nearly stopped when she saw the familiar face.

"What are you doing here?"

Chapter Four

Rodney Kyle stood before her, clad in a navy blue business suit. His blond hair was cut above his ears, and his blue gaze penetrated her.

"I missed you."

Her nerves skittered across her skin. *Now what? Sam is in my bathroom, for God's sake.* At least he was getting dressed. What time was it? She had no idea. Dawn had already broken when she awoke.

Rod leaned in for a kiss. She turned her head and his lips slid over her cheek.

"Some greeting," he said.

"I'm sorry, it's just—"

The whoosh of a toilet flush screamed in her ears.

Rod's eyebrows shot up.

"My mother," Sydney said, her voice shaking.

God, Sam, please don't come out of the bathroom!

No such luck. The squeak of the bathroom door brought Sam into the room.

His smile turned downward when he rested his gaze upon Rod. "Uh, who's this, Syd?"

Rod strode forward, brash and businesslike as ever. He held out his hand. "Rod Kyle. Sydney's fiancé."

Sam left Rod's hand in midair. He turned to Sydney. "What the fuck is going on here?"

"This isn't what it looks like," Sydney said.

She wasn't sure which man she was talking do. Did it make a difference?

She wasn't in love with Rod. She'd planned to break if off with him after the rodeo. After she won a purse. Even if she didn't. But how could she get Sam to believe that now?

And how could she explain this to Rod? She'd hoped for an amicable parting. That wouldn't happen now.

Sam, though fully clothed, was clearly disheveled. What would Rod think? Especially since she'd told him she was saving herself for marriage?

And Sam?

She looked like a little slut cheating on her fiancé.

And that's exactly what she had done, her own feelings aside. She should not have slept with Sam while she was still engaged to Rod. She should have broken up with Rod before she came here. She'd meant to. Why hadn't she just grown some guts and done it?

"I'm thinking it's exactly how it looks," Sam said. He took his Stetson from the desk. "Thanks for a good time. I'm outta here." He slammed the door behind him.

"Who the hell is he?" Rod asked.

"A friend. A brother of a friend, actually." At least that was the truth.

Rod grabbed her hand. "Where's your ring?"

"At home. In my safe. You know I don't wear jewelry when I compete."

"A good excuse to leave it home, isn't it?" Rod's lips twitched. "Did he spend the night here?"

How had she made such a mess of things? The last five years had been the most wonderful and the most terrible of her life at the same time.

How had it come to this?

"I asked you a question," Rod said again. "Did he spend the night here?"

Sydney shook, afraid. Rod was not a violent person, at least as far as she knew, but he was a powerful businessman. He could hurt her in worse ways than physically.

She slowly nodded her head.

"I see."

"I'm sorry, Rod."

"Sorry?"

She nodded again. "Yes. I never meant to hurt you."

"Hurt me? You think a little slut like you could hurt me?"

She shuddered. His words shouldn't hurt, but they did. They rang with truth. "I'm afraid I can't marry you." She turned away from his gaze.

"Why not?"

Sydney's neck whipped around. Had she heard right? "Excuse me?"

"I said, why not? You don't think I've been faithful to you all this time, do you? A man has needs. You said you wanted to wait until we were married. Although obviously you got over that last night."

"You mean you—"

"Of course. Don't be naïve. As far as I'm concerned, the engagement can proceed as planned. I never planned on being faithful to you."

She stood, her body numb. "Are you kidding me? This is the kind of marriage you wanted?"

"This *is* marriage, dear. My own parents have been married nearly forty years, and they've both had strings of lovers. My father likes twenty-something blond girls. Ironically, so does my mother."

The reality of the rich—way more information than she wanted. "Rod, I'm really glad I haven't hurt you."

"You don't have the power to hurt me."

"Be that as it may, I'm glad I didn't. But this engagement is over."

"No, it's not."

"I'm sorry, but I'm afraid it is."

He stalked toward her. "The announcements have already been made in all my circles. It is not over."

"But I don't love you."

"I don't love you either."

"Then what's the big deal?"

"You are the kind of wife I need. Beautiful to the eye. From a modest background, so you're attracted to money. You're tall and athletic. You'll bear me strong heirs. You'll be a good hostess."

Anger boiled under her skin. "I'm more than just arm candy, damn it."

"Darling, you are the ultimate arm candy, but I'm afraid that's all you are."

Why did his words cut her? She didn't care, but it still hurt to be spoken of in that manner. "Why does it matter? If that's all I am, I'm easily replaced."

"I'll lose face. And I don't take kindly to that. My parents have gone to a lot of expense and trouble for our impending marriage. Besides, you have value you can't even fathom."

What the hell does that mean? "Your parents are richer than God. They won't care. And I don't care what kind of value you think I have. I'm not marrying you. You can't make me."

Rod shook his head. "Fine. Have it your way."

"Why did you come here?"

"I told you. I missed you."

"That's crap. You just admitted you don't love me. You just wanted to see what was going on. You want to control me."

The man was a control freak in his business. Clearly he was also a control freak in his personal life. How had she gotten involved with him?

Unfortunately, she knew the answer to that question. *Money.*

Sydney and her parents were carrying some major debt. Rod had been her savior. But right now, money didn't matter to her. She wanted out.

"I think you'll change your mind. But for now, if we're no longer to be married, I guess I don't have to worry about controlling you."

"That's right. Now get the hell out of here." She pushed him out the door and slammed it shut.

Rod's words stung because they were mean, but not because they'd come from him. That realization made her even more comfortable with her decision to break it off. She hadn't wanted to hurt him, and she hadn't. For that, she was glad.

Now, what to do about Sam?

She couldn't have a life with him. That was out of the question. But she didn't want to hurt him. She didn't want to hurt anyone, but especially not Sam.

She wanted him to know that last night had meant something to her. That their time five years ago had meant something.

That she'd never forgotten him, and she never would.

How, though, could she convey that while also telling him she couldn't see him again?

* * * *

How could he have misjudged her?

Sam raked his fingers through his disheveled hair. He needed a shower. He drove up to his small guest house on Zach and Dusty's ranch and took refuge inside.

He inhaled. Pears. Musk. Sex. He could still smell her. Yep, he definitely needed that shower. And it needed to be a cold one. Even now, his cock still throbbed for her.

As the lukewarm water streamed over his tired body, images of Sydney's dark, brooding eyes haunted him. She'd been acting strange yesterday, no doubt. Yet after they'd made love, he'd been sure he imagined it.

No such luck.

The woman was like a disease. She got into his body and wreaked havoc.

The sex had been amazing, though. He connected with her on a level unknown to him with any other woman.

He was tired of trying to replicate the feelings he'd had when he was with Sydney. He'd tried for five years, to no avail. He was done trying.

Sam O'Donovan would live out his life as a bachelor. Yes, he'd always wanted to be a father, but he could still be a father figure. He didn't need his own kids. He'd dote on Seanie and his cousins on Zach's side. Dallas and Annie had four adorable kids, and Chad and Catie had a beautiful little girl named Violet. They all loved their Uncle Sam. Or Uncle Sammy, as Dallas's girls, Sylvie and Laurie, called him.

In a flash, an image of a smiling little boy with sandy brown hair and dark brooding eyes soared into his mind.

His son with the woman he loved.

Loved?

Make that the woman he'd never have.

The child he'd never have.

He let grief consume him for only a few moments. Then he washed his hair, stepped out of the shower, and dried off.

Sam wasn't one to wallow in misery. He'd had his share of it, losing his mother when he was only ten, his father years later. Nearly losing his baby sister. If he'd wallowed in it, he would have had a shitty life.

Still, life had grown stale.

He needed a change. He'd hoped against the odds that Sydney might be that change.

Nope. Not to be.

He dressed quickly and headed over to the main house to see Dusty. She and Zach were sitting at the table, drinking coffee.

"Glad I caught you," Sam said. "I thought you all might have headed over to the grounds already."

"No, not for a few hours yet," Zach said. "Have a seat. Want some coffee?"

"Don't mind if I do. Don't get up. I'll get it." Sam poured himself a cup and sat down next to his sister.

"Rumor has it you left the party with one Sydney Buchanan last night," Dusty said.

"Rumor has it that's none of your business, little sis."

Zach smiled. "Give the man a break, darlin'. You know men don't kiss and tell."

"This isn't a man. He's my brother," Dusty said. "Now spill it."

"There's nothing to spill," Sam said. "I gave her a ride home."

"Now I know darn well you and Chad hooked up with Syd and her friend at the stock show that time. You remember, don't you, Zach?"

"Dust, you're gonna have to give your big brother a break here. He clearly doesn't want to discuss this."

"There's nothing to discuss, and that's final." Truer words had never been spoken. He and Sydney were over. Heck, they'd never begun. Sam took a long drink of the coffee. Good and strong, just as he liked it. "Case closed."

Dusty sighed. "Fine. I understand."

"In that case, Dust and I have something we need to talk to you about," Zach said.

Sam took another sip. "Yeah? What is it?"

"Well, our ranch foreman is retiring, goin' down to Arizona with his family."

"Sorry to hear that."

"We need a new foreman, and Dust and I think you might be the perfect man for the job."

Sam perked up. "I'm listening."

"You wouldn't have to sell the Double D, Sam," Dusty said. "You could have your foreman run it. It's a small operation, and you'll be making more than enough here to keep it running. I know you don't want to sell it. It has sentimental value to both of us."

He set his mug on the table. "I'm not sure it's a good idea to do business with family."

"Which is why I'm offerin' you a cut," Zach said. "That way, you'd be an owner of sorts. Dust and I have discussed this at length with Dallas and Chad and their wives. We all agree you're who we want."

"Plus, it'd be great to have you here, Sam," Dusty added.

A new place. A new job. New challenges. New people to meet, and family to spend time with. It might be just the cure for a life that had grown stale.

Sounded like a gift dropped from heaven.

"I'll definitely give it some thought."

"Please consider it," Dusty said, refilling his coffee. "Zach and I would love to have you here."

"And make no mistake," Zach added, "this ain't nepotism or anything. This was actually my idea, not Dusty's. You are the best man for this job. I don't offer just anyone a share in my ranch, not even my wife's brother. I offer it to you because I know you'll earn it."

Sam opened his mouth to speak, but the doorbell interrupted him.

"Stay put," Dusty said to Zach. "I'll get it."

A few minutes later, Dusty returned with Sydney Buchanan at her side.

Sam's heart leaped.

Then dropped to his belly.

He stood. "I need to get going. Thanks for the coffee."

"Can't you stay for a few more minutes?" Dusty asked.

"Wish I could, Sis, but I've got stuff that can't wait." He grabbed his hat and nodded to Sydney. "Nice to see you again, ma'am."

He walked out the door without looking back.

Too bad his heart was still in the room.

* * * *

"Sit on down," Dusty said to Sydney, "and I'll get you a cup of coffee. You want some coffee cake? Seraphina left a nice one. She took Seanie out for the day."

"Oh, no, thank you." The cake looked delicious but it would taste like sawdust. She couldn't eat right now.

Sam had run from her like an ant from a grasshopper. Not that she blamed him.

She hadn't thought it would cut into her heart like this, though. *Crap.* Of course she had. That was a big ol' lie.

Zach rose. "I'll leave you ladies to your girl talk. Got work to do." He gave Dusty a quick kiss. "See you later, darlin'. And nice to see you, Sydney."

"You too." Sydney sat down and took a sip of the coffee Dusty had given her. "I hope I'm not intruding."

"Not at all. I'm glad to have the company."

"I was hoping we could talk."

"Of course. What's up?"

"I know we don't know each other that well. But really, you're my only friend here. I'm actually surprised you remembered me yesterday."

"How could I forget the woman who beat me in that race?" Dusty smiled.

"You should have won."

"Nah. It turned out the way it needed to turn out. Sometimes it takes a while to see the ultimate plan, but it eventually surfaces."

Does it?

The last five years had been a both a blessing and a hardship. Sydney wasn't sure where she was going next. At least she wasn't marrying Rod. That whole relationship had been a mistake, further evidenced by his visit this morning.

"I'm glad you see it that way."

"I do." Dusty patted Sydney's arm.

The warmth of friendship infused her. Could she really talk to this woman? After all, she was Sam's sister. But she had no one else, and she needed Sam to know the truth. Or at least part of it. She'd start with Dusty.

"I suppose it's no secret that your brother and I met five years ago in Denver."

"Yes, I remember. We all sat together for a few minutes at the Bays' party at the Windsor."

Sydney nodded. "Sam and I, we spent that night together."

Dusty remained silent.

"I hope that doesn't shock you."

"Shock me? Goodness no. I know my brother's not a monk. I just don't really know what to say. But truly, I don't think less of either of you for it."

"Thank you. I appreciate that. The thing is, we hooked up again last night, but…"

"But what?"

"You may think less of me now."

"Why is that?"

"Well, someone showed up this morning and interrupted us."

"Why would that matter?"

"Because of who it was." Sydney cleared her throat. "My fiancé."

Dusty's eyebrows shot up.

"But please believe me," Sydney continued, "Rod and I were over. I was going to break up with him as soon as I got home. In fact, I should have done it sooner. At any rate, it's done now. We broke up this morning."

"He ended it because he found you with Sam?"

"No. Oddly, he was okay with that. If you knew his family, you'd understand. I was the one who ended it."

"Why?"

"Because I don't love him. I never did. Rod is the heir to a huge hotel business in Carson City. He offered financial security."

Dusty nodded. "I understand."

"You do?"

"Yes, I do. Believe it or not, I was once in financial trouble myself. I know how it feels. I nearly sold my Regina to get money I needed."

"Regina?"

"My barrel racing mare."

"Oh! She's a beautiful horse."

"Thank you. Yes, she is."

Sydney sipped her coffee. "Rod came into my life by accident. I applied for a job at his office. I didn't get it, but I caught his eye. He recognized me from a magazine article on the WPRA. He wanted a woman who had a recognizable name and a good face and body to be arm candy. He also liked the fact that being a barrel racer, I wasn't all that financially secure. That was evident when I applied to work at his company."

"I see. So he asked you out?"

"Yes. It was a whirlwind courtship. I think his daddy told him it was time to get married or something. Within a month, my face was plastered all over the society pages in Carson City. Hotel heir Rodney Kyle and his fiancé, barrel racer Sydney Buchanan. We were the talk of the town."

"Did you love him?"

Sydney shook her head. "No. And I found out today he never loved me either. This was to be solely a business arrangement."

"Do you still need money?"

"Yes, but I'm hoping to win a purse here."

"I think there's a good chance of that."

"I sure hope so." She sighed and took another sip of coffee. "I'm sorry I hurt your brother. I never meant to."

"Sam's a big boy. He'll be okay. Just talk to him."

"That's the thing." Her voice cracked and she steadied it. "I can't talk to him. I can't ever see him again.

Chapter Five

"That's a good boy." Sam smoothed the jet-black horse's mane.

"He's a beauty, ain't he?"

Sam turned to see Zach. "Yeah, he is. What's his name?"

"Midnight."

"It fits."

Zach nodded. "Want to take him out?"

"I was hoping to, thanks. I need to get out of here for a while."

"Something wrong?"

Sam wasn't one to talk about his problems. He wasn't a woman, for God's sake. But Zach was his brother-in-law and a good friend. "Sydney Buchanan."

"I figured as much, the way you hightailed it out of there this mornin'. What's going on?"

"I suppose it's no secret that she and I hooked up in Denver. You know, back when you and Dusty hooked up."

"Yeah. Did Chad ever tell you about the problems he had with the woman he hooked up with that night? Linda?"

"Yeah. I'm glad that all worked out for the best."

"Me too. Though it came at a rotten time. Right after our ma died."

"I know. I'm sorry." He gave Zach a pat on the back.

"Water under the bridge. Chad's happy as a clam now with Catie."

"I know." Sam chuckled. "I wasn't sure I'd ever see him settle down. He did love the ladies."

"Now he loves one lady. He's as smitten as can be with his wife and baby daughter."

"They're both beauties, that's for sure."

"So what's going on with Miss Buchanan?"

Sam cleared his throat. "Thing is, I'm no Chad McCray, but I've had my share. But that night with Sydney stands out as the best."

"Yeah?"

"I thought maybe I was just having fond memories of my one and only one-night stand. But she and I got together last night, and it was just as good. Better, even."

"And that's bad because…?"

"You don't know the half of it."

"Tell me."

"She's engaged. A little fact she neglected to tell me."

Zach raised his eyebrows. "I don't recall seeing a ring on her finger."

"That's because she wasn't wearing one. But she's engaged to some pretty-boy businessman. He showed up at her hotel room this morning while I was still there."

"How did she explain your presence?"

"I haven't the foggiest. Didn't stick around to find out."

"Well, if you want to know what's going on, go on up to the house. She's having coffee with Dust."

Sam shook his head. "Can't. She flat out lied to me. Who has sex with another man when she's engaged? That's crazy shit."

"Maybe there's an explanation."

"What kind of explanation can there possibly be?" Sam shoved his hands in his pockets. "We had great sex. Twice. But great sex doesn't make up for a lack of trust."

"Are you looking for something with this girl?"

"I thought I might be. Hell, I don't know. Life's gotten kind of boring, Zach. Which is why"—he took a few steps forward and held out his hand—"I've decided to take you up on your offer. Coming here to Colorado, being near my sister and nephew, might be just what the doctor ordered."

Zach shook his hand. "Good. We're all thrilled to have you on board here at McCray Landing. When can you start?"

"After the rodeo, I'll head back to Montana to make sure the Double D is taken care of. I think I can persuade my foreman to take over. Once things are settled, I'll get down here as soon as I can."

"Would you like to see the house for the foreman?" Zach asked. "It's vacant. You can move in anytime."

"I'd love to."

"Good. You saddle up Midnight there, and I'll get Attila ready. We can ride on over and take a look at it."

Yes, this would be just what he needed. Once the rodeo was over and Sydney Buchanan went back to Nevada, he could concentrate on starting his new life.

* * * *

Dusty's mouth dropped open. "What do you mean you can't see Sam again?"

Sydney's heart ached. Sam was amazing, and such a nice man. And she adored Dusty and her little boy.

God, her little boy.

Some hurts never healed.

"It's not something I can talk about."

"I guess I don't see the problem. You broke up with your fiancé. You're a free woman now."

"But I neglected to tell Sam I was engaged."

"So?"

"Well...we spent last night together."

"You told me that. And yes, the guy showed up. But you can just explain to Sam that you were planning to break up with him, which is the truth."

"Still—"

"My big brother is a great guy, Syd. If he's interested in you, don't let him go."

"I don't want to."

"Then don't. Whatever's going on, be honest with him. If he cares for you, and I think he does, he'll help you. He was there for me all those years when I needed him. He sacrificed his own happiness so I was taken care of."

Sydney nodded. She'd known for a while that Dusty had been ill when she was younger. "Your leukemia."

"Yeah. It's also the reason I can't have more children. It left me nearly infertile. Sean was a gift from heaven."

"Oh, Dusty, I had no idea. I'm so sorry." Here she was complaining. How selfish could she be?

"Don't be. I'm fine now. I'm ten years out and considered cured. But my point is Sam was there for me when I needed him. He took care of me. My father passed away during that time, and Sam was all I had. So when I tell you he's a special man, I'm not just saying that because he's my brother."

Sydney looked at her lap. Sam *was* wonderful. She'd always known that. Sometimes she looked back at her life and wondered why she'd made the decisions she had.

Perhaps he'd forgive her for not telling him she was engaged.

But other things could never be forgiven.

"I'm sorry to keep you so long," Sydney said, rising. "I need to get to the rodeo and warm Sapphire up. I've got a race this afternoon."

Dusty took her hand. "I'm glad you came over. Whatever is bothering you, I promise it will work out. Trust me, I've hit rock bottom before and come out swinging. You will too."

Sydney wasn't so sure, but she smiled halfheartedly. "Thanks."

"And I'll be there cheering you on in the stands this afternoon. Good luck."

"Thanks. That means a lot." She walked out the door and drove away.

* * * *

Sydney took a deep breath and smoothed Sapphire's soft white mane. She hadn't hit her personal best of 14.1 in seven years. She was last to go in the competition, which only made her more tense. But at least she knew what she was up against. So far, the fastest time belonged to a local girl at 14.5. She could still take first, but it would require intense concentration and perfect form.

She had to win. She needed the money. Especially now that Rod was out of the picture for good.

One more deep breath and she closed her eyes. In her mind, she and Sapphire ran like the wind, skating around every barrel with perfect ease.

She opened her eyes, signaled to the judge, and then kicked into high gear. She and Sapphire crossed the electric eye and raced toward the first barrel. Sydney clenched her teeth as she set the mare up to turn the first barrel without knocking it over. Then, in a whirlwind, Sydney took Sapphire around the first barrel perfectly. Pursing her lips, she looked straight ahead and galloped toward the second, taking Sapphire around in the opposite direction. Excellent. One more to go. Running toward the backside of the arena, she and the mare aimed toward the third and final barrel, the sweet rush of adrenaline empowering her.

Yes, yes, she was doing it! Sapphire was in fine form as she rounded the last barrel.

Thundering applause echoed from the stands. She ignored it. Only the race mattered. She and Sapphire were alone in the universe. Alone to conquer the world.

A microsecond later, Sapphire rounded the final barrel and they headed back down the center of the arena.

She crossed the electric eye but didn't see her time.

Had she made it?

Had she beaten 14.5?

She didn't know. But right now it didn't matter. Sapphire had worked hard and needed Sydney's attention. She dismounted and petted the mare's nose. "Great job, sweetie."

Within a few seconds, the local girl, Sandra something or other, approached her. "Good race."

"You too."

"Congratulations. Fourteen-three is a great time. "

I won? Warmth flooded her. "Thank you."

"It's a fine purse you'll be getting."

"Congratulations to you, too. You had a great score."

Sandra smiled. "Thank you. See you next race."

Sydney's heart leaped. She'd done it! Not her personal best, but as close as she'd gotten in seven years. All those hours working with Sapphire had paid off.

She led the mare to the grooming area and got to work. Soon her parents and Duke joined her.

"That was great, Sassy!" her little brother exclaimed.

Sydney smiled. When Duke had been learning to talk, he couldn't say Sydney, so he called her Sassy. It had stuck. Though he was five, they all still used the nickname. She pulled the little boy into her arms and kissed his apple-red cheek. He was such a beauty, with light brown hair and dark walnut eyes.

"One day you'll be the best bronc buster in the world."

Duke turned to his mother. "Can't I please do the mutton busting, Mama?"

"You're still a little too young," his mother replied.

"I'm five. I'm allowed."

"Now we promised Mama you wouldn't do it till you were six, " Sydney said. "Next year will come soon enough."

"It's bad enough I had to watch you and Blake fall off animals and nearly kill yourselves when you were older than Duke. Let me keep my baby for one more year."

All the talk meant nothing to Duke, who sulked in Sydney's arms.

"Don't worry, partner." His father patted his head. "You'll be big enough next summer."

"Sydney!" Dusty ran forward, dragging Sean by the hand. "You were incredible. Congratulations!"

"Thank you," Sydney said. Her nerves ricocheted. Now what? It would be rude not to introduce her family. "These are my parents, Roy and Carrie Buchanan, and this is my baby brother, Duke."

"It's wonderful to meet you." Dusty held out her hand. "I'm Dusty McCray, and this is my son, Sean."

"One of the infamous McCrays." Roy Buchanan smiled. "Great to meet you."

"I'm so sorry we missed you at our gathering last night."

"Yes, well—" Roy cleared his throat. "Duke here wasn't feeling all too well, but he's much better now."

"I'm glad. He and Seanie look about the same age. We'd love you to bring him over while you're in town. I'm sure they'd get along great."

"Thank you so much for the offer," Carrie said. "We'll take you up on it if there's time."

"Even if you can't, we're having another big party at the end of the rodeo. If you're still in town, you must come."

Sydney fidgeted. Why did Dusty have to have another party?

Before Sydney could formulate an excuse not to attend, Dusty spoke again. "There's my brother. Sam! Over here!"

Good God, no.

Sam loped up, black Stetson on his head, his sandy hair curling along the outside. His gorgeous physique was apparent in his black western shirt and dark denim jeans. Was that the outline of his sculpted abs under the shirt? Sydney's heart raced.

Sam smiled.

It wasn't a real smile. It looked pasted on.

"Good afternoon." He removed his hat.

"Sam, these are Sydney's parents, Roy and Carrie," Dusty said. "And this gorgeous little creature is Duke."

"You have a little brother?" he said to Sydney.

She looked down. "Yes."

"He's a mighty fine-lookin' young man."

"Thank you," Duke said with a smile.

"I'm sure you're right proud of your big sister." He turned to Sydney. "That was an amazing race."

Her cheeks warmed. "Thank you." She turned. "If you'll excuse me, I need to take care of Sapphire."

"Of course," Dusty said. "We'll see you later." She and Sam walked off, Sean in tow.

"We'll meet you down by the concessions," Roy said, taking Duke.

"Okay, I'll be there in about half an hour, soon as I get her settled."

A few minutes later she was currying Sapphire. Her mare was beautiful, pure white. She'd wondered, when she bought her, why the previous owner had named her Sapphire.

No longer. The name fit. The mare was a jewel.

"Hello."

She turned toward the deep timbre. She didn't have to. She knew exactly who it was.

Sam O'Donovan.

She cleared her throat. "Hello."

"Congratulations again on the race."

"Thank you." She went back to work on Sapphire. "Is there something you wanted?"

"Yes."

She looked back up at him. Why did he have to be such a beautiful man?

And why couldn't her heart stop pounding?

"What?" she asked.

"This."

He stalked forward, grabbed her, and crushed his mouth to hers.

Chapter Six

Sydney couldn't let this happen. She knew that, in her rational mind.

Problem was, her rational mind didn't control this part of her.

Right now she wanted this kiss. Wanted Sam with an astounding passion that surprised even her.

When he ripped his mouth from hers, she whimpered at the loss, but his nips and kisses on the nape of her neck soothed her.

"Oh God," she whispered.

"I want you," he said against her neck. "I want you so much."

"I want you too."

Sam pressed his mouth on hers again. The kiss was demanding this time, almost punishing. He took from her, marked her.

When he paused to take a breath, his gaze penetrated her. For a second, she could actually feel it boring beneath her skin.

"Why?" he said. "Why didn't you tell me?"

Her tummy plummeted. "What?"

"That you were engaged? I thought we had something special. Last night was just as amazing as it was five years ago. Can you stand there and tell me you didn't feel something?"

She gulped. Shook her head. "I felt a lot. I... You have no idea how much I felt."

"Why did you do it?"

She averted her gaze. "I don't know."

That was a lie. She *did* know. She could at least tell him that much.

He cupped her cheek and returned her gaze to his. "Look at me, damnit."

"I'm sorry," she choked out. "I *do* know why I did it. I did it because I wanted you. Because I've never forgotten what it was like with you."

"But your fiancé—"

"Is gone. I broke up with him this morning."

"Don't you mean he broke up with you? I'm sure you had a hell of a time explaining who I was."

"Actually, no. I did the breaking up. I had planned to do it before I came here but I didn't. I'm not sure why. But I did it this morning. He was willing to forget the whole thing."

Sam arched his eyebrows. "What?"

"That's the kind of guy he is. It was never going to be a marriage in the real sense. I never even had sex with him."

"What?" Sam said again.

"I never had sex with him. I told him I was saving myself for marriage. I haven't had sex with anyone since—" She clamped her hand over her mouth.

"Since when, Sydney?" Sam gripped her shoulders. "What are you trying to say to me here?"

The truth burst from her lips. "Since *you*, damnit! I haven't had sex since that night with you five years ago."

His brown eyes smoked. "Is your horse taken care of?"

"Yes. I just finished."

"Good. You're coming with me."

* * * *

Sam's lovemaking was forceful, as though he were marking her, making her his.

Yet it was wonderful at the same time. Sydney wanted to be his. Wanted the passion and desire she'd only experienced with this man.

Could she dare have it?

As she straddled atop him, his cock embedded deep inside her, his fingers pulling her hard nipples, she thought, for an instant, that it could work.

He wanted her. That was obvious.

"Ride me, sweetheart. Just like that."

His deep voice was so sexy.

"God yes, Sam, I love how you feel inside me."

"I love it when you talk like that, baby. You make me hard." His hips rose from the bed and he pushed farther into her.

Sydney reached down to her own special spot and began rubbing in time with Sam's upward thrusts.

"Yeah, sweetheart, you're so hot when you touch yourself there. God, you're beautiful."

"You're beautiful too, Sam. So gorgeous. I've never seen a more beautiful man."

He thrust into her. "Never like this. Never before or after you."

He had no idea. "Amazing with you. Only with you."

"I'm gonna come, baby." He thrust harder.

As his shaft pulsed within her, her own orgasm blasted through her veins like boiling honey.

So good. So right.

Could she have this? Could it work?

They hadn't said a word as they rushed to her hotel room. It wasn't far from the rodeo arena. He'd dragged her by the hand up to the room and nearly thrown her on the bed. Frantically they'd stripped each other, and within seconds she was on top of him, impaled on him.

Now she slid off him, mourning the loss of his cock. She lay down next to him.

He propped up on one shoulder and looked at her. "We need to talk."

Oh God. She waited.

He cleared his throat. "I want to be able to trust you."

"I know."

"You should have told me you were engaged."

"You're absolutely right. And I shouldn't have gone to bed with you while I was engaged to someone else, even if I was intending to end it."

"You're right."

"This isn't an excuse, but…I couldn't resist you, Sam. I couldn't resist you five years ago, and I couldn't now. I'm not afraid to go after what I want, but I'm not the type who goes around having one-night stands."

"You invited me to your room that night, Sydney."

"I know. And it wasn't like me at all. There was something about you."

He nodded. "I understand, believe it or not. I never believed in chemistry before. I never believed in love at first sight."

Her heart lurched. "Love at first sight?"

"I'm sorry. I don't want to scare you."

Adrenaline spiked through her. "I'm not scared, just a little confused. What exactly are you saying?"

"We know little about each other, but I can tell you one thing. I have never in my life felt the way I do when I'm with you."

"Neither have I."

"Then is it love we're feeling?"

"I don't know."

"From my end, it sure seems to be."

Warmth flooded her. Did he truly love her? Could it possibly happen? Even with everything else she hadn't told him yet?

He caressed her cheek. "I love you, Sydney."

She shouldn't say it back. It would just make things harder, but the words tumbled off her tongue. "I love you too, Sam. God, I love you so much."

She meant the words with all her heart.

It was now or never. She had to level with him. He deserved the truth. She might lose him, but she could no longer live the lie.

"Sam, I need to tell you something."

"What is it, baby?"

A knock on the door interrupted her. "Who could that be? I know Mom and Dad were keeping Duke at the rodeo to watch the rest of the events. He already had his nap before my race."

"Whoever it is, get rid of him," Sam said, pressing his lips to hers. "I want you back in this bed."

She smiled. Saved by the knock. For now at least. She pulled on her robe and opened the door.

"Hello, darling Sydney," Rod Kyle said.

"What are you doing here?"

He pushed past her and walked into the room. Sam, still naked, jumped to his feet.

"For God's sake, put some clothes on," Rod said, turning his head.

Sam hurried into his jeans. "What's going on, Sydney? I thought you two were over."

"We are. Why are you here, Rod?"

"I did a little digging today, and I found some stuff that I thought you might find interesting."

"Nothing you have to say interests me," she said. "Now leave, please."

"Not until I say what I came to say."

"You heard the lady," Sam said. "Get the hell out of here."

Rod was no match for muscular Sam. Yet he didn't seem fazed.

"You and your friend here might be interested in this." He handed a paper to Sydney.

She gulped. "Oh God."

"What is it?" Sam ripped the document out of her hands.

He scanned the paper. "A birth certificate. Baby Boy Buchanan? With you as the mother?"

Her heart sank. Now he knew the truth, and it wouldn't take long for him to put two and two together.

"September first? Five years ago? And you haven't had sex with anyone since me?" He stalked toward her. "Goddamnit, you had my baby, and I never even knew it!"

Chapter Seven

Rod smiled a smug grin. "This just keeps getting better. I didn't expect this turn of events. I just thought you had a child when you were a young maid of nineteen."

"Nineteen?" Sam reddened. "You were only nineteen? That makes you twenty-four now?"

"Nearly twenty-five. Next month, in fact."

"Christ." Sam raked his fingers through his hair. "Where is he? Where is my son?"

She trembled, tried to keep her voice calm. "He was put up for adoption."

"Why didn't you contact me? I would have helped. I would have taken the child. I would have—" He plunked down on the bed, his eyes wet and sunken. "I've always wanted kids."

Sydney ran to him and touched his cheek.

He pushed her hand away. "Don't touch me."

"Sam, I love you."

"I don't want to hear that right now."

Her heart breaking, she rose and stalked toward Rod. "Why did you do this? I mean nothing to you. You admitted that this morning."

"I don't like being rejected. Rodney Kyle doesn't get rejected, certainly not by the likes of you."

"I was only some stupid trophy wife to you," Sydney said. "Why does it matter?"

"You're the wife I want, and I mean to have you."

"Too bad. You can't have me. You think you can show up with this birth certificate and turn my life upside down? And I'll take you back?"

"You might. If you want to keep this little tidbit of news from getting out."

Clearly he didn't know everything. She'd have to tread carefully.

"Why should I care if it gets out?"

"I can see there's a problem with my plan. I thought perhaps you'd want to keep the news from the father. I had no idea I'd find the actual father in your bed."

Sam finally spoke. "Don't talk about me like I'm not here, asshole." He stood. "I'll make you a deal, Kyle. You're obviously good at finding information. Find out where my child is, and I won't smash your face into this wall."

Sydney froze. *Oh God.*

"Should be easy enough," Rod said. "I'll get right to it. I do value my face, after all. But not until Sydney agrees to reinstate our engagement."

Sydney looked pleadingly at Sam.

"What?" His eyes flashed anger. Rage. "I don't give a fuck what you do. You gave away my child."

Nausea crept into her throat. How could this be happening? "You just said you love me."

He sniffed. "I'll get over it." He put on his shirt and boots and grabbed his hat.

He went to the desk and scribbled something on a piece of hotel stationery. He handed it to Rod. "Here's my name and number. Find my kid. If I don't hear from you within twenty-four hours, I swear to God I'll hunt you down and kick your ass into next year."

He put his hat on and left.

"What will it take for you not to find the kid?" she asked Rod.

"Since I have no desire to have that Neanderthal pummel me, I don't see why I shouldn't acquiesce to his request. What do you care? Don't you want to know where your son is?"

What could she say to that? "It's not that I don't want to know. I just can't dredge up that part of my life. It's too painful."

"What will you do for me? Marry me?"

God no, she couldn't. She loved Sam. *Damn it, I love Sam so much.*

"I'm sorry. I can't marry you, Rod. For the life of me, I don't know why you want me."

"This is a blemish, that's no lie. I don't relish having bastard half siblings of my own flesh and blood running around."

"See? Good. You don't want to marry me."

"So there's no reason not to honor the man's request, is there? He has a right to know where his child is."

Sydney clenched her fists, her heart pounding. "Damn you! Why do you want to do this? Why are you trying to hurt me?"

Rod smiled sardonically. "Because I can."

She pushed him out the door and slammed it. He was pure evil. How had she gotten involved with the likes of him?

Money.

It all came down to money.

The purse she won today would help. They weren't destitute after all, but the small Buchanan ranch needed help. Right now they were being forced to sell off their livestock, and a ranch couldn't exist without its stock.

Her big brother, Blake, had abandoned them long ago, but she would not. Her parents deserved better. Duke deserved better.

Duke.

Such an angel.

She walked to the bathroom and took off the robe. She needed a shower.

* * * *

Goddamn her to hell!

Sam drove back to the rodeo at top speed.

Once there, he walked through the crowds, looking for Sydney's parents. He'd find out once and for all what the hell was going on.

Maybe they didn't even know she'd had a child.

Well, too bad. Today they'd find out. If they had any information about his kid, they were damn well going to give it to him.

God, where were they? The damn place was so fucking crowded.

"Hey, Sam!"

Crap. Dusty. He loved his baby sister, but he did not have the time right now.

"What is it, Dust?"

"Did you have a chance to talk to Sydney?"

What was that about? "I don't have any desire to talk to her."

"Listen, she told me all about her engagement. She's not in love with that guy, and she was going to break up with him anyway. Did you know they never even had sex?"

"I don't care right now. I'm sorry, Dust, but I'm busy."

"You don't care? You don't seem like you don't care whenever you're with her. The chemistry between you two is palpable."

He looked above Dusty's red-gold head, scanning for the Buchanans. "The chemistry between us, if it's even there, is not any of your business. Right now I have to find some answers."

"Answers about what?"

He turned and faced his sister. What the hell? She'd find out anyway. "About my child, Dusty. Sydney had my child five years ago and gave it up for adoption."

Dusty's eyes widened. "What?"

"It's true. I just found out."

"You mean Seanie has a cousin? Who's almost his exact age?"

"Yes, Sis, that's exactly what it means. Where's that genius IQ of yours today? This isn't rocket science."

"I need to sit down." Dusty visibly trembled.

He took his sister's arm and found a bench with one empty spot. "Stay here," he said. "I'm sorry. I didn't mean to upset you. But right now I need to find Sydney's parents."

"Give me a minute," Dusty said. "I know where they are. I saw them a while ago. They're in the stands."

"Where?"

"To the north."

"Thanks, Sis. I'll go find them."

"I want to go with you."

"I need to do this alone. I'll tell you what I find out."

His heart beat like a drum against his sternum. A child. He had a child.

A son.

A little boy.

What might he look like?

A mini Sam? A mini Sydney? A combination?

He made his way to the north stands and scanned the crowd. *Damnit, where are they?*

And then he spied them, Roy and Carrie, with little Duke sitting between them. He sprinted up the stairs, nearly knocking over a hot dog vendor.

"I need to talk to you two," he said.

"Goodness," Carrie said. "Oh, yes, you're Dusty's brother."

"Yes. Sam O'Donovan. I want some answers."

"Answers about what?" Roy said.

"About my son. Where the hell is my son?"

Carrie's pretty face, so like Sydney's, whitened. "Roy—"

"I'll take care of this, Carrie." He turned to Sam. "Come with me, and we'll talk."

"No," Carrie said, "I'm coming with you."

"You stay here."

"No, damnit. I'm coming with you." She stood up and lifted her son into her arms. "Let's get the hell out of here."

Finding a quiet place to talk was nearly impossible, but they found a spot where the noise wasn't so loud. Carrie sat down on a bench with Duke, and Roy took Sam around a corner and lowered his voice.

"Now, young man, what's this about?"

"Your future son-in-law, Rod Kyle, came by with some news today. It seems Sydney had a baby five years ago."

He didn't seem surprised. Clearly he already knew.

"Yes. And?"

"I happen to be the child's father."

Roy's eyebrows shot up. "Are you sure? She never told us who it was."

"Why wouldn't she tell you?"

"She probably didn't want us to go hunting you down."

Sam forced his teeth to unclench. "I wish she would have. I want my child."

"He's been adopted into a loving home."

"How do you know?"

"It was an open adoption."

"Then you know who has him. Tell me."

He shook his head. "I can't."

"Why not?" He grabbed the collar of Roy's shirt. "Damnit. I have a right to know where my child is!"

Roy stared into Sam's eyes. "I'm sorry, son. I can't give you any information."

"Why not?"

"Because he's with parents who love him very much. If you do anything to challenge that relationship, the only person harmed will be your son. The parents will suffer, but the child will be the ultimate loser."

"Damnit!" Sam punched the wall. His fist went through the drywall. His knuckles bled, yet he felt no pain.

No pain at all.

Only anger.

At Sydney.

At Roy.

At Carrie.

He walked away from Roy and turned the corner. Sydney's mother sat with Duke. He was a beautiful child. He had Sydney's eyes.

And sandy brown hair.

Oh my God. Was it possible?

He left Roy standing and stalked toward the woman and child. He eyed Duke up and down. Could it be?

When he noticed the little boy's hands, his heart nearly leaped out of his chest.

They were tiny replicas of his own.

Chapter Eight

Carrie shielded the child against her chest. "Back away," she warned.

Sam steeled himself. He had to think of Duke.

Roy strode forward. "Sam, what are you doing?"

"You were right in the first place," he ground out, trying his damndest to stay calm, to not alarm the child. *His* child. "We need to speak alone."

"Take Duke back to the hotel, Carrie," Roy said calmly.

"But the car... How will you—"

"I'll find a ride. Just go. Now."

Carrie stood and ushered Duke away.

Roy sank down on the bench that they had vacated. "Do you really want to turn his life upside down?"

Sam grabbed Roy by the collar again, bringing him to his feet and slamming his back into the wall. "You have turned *my* life upside down, goddamnit."

"I am sorry." Roy's dark eyes misted. "Let go of me, please."

"Why should I?"

"Because I didn't know he was yours. Sydney never told us."

She didn't? Sam let go and pushed Roy back down on the bench. "Now start talking. You owe me that much."

"She was young, only nineteen. She was a champion racer. She couldn't keep a child."

"So what? Maybe I could have."

"She never told us who you were. I think because she knew we'd try to contact you. Carrie and I always felt the father had a right to know."

"Why wouldn't she tell you?"

"I don't know. That's something you'll have to ask her."

"I'm never speaking to her again. So you'll have to tell me."

Roy shook his head. "I told you. I don't know."

"How did you end up with him?"

"Sydney was too young to take care of a child. But she didn't want to give him up. Carrie and I were becoming empty nesters. Blake had left while Sydney was pregnant, and Syd was nineteen and ready to fly on her own. We were still young enough to be good parents. It made sense."

"Well, it doesn't make sense to me."

"We love him as our own. He's our child, and our biological grandchild. He's had a good life. He's happy."

"What makes you think he wouldn't have been happy with me?" Sam's voice cracked.

"Maybe he would have. I don't know. But did you want to raise a child alone? Your son has a mother and father who adore him and a big sister who couldn't love him more."

"And when were you planning to tell him that his big sister is actually his mother?"

"I don't know." Roy sighed. "Eventually we did plan to tell him."

"I want to spend some time with him."

"That's not possible."

"I'll drag your asses to court, then. The kid is my flesh and blood."

"Are you absolutely sure he's yours?"

"Are you kidding? Take a good look at me."

Roy perused him and nodded soberly.

"And even if we looked nothing alike, I have further proof. Sydney has admitted to me that she hasn't been with anyone since we were together five years ago. He has to be mine."

"Thank God."

"Thank God? Are you kidding?"

"You don't understand. I mean thank God she didn't sleep with that slime Rodney Kyle."

"She broke up with him today."

"Thank God again. She was only with him for his money."

"She needs money?"

"Our ranch isn't doing very well. It's the economy and all."

Sam understood. God knew he'd been there. He'd only gotten the Double D out of trouble in the last couple years. But damnit, he didn't want to feel sorry for these people.

They'd stolen his child, for God's sake.

"I'm sorry," he said, despite his anger.

"Sydney didn't want the ranch to go under," Roy continued. "She wanted it for Duke. The ranch has been In the Buchanan family for three generations."

"I want a DNA test, pronto."

"I won't put him through that."

"Fine." Sam stopped himself from putting his fist through the wall again. Wasn't easy. "I'll get a court order. Then you won't have a choice."

"Do you really want to do this to the child?"

"What about me? Don't I have rights?"

Roy nodded. "Of course you do. But he's five years old. He's secure in his life, his family."

"Why didn't anyone try to find me?"

"I told you. Sydney never told us who the father was."

"Why the hell not?"

"You'll have to ask her that."

"I plan to ask her plenty. So much for never speaking to her again." He took off his hat and raked his fingers through his hair—hair just like Duke's. His son. "Where the hell is she?"

"I don't know."

He'd left her at the hotel. He didn't want to see her, but she was the only one who could answer these questions.

She was the last person he wanted to see.

And the first person he wanted to see.

Goddamnit.

He loved her.

How had it come to this?

Yes, his life had gotten stale. He'd wanted to shake things up. But not like this.

He left Roy and walked out of the arena toward the parking area.

And who should be walking toward him, but sharply dressed businessman Rod Kyle.

"Ah, Mr. O'Donovan, just the man I was looking for. I've found your answer for you, and even *you* won't believe where your son is."

"He's here in town." Sam gritted his teeth. "He's Sydney's little brother." Then he hit Rod square in the jaw. Felt damn good, even with bleeding knuckles.

Rod fell backward, rubbing his face. "Hey, we had a deal."

"The deal was you find out where my son is."

"I did."

"Not quick enough. I figured it out without you. Now get the hell out of my sight before I do some real damage."

Sam found his rental car and drove away. The rodeo was still going on, but Zach's brother Dallas would be home. Dallas didn't compete like his two younger brothers. He was a shooter at heart. He'd be at the ranch. It was near suppertime.

Dallas was one of the only two attorneys in Bakersville. The other was Chad's brother-in-law, Harper Bay, but he was busy planning a wedding in less than a week. Dallas was Sam's best bet.

He drove to Dallas and Annie's ranch house on the McCray property, walked up, and knocked.

"Hello there, Sam," Annie McCray said in her biting Jersey accent. "Nice to see you."

"Is Dallas at home?"

"Yeah, he sure is. Come on in. We're just finishing our dinner."

"I'm sorry to intrude. I have a legal problem."

"No intrusion. Let me get the kids out of your way, and you and he can talk. Come on in to the kitchen."

After they said hi to their Uncle Sammy, Annie took Sylvie and Laurie by the hands and escorted them into the family room where the babies were sleeping in their bassinets. "Sam's here to see you, hon. Legal talk."

"What can I do you for, Sam?" Dallas asked, standing. "You want to sit down?"

"Do I ever." Sam plunked his ass in a chair.

"Coffee?"

"Got anything stronger?"

Dallas smiled. "That bad, huh? How about a Macallan, neat?"

"Sounds like nectar of the gods."

Dallas poured two drinks and sat back down at the table. "So what's going on?"

"I need to get a court order for a DNA test."

"What for?"

"You know the Buchanans, right?"

"Blake and Sydney, yeah. And their parents are here for the rodeo too."

"Along with their little boy. He's about Sean's age."

"Duke, yeah. I've seen him."

"Well, here's the thing." He cleared his throat. "Little Duke Buchanan is my son."

* * * *

"Well, Sydney," Roy Buchanan said when Sydney opened the door to her hotel room. "You've got yourself in quite a mess now."

"I know, Daddy." She sniffed.

"You've been crying."

"Of course I have."

"Tell me what's going on."

"It's that jerk, Rod. He found Duke's birth certificate. He brought it over here and confronted me while Sam was here. Sam put two and two together and figured out he was the father."

"Sam O'Donovan. A good man from a good family. Why didn't you tell us who the father was?"

"I had my reasons. Don't worry, Daddy, he doesn't know where the child is. But I'm afraid he will soon. He asked Rod to find out for him."

"Rod's quick, then. Or Sam figured it out on his own. He confronted your mother and me this afternoon at the rodeo."

Sydney cringed, resisting the urge to swat away the invisible insects crawling on her skin. "Oh, Daddy. What are we going to do?"

Roy sat down and cupped his head in his hands. "I don't know, Sydney. I just don't know."

"I can't let anything happen to Duke."

"Good, I'm glad to hear you say that. Duke is the most important thing here. We must consider what's best for him first and foremost."

"Of course." Sydney's blood turned to ice. "That's what I've always done."

"Not always, Sydney."

"What do you mean?"

"Why didn't you tell us back then who the father was? Then maybe all this turmoil could have been avoided. Sam would have known. He would have had a choice to be in Duke's life."

"I didn't want him in Duke's life."

"Why, Sydney? Why didn't you want the father to know about his child?"

* * * *

"I see," Dallas said after Sam had explained the situation. "All this time you never knew he existed."

"Not at all."

"And had you known at the time, would you have wanted the child?"

Sam rose, shoved his hands in his pockets. "How the hell should I know? That was over five years ago. I know I want him now."

"Why do you want him now?"

"I've always wanted kids. Just never found the right woman."

"And is Sydney Buchanan the right woman?"

He sat back down with a plunk. "I don't know. Shit, a mere five hours ago I was sure she was."

"Are you in love with her?"

"I was five hours ago, before all this shit hit the fan."

"You have a child with the woman you love." Dallas smiled. "That's a beautiful thing. The rest can be worked out."

"Dallas, my child is five years old! I've missed a half decade of his life. I didn't hear his first word. I didn't see his first smile, his first step."

"I understand." Dallas looked toward the family room where the girls were playing. "Believe me, I understand."

"I have rights, damnit. I want to know my son."

"The child legally belongs to the Buchanans. They adopted him. I'm assuming they went through all the legal channels."

"What if they didn't?"

"I suppose it's possible that Sydney just let her parents raise him."

"She said she was only nineteen when she had him. I can't believe she was that young when we met. She seemed so much older. She was a champion barrel racer. Dusty was twenty-three at that time."

"And you were?"

"Twenty-seven. I feel like I robbed the cradle."

"She was legal, Sam. You didn't do anything wrong."

"I know that." He shook his head. Emotion coursed through him. "Damnit!"

"First thing is to find out if the Buchanans *are* Duke's legal parents. If they are, this is going to be more difficult. I won't lie to you. If they're not, and Sydney is the legal parent, it will be easier for you to get paternal rights."

"Can you find that out?"

"Where was the child born?"

"Hell if I know. Nevada, probably." Sam took a drink of Scotch. "That's where they live now."

"That's a start. We can search the records."

"How long will that take?" Sam asked.

"I don't have an office. I'm not a practicing lawyer. I'll have to call someone in Denver. But there's an easier way to get this information."

"And what might that be?"

Dallas cleared his throat. "Ask Sydney."

"Are you kidding? She's hardly proved herself trustworthy. First, she neglected to tell me she was engaged to some effeminate businessman, and now this? I'm not taking her word for anything."

"All right. Fair enough. Her parents, then."

"I doubt they'll cooperate. I was pretty hard on Roy at the rodeo."

"I'm sure he understands. This is a lot for you to deal with."

Sam nodded. Finally, someone who understood, or at least tried to. "They see me as a threat. They're probably afraid I'm going to take Duke."

"Are you?"

"I just might. He is mine, after all. I was never given a choice in the matter."

"How do you think that would affect them?"

Sam clenched both his fists in his unruly hair. "It'll hurt. I know that. This isn't their fault. According to Roy, Sydney never told them who the father was."

"Hmm. Why didn't she?"

"Do you honestly think I have a clue? I don't know anything about that woman."

"Only that you love her."

"Love her?" He unclenched his hair. "She's a completely different woman than the one I thought I loved earlier today."

"I see."

"So what are my chances? What do I need to do?"

"We can get a court order for a DNA test, but that's not your main problem."

"The DNA will show he's mine. Sydney admitted to me that she hadn't been with anyone since she was with me over five years ago, and the child was born after that. Plus, have you seen him? He's definitely my son."

"Have you told Dusty?"

"No. I haven't told anyone. Just you."

Dallas sighed. "I feel for you, I really do. But like I said, there's a bigger problem than proving that he's yours."

"What's that?" Sam asked.

"Whenever a child is involved, the courts focus on one thing and one thing only—the best interests of the child in question."

"How can I not be in his best interest? I'm his father."

"He's a child of five. The only parents he's ever known are the Buchanans. To take him from them would scar him. He's just a little boy, Sam."

"Damnit." He pounded his fist on the table. "This isn't fair."

Dallas nodded. "I agree with you. It's not fair. It's not fair to you, and it's ultimately not fair to Duke. He should be able to know his biological father if that father wants to be known. But right now he's a little boy, and if you take his mommy and daddy away from him, he'll be devastated."

Sam sighed heavily. Dallas was right. "What then? What are my options?"

"Your best option right now is to talk to Sydney. If she won't talk to you, talk to her parents. Most likely they're the legal parents and will make the decisions. Tell them you want to know the child, be a part of his life."

"They'll tell me to fuck off."

"What makes you say that?"

"They damn near already did."

"They were reacting, just as you were. They were scared you were going to take away the child they love."

"But—"

Dallas stopped him. "Trust me. If I felt there was the tiniest chance someone might take away one of my children, I'd react with all the anger in me to make sure it did not happen. That's how much a parent loves a child."

"I love him."

"You may. I don't know. But Sam, you didn't even know he existed yesterday. These two have raised him since he was an infant. They've fed him, housed him, clothed him, watched him grow. You represent a huge threat."

"I just want my son."

"You need to take yourself out of the equation right now. Yes, you were wronged. What Sydney did to you was wrong. But right now you have to think about the boy."

"Yes, I know." He pounded the table again. "Damnit."

Annie entered the kitchen. "Everything all right in here?"

"Yeah, Dr. Annie. I was just leaving." Sam stood.

"You don't have to go," Dallas said. "You want another drink?"

Sam looked down. He'd hardly touched his Scotch. He downed it and let the peaty alcohol burn his throat. Good stuff.

He thanked Dallas and Annie, told them he'd be touch, and drove back to his house near Zach and Dusty's.

Why hadn't Sydney told her parents he was the father?

He didn't know, but he was damn well going to find out.

Chapter Nine

Two days later, Sam still hadn't contacted Sydney or his son. He wasn't sure what the right course of action was. All he knew was that his heart had been broken, and he'd never let another woman in again.

What he would give to have his stale life back...

Why had he decided he needed to shake things up? Life in Montana was good. He was alone, but he wasn't lonely. He had his housekeeper and his hands, his dogs, cats, and livestock.

He'd missed his first bronc busting competition. His heart just wasn't in it. He no longer needed the cash. He was only doing it for fun.

Right now, Sam didn't really feel like having fun. He'd been doing ranch work for Zach, helping out where needed. Might as well get used to the place. He'd taken his meals alone in his little guest house, but he knew Dusty wouldn't put up with that much longer. If it weren't for the rodeo keeping her busy, she'd have rooted him out before now.

Speak of the devil. Dusty peeked through the window and a knock sounded on the door.

"Hey, stranger. Where've you been the last few days?"

"Just hangin' out."

"Why didn't you compete?"

"Didn't much feel like it."

"Oh." She didn't press it. *Thank God.* Then, "What's going on, Sam?"

He sighed. "I can't hide anything from you, can I?"

"Nope."

"Sit on down," he said. "It's a long story."

They sat together at the small table in the kitchen while Sam poured out the saga. After Dusty got over the shock, she gave him a hug.

"So Duke is Seanie's cousin."

"Pretty much."

"Why didn't Sydney tell you?"

"I have no clue. She didn't even tell her parents who the father was."

"Have you talked to them?"

"No. Not in a few days. I got some legal advice from Dallas, but I just haven't had the stamina to deal with it. It's going to be confrontational and ugly. It's not fair. I just want to see my son. To know him."

"I want you to come to dinner tonight."

"Why?"

"We're having a guest you need to talk to."

"Trust me, unless it's little Duke Buchanan, I'm not interested."

"Oh, I think you'll be interested in this person."

He sighed. "Who is it?"

"Thunder Morgan."

Ha. Any other time he'd jump at that chance, but not right now. "I'm not in the mood to discuss bronc busting, even with one of the greats."

"That's not why you need to talk to him."

"What the heck are you talking about, Dust?"

She winked. "Come to dinner and find out."

* * * *

Sam had missed his first bronc busting event, and Sydney was worried.

How she missed him! Rod had been by twice, flashing more papers in her face about Duke and his birth and adoption. So now everyone knew. So what? It didn't matter. She'd already lost Sam. Her priority now was Duke. She had to protect him. He was a happy little boy, and she intended to make sure he stayed that way.

They'd spent a morning at the rodeo, eaten there, and Duke was exhausted and cranky. Carrie thought his forehead was slightly warm, so he was in his room with his mother now, napping. Roy sat across from Sydney at the table in her hotel room.

"Time to start talking, baby girl," Roy said. "I need to know why you wouldn't tell us who the father was. Sam O'Donovan is a good man from a good family. He would not have done wrong by you or Duke."

"It wasn't easy telling you the baby was a result of a one-night stand. No girl wants to tell her daddy that."

"No daddy wants to hear it, trust me. But at least now I know he was a good man. An upstanding man. Not some fly-by-night loser."

"You thought that?"

"Sydney, we didn't know what to think."

She sighed. "Yeah, I guess I can understand that."

"So start talking now, baby girl."

"Oh, Daddy." She took a drink of the iced tea in front of her. "It's not a long story or a particularly interesting one. It's actually really sad."

"I'm listening."

"How much do you know about the O'Donovans?"

"The girl married the middle McCray boy. They have a son. That's about it. We haven't been back here in a while. We certainly weren't welcome to visit Blake while he lived here."

"Yeah, I know."

"So what's the story?"

"I didn't know this at the time, of course. Sam and I did talk that first night, but not about anything really personal. Mostly about the rodeo and stuff. We seemed to have a lot in common, and I liked him a lot."

"So?"

"When I found out I was pregnant, I did some research on the O'Donovans."

"Yes?"

"I found out they had a sad history. Their daddy was a ranch hand for Jason McCray when they were little. Their mama died of leukemia when Sam was only ten. They moved to Montana to their grandparents' ranch so she could die there."

Roy nodded. "That *is* sad."

"It gets worse. When Dusty was eighteen, she got the same kind of leukemia. Her dad mortgaged the place to the hilt to pay for her treatment. Luckily she survived, and obviously she's fine now. But their dad committed suicide after nearly bankrupting their ranch. I didn't know till later that Dusty had married Zach McCray and she was fine. At the time, I thought Sam had to take care of her and the ranch. I just couldn't saddle him with another responsibility."

"But baby, that was not your choice to make."

"I knew enough about Sam to know he'd sacrifice everything to do the right thing, even if he didn't love me and didn't want a child. I thought I could spare him that. And I knew you and Mama had tried to have another child a few years before without any luck."

"How did you know that?"

"Mama told me."

"Yes, we did want another baby. Since we married so young, we were still young enough. But it didn't happen."

"I could make that happen for you. You've been great parents to Duke."

"He's a blessing, that's for sure. We won't give him up without a fight."

"I know that." She fiddled with strands of her hair. "I never thought I'd see Sam again. And I certainly never thought he'd find out about Duke."

"Sydney, you had to consider the possibility."

"He says he tried to look me up after that first night."

"It's not surprising that he didn't find you, especially if he didn't look too hard. You were on bed rest for a lot of the pregnancy and you got off the rodeo circuit for over a year after that."

"I know." She shook her head. "I had no idea he'd want to see me again. I mean, I figured it was just a one night thing for him."

"Was it that for you?"

She shook her head again. "No. Please believe me, Daddy, it was my first and last one-night stand."

"So you thought he was special, then?"

"Yes, I did, and I was right. He *is* special. And I've blown it for eternity."

"I won't sugar coat it, baby girl. You have made a mess of things. Not only for yourself and your mama and me, but mostly importantly for your innocent baby brother."

"I know. And I know we can't tell him what's going on. He won't understand."

"No, he won't."

"Oh, Daddy, what am I going to do?"

"I think you need to talk to Sam. Tell him the truth, exactly what you just told me."

"Will you come with me?"

Roy shook his head. "You're a grown-up, Sydney. You need to do this yourself. Clean up your own mess. Once we see how he reacts, I will certainly get involved, but for now, he deserves to hear the truth from you."

Sydney nodded. Her father was right, of course. "I will call him."

"No."

"No?"

"You will drive over to the McCray ranch and see him face-to-face, Sydney. That's the only way. He deserves that much."

"Okay."

There was only one problem.

Sam would not want to see her, let alone listen to her. But she'd cross that bridge when she got there. She looked around for her purse as her father opened the door to leave.

Standing in the doorway was Carrie, holding a listless Duke.

"Roy, there's something very wrong." Tears welled in her eyes. "He's burning up, and look at him! He's hardly moving."

"Now, Carrie, don't fret. He's probably just tired."

"Feel his forehead, damnit."

Sydney ran toward them while her father kissed the little boy's forehead.

"Hmm, he is pretty hot," Roy said. "Did you bring a thermometer with you?"

"No, I didn't. I don't usually travel with one. My God, what kind of mother am I?"

"You're a great mother, Mama," Sydney said. "We'll just go on down to the pharmacy and get a thermometer and some children's ibuprofen, okay? He'll be fine."

"You two don't understand. This isn't a normal fever. He's had fevers before. A mother knows her child."

Sydney's heart jumped. *She* should be the one knowing when Duke was sick. She was his mother.

No. She was his sister. The woman holding him, crying over him, was his mother.

What was she going to do? If her parents lost Duke to Sam, they'd be devastated. It would be all her fault. Either her parents would hate her or Sam would.

No matter. Duke was the important thing right now.

"Okay, Mama. There's a doctor's office on Main Street. Let's just go on over there and see if he can take a look."

Carrie nodded. "I'd feel much better if we could have a doc look at him, Roy."

"All righty then, let's do it. Here, give him to me." Roy took the floppy little boy and the three of them drove the five blocks to Main Street.

They went in. "It's nearly six o'clock," the nurse said. "We're closing soon."

"Please," Carrie begged, "could he look at my son? He's burning up, and he's not acting right."

The nurse smiled. "Of course. Doc Larson never turns away a child in need. Wait here and I'll let him know you're here."

In a few moments, a bespectacled gray-haired man appeared. "Hello there. Bring the tyke on back and let's have a look."

"You stay here, Syd," Roy said.

"Please, let me," she begged. "He's—"

"All right. I understand." The three of them accompanied the doctor to an examining room.

"Hello, little fella," Doc said. "What's your name?"

"He's not very responsive," Carrie said.

"Can you tell the doc your name, son?" Roy asked.

"Duke," he said softly, his little boy treble stabbing Sydney's heart. How had she given up her baby?

"Duke, I'm going to have your daddy put you on the table here, okay?"

"'Kay."

Roy laid the little boy on the examining table, and Doc Larson inserted a thermometer in his ear. When it dinged, he looked at it and frowned.

"What?" Carrie asked frantically.

"Nearly 105. Is he prone to high fevers?"

"Not usually." Carrie's voice shook. "He usually never goes above 103, and that's only when he's really sick.

"Well, that alone isn't a huge worry," Doc said. "It's probably just a virus. I've seen some nasty ones going around. Let's get his shirt off and take a look and a listen."

Carrie pulled Duke's T-shirt over his head.

Doc put his stethoscope in his ears and placed the bell on Duke's chest. Then he turned. "How did he get this bruise?"

"What bruise?" Carrie asked.

"This one." Doc indicated a quarter-size bruise on Duke's side.

"I'm not sure. We were at the rodeo all morning, till about two."

"How was he at the rodeo?"

"A little cranky. And he didn't seem to sleep well last night. Tossed and turned a lot."

"Can we get the rest of his clothes off? I want to take a look."

"Of course."

Duke whimpered as Carrie undressed him. Doc Larson took a look.

"Here's another bruise on his thigh, but I don't see any more. Has he fallen in the last day or so?"

"Not that I recall," Carrie said.

"Is he an unusually rowdy and rambunctious little boy?"

Roy wiped his forehead with a bandana. "He's a little boy, Doc. Of course he's rowdy and rambunctious. But he's been a little under the weather the past few days. We thought he was just catching a cold, but this fever's got us worried."

"Duke," Doc said, "see this bruise on your leg here?"

"Yeah."

"Can you remember how you got it? Did you fall down? Did something hit you in the leg?"

"I don't know."

"You can't remember anything that would have made you get a bruise?"

"No."

"It's okay, precious," Carrie said, rubbing his back. "So what do you think, Doc?"

Doc Larson's face was stern. "Honestly, it's probably nothing. As I said, there's some nasty crud going around right now. Viruses that cause fever and aches. I've seen a lot of kids with it. But Duke's fever is darned high."

"So what do we need to do?"

"I'm going to give him a little something to get the fever down, that's for sure, but I gotta say, I don't like those bruises."

"Little boys get bruises."

"You're traveling, though, and he's been in your sight at all times since you've been here, right?"

"Yes."

"Then you or he should know how he got those bruises."

"It's only two bruises," Carrie said, her voice still shaking.

Sydney's heart dropped to her belly.

Fever. Bruising.

Leukemia.

"I think we can let it go for twenty-four hours," Doc said. "I want to see him again tomorrow. The ibuprofen should get the fever down. Repeat the dosage every six hours. Keep liquids in him and make sure he gets lots of rest."

"Doc?" Sydney stepped forward.

"Yes, young lady?"

"I think you should know something."

"Of course. What is it?"

"Both his paternal grandmother and aunt had—oh God—leukemia."

Carrie's hands whipped to her mouth. "Sydney, what are you talking about?"

Doc Larson's expression went grave.

"Carrie, take Duke out of here," Roy said.

"Roy—"

"Just do it, please. I'll explain everything as soon as I can."

Carrie dressed Duke quickly and left the room.

"Doc, Duke is not my wife's and my biological child. He's our grandchild. May I speak confidentially?"

"Absolutely," Doc said.

"Sydney is his mother, and the father is a man named Sam O'Donovan."

"Sam? I know his sister, Dusty, well." Doc's face went white. "Dear Lord."

"That's why I told you," Sydney said. "I'm so afraid."

Doc scribbled some notes on a pad and handed it to Roy. "Take the boy to Denver. He needs some blood work pronto."

"Okay, Doc. We'll take him first thing in the morning."

Doc's eyes softened as he touched Roy's arm. "Take him now."

Chapter Ten

The dinner at Dusty's with Thunder Morgan had been pleasant. He regaled them with tales of his bronc busting days, and Sam smiled and laughed, almost forgetting about Sydney and Duke.

But not quite.

Now they sat in the family room, having an after dinner drink.

"Thunder," Dusty said, "would you mind telling Sam a little about you and Amber?"

Sam jerked his head. Amber was Thunder's daughter, right? Why would Dusty think he needed to know anything about that?

"Not at all," the man said. "What would you like to know?"

The woman was about to be married to Harper Bay. Surely Thunder couldn't think Sam was interested in her. What the hell was Dusty doing?

"I'm not sure what I want to know myself," Sam said. "What are you getting at, Dust?"

"It's common news around here, and neither Thunder nor Amber mind talking about it. I thought their circumstances might interest you."

"Uh, well—" Sam didn't want to be rude, but he couldn't imagine why he'd be interested in their "circumstances."

"Sam has had an issue come up in his life, and I think he'd benefit by hearing about you and Amber."

"All right." Thunder cleared his throat. "I only met my beautiful daughter a little over two months ago."

Sam jerked forward. "What?"

"Yup, it's the truth. I had one night with her mother twenty-some years ago. I never even knew Amber existed till I met her."

"And you're sure she's yours?"

"Absolutely." He nodded. "I recalled her mother. And Amber, though she looks an awful lot like Karen, definitely has my eyes. That was all the proof I needed."

"Really?"

"Yes. But Amber wanted to be sure. She didn't want to force herself on me. Heck, she wasn't forcin' herself. I was glad to have her. Never did have a family of my own. But it was important to her, so we had a DNA test."

"And she's definitely yours?"

"Yep. Definitely. I couldn't be happier or more proud to have her in my life."

"Wow." Not only was Thunder Morgan his all-time idol, but they had more than bronc busting in common.

"Dusty," Zach interjected, "maybe we should let these two talk."

"Oh, it's okay," Sam said. "I don't mind if you're here. I assume Dusty told you everything anyway, right?"

"Yes," Zach said, "and I know you don't have any secrets from your sister, but let's give them a little privacy, okay, Dusty?"

She nodded. "We can go read Seanie a story."

They left the spacious family room, leaving Sam alone with Thunder Morgan.

"So," Thunder said, "I take it there's a reason why your baby sis wanted you to know about Amber and me."

"Yeah, there is." Sam cleared his throat. "I'm kind of in a similar situation right now."

"Well, son, don't just sit there stuttering. Tell me what's going on."

He poured out the story of Sydney and Duke.

"In a way, you're luckier than I was," Thunder said. "You know about your boy now. I missed twenty-two years of my baby girl's life, a life I could have helped make a lot better. She had some rough times."

"What's your relationship with Amber's mother?"

"Well, that's kind of a sad thing. Karen—that's her name—isn't well. She's in rehab for alcoholism right now, and she's also gettin' psychotherapy and medication. She's been diagnosed with bipolar disorder and borderline personality disorder.

"Oh, wow. I'm sorry to hear that."

"Amber didn't have it easy, growin' up with Karen. I feel a lot of guilt about not being there for her. Or for Karen, for that matter."

"But did you even know you had a daughter?"

He shook his head. "No, I didn't. Evidently Karen tried to contact me after Amber was born, but I never got the message. I was livin' with a woman at the time who told Karen never to call me again. The woman was obsessed with me. I later got a restraining order against her."

"Wow." Sam shook his head. "But you shouldn't feel guilty. You didn't even know she existed."

"Doesn't matter. She's mine. I could have made her life easier."

"Does she blame you?"

"No, absolutely not. She understands. She's a wonderful young woman."

"Then you shouldn't blame yourself."

Thunder nodded. "Objectively I know that. But it's easier said than done."

The ache in Sam's heart eased a little. But only a little. "At least I know my boy has had a good life so far."

"That's something to be said, for sure," Thunder agreed.

"But I can't help but be really angry," Sam said. "I wasn't even given a choice to be a part of his life."

"Nor was I."

"I know, I know. And you missed a lot more than I did. Don't you resent Amber's mother for not telling you?"

"Like I said, she tried to tell me once. The woman scared her enough to never try again. And Karen's illness helped her keep that promise. She was paranoid."

"I'm sorry you missed so much."

"So am I. I feel a lot of guilt over Amber's tough life. But she sets me straight. She's so loving and giving. I wish I had been there for her when she needed me, but I'm here now, and right now, the best thing I can do for Amber is see that her mother gets the help she needs."

"You're a very forgiving man."

"Nah, there's nothin' special about me. But when you get to a certain age, you realize that resentment only breeds more resentment. So I've chosen to focus on now. Amber still needs a father—maybe not the same way she did when she was a little girl, but she needs me. And I sure as heck need her."

"What should I do? My son is only five. If I uproot him, he will suffer."

"That's a tough one, for sure," Thunder said. "I wish I had an answer for you."

Sam stood and paced in a circle. "I'm so angry."

"I can't tell you what to do about your son. My situation is totally different. Amber's an adult and can make her own decisions. But I can give you this advice. Let the anger go, Sam. If you truly want a relationship with your boy, the anger will only hold you back."

Sam walked to the bar and refreshed his drink. "You need some more?" He held up the bottle of Scotch.

"Nope, I'm good for now."

"I just wish I knew what to do."

"Do you care for the child's mother?"

Sam took a stiff belt of the Scotch. "I thought I did."

"And now?"

"Now I don't know. Sydney's amazing, but she's lied to me twice now."

"Twice?"

"When I ran into her again at the rodeo a few days ago, we hooked up. After that, I learned she was engaged."

"Oh, Jesus."

"Yeah. He showed up while I was still in her room. She broke up with him and later told me she'd been planning to end it anyway, but still, it was dishonest."

"Yes, it was."

"But that was nothing compared to this. She's kept my son from me for five years."

"She may have had a reason. Have you asked her?"

"She can't possibly have any reason that would make any sense."

"She obviously didn't keep the child. She let her mother and father adopt him."

"Yeah. They legally adopted him. Dallas McCray looked into it. He called this morning with that piece of news. It might have been easier for me if they were just raising him and he was still legally Sydney's child. It'd be easier for me to assert my parental rights in that case."

"But now he has a legal mother and father who love him."

"Yes, and more importantly, who *he* loves. What kind of horrid man would I be to take a baby away from his mom and dad?"

"I wouldn't call you horrid."

"I feel like one big asshole. But I want my child, Thunder." He sat down and cupped his head in his hands. "I just don't know what to do."

"And as for Sydney?"

Sydney. What a mess. "A couple days ago I thought I was in love with her."

"Love? In this short time?"

"Yes, damnit. I know it sounds ridiculous, but I've never dated anyone who makes me feel the way she does. Or did. Or does. Aw hell, I don't know what the fuck I'm saying."

"Son, I'm going to give you some advice, and it's up to you whether you take it."

"All right. I'm listenin'." Why not? He sure as hell didn't know what to do. Maybe Thunder had some answers.

"I gave my life to the rodeo. Hell, I had my one nighters—that's what Amber's mother was. I'm not proud of it, but I was a young cowboy and women liked me. My life was on the road. I traveled all over and won purse after purse. I had a good life, had all I wanted, but it got mighty lonely comin' home every night."

"Are you saying you have regrets?"

"Would I do it differently if I could?" He shook his head. "I don't know. Knowin' what I do now, yes, I think I would. I retired a few years ago, as you know, and I was livin' alone on a ranch on the western slope. Life was good. Peaceful. But I can't tell you what a glow Amber has brought to my life. I'm giving her away at her wedding Saturday, did you know that? I've only been her father for two months and she's lettin' me have that honor."

Sam nodded.

Thunder continued, "People, son. Family. Those are the precious things in life. If you think you love this woman, this woman who gave birth to your child, you owe it to yourself to give it the shot it deserves."

"What if it doesn't work?"

"There are no guarantees in life. You know that better than anyone, being a bronc buster. There's no guarantee you aren't gonna bust a rib or worse when that stud bucks you off."

Sam nodded. The man was right.

"So my advice to you is to go get her."

What about Duke? Sam opened his mouth to say as much, when Dusty came rushing in.

"Sam!"

"What is it?"

"Sydney just called." Her eyes filled with tears. "They've taken Duke to Denver to the hospital." She doubled over, her breath coming in rapid puffs.

"Take it easy, darlin'," Zach said, helping her to the couch.

"What, Dusty? What's wrong with Duke?"

Zach looked up, his eyes sober. "They think he might have leukemia."

Chapter Eleven

Sam drove to Denver at top speed. When he reached the hospital, he parked quickly and ran inside.

Roy was waiting in the emergency room waiting area. "Carrie and Syd are in with him. His fever's come down quite a bit, thank God, and he's much livelier now."

That's a good sign, right?" Sam said.

Roy shook his head. "Hell, I don't know. I wish I knew what was going on. My little boy has a fever and some bruises, and all of a sudden we're talking about the C word? I can't deal with this. Four days ago I didn't know who his biological father was, and now I find out leukemia runs in the family."

"Leukemia isn't usually hereditary," Sam said. "At least that's what they've always told us. It was just bad luck that both Ma and Dusty got the same disease."

"Yes, the doctors here have assured us of the same thing. Still, Doc Larson seemed very adamant that we bring Duke in tonight once he found out about your mother and your sister."

"Doc Larson's a small-town doctor. He's a good man, but he probably isn't up to date on his research. Plus, leukemia is highly curable."

"But your mother..."

"She didn't make it." Sam gulped. "But that was a long time ago. Treatment is better now. And look at Dusty. She's healthy as a horse."

Carrie came out white-faced. "They've drawn all the blood. It's going to take a few hours to get the results. Hello, Sam."

Sam stood. "How is he?"

"He's better." Her face was streaked from tears. "Sydney is sitting with him now."

"May I see him?"

"He doesn't even know you," Carrie said.

"Carrie," Roy said, his voice soft yet stern. "He needs to see the child. Try to understand."

Carrie nodded. "Go on in."

Sam walked into the room and the sound of childish laughter was like a symphonic concerto to his ears. Duke was laughing. Sydney, her face swollen and puffy, her brooding dark eyes sunken, smiled at the little boy. *SpongeBob SquarePants* played on the television.

"Hello," Sam said.

Sydney looked up, startled. "Sam." She wiped her nose. "Hello."

"How's the little fella doing?"

"He's actually doing better. We're just waiting now."

"Your mom told me."

"Who's that, Sassy?" the little boy asked.

"Sweetie, this is a good friend of mine," Sydney said. "His name is Sam."

Sam smiled and walked forward, holding out his hand. To his surprise, the boy took it, shaking like a man.

"I hear you've been a little under the weather," Sam said.

"Yeah. They poked me and took blood out of me."

"Well, that didn't bother a big boy like you, did it?"

"Nah. Mama and Sassy cried, but I didn't."

Sam ruffled Duke's hair—hair so like his own. "So what's on the tube?"

"Duke's favorite," Sydney said. "SpongeBob."

They watched television for a few minutes, saying nothing, until Roy and Carrie came back into the room.

"Sydney," Roy said, "you take a break for a while. Mom and I will stay with Duke."

Sydney nodded and stood up. She glanced at Sam. Was he supposed to go with her?

Fine.

"Good to meet you, Duke," he said. "I'll be back to check on you later, okay?"

"Okay." The boy smiled.

Sam's heart melted. His son was a beautiful child. He had to be okay. He just had to be.

Sam wasn't sure what to say, how to act around Sydney. One look at her and he knew he loved her. Feelings didn't turn on and off like a water faucet. No sirree. And something else was evident as well. This woman loved her son—her brother—however she thought of him.

This was killing her. As much as it was killing him.

"You want some coffee?" he asked.

She nodded. "Sure."

"Go on and sit down in the waiting area. I'll go get it."

Sydney took his arm. "No. I'll come along with you if you don't mind. I just can't sit anymore. I feel like I'm just sitting around waiting for bad news. I hate it."

Sam nodded. His gut clenched and he felt helpless, as he'd felt so many times before in similar situations. He knew how Sydney was feeling. He'd done his share of waiting around with Dusty for results. It was damned hard.

They walked out of the ER and through a walkway that led to the regular hospital. That area was quiet. It was late, and visiting hours were over. Sam scoped out the coffee shop.

"Damn. It's closed."

Sydney let out a huff of air. "Just my luck." She leaned against a wall next to a supply closet. "Sam?"

"What?"

"Would you please hold me?"

He wanted to hold her until the end of time, but what good would it do?

God, I love her. Love her with all my heart. But he could never be with her.

Yet she was still the mother of his child, and she needed comfort.

He took her in his arms and held her body close.

She was tall, nearly six feet, he guessed, and fit perfectly against his own six-feet-three-inch frame. Her ample breasts pressed against his chest. How good it felt to hold the woman he loved.

The woman he loved and could never have.

She let out a sniff. "I'm so scared, Sam."

"I know, sweetheart. I'm scared too."

"How are we supposed to get through this?"

He shook his head. "I don't know. You just do, I guess. I remember waiting around with Dusty for blood tests. Wanting to do something but knowing I couldn't do anything. Wishing it were me instead of her. It's horrible."

"That's just how it is."

"I know, and I'm sorry you have to go through it."

She lifted her head and gazed at him, her dark eyes sunken and sad. "You really do know."

"Yes."

"You poor thing. God, you poor thing!"

"It's okay."

"No, it's not even close to okay. I'm so sorry, Sam. I'm so sorry for everything."

"Don't worry about that now. Let's focus on Duke."

She nodded, and then, out of nowhere, she wrapped her arms around his neck and pulled him into a kiss.

Her lips smashed to his with a force so raw, he wasn't sure he'd experienced anything like it. She trailed her tongue across the seam of his lips, looking for entrance. He granted it, and her mouth had never tasted sweeter. Their tongues met and dueled, tangled together in a kiss of passion, of desire, an expression of life.

Sam backed her up against the wall and pushed into her, his erection straining against his jeans.

She met him eagerly, pushing into his hardness, spreading her legs so that his thigh was between them. She begin to writhe against his jean-clad thigh, rubbing herself.

What a turn-on! But how could he be turned on right now, when so much else demanded his attention?

Yet it made perfect sense. Here they were, loving each other, validating their lives.

He forced his thigh upward and she groaned. He rubbed it against her vulva, matching the thrust of his tongue in her mouth.

He had to have her. Had to have her now. Right here in the hospital hallway. He didn't care who walked by, who might be in the next room.

Room.

The supply closet.

He jiggled the doorknob and it opened.

"In here, baby," he said.

The small room was dark and smelled of pine, but he didn't care, nor did Sydney seem to. He unzipped her jeans and thrust his fingers into her heat.

Soaking wet for him. He thought he might cream for her right there.

"Sam, Sam, I need you," she whimpered into his shoulder.

"It's dark in here, sweetheart. Take off your boots and jeans. I'd do it for you but I can't see."

Fabric rustled. He fumbled with his own belt and jeans and pushed them down to his knees. When she came toward him, he lifted her and placed her on his rigid cock.

"Oh God." She sighed.

"Yeah, baby. God, you have no idea how much I need this."

"I have a pretty good idea," she said.

She clung to him, and he held onto her with his strong arms and moved her up and down upon his hardness.

Her sleek warmth gloved him like no other. If only this could last forever. If only.

He wanted her to come, but he couldn't let go of her to touch her clit. As if reading his mind, she snaked one arm between their bodies and began to stimulate herself.

And he was even more turned on than before.

He lifted her soft body up, to the tip of his cock, and lowered her down to his base.

Sweet sensation.

Sweet fuck.

No.

Sweet love.

This wasn't a fuck. This was making love.

He was making love to his woman in a hospital supply closet, but it didn't matter. It was love, pure and simple, and it was a validation of the life that flowed through their veins.

"Sam, I'm coming. I'm coming!"

Sydney's warmth throbbed against him, and he let himself go.

The convulsions started at the base of his cock and shot through as he shot into her. His veins pulsed, his muscles contracted. His whole body went rigid, relaxed, and went rigid again. When he wasn't sure he could stand any longer, he had to let Sydney go.

"I'm sorry, baby. I have to put you down."

Her legs slid down his thighs. "It's okay. God, it's okay. That was amazing."

"Yes, it was." *God, it was.*

"You are amazing, Sam. It's you. It's not the act. It's you."

He wanted to say the words back to her because he meant them with all his heart. How could he live without her?

Could he forgive her?

What about Duke?

Duke.

His baby son might be very ill right now. How had he gotten so out of control that he was fucking in a closet when his son might be gravely ill?

"Jesus," he said. "What the fuck are we doing?"

His eyes had adjusted to the dark. Sydney was pulling on her boots. "Making love, I think."

"Sydney, our son is in the hospital. We have no right to be acting so foolishly. What were we thinking?"

She sighed. "I was thinking I wanted to be in your arms. Is that so wrong?"

"When our son is lying in a hospital bed and when we have many issues to work out between us—some of which I don't think can ever be worked out—yes, it's wrong. It's selfish and wrong."

"I didn't see you stopping me."

He sighed. She was right, of course. He should have kept his head—the one *above* his shoulders. "Well, I'm stopping you now."

"Now? What good does that do? What's done is done. You got your rocks off just like I did. Admit it, you wanted it as much as I did."

Of course he did. But damned if he'd admit anything to her.

He pulled his pants up and buckled his belt. "We'd better hit the restroom before we go back to the ER. To make sure we look okay."

"I already look like shit. I've been crying and worrying for the last several hours. My parents will understand that."

She was right again. "Fine. Let's just get back there. Now."

They walked back in silence and sat down in the waiting area of the ER.

Within five minutes, Roy came out to find them.

"You two come on back now," he said. "The doc's on his way with the results."

Chapter Twelve

Sydney's heart dropped to her stomach. She gulped. *Please, please let him be okay. I'll do anything. I'll give up anything. Anything as long as he's okay.*

The doctor entered with Duke's chart.

"Mr. and Mrs. Buchanan," he said.

"Please don't beat around the bush," Carrie begged. "What's going on with our little boy?"

Duke had fallen asleep in the bed and appeared comfortable.

"I'm not going to beat around the bush. The news is good. Duke's blood counts came back in the normal range."

Sydney fell into Sam's hard body.

"And that means?" Roy said.

"It means Duke has a virus. He'll be good as new in a few days. Keep him rested and push fluids. Give him ibuprofen for the fever as needed."

"But the bruises," Carrie said.

"He's a little boy. Little boys get bruises. It's not uncommon for a little boy to not know how he got a bruise."

"But Doc Larson—"

"Doc Larson did the right thing by telling you to come here, especially with the medical history. Although as I said before, blood cancers are rarely hereditary. I'd like you to repeat the blood work in a month, just to make sure. I'll write out the instructions for your pediatrician at home."

"Thank you," Carrie breathed. "Thank you so much!"

Sydney burst into tears.

"He's okay, sweetheart," Sam said. "He's okay."

"I know that. It's just… I don't know."

"You're letting down," the doctor said. "Completely understandable and normal. I'm so sorry you had this scare. But Duke is just fine."

"Should we get him home to Nevada right away?" Carrie asked.

"There's no reason why you can't continue your visit," the doctor said. "It's really up to you. He'd be more comfortable at home, of course, but the travel might be difficult for him. If you stay, he'll be on the mend by the time you leave, and the trip will be much more comfortable for him."

"I have another barrel race the day after tomorrow," Sydney said, "but I'd feel better if you and Daddy took Duke home."

"Well, we can't go anywhere tonight," Roy said. "Let's get him back to Bakersville to the hotel and make sure he gets a good night's sleep. We can make that decision in the morning." He held out his hand. "Thank you so much, Doctor."

"You're most welcome." He handed Roy a paper. "Here's the instructions for your pediatrician. You all have a good night."

Carrie picked up a sleeping Duke.

"Just a minute, Doctor," Sam said.

"Yes?"

"I assume you still have Duke's blood sample?"

"Of course. It's in the lab."

"Then I want you draw some of mine. I want a DNA test."

"Excuse me? I'm not sure I understand."

"He's my son. I want proof."

Sydney's stomach tumbled. "Please, Sam, not right now."

"Right now's the perfect time. He's already had his blood drawn so we don't have to poke him again. And he's sleeping. He can't hear us."

"I can't run another test without parental consent." He turned to Roy and Carrie. "Are you okay with this?"

"No," Carrie said. "I am not."

Roy soothed her. "Carrie, it will happen sooner or later. If we do it now it saves Duke an additional pinprick."

"You realize insurance won't cover this," the doctor said.

"I can pay you cash money right now," Sam said. "Or put it on a credit card. I don't give a damn what it costs."

"All right. We're not in the habit of drawing blood for paternity tests in the ER, but since you're here, I can arrange it. You come with me." He nodded to Sam. "I'll send a nurse in with paperwork for you to sign," he said to Roy and Carrie.

Sydney plunked down in a chair, feeling utterly defeated. "I'm sorry," she said to her parents.

"What are we going to do?" Carrie sobbed.

"Look," Roy said, "the most important thing is that Duke is okay. Our little boy does not have leukemia. Grasp that concept, and everything else is nothing."

"Everything else is *not* nothing," Carrie said. "That man wants to take our son."

"Lower your voice." Roy put his fingers against his lips. "Do you want to wake him? Now just settle down. We have to accept that Sam is going to be a part of Duke's life. There's nothing we can do. He's the child's father."

Sydney sat, numb and silent.

A nurse entered. "Here are the papers for you to sign."

Roy scribbled his signature.

"I can't believe you're letting him do this," Carrie said.

"If we don't, he'll just get a court order. Duke's blood has already been drawn."

"There's no need," Sydney said. "Only one man can be the father, and it's Sam. You can trust me on that."

"He needs to know for sure, and I don't blame him."

"But this will only help him," Carrie said. "It will give him the ammunition he needs to take Duke away from us."

"No one is taking Duke away from us. You can count on that," Roy said. "Now simmer down."

Sam returned, a Band-Aid in the crease of his elbow. "I'll get the results in a few days."

"I hope you're happy," Carrie said.

"As a matter of fact, I am," Sam said. "I'm happy that Duke is not seriously ill. I've had enough catastrophic illness affecting people I love to last a lifetime. I really didn't want to go through that again."

Carrie lowered her gaze, and Sydney felt bad for her mother. Sam had shamed her a little.

"Do you mind if I ride back with Sam?" Sydney asked. "We need to talk."

Her father understood. She could tell by the expression on his face. "Yes, that's fine, baby girl."

"Well, I don't know—" Sam began.

"Please, Sam. Just give me the ride to Bakersville. It's only an hour or so."

Sam sighed. "All right. We can stop and grab a bite on the way. Suddenly I'm famished."

Sydney's tummy tightened. She wasn't famished. Not hungry at all. Gratitude filled her for her little boy's health, but still so much remained unresolved.

Maybe the drive home with Sam would resolve some of it.

She hoped, at least.

* * * *

"So you expect me to believe that you didn't tell your parents who the father was because you didn't want to lay a child on me? With all my other problems?"

Sydney gulped. She'd never expected him to question her reasons why. They were the truth, after all. "I was young. Those were my thoughts at the time."

"Unbelievable."

"Plus, you hardly knew me. It was a one-night stand. Did you really want me coming to you with news of a baby?"

"I don't know, Sydney. I'll never know how I would have felt, because you didn't let me have the chance to feel anything, did you?"

He was right. What could she say? Except, "I'm sorry, Sam. I'm so sorry."

"Doesn't cut it."

"I know that. But I am sorry. Truly."

"You know, I could almost understand if you'd had the baby and then put him up for adoption. I'd still be upset, but I could at least understand. You weren't ready for a baby. You didn't think I'd want him either. Course you'd have been wrong about that, but I can at least see the reasoning. But that's not what you did. You had the baby, didn't tell me, and gave him to your parents to raise."

"They wanted another child. My mama was only seventeen when Blake was born, twenty when I came along. She was only thirty-nine when Duke was born. She and Dad had tried to have another child for several years, but it didn't happen. Duke was a godsend for them."

"Maybe he would have been a godsend to me. Did you think of that?"

"No. I didn't, and I'm sorry. I thought it was a one-night stand and you wouldn't want the baby."

"You were wrong."

"I realize that now." Memory washed over her of that incredible night together, the night that had resulted in their beautiful son. How could she make him understand when she wasn't sure she understood herself?

"You got the best of both worlds, didn't you? You got the baby without the responsibility. Instead of being the responsible parent, you get to be the doting big sister."

Guilt rolled through her like hot lava. It was true. She couldn't deny that she liked being a part of Duke's life. Giving him away to strangers would have been too hard. But she couldn't say these words to Sam.

Didn't matter. He already knew anyway.

They drove the rest of the way in silence, until Sydney noticed they'd passed through town and were into ranching country.

"Where are we going?"

"Aw, fuck," Sam said. "I was on autopilot. We're heading to Dusty and Zach's ranch. Shit, now I have to turn around. We're almost there, too."

"No matter. You're exhausted and so am I. Are you staying at a guest house?"

"Yeah."

"Is there more than one bedroom?"

"Yeah."

"Just keep going then. I'll sleep in the other bedroom."

"Look, it's no problem to go back."

"Sam, please. We've both been through the wringer tonight. Let's just go to bed."

He relented and kept driving.

* * * *

Sydney woke in the darkness. A warm body had snuggled against her back, spoon fashion. She jerked.

"It's just me, baby," Sam said. "Go back to sleep."

She smiled and curled against him.

When she opened her eyes to dawn streaming through the window, he was gone.

The smoky aroma of bacon wafted into her room. She rose and pulled on her jeans and shirt and traipsed out to the kitchen.

Sam stood at the stove in jeans, shirtless, his bronze muscular back a sight to behold. Had a more beautiful man ever been made?

"Good morning," she said.

He turned. "Morning. Coffee's made. Help yourself."

Was that it? Was he going to say nothing about the fact that he'd slept against her last night?

"Uh, okay. Thanks."

She fumbled in the cupboards until she found a mug and poured herself a cup.

"Like scrambled eggs?" he asked.

"Love 'em."

"Good. They'll be ready in a minute or two."

So this was how it was going to be. *Fine. I get it.*

He set a plate of eggs in front of her, and the doorbell rang.

"Excuse me for a minute."

In walked Dallas McCray, the oldest of the McCray brothers. Sydney remembered him.

"Sydney, this is Dusty's brother-in-law Dallas," Sam said.

"We've met. Nice to see you."

"You too," Dallas said. He turned to Sam. "You want me to come back later?"

"No. This concerns her. Sit on down. I'll get you some coffee."

What on earth was going on?

"Dallas is an attorney," Sam said.

"I'm a rancher with a license to practice law," Dallas said. "I don't claim to know everything about the law."

"You know enough for me," Sam said. "What did you find out?"

"To proceed with anything, you'll need to get a DNA test."

"Already done."

"What?"

"The DNA test. Got it yesterday. I'll have the results in a few days."

"How'd you manage that? I thought we'd need a court order."

"Circumstances. I was in the right place at the right time."

Sydney widened her eyes. "I can't believe this. What the hell is going on?"

"I'm going after my rights, Sydney."

"Meaning?"

"I want my son."

"You can't possibly be serious. You're not taking him away from my parents. I won't let you."

"You gave away your parental rights. I did not."

"And you agree with this?" she said to Dallas.

"I'm just the lawyer here. It's not my job to agree or disagree. It's my job to answer his questions about the law, and that's what I'm doing. He already knows I can't represent him in any kind of legal action. I have a ranch to run."

"Then who's representing him?

"A friend of mine in Denver. Richard White. He's a family lawyer. He specializes in this kind of stuff."

"How much is this costing you?" she asked Sam.

"Don't righteously care," he said. "Hang the cost. I want my kid."

"Don't put the cart before the horse," Dallas said. "We can't do anything until we get the DNA results."

"I can guarantee what the results will be. And so can you, can't you, Sydney?"

Her cheeks warmed. "He's the father," she said. "I haven't been with anyone else." She turned to Sam. "After everything we went through last night, I can't believe you still want to do this."

"Last night only clinched it," he said. "Last night proved how fragile life is. I'm glad as hell Duke isn't sick, but damnit, anything can happen. Last night drove home that you never know what tomorrow may bring. I want to know my son now, because only God knows how much more time he and I have together."

Sydney opened her mouth to speak but shut it quickly. What could she say to that? He made a damn good point.

"Tell me," Sam said to her. "If you were in my place, what would you do? Say you had a kid out there you just found out about. Wouldn't you want to get to know him?"

"I...I don't know. The situation is completely different. I'm a woman. If I had a kid out there, I'd know it."

"I think you just made my point. You can't even begin to understand how I feel, can you? Women think they can make all the decisions because they have the babies. Well, I'll grant you the fact that it's your body. If you had decided to abort the baby, I wouldn't have had any say in it."

Sydney gasped. "I could never have done that."

"I'm not saying you could have." Sam's tone softened a bit. "I'm just saying it was your decision. But that baby is half mine, and the minute he came out of your body, he stopped being solely your business."

"Fathers do have rights," Dallas said.

Sydney pounded her fist on the table. "I understand all that."

"Then what's the problem?" Sam said, still softly. "I'm just asserting my rights."

"Can't you at least talk to my parents? Maybe we can all work something out."

"That's an option you haven't considered, Sam," Dallas said, "and it's something that makes real sense from where I see it. Remember, the court will consider what's in the best interest of the child, not the parent. You can love that boy all you want, and you can want to be with him and raise him all you want, but if the court thinks leaving him with the Buchanans is in his best interest, that's what they'll do."

Sam raked his fingers through his hair. The taut muscles in his forearm tightened. *Good. Dallas had made him think.*

"Without the court involved, I have no way of knowing they'd keep any agreement we made between us."

"My parents are good people," Sydney said. "They would keep their word."

"And just how do I know that? I don't know your parents. How do I know they're trustworthy?"

After all, their daughter sure isn't. A knife sliced into Sydney's heart as she heard the words Sam didn't say.

And it was the truth. She hadn't been very trustworthy. She hadn't told him about Rod. And way more importantly, she hadn't told him about Duke.

Dallas took a sip of his coffee. "This is clearly getting personal between the two of you. I think I should leave." He stood.

"You don't have to go," Sam said.

"Yes, I do," Dallas said. "You two need to come to some kind of understanding. If you don't want to do it for yourselves, do it for Duke." He left.

"Damnit, Sydney!" Sam gripped the edge of the table with both hands.

"What?"

His eyes blazed. "It's not a crime to want to be a part of my son's life. Why can't anyone understand that?"

"It's not that we don't understand..."

"What then? What is it?"

She tried to smile. Didn't quite make it. "We just all love him so much."

Sam seemed to soften a little. "I know that." He sighed. "I really do know that, Sydney."

Reality hit her. He did understand. Just like she understood how he was feeling, how he wanted to be a part of Duke's life. If only she had handled the situation differently from the beginning. Then he wouldn't think her untrustworthy now.

She reached forward and covered one of Sam's hands with her own. His brown gaze shifted to hers

"I'm so sorry," she said, "about all of this."

He nodded. "Yeah, me too." He ungripped the table, moved toward her, and helped her to her feet. "Sydney." His voice was rough as it cracked.

"Yes?"

"Will you come to bed with me?

She nodded.

Chapter Thirteen

He picked her up and carried her to the other bedroom, presumably his, and tossed her on the bed. Fire burned in his eyes. He was going to be rough.

But she was ready for it. She wanted him to take her. Make her his.

He ripped off her clothes quickly and with a vengeance, until she lay nude upon the bed. Sam, still fully clothed, rose and went to the dresser. He returned with two red bandanas.

"Grab the headboard," he said.

Sydney jerked. "What?"

"Did I stutter? Grab two of the bars on the headboard. Make sure you're comfortable. You'll be in this position for a little while."

The bandanas. *Oh God, he's going to tie my wrists to the headboard.* Fear rushed through her, accompanied by a strange arousal.

"Sam, I don't think—"

"I don't recall asking what you thought. If you don't want to do this, you can leave."

"You mean I'm free to go?"

"Of course you're free to go. I'd never keep you against your will. What kind of man do you think I am?"

Up until now, she thought she'd known. She'd never imagined him tying her up. Had he been a calf roper? She couldn't remember.

I should go. I should run like the wind out of here. But a force like the strongest magnet kept her supine on the bed.

"So you're staying?"

She nodded. She most likely needed her head examined, but she was staying.

"Good." His voice was husky, stern.

He would not hurt her. She trusted him.

She understood now. He didn't think she was trustworthy.

He would prove to her that *he* was.

He regarded her, his eyes blazing. He sat down next to her and blindfolded her with one of the bandanas.

She was not expecting that. She thought he'd use them to tie her wrists to the headboard.

The cotton fabric brushed against her skin as he tied first one and then the other wrist to the headboard.

His lips brushed her ear. "Do you trust me?" he whispered.

Warmth flooded her veins. "Yes. I trust you, Sam."

"Good." He tightened the fabric around both wrists.

Her body burned. Electricity crackled between them and her veins popped with energy. Excitement overwhelmed her. She was scared, her nerves hopped within her skin, but she was turned on. Oh, so turned on.

She lay still for several minutes, wondering what he was up to. When she thought she could stand it no longer, coldness touched one nipple.

Ice. He was rubbing an ice cube over her nipple.

"Relax, baby," he said softly. "I won't hurt you."

She nodded. "I know."

"Enjoy the sensations."

She breathed in, breathed out, willed her body to relax.

The ice on her nipple melted, and droplets of water tickled the flesh of her breasts as they oozed downward. The ice touched her other nipple, and this time the sensation wasn't so abrupt. It was cold and harsh, yet her nipple hardened and strained upward. She wanted the warmth of his lips to soothe the cold.

But his lips didn't come. Only the ice melting and drizzling down her breast like the frosting on a hot cinnamon roll.

With both nipples cold and hard, the ice disappeared.

"Oh!"

It had reappeared within in seconds…on her clit.

"Easy, sweetheart," he soothed. "Hold still."

Her knees buckled.

"I said hold still." His voice was stern this time. It left no question that he meant to be obeyed.

She obeyed.

Images of him tying her feet to the foot of the bed swirled through her mind. And her nipples hardened even further at that thought.

The ice cube smoothed back and forth over the folds of her flesh.

"Mmm, it's melting fast. You're so hot down here."

Again, the icy coldness made her long for the heat of his lips, his mouth.

Again, they didn't come.

She needed to be touched by a human hand, mouth, lips. No more ice. She wanted human contact. Sam contact.

The ice melted into oblivion, and then…ah, yes. His tongue found her. Finally.

He flicked it over her hard bud and she wrapped her legs around his muscular back. His skin was warm and smooth, and though she couldn't see, she knew it was glowing and beautiful.

"Sam, yes, yes." Her voice seemed to come from without her. Funny how taking away her vision made her voice seem distant. He continued licking, and then fingers closed around each of her nipples. He was playing with them while he pleasured her.

Holy Christ, it felt good. Not knowing what he'd do next was oddly exciting. Oddly arousing.

His tongue darted in and out of her wetness. When he clamped his lips around her clit, an orgasm burst through her.

Crazy bursts, like fireworks. No build up this time. She was coming, just coming, out of nowhere. And God, it was good.

"Yeah, baby, come for me." His fingers continued to work her nipples as he soothed her clit with his tongue after her climax. "Come for me again."

And as though he demanded her obedience with mere words, she burst into flames once more.

Once more he brought her to climax, until she was begging for him to let her go. "Please, Sam, I want to touch you."

Soon his warm hands fumbled with the bandanas at her wrists. "Oh, thank you." She breathed. "I need to touch you. Feel you."

She reached upward when her hands were free, but he was nowhere. "Can I take off the blindfold?"

"No," his stern voice said. "Turn over."

"On my belly?"

"Yes. Turn over on your belly and then grab the headboard again."

Her body thrumming, she did as she was told. He retied her hands as she lay prone on the bed.

"Sydney, you have one beautiful ass."

"Thank you." *I think*. What else could she say? He had one fine backside too, but not being visually aware of it at the moment, she didn't state that fact.

One finger breached her wet channel.

"Ahhh," she moaned. *Perfect.*

In and out he stroked her, so slowly she thought she might go mad.

"Pull your knees up under you," he said.

She obeyed, and he added another finger. This position allowed him to go deeper, stretching and probing, filling an emptiness she hadn't known existed.

She thought she might come right there.

Again.

"Oh!" Cold again, this time against her secret opening.

No one had ever touched her there. Yet no fear consumed her. She trusted Sam.

It was another ice cube, and as it melted and the tiny rivers of water trickled between her cheeks, tickling her, she sighed. She'd never known this kind of play could be so fulfilling.

If her hands were free, she could reach between her legs and stroke her clit. She'd come for sure.

But her hands weren't free. Desire to touch herself, to touch Sam, built within her until she thought for sure she'd explode.

"Sam, please! Let me go. I need to…I need…"

"No." Still stroking her with his fingers, he replaced the ice cube with his tongue.

Ah God, soft warmth. He licked her there, in that private place, and she was thrilled. Electricity sizzled through her veins. How could this feel so good? So right?

"Mmm." His voice vibrated against the sensitive skin of her crease. "You're sweet."

The feelings coursing through her were entirely new, things she'd never imagined feeling. Images swirled through her mind's eye, of Sam taking her in her ass. Would he? She didn't know. Would she let him if he wanted to?

Oh, yes. She would.

"Ah, God!" The fingers of his other hand found her swollen clit. Only a few strokes, and the sparks coursed through her again.

How many orgasms could her body take before it shut down and couldn't take any more? She had a sneaking suspicion she would find out today.

Swirling images funneled through her mind. She and Sam riding horses together across the sprawling acres of the ranch—she and Sam making love in her hotel room at the Windsor that first night five years ago—kissing and licking Sam's cock until he exploded against her tongue—a Colorado sunset with Sam, the pink-and-orange clouds forming a heart over the mountains as they held hands, kissed, vowed to love each other forever.

All from being blindfolded, sensory deprived.

"More," he said to her. "Come for me again."

"Sam, please, I—"

"Come!" he commanded.

She imploded into the bed, her body sinking downward, floating on the bottom of a lush green sea. She was a mermaid, swinging her tail and laughing at sea creatures as her body moved inward, outward, in and out of itself.

Throbbing, pulsing, convulsing, materializing and dematerializing.

"Sam, please. I have to touch you!"

He thrust his cock into her.

He started slowly, rocking back and forth into her tight channel. In. Out. In. Out.

Oh. My. God.

She wouldn't come again. She couldn't. She knew that. But still, he felt so wonderful inside her, filled her, completed her.

"You feel so good on my cock, sweetheart," he said. "So damn good."

She moved her hips back and forth as best she cold, trying to take in more of him.

"God, I could do this forever," he said. "Your body takes mine so perfectly."

Her head sank farther into the pillow, her eyes clenched shut under the blindfold. How she loved this man.

How she trusted this man.

Trust.

She needed to find a way for him to trust her.

She needed to be with him, but it would never work unless he trusted her. She'd betrayed his trust twice. Now, as he made love to her while she lay at his mercy, thrusting into her and giving her pleasure, she vowed he would trust her again.

Somehow.

Chapter Fourteen

"I didn't know you were into that kind of sex," Sydney said, resting her head on Sam's chest.

"Truthfully, neither did I." He chuckled. "But I liked it. It was a real turn-on."

"What made you want to try it today?"

"I wanted to show you that you can trust me."

She nodded, his skin warm against her cheek. "I trust you, Sam."

He didn't say it back, and she didn't expect it. She'd have to earn that.

She'd find a way. She had to. She loved this man, and she damn well was not going to live without him.

"I want to help you, Sam."

"With what?"

"Trusting me."

He sighed. "Sweetheart, I want to trust you more than anything in the world."

"What if I helped you work it out with Mom and Dad so you could see Duke?"

He sat up, pushing her off his chest. "You still don't get it, do you?"

"Get what?"

"I don't want to just see Duke. I want to raise Duke. He's my son."

Sydney's heart sank. Nothing had changed. He was still determined to take Duke from her parents.

"They love him."

"Of course they love him. They're his grandparents. I fully expect them to be a part of his life. But your father is not his father. I am."

"Oh, Sam. Please."

"Please what? Give up my child? I can't, Sydney. I can't."

"I want you to be part of his life. And so do they."

"Part of his life isn't good enough."

"You heard what Dallas said. The court will consider what's in the child's best interests. They won't uproot him. They'll probably give you some kind of visitation, but they won't take him away from the only parents he's ever known."

"I don't care. I have to try."

"Why? Why can't we just talk to my parents?"

"Because if I don't try, I'll never forgive myself. I've always wanted kids, Sydney, and here I find out I actually have one. A beautiful little boy. I love him, Sydney. I loved him as soon as I found out about him, but last night, seeing him lying in that hospital bed, possibly dying, I knew he was mine. My heart cried out for him. I wanted only to protect him. To take away any pain he might ever feel."

What a wonderful man. He would indeed have made an amazing father. But she had to clue him in on something. "Sam, you can't take away every pain he might ever feel. No one can. Your parents couldn't do that for you, could they?"

Sam sighed. "You're right. They couldn't. They didn't."

"No parent can."

"But I should be there for him. I love that child. I don't even know him yet, but I love him."

Sydney summoned all her emotion, all her love for Sam, and met his gaze. "Then please don't hurt him."

He looked away from her, rose, walked out of the room, and then back in. His eyes were wet, and a streak ran down each of his cheeks.

"All right, Sydney," he said. "Let's talk to your parents."

Still naked, she jumped off the bed and ran into his arms. "Thank you, Sam. You won't regret this, I promise you. You can trust me on that."

* * * *

Sam drove Sydney back to the hotel so she could get over to the grounds and work Sapphire. They had a race the next day. Sam agreed to wait a day or two before talking to her parents. He wanted Duke to get over the virus he had, and he wanted to wait until the DNA test results came in. They could be in as early as this afternoon, though he figured tomorrow was a safer bet.

He worked his horse a little, thinking he might actually compete tomorrow as planned. After all, he'd already missed one competition. His heart wasn't really in it, though. He had other stuff on his mind. Besides, with the new job he was taking with Zach, he no longer needed purse money.

Then, out of the blue, it hit him—what he wanted to do this afternoon. He went to the main house to talk to Dusty.

"Is Seanie home?"

"Yes, he's outside having a riding lesson with one of the hands."

"Good. When will he be done?"

"In a half hour or so. Why?"

"I'd like to spend the afternoon with my nephew."

"That's sweet, Sam. I'm sure he'd love it."

"We could go fishing. Or I could take him up to the rodeo to watch some of the competitions."

"He'd love that. Why don't you plan on it? Are you hungry? I can make you a sandwich."

"Yeah, as a matter of fact." Sam sat down at the kitchen table.

Dusty grabbed some deli meat out of the fridge. "It's such good news about Duke. I was really scared."

Sam nodded. "I was freaked."

"I was worried that our stupid DNA was going to make his life hard."

"You know you didn't need to worry about that. We've heard it a hundred times. There's no indication anywhere that leukemia is hereditary."

"I know, but first Mom, and then me." Dusty shook her head as she spread mustard on two slices of bread. "It sure seems to be in our family."

"Luckily, you are cured. And Duke is clean. Thank God."

"I shook all last night till we got your call."

"I know, Dust. I'm sorry."

"Don't be. It's part of my life. Every time I take Seanie in for a sick visit, I'm scared to death they're going to say he has the damn thing."

"Sean is fine. He'll always be fine. And so will Duke."

"God, I hope you're right." She set the sandwich on a plate and placed it before him.

He smiled. "Of course I'm right."

"Eat your sandwich. Sean'll be done soon, and you can have your uncle's outing."

Mmm, good old McCray roast beef. And a date with his nephew. Just what he needed. Some five-year-old boy time.

If he couldn't lavish his love on his son, he could lavish it on his adorable nephew.

* * * *

Sydney ached with exhaustion. She and Sapphire had had a good workout. She'd gone back to hotel, taken a long hot shower, and decided to check in on Duke.

She walked down the hall and knocked on the door to her parents' hotel room.

No response.

Had they gone out? Hmm. Duke was surely still not himself. When Sydney had called this morning, her mother said he'd slept well and was doing better, but Sydney had assumed they'd be staying in today.

She called her mother's cell phone. No answer. Her father's. No answer. Well, if they were at the rodeo, no doubt they couldn't hear the phones over all the commotion.

This was good news. Duke was obviously feeling better. Sydney checked her watched. Nearly dinner time. No wonder her tummy was putting up a fuss.

She had a great idea. She'd call Sam and invite him for dinner. They could go to the Blue Bird on Main. Too bad she didn't have a kitchenette in her hotel room. She'd love to cook for him.

But wait, he had a kitchen in his guest house. Would it be presumptuous to invite herself over to cook him dinner? Heck, they'd shared stuff a lot more intimate that a home-cooked meal this morning in bed.

She dialed his number and her pulse raced when he answered.

"Hi, Sam. It's me."

"Hello, Sydney."

"I was wondering…well, Duke's doing better and Mom and Dad took him out, so I was thinking… Would you like to have dinner with me?"

"I'm afraid I have company right now," he said.

"Oh." Her heart sank. "I'm sorry. I didn't mean to interrupt."

"You're not interrupting. I was about to cook a great meal of mac and cheese for my nephew. We would love to have you join us."

"Oh." *Thank God. He's not with another woman.* "I don't want to intrude."

"Who's intruding? Sean and I had a fun afternoon riding horses together. And now we're famished, aren't we, buddy?"

Childish laughter rang in the background.

"Well, then, I'd love to join you. But I was hoping I could cook you dinner."

"I'm afraid Seanie has his heart set on Uncle Sam's famous mac and cheese, but you could make dessert."

"Perfect," Sydney said. "I'll pick up groceries on the way. What would you like?"

"Let's ask the guest of honor. What would you like for dessert, bud?"

"Something chocolate!"

Sam laughed. "Did you hear that?"

"I sure did. I know just what to make. One of my specialties. I'll be there in an hour."

"Mac and cheese should be almost done by then."

They hung up and Sydney headed to the grocery and purchased ingredients for chocolate mousse. It didn't take long to make, and it could chill while they ate.

"Oops," she said out loud. Chocolate mousse had raw eggs in it. Not the best for a five-year-old. Now what? She'd promised chocolate. She grabbed cocoa, eggs, sugar, and a pint of premium vanilla ice cream.

Flourless chocolate torte to the rescue. All she needed was a round cake pan. Hopefully the guest house had one.

On second thought, she headed to the housewares section and grabbed a disposable foil pan just in case.

And off to Sam's.

She found herself humming a lively tune as she drove, looking forward to spending time with Sam and his nephew. It would be almost like—

Almost like she and Sam making dinner for Duke—had she told him and had they decided to raise him together, of course.

She'd made what she thought was the best decision at the time. No use crying over spilled milk.

She arrived to a smiling Sean on the front stoop. He had hair like his mother and light blue eyes. A beautiful little boy, just like her Duke.

"Are you Sydney? Uncle Sam said you were coming."

"Yes, I am. And you're Sean. I remember you from your mom and dad's party."

"You're pretty."

"Why thank you."

"Come on in."

"Thank you very much."

Sean led the way. "She's here, Uncle Sam, and she's pretty!"

Sam's laugher rang from the kitchen. "Yes, she certainly is."

"Mmm. It smells great in here. The savory aroma of cheddar cheese wafted to her nose.

"It's almost ready."

"Okay. I just need about ten minutes to whip up my dessert. It can bake while we eat."

"Have at it. The kitchen is pretty well-stocked. Sean and I will stay out of your way."

Sydney put together her flourless torte with ease and got it in the oven. By the time she was done, Sam was spooning out globs of piping hot mac and cheese onto plates.

He poured a glass of milk for Sean and opened a bottle of Gewürztraminer and poured two glasses. He handed one to Sydney. "I hope you like white wine."

"I like most wine," she said. "Thank you."

They sat down and dug in.

"Mmm, this is delicious," Sydney said.

"My own personal recipe. I've been on my own up at the ranch for the last five years. I had to learn to cook. This is actually made with four different cheeses."

"Let me guess. Cheddar, of course, Monterey jack, parmesan, and…"

"It's the last one that always tricks people up."

"Wait a minute, I'll get it." She took another bite. "Is it Roquefort?"

"You're as smart as you are beautiful." He grinned.

"What's rockport?" Sean asked.

"It's just a kind of cheese," Sam said. "It's good, isn't it?"

"Yum," he said, holding out his plate. "Can I have more?"

"You sure can."

"I'll get it, Sam." Sydney stood. "You want more milk too, honey?"

"Yes, please."

She rose a few moments later to take her torte from the oven. "This needs to cool for a few minutes. Then we'll have it hot with a scoop of vanilla ice cream on top. Does that sound good?" she asked Sean.

"Sounds great!"

She smiled. What a cutie! He was so much like Duke. They were cousins after all. She couldn't wait for the two of them to get to know each other.

Sean got up to run around and Sydney asked Sam, "Did you hear about the DNA test yet?"

"No. Tomorrow, probably."

"Well, you and I both know what it'll say."

"Yes, but I want to have it in hand before I talk to your parents. I agreed to do this, Sydney, but only if they're willing to be fair."

"They'll be fair," she said, hoping to God she was right. "They won't want to put Duke through a lawsuit or anything."

Sam shook his head. "I don't want to do that either. I really don't. I'm just not sure there's any other way, especially if they won't cooperate."

"They'll cooperate. The only thing is, you're going to have to meet them halfway."

"I just wish you'd told me five years ago. Then we wouldn't have this problem."

"We've been through that, Sam. I made the decision I thought was right at the time."

"You made a mistake."

"Yes, I can see now that I did. But that's all hindsight and retrospect. At the time, I had no idea you'd want to know. I thought I was doing you a favor."

"Yes, I've heard your side of it. We don't need to go there again."

She sighed. "Let's have our dessert. Go on and call Sean in, and I'll serve it up."

Sean pronounced the dessert a success, and Sydney laughed as she wiped the chocolate off his cute little face.

"It's getting about to be your bedtime, bud," Sam said.

"No, I don't wanna go."

"Why doesn't he spend the night here with you?" Sydney said.

"Now that's a good idea. Would you like that, partner?"

"Eggs and hash browns in the morning?"

"Of course."

"Then yeah! Can Sydney stay too?"

Sydney's cheeks warmed. She'd like nothing better than to spend another night with Sam, but not with his little nephew in the house. It wouldn't look right.

"Not this time, I'm afraid," she said. "I need to be getting back to my hotel. I'm competing tomorrow." She looked at Sam. "Aren't you competing tomorrow?"

"I've decided not to," he said.

"Really? Why not?"

"I'm moving here as soon as I get things settled at the ranch in Montana."

"Moving here? Why?"

"Uncle Sam's gonna live here with us," Sean said.

"Zach offered me a job as ranch foreman along with a nice ownership interest. I couldn't turn him down. Plus, I'll get to see my sis and this little guy a lot more often." He grabbed Sean and gave him a rough noogie.

Sean laughed, squirming. "Stop that!"

"What's that have to do with not competing tomorrow?"

"I'm thirty-three years old. I've broken a few ribs over the years, strained a lot of muscles. I'm not the competitor I was ten years ago. It's time to say goodbye to that life. I've got a chance to make a great living out here, and I want to focus on that."

Sydney nodded. She couldn't imagine giving up racing. Of course she was younger at twenty-four. But Dusty had given it up at twenty-three when she got pregnant with Sean.

She didn't need to think about that. She wasn't pregnant. Hadn't been in a while. And she didn't have a family to think about other than her parents and Duke, and they relied on her purse money.

But had she made the right choice? Maybe she should have stopped racing long ago and raised her son.

She'd been young, no doubt. But she'd also been selfish, and her selfishness was coming back to bite her in the butt. She'd made things much harder on her parents and Duke than she'd ever intended. And on Sam. And even on herself.

For a moment again, she imagined Sean as Duke and herself and Sam as the happily married parents.

Could it have happened then?

She sighed. She'd never know.

She stood. "As much as I hate to say goodbye, I have to be going. Thank you so much for dinner," she said to Sam. Then, to Sean, "I had a great time hanging out with you. I hope we can do it again sometime."

"Okay, as long as you bring chocolate."

She laughed and ruffled his hair. "It's a deal."

"I'll walk you out," Sam said.

"You don't need to bother."

"It's no bother. The critter'll be fine in here for a minute, won't you?

"Yup."

He walked her to her car and took both hands in his. "I'm glad you came. Dessert was delicious. But"—he leaned in—"not half as delicious as you are."

He pressed his mouth to hers in a soft kiss.

She parted her lips and the kiss deepened, but he pulled back. "I have to get back inside."

"I know."

"I'm glad you came."

"Sam, I hope you know we will work this out somehow. My parents are not unreasonable people."

He nodded. "I've given you a hard time. I don't mean to. It's just—"

She put her fingers to his mouth, silencing him. "Don't. I understand. Good night."

"Good night."

He stood outside until she had backed out and was on her way down the winding road of the McCray Ranch, heading toward the county road.

She pulled out her cell phone and hit her mother's number on speed dial. She'd be back at the hotel soon, but she wanted to check on Duke.

"What?" she said aloud.

Her heart sped up and her throat constricted. Nausea worked its way up her esophagus. Quickly she hit "end" and redialed, this time punching in the actual numbers.

Her tummy plummeted as she listened to the same message.

This number is no longer in service.

Chapter Fifteen

She pulled to the side of the road, frantic, and tried her father's number.

Same message.

She gunned the engine and sped back to the hotel. She rushed in and stopped at the front desk. "Roy and Carrie Buchanan and their son—did they check out?"

The clerk checked his computer. "No, ma'am. They're scheduled to be here six more days."

Thank goodness.

Must be a glitch with one of the cellular towers in the area. She took the elevator up and walked to her room. She wanted to check on Duke, so she crossed the hall to her parents' room and knocked.

No response.

She knocked louder. It was after ten o'clock. They couldn't still be out with Duke, could they? After he'd been so sick just the night before?

She knocked again, this time nearly putting her fist through the door. "Mom, Dad." She didn't want to yell. It was late, and some of the other guests were no doubt in bed.

She let out a breath. Those invisible bugs were crawling up her arms again—something didn't feel right about this. But surely her parents were taking good care of Duke. They probably ran into some friends or something at the rodeo and were up talking. Duke was no doubt snoozing on his mother's lap this very minute.

Sydney was exhausted herself, and she had a competition tomorrow. Best get to bed.

She went to her own room, undressed, washed up, and fell into bed.

She'd check on her baby in the morning.

* * * *

At the first light of dawn, Sydney woke, her heart pounding.

What was going on?

She couldn't remember having a nightmare. Why was she so on edge?

Duke. She was worried about Duke. She pulled on a robe, walked across the hall, and knocked again on her parents' door. Still no answer.

This was getting freaky.

She went back to her room and tried both of their cell numbers again. She got the same troubling message. Their numbers were no longer in service.

That nauseated feeling plagued her again.

Something was very wrong.

She called to the front desk and found her parents had still not checked out.

Then she called Sam. Just to say good morning, she said in as cheery a voice as she could muster. She didn't want to alarm him. It was just a test to check the cellular service in the area, which was obviously working just fine.

Her heart sped. What the hell was going on?

She'd taken the rental car yesterday. Where were they?

Suddenly, she had a terrible thought. What if they were in their room and couldn't get to the door? Oh no! What if something horrible had happened?

She nearly lost what little was left in her stomach as she pulled on some jeans and a shirt and raced down to the front desk.

"I need you to open my parents' room," she said.

"Ma'am?" The clerk looked at her with a concerned face.

"You've told me they haven't checked out, but I don't have a clue where they are. They didn't answer last night and they're not answering the door this morning. They're not answering the phone."

"Maybe they stayed out all night. Sometimes, adults do that."

"Not adults with a five-year-old little boy. Please do this for me. Humor me."

"Okay, okay. I'll have someone from security check it out."

A few minutes later, Sydney followed a security official to the door of her parents' room. He knocked firmly. "Mr. Buchanan? Mrs. Buchanan?"

"I told you they're not answering."

"All right, miss, simmer down. We're going in." He slid a card through the lock and opened the door.

Sydney rushed past him into the room.

Her heart dropped. No suitcases in sight. The beds had been made, obviously by housekeeping yesterday. They had not been slept in.

She ran into the bathroom. Nothing but a few half-used bottles of hotel shampoo and lotion. Everything else was gone.

What on Earth?

"Looks like they left, ma'am," the security guy said.

"But they didn't. The clerk said they didn't check out."

"Then they didn't check out but they left anyway. It happens."

"You don't understand. They're booked here for five more days. For the rodeo."

"I guess they decided to go home."

"But they would have told me." She plunked down on one of the beds. "This isn't good. This isn't good at all. Something is definitely wrong."

"I wish I could help you, but I need to get this room closed back up. I'll need to notify the front desk. They may have skipped out on their bill."

"They didn't," Sydney said, her head in her hands. "They prepaid for the rodeo. Oh my God."

"I'm sorry, ma'am. I don't know what else to say."

"It's all right. Just go."

"I need to ask you to leave this room."

"Can I just look around first? See if they might have left something behind? I need to know what's going on."

"Okay, you can have ten minutes."

She used every millisecond of those ten minutes, scouring every millimeter of the room for something—anything—to clue her in on what had happened.

Nothing.

No evidence of any struggle. No evidence of anything at all, except that they were gone.

"Thank you," she said to the security guy. She walked soberly back to her own room.

She dialed the land line to their home in Carson City. No answer, of course. If they'd driven, they wouldn't have gotten back there yet. Or maybe they would have if they'd driven all night. Or they could have caught a red-eye flight.

God, now what?

If they flew, the airport would have those records, right? But would she be able to access them?

Where were they?

Visions of a masked gunman taking them hostage tormented her. Perhaps they were bound and gagged at this very moment in the back of a truck somewhere.

Perhaps Duke... *Dear Lord, Duke!*

Who could help her?

Sam. Sam would help her.

Her skin chilled when a horrible thought crossed her mind.

What if her parents had skipped town with Duke? To keep Sam away from him?

They wouldn't.

Would they?

No, of course not. They were also keeping Sydney away from him, and they would never do that.

Yet none of this made sense. If they'd been abducted, their cell phones would still work. They might not answer, but the numbers would still go through.

More importantly, there'd be evidence of some sort of struggle. Something would have been left behind. Maybe the gunman had made them pack everything up—

No.

Her body went limp. In her heart, she knew the truth.

They had left.

Her parents were good people. They wouldn't have done this if they hadn't thought it completely necessary. Desperation had obviously fueled them.

What could she do? She could wait for them to show up at home. They'd have to answer the land line sooner or later.

If, indeed, they went home at all.

The thought nagged her. If they'd canceled their cell numbers, they probably weren't headed home.

They were headed somewhere else. Somewhere Sam—and no one else—would ever find them.

Sydney buried her face against the palms of her hands. How had it all come to this? She swallowed. She could go after them, look for them. Not bother Sam until she knew something concrete.

No. She couldn't do that to Sam. She couldn't keep this from him. Not only would he have one more reason not to trust her, but more importantly, this was Sam's business. He had a right to know.

She'd taken away his rights five years ago. She could not do it again. She had to find Sam and tell him.

Her heart sank when a truth struck her in a black haze.

She'd tell Sam what happened—that her parents had skipped town and taken Duke with them. That they hadn't told her they were leaving and they'd canceled their cell phone numbers.

It was the truth and nothing but the truth.

There was only one problem.

He wouldn't believe her.

Chapter Sixteen

"How could they?" Sam paced around the living room of his guest house. "How could they just pack up a sick little kid and leave?"

"I don't know, Sam. I guess they thought they had no choice."

"Why don't you tell me the truth for once, Sydney," he said. "You sent them on their merry way, and now you're lying to me, aren't you?"

Just what she'd been afraid of. He didn't believe her. "I swear to you that's not true. Call the hotel if you want. I was frantic this morning looking for them. Their cell phones have been disconnected, for God's sake. I had nothing to do with this."

"You never wanted me in the picture from the beginning."

"That's not true!" Tears streamed down her cheeks. "I've explained all that."

"Why should I believe any of this?"

She sat down. What could she say? " Sam. I can only tell you it's the truth."

"If you were in my shoes, would you believe it?"

She shook her head. "I honestly don't know. And that's the cold hard truth."

He softened a little. The fire in his dark eyes turned to ash. "God." He sat down on the couch and buried his head in his hands. "This is all my fault."

Sydney went to him, tried to comfort him, but he shook her away. "Don't."

"It's not your fault, Sam. It's mine. This all began when I made a horrible mistake. I chose not to tell you about Duke, and I chose not to tell my parents who the father was. I thought I was protecting you, but I see now that I was young and naïve. I'm sorry. You had a right to know your son."

No response.

She put her arms around his shoulders, tried to hold his unresponsive body. "I love you, Sam. I have never stopped loving you."

Still no response.

"We will find them, and we will work something out."

He lifted his head. "You said they'd be willing to talk to me."

She shook her head. "I thought they would. This behavior isn't like them at all. I'm not sure why they left, but they must have thought they had good reason. I can guarantee you one thing. They would never in a million years harm Duke. We can at least know that he's safe."

"We need to call Dallas. Or the cops."

"No. Dallas and the cops can't do anything. They are Duke's legal parents. In the eyes of the law, they haven't done anything wrong."

"I can't accept that. Damnit." He stood. "I'm calling Dallas."

Sydney sat, numb, as he spoke to his brother-in-law for a few minutes. When he hung up, his eyes were glazed over.

"You're right. The cops won't touch this. We have nothing to stand on."

"I'm sorry."

"Our only option is to hire a private investigator. Chad knows a good one who he uses all the time."

"I don't think we need a PI. We can find them. Where could they go? They don't have a lot of disposable cash.

Most of our money is tied up in the ranch. We're not in financial straits or anything, but we're not rolling in it either. I wanted to win a few purses here because we can really use the money."

"Aren't you supposed to compete today?"

She nodded. "I can't. Not now. My head's not in it." She hoped he understood, though she could use the money now more than ever.

Man up, Syd. Her father's voice spoke in her thoughts. He'd said those words to her older brother, Blake, many times, but never to her. They rang true for her now.

She stood. "I've changed my mind. I have enough time to get over there and get ready. I'm competing today. We need the purse money to find Duke."

He nodded. "I've got my job here, but of course I haven't gotten paid yet. Most of my money is tied up in the ranch in Montana. I'm in the same boat your parents are, but I think I know where I can get some fast cash."

"How?"

"I'll ride Zach's bull."

Sydney jerked. "You're crazy! That bull almost killed both Dusty *and* Zach five years ago. I won't allow it."

"You won't allow it? Oh, that's rich."

"You're not a bull rider. You're a bronc buster. There's a huge difference."

"It can't be that different. I'm a hell of a bronc buster. Besides, what makes you think you have any say in it?"

"Because I love you, that's why!" She threw her arms around him and crushed her lips to his.

It was a kiss of not only passion, but fear and anxiety. They were both worried about Duke.

Electricity pulsed between them. Sam lifted her in his arms and they continued kissing, their lips and tongues sliding together in lustful rhythm.

Sydney pulled away. "I'm sorry. I know now isn't the time for this. We have to figure out what we're going to do. Plus, I have a competition this afternoon."

"There is time. I will take you to the rodeo. Now is the perfect time for this." He lifted her in his strong arms and carried her to his bedroom.

No bandanas tying her to the bed posts this time. No angry, punishing kisses. This was slow, sweet love. They kissed for a long time and then slowly undressed each other.

When Sam entered her, tears welled in her eyes. Emotion so thick she could almost see it swirled between them. She hadn't known she'd been so empty until he filled her at that moment.

She loved this man.

Suddenly, she knew she always had.

It was because of her love for him that she hadn't told him about Duke. She hadn't wanted to wreck his life, to trap him. He would not understand her logic. She wasn't sure she understood it herself. She only knew the truth of it in her heart.

His thrusts became harder, and even without the clitoral stimulation she thought necessary, an orgasm rose within her.

They came in unison, panting and heaving, until they were a mass of naked limbs tangled together, breathing heavily.

"That was amazing," Sydney said.

He grunted, his eyes closed.

"I have to get to the rodeo."

"I know. I'll take you." He didn't move.

"It's okay. I can get there myself."

"No, I want to go with you. We can talk on the way about what we're going to do."

"All right."

They showered in each other's arms and then dressed. After a quick stop at the hotel for Sydney's racing clothes, they got to the rodeo without much time to spare. Sydney had given Sapphire a workout the day before so the mare was in good shape.

She needed the purse.

She couldn't let Sam ride that huge-ass bull.

Sam left her to prepare Sapphire. He'd be in the stands, he assured her, cheering her on.

Sydney groomed Sapphire, trying like hell to concentrate on the race. Her visualization was stunted. She couldn't picture the race. She couldn't picture winning.

Instead her mind conjured images of her baby boy on the run with her parents. She'd failed Duke, and she'd failed Sam. What was she going to do?

Right now Sam seemed rational, but who knew what would happen when they finally caught up with her parents and Duke?

Damn it, Sydney, focus!

She tried to concentrate on Sapphire. Nope, wasn't working. She continued grooming on autopilot, knowing full well she should be bonding with her mare instead of ruminating. The race and the purse depended upon her and Sapphire being in perfect sync.

"That's my girl," she said to the horse. Normally she talked in soothing tones while grooming. She hadn't today. She hoped Sapphire would be okay.

Once finished, she and Sapphire headed to the arena to await the start of the race. Sydney was set to go second to last.

One by one, she watched the other racers, each time thinking they did something better than she did. She had beaten most of these racers the other day, so why was she doubting herself?

Because now there was something more at stake. Not just the purse.

Duke.

Sam.

The two most important people in her life.

She'd never have a life with both of them. Duke was her parents' son now. The most she'd ever get as the birth mother was visitation, and she could have that now as his big sister. What would Sam get?

Probably nothing.

Of course, if he married her, he could be Duke's brother-in-law. Sydney shook her head. That wouldn't be enough for Sam. And though he professed to love her, he would never marry her just to have his son. He was too honorable for that.

He had to trust her first.

She had to find a way to make him trust her.

How? How could she? She'd betrayed him in such a terrible way already. She'd kept him from his son. She wasn't sure she could ever forgive herself.

And now her parents, her beloved parents, had run rather than face losing the little boy they adored.

She had gotten herself, her son, her parents, and the man she loved into one fine mess indeed.

"Syd, you're up next," Sharla Perkins, the racer behind her, said.

Sydney jerked out of her stupor. She hadn't even seen the racers ahead of her go. She had no idea what kind of competition she was up against.

She and Sapphire headed forward.

"Next up is Sydney Buchanan of Nevada," the announcer, Mark, said. "Sydney won a handsome purse in her first race. Let's see what she can show us today."

Yeah, let's see for sure.

She closed her eyes. But instead of images of her and Sapphire, working as one, only dark visions of her parents running away appeared.

Sapphire. Must see myself with Sapphire. Why isn't this working?

No more time to stall. She had to go.

She opened her eyes, signaled to the judge, and raced forward. With the force of a tornado, Sydney took Sapphire around the first barrel perfectly. She looked straight ahead and galloped toward the second, taking Sapphire around in the opposite direction. Thank God! One more to go. She aimed toward the final barrel.

Thundering applause rushed from the stands. She could do it. She was doing it. Sam was out there watching. She'd do it for him, for Duke, for all the mistakes she'd made.

God, the mistakes…

A millisecond later, Sapphire knocked down the final barrel.

Her throat constricted, Sydney raced back and crossed the electric eye. She didn't see her time.

It didn't matter anyway. Even if she'd made her personal best, the barrel would cost her a five second penalty. She wouldn't place.

She dismounted and petted the mare's nose. "Great job, sweetie."

A local girl approached her. "Tough break," she said.

Sydney tried to feign nonchalance. "It happens."

The girl smiled and went on her way. Sydney took Sapphire back to the stalls and cleaned her up.

After she'd taken care of the mare and blown the congestion out of her nose, hoping she'd shed her last tear, she went out into the stands to find Sam.

She walked for a while, her brain in a haze, seeing only blurred faces in front of her. No blurry Sam. When she'd nearly given up, he appeared.

"Lord," she groaned under her breath.

Next to him, jabbering in his ear, was none other than Rod Kyle.

Chapter Seventeen

"Look," Sam said, "I'm not interested in all the documentation you have. I know the kid is mine. The DNA results will be in today, tomorrow at the latest. In fact, they might be in right now. I haven't checked my phone in a while."

"What I'm trying to tell you is that Roy and Carrie Buchanan are not who they seem to be," Rod said. "I thought for sure you'd be interested."

"You think I'd trust anything you told me?"

"Look, I get that Sydney's not going to marry me. I'm not thrilled about the gossip and shit it's going to create. My father had his own reasons for wanting me to marry her, and her family had a lot to do with it. He's livid about the broken engagement."

"What the hell would her family have to do with it? And why the fuck does your father care who you marry? Jesus Christ."

"That's what I'm trying to tell you. I found some information—"

"What exactly have you found, then? And why were you looking?"

"Fair question. I started looking to find a way to keep Sydney from breaking our engagement. My father wanted the marriage more than I did, and my father doesn't ever do anything without a reason, so I dug deeper."

"Say I want this information," Sam said. "What's it going to cost me?"

"You need to leave Sydney. Give her up."

Sam shook his head. "You're dreaming. I have a child with that woman."

"But you're not in love with her."

"That's none of your goddamn business."

Rod's meticulously groomed eyebrows shot up. "Shit, are you telling me you've fallen for that manipulative little tramp?"

Sam grabbed Rod's collar. "You want another punch in the face? 'Cause I can sure arrange it."

"Ease up, ease up."

Sam let him go.

Rod rubbed his neck. "Christ. What a mess you've gotten yourself into."

"Nothing like the mess you're gonna be in if you ever say anything like that about Sydney again."

"Fine, fine." Rod rubbed his jaw. "Are you willing to give her up?"

"It depends on the information. Why don't you give me a preview, and I'll think about it?"

"Fair enough." Rod moved closer to him. "Sydney has an older brother."

"Yeah. Blake. He worked for one of my brothers-in-law for a while. But I already know that. Anything else?"

"Blake had a falling out with his parents some time ago. He left their ranch to make it on his own. He lived here for a while, working for your brother-in-law, and then got caught up in a scandal involving the mayor's daughter."

"Yeah, yeah, I know all that. The mayor went to prison for shooting Blake. The daughter miscarried. Tell me something I don't know."

"From here, Blake went to San Antonio and got into some real trouble with crime bosses in high places."

"So?"

"So I'd bet you don't know what caused the falling out in the first place. Why Blake left his parents."

"Probably because he's an asshole and they kicked him out. The guy's clearly a loser."

"That may be, but it has nothing to do with why he left. Blake wasn't kicked out. He left of his own accord."

"Why?"

Rod's lips curved into a sickening smile. "That's the information I have. Roy and Carrie Buchanan are not what they seem."

"Yes, you already said that."

"So will you leave Sydney?"

For that? For "Roy and Carrie aren't who they seem to be?" Not only no, but hell no.

"No, I will not leave Sydney. Now get the hell out of my sight."

"Speak of the devil," Rod said.

Sydney approached. The sadness in her dark eyes nearly broke Sam's heart.

"Nice race," Rod said.

"Fuck you," Sydney said.

"Get out of here," Sam said to Rod. "I have no more use for you."

"You have no idea what you're dealing with," Rod said.

"Then I'll figure it out on my own. Now go, before I kick your ass into next year."

Rod shrugged. "Don't say I didn't try."

"What's going on?" Sydney asked when Rod had left.

"He's a pain in the ass, but he did say something worthwhile."

"What's that?"

"I'm not sure yet. We need to talk to someone."

"Who?"

"Your brother."

"I haven't talked to Blake in years."

"He's here in town, isn't he?"

"I have no idea. Last I heard he was in San Antonio."

"No, he came back here. Harper and Amber know him."

"They're busy with wedding plans."

"True. But we can easily find him. He used to work for Chad. I'll give him a call."

"Okay. Whatever you think is best," Sydney said. "I'm going to call the foreman at our ranch and see if Mama and Daddy have come home yet. They're still not answering the land line. I'm going to call our neighbors, too."

"You do that. But first—" He pulled her to him for a hug. "I'm sorry about the race."

"No, *I'm* sorry. We needed that money, Sam."

"We'll make do. I have credit cards and a good job with Zach. We'll be fine."

"I have my purse money from the race the other day. It's in the safe in my room."

"Good. We won't use it unless we have to."

"I want to use it. This is all my fault. I want to help."

"That's sweet of you. All right. Let's make our phone calls, and then we'll go grab a bite to eat and figure out what to do next."

* * * *

Blake hadn't changed a bit.

He was still a good-looking and feisty cowboy, though he seemed a bit more humble. Clearly he'd been taken down a few notches over the last several years. Happiness swelled in Sydney's heart. She hadn't realized how much she'd missed him.

Sam had gotten his number from Chad, and Blake had agreed to meet them for dinner in the privacy of Sydney's hotel room. They ordered pizza, and Blake came with a six pack of Bud.

"It's good to see you, Sis," he said. "How are Mom and Dad?"

Sydney let out a sigh. "They're fine, as far as I know."

"What's that supposed to mean?"

"We'll get to that," Sam said. "Right now we have a lot of questions for you."

"Starting with why you left home," Sydney said.

Blake took a long drink of beer. "That's a story for sure. Why, though, do you want to know now? It's been a while since I've been gone. You were expecting, I believe, when I took off."

"Yes."

"What happened to the baby?"

"It's a long story. But first you need to know that the baby is Sam's."

"What? You fucked my baby sister and left her pregnant?" Blake stood.

"Stop, stop," Sydney said. "I was a willing participant, and he didn't even know I was pregnant."

"I heard Mom and Pop adopted a kid after I left. Was that...?"

"Yeah."

"I see. Well, spit out your story then, Sis. If you expect me to be honest with you, I expect to know why you're asking."

"Fair enough," she said.

After she and Sam had told the story, Blake opened another beer.

"Any more pizza?" he asked.

"We can order more."

"Nah, I'm fine. That's a heck of a story. Mom and Pop flew the coop, huh?"

"That's what we're assuming. Evidently they thought Sam would try to take Duke away from them."

"Yes, I can see where you might think that."

"What other reason would they have for leaving?"

"Probably none. Unless they thought you were about to uncover some stuff."

"Uncover what? What on Earth are you talking about?"

"Okay. I'm going to tell you why I left. Why our parents and I are no longer on speaking terms. And just so you know, I've missed you, Sis."

"I've missed you too."

"This is all great, but could you start talking please?" Sam said.

"Mom and Dad aren't who they appear to be," Blake said.

"That's just what Rod said." Sam opened a second beer. "What are you talking about?"

"Who's Rod?"

"My ex-fiancé," Sydney replied. "Evidently he did some digging on me and inadvertently found out something about Mom and Dad. He tried to get Sam to pay for the information, but he wouldn't. Rod's the one who told us that you weren't kicked out—that you left of your own accord."

"Rod's right."

"What could be so bad that you left your pregnant little sister behind?" Sam said.

"I felt bad about that," Blake said, "and I still do. But as long as you didn't know what I knew, I figured you were okay. But I can't tell you how much I've regretted leaving you there."

"Know what?" Sydney's heart lurched. "What in the world are you talking about, Blake?"

"Mom and Dad have kind of a Romeo and Juliet story," Blake said. "They were the children of feuding houses."

"What?"

"Didn't you ever think it was weird that we never knew our grandparents?"

"I guess I never thought about it."

"Both of our grandfathers are criminals, Sydney."

Sydney sat, numb, her mouth in an oval.

"Big bad criminals. Mafia."

No, couldn't be. "The Buchanans and the Ciancios? They're mob families?"

"You are as naïve as I was. I'd never heard of either family, but then we grew up in rural Nevada. We were ranch folk. We went to county schools. But yes, the Buchanans and the Ciancios are both mob families out of Chicago."

The pizza in Syd's stomach threatened to come up. "But our ranch—it's been in the family for generations."

"Nope. Dad bought the ranch."

Sydney's body felt limp. "He lied?"

"Syd, he's been lying to you for years."

"I can't believe it."

"Irish and Italian mob don't mix. But Mom and Dad fell in love. They weren't much older than the real Romeo and Juliet. Plus, Dad especially hated the mafia life. This gave him a great excuse to leave it behind."

"I wonder why their parents never came after them," Sydney said.

"Why would they? They weren't causing any trouble. They just wanted to be left alone."

"I guess that makes sense." Sydney took a drink of water. Sense? Really? None of this made any sense.

"So this trouble you got into in San Antonio?" Sam said.

"With a distant cousin on my mother's side, Paul Donetto. I figured I'd be safe, being family and all. I found out family doesn't mean jack to these people. When Michael killed Fredo in *The Godfather*, that was pretty close to reality."

Icy worry gripped Sydney's neck. "Are you still in trouble?"

"No. Donetto and I are even. I'm in no danger. I can't talk about it to you. There are things I'm not at liberty to divulge because I made promises to people. To friends."

Sam snorted. "You have friends now?"

"Yes, I do have friends, believe it or not." Blake turned to Sydney. "I'm telling you that Mom and Dad didn't kick me out. I left."

"Okay. Now tell us why," Sam said. "Just because Roy and Carrie came from criminals doesn't mean they *are* criminals. Why is this important?"

"In a perfect world, it wouldn't be. They'd have gone off together and made their own lives and left it all behind."

"Isn't that what they did?"

"They tried."

"And?" Sydney gulped.

"They couldn't cut it. The ranch was never very profitable. The best thing they did was get you and me trained in rodeo arts. We actually have some talent, though God knows where it came from. A long line of mobsters who could make a living in the rodeo, I guess, though they'll never know it."

"You're digressing," Sam said.

"Sorry." Blake opened another beer. "I never had any reason to suspect anything, and I didn't, but one day I was tooling around in Dad's office, looking for a paper clip. I pulled the flat drawer of his desk out a little too hard, I guess, and it ended up on the floor. As I was putting it away, the bottom gave way. Or should I say, the false bottom."

Sydney's ear perked up. "What?"

"A false bottom. Underneath the drawer was a small compartment about half an inch thick. And in it were some papers." He shook his head. "I shouldn't have looked, but I did. Curiosity go the best of me."

"What were they?"

"Bank accounts. In the Cayman Islands."

"So what?"

"The Cayman Islands are a place where people keep money that isn't necessarily obtained legally, Sydney," Sam said. "They have very strict bank secrecy laws and very strict penalties for unauthorized disclosure."

"Can't anyone bank there anyway? Like in Switzerland?"

"Of course, Sis, but an offshore account in the Caymans is a major red flag for someone like Dad, who basically, as far as I knew, was a rancher making a modest living."

"So you found the account. So what?"

"I found the account. What was also interesting was the amount of money in the account."

"How much? Ten or twenty thousand?"

"Try nine hundred thousand," Blake said. "Here was an account in our father's name with nearly a million dollars in it, and all this time we'd been living so frugally. Not that I minded, but sheesh, you and I would compete and turn over our purses to them. Was that fair?"

Sydney shook her head. "Doesn't seem to be. Do you know where the money came from?"

"I confronted Pop about the whole thing. He told me it was none of my goddamned business and to get the hell out if I didn't like it."

"So you left."

"Not yet. I went to Mom."

"What did she say?"

"She told me about how they'd met and fallen in love when they were still kids. How they'd run away and gotten married and had me soon thereafter. They'd wanted no part of their families' criminal activities."

"So where did the money come from?"

"It's Pop's money, from a trust fund from his mother."

"And they wouldn't use it?"

"No. He told Mom it was dirty money and he wanted no part of it."

"Then why didn't they just give it to charity or something?"

"I asked that same question. She said Pop refused to. He said they never knew when they might need it."

"Oh God." Sydney's heart fell to her tummy. "They took Duke away. They might have even left the country with all that money."

"Yes, they might have. But there was still one thing that didn't jibe. The account papers showed multiple withdrawals from the account. So if Dad refused to use the money, who made the withdrawals?"

"Did you ask Mom?"

"I did. She said I must have misread the statements. There hadn't been any withdrawals. Then she refused to discuss the matter further." Blake shook his head. "You can think what you want about me. I'm no Einstein, but for

God's sake, I can read an account statement. Money had been withdrawn."

"Are you sure it was trust fund money? Mom and Dad weren't doing anything illegal, were they?"

"I wish I knew, Sis, but I don't."

Dear God.

"I didn't have the money myself to go looking into that kind of stuff. I got myself into some trouble, as you know, and every last cent I made went to bail myself out of that. All I knew is that I wanted no part of them. They let that money sit there when we had some lean years as kids, Syd. Do you remember?"

She remembered all too well. "I'm sure they had their reasons."

"Yes, they had their reasons," Blake said, "and obviously they thought those reasons made logical sense at the time. But it burns my ass that they had this money. I wanted to go to college. So did you. Remember? We could have gone to any school we wanted. They had the money. But we didn't get to go, and someone, either Mom or Dad, had been withdrawing money from that account during those years."

"We can still go to college, Blake."

"Sure we can, if we have the money. I don't have the money right now, do you?"

Sydney rose and got another bottle of water from the mini fridge. "All I have is the twenty grand in my safe from my purse the other day. I've given everything else to Mom and Dad."

"Why, Sydney?" Blake asked. "You're of age now. You don't have to give them your money."

"I do it for Duke," Sydney said. "They adopted him and took responsibility for him. I wanted to do my part."

"We have to find them and find Duke," Sam said.

Blake rubbed his temples. "They could be anywhere, anywhere at all, if they dipped into that money."

"But the money's in the Caymans." Sydney took a sip of water. "How could they get it?"

"Online transfers, wirings, any old way. It's easy as pie to transfer money these days."

"But they didn't bring a computer, and a transfer could be traced." Sam stood and paced. "There's no way they could have— Oh my God."

"What, Sam? What?" Sydney's pulse raced.

"When was the last time you looked in your safe, Sydney?"

"Not since I put the money there. You don't think—"

But she knew exactly what Sam was thinking, and by the look on Blake's face, he was thinking the same thing.

She gulped as she keyed in the code to her safe.

Before she opened the door, she knew.

Her money was gone.

Chapter Eighteen

This is all my fault. This is all my fault.
Sydney couldn't breathe.

A noose was squeezing her neck. Her throat constricted. Sharp fingers of acid climbed up her esophagus, threatening to choke her.

"God, what should we do?"

Blake's voice. That was Blake's voice.

"She'll be okay."

Sam's voice. *Ah, the soothing timbre of Sam's voice.* Her man. Her love.

Warm hands caressed her, dulcet tones soothed her. "It will be okay, sweetheart. We'll figure this out. We'll find our son."

Sam lifted her away from the empty safe and laid her on the bed. "Get her some more water," he said to Blake.

No water. Just Sam. Only need Sam.
And Duke. Want to see Duke.

Until now, Sydney had been sure of one thing—her parents would never hurt Duke. She'd seen the fear in her mother's eyes when they thought Duke might have leukemia. It had mirrored her own.

And her father, what had he been thinking? He had started to come around where Sam was concerned. He seemed ready to work something out.

Yet they'd left.

Only one explanation made sense. Her mother had wanted to leave. Roy Buchanan loved his wife and gave her whatever she wanted if it was within his power to do so.

Carrie was the one who was scared of Sam, not Roy.

She must have talked him into leaving.

Only one other thing could have made them leave. If they thought harm could come to Duke by staying.

But in leaving, they'd taken Duke away from Sydney as well.

From Sassy.

Tears erupted in her eyes. She wanted her baby boy. Why, oh why had she given him up?

She'd taken the easy way out. She'd given him up without really giving him up. Duke got parents who loved him and a "big sister" who doted on him.

Sam was the real loser here. He hadn't had a choice in the matter.

She had to fix this. For Duke and for Sam.

They will not harm Duke, they will not harm Duke. She repeated the mantra in her mind.

"What should we do now?" Blake said to Sam.

"I don't know. We have to find Duke. I'm scared for him now. You don't think your parents would—"

"No." Blake shook his head. "They never harmed Syd or me. They were good parents. They just never told us the truth."

The apple didn't fall far from the tree. She hadn't told Sam the truth. She felt like shit.

"Sydney?" Sam caressed her shoulder. "Are you feeling better?"

Better? That was a laugh. It would be a long time before she felt anything close to better. But she nodded anyway. They had to get on with it. "I can't believe they stole my money."

"They've been stealing our money for years, Sis," Blake said, "when they had near a million dollars in the bank."

"But they were good parents. They loved us."

He nodded. "They did, I think."

"It killed them when you left."

"I'm sure it did," Blake said, "but I hope you'll excuse me if I don't feel a whole lot of remorse about that."

Sydney nodded. She'd have a hard time forgiving her parents for what they'd done. She didn't want to hold a grudge against Blake. She had her brother back, and she wanted to keep him.

"If I'd known, Syd…"

"Known what?"

Blake cleared his throat. "If I'd known you were going to let them adopt your child, I would have come back. I would have told you." He sat down on the other side of the bed, next to her. "I'm sorry."

"I'm sorry too, Blake. You were a good brother. I should have known you had a good reason for leaving."

"It wasn't good enough. It wasn't good enough to leave my pregnant sister there."

"It's okay. We've both made mistakes. Now it's time to correct them. Will you help Sam and me find Mom and Dad?"

"Sydney," Sam said, "I'm not sure he should be involved."

"Why not?" Blake asked. "They're my parents, and the little tyke is my nephew. I wasn't there for Sydney when I should have been. I want to be there for her now."

Sam nodded. "All right. If you can help in any way, we'd appreciate it."

"I'm afraid I don't have much money to offer."

"So we're all broke," Sydney said. "Where does that leave us?"

"It leaves us my credit cards," Sam said. "I've got a little bit in the bank."

"I've got a little in the bank too," Blake said, "but I'm afraid it's damn little."

"You're both wonderful," Sydney said. "I have nothing. They stole my purse money."

"It's okay," Blake said. "You didn't know they'd do that."

"I still can't believe it."

"I can. And you will someday, trust me."

Sam shook his head. "I can't believe I was such a bad judge of character. I really thought they were good people."

"So did I," Blake said, "and in a way, they are. They just grew up around criminals. I think they're good in their hearts, but look at the examples they had."

"At least they set good examples for us," Sydney said.

"I won't argue with that, for the most part," Blake said. "But once we were old enough to handle it, they should have told us the truth about their backgrounds."

Sam nodded. "I agree. If you had known, Sydney, you would never have let them adopt Duke."

"Probably not," Sydney said. "But Duke has had a good life up until now. He's a happy little boy."

"A happy little boy who is now God knows where," Blake said. "For all we know, they've cut his hair off or dyed it so no one will recognize him."

"No! Not his beautiful hair." Sydney burst into tears. "His hair is just like yours, Sam."

Sam caressed her forearm. "It'll grow back. We'll find him."

Yes. They'd find him. They had to.

But there would be a cost.

The mother and father she'd loved and adored for twenty-four years were now strangers to her.

* * * *

"Let her sleep," Sam said to Blake. "We can figure this out in the morning."

"I still can't get over them taking her money right out of her safe. How did they figure out the combination?"

Sam shook his head. "Got me. Maybe they know the numbers she uses. Hell if I know."

"They could have gotten security to open it."

"Nah. Sydney talked to security in depth when she couldn't find her parents. They would have told her. Plus, Sydney's an adult. Security can't open a safe for anyone else, not even her parents."

"Yeah, you're probably right."

"Do you have any idea where they might go first?" Sam asked.

"Nope. Maybe to the Caymans to get the money. They were smart not to try here. They know that I know about the account and that we'd try to trace it."

"So I suppose the fact that you know is going to make them harder to track."

"I'm afraid so. Sorry about that."

"Don't be. If not for you, we'd have no idea where to start. Sydney called the folks on the neighboring ranch. They said as far as they knew, your parents hadn't returned. They were going to go over and check. I don't think they've called her back yet." Sam scratched his head, thinking. "There's something that just doesn't quite seem right to me about this situation."

"What?"

"I can't believe your parents considered me that big of a threat. I mean, they're the legal parents, and Dallas McCray told me that courts will consider the best interest of the child first, before my interests or anyone else's. Duke has been living with them his whole life, and to uproot him would not be in his best interests. I love my son, and I want him, but even I can see how the court would see this."

"Yeah. So?"

"So why would they run? They don't seem the type."

"But they are the type, Sam. They ran from their families when they were young so they could be together."

"Yes, but their families are criminals. I'm not a criminal."

"But you pose a threat, just like their families did. It really makes perfect sense if you skew your reasoning just a little."

"You mean think like people who were raised by criminals."

"Exactly."

"I suppose so." Sam paced the floor. "And when you explain it that way, it does make sense. Still, it just doesn't feel right."

"Okay. Say I'm wrong. Say they didn't run. Then what could have happened?"

Sam plunked on a chair. "That's just it. I'm not sure."

"Is there anyone else who might have an interest in Duke? In my parents?"

"Only your grandparents, but they've left them alone all this time." Sam let out a huff of air. *Think, Sam. Think.*

And a light bulb lit over his head.

"There is one other person."

Chapter Nineteen

No, no, no! You can't have my son!

Sydney struggled against the arms holding her, jerking her.

She opened her eyes. Sam sat next to her, gently tugging on her.

Thank God. It had only been a nightmare.

"I'm sorry to wake you, sweetheart, but Blake and I need to talk to you."

She rubbed the sleep out of her eyes. "Okay. What about?"

"Rod Kyle."

"Rod? Why? He's old news."

"We're not so sure, Sis," Blake said. "Sam and I have been talking, and it's not completely out of the realm of reality that he might be involved in this."

"He has no interest in Duke."

"No, but he has an interest in you."

"He'll get over me. He doesn't love me. He never did."

"No, but he's used to getting what he wants, and for whatever reason, right now he wants you."

"He's not going to get me."

"I know that, but it's not only him. It's his dad. His dad wanted the marriage. You saw him talking to me after your race, remember?"

"Yeah."

"He knows about your parents. He told me they weren't who they seemed to be. He offered me information on the condition I stay away from you."

"Goddamn him!"

"Hold the phone. I told him to fuck off. But it's clear now that he knows about your parents and their links to the criminal families. Do you think it's possible he could have something to do with their disappearance?"

Sydney shook her head. "I doubt it."

"Are you sure?"

"What would he have to gain by forcing them away? Me? I don't think so. He knows about Duke, and he knows how much I love him."

"Yes, but think about it. He could be trying to make things worse for us. He already knows you've lied to me twice."

"I don't know. Maybe." Sydney rubbed her temples. Her brain was mush right about now. She didn't want to think about Rod Kyle. Or her parents, for that matter. Their relationship would never be the same. She just wanted Duke.

How could she have made such a mistake? She'd given her little boy—her most precious thing on the planet—to her parents. She'd trusted them with him.

And now this.

"I think we need to contact Kyle," Blake said. "Sam may be onto something."

"Whatever you two think is best." Sydney yawned. Her body needed sleep. Her brain needed sleep. But when she did sleep, it was fitful, fragmented with nightmares and horrific visions.

"I need to get back to the ranch," Sam said.

"I should be going too," Blake agreed. "It's late, and we have a lot to do in the morning."

"You guys aren't really thinking about leaving me alone? Please don't." Fear, though she knew it irrational, coursed through Sydney's veins.

"I need Kyle's phone number," Blake said.

"Look in my cell." Sydney tossed it to him.

Blake fiddled with the phone and entered a number into his own. He tossed it to Sam. "You want it?"

Sam nodded. "I'm going to call him tonight, on the way home."

Christ, he really is leaving me. "Please, Sam. Stay with me."

"That's my exit cue," Blake said. "I don't need to watch my little sister get it on."

Sam let out laugh that sounded forced. "Nothing's happening." He tossed his cell phone to Blake. "Put your number in mine. I'll contact you in the morning."

Blake put in the number and then tossed the phone back. "Sounds good. Take care of her, will you?"

"I will."

Good, maybe that meant he was staying.

Blake shut the door behind him.

"I'm going to go out in the hall for a few minutes and call Rod," Sam said.

"Stay here. You can put him on speaker." No, she didn't want to talk to Rod. She'd rather be hung by her toenails on a clothesline, but she had to know if he knew anything.

"Let me handle this," Sam said. "You relax. I promise I'll tell you everything."

She relented. Relaxing was out of the question, of course, but not dealing with Rod sounded like heaven on Earth at the moment.

Sam left the room.

Sydney lay on the bed. She wanted to cry. She wanted to cry for her parents whom she didn't know at all, it turned out. She wanted to cry for her big brother, who'd had a reason for leaving after all. She wanted to cry for Sam, from whom she'd kept such a terrible secret for so many years. How would he be able to trust her? And mostly she wanted to cry for her beautiful little boy whom she might never see again. Might never hear his bubbly laughter, might never hear his sweet little voice call her "Sassy."

Was she truly all cried out? Had she become numb?

Sam entered about ten minutes later. "He says he has no clue where they are. But get this, he's offered to help us locate them."

"Don't trust him," Sydney said.

"Don't worry. You want to know his price for his help?"

"What?"

"You."

Sydney's tummy tumbled. What was it with this guy? Couldn't he take no for an answer?

But she sighed. "Take his help if you need it, Sam. I will go back with him if it means Duke comes home safely."

"No, you will not. Besides, I don't believe for a minute that he knows anything. He let something slip that made me figure out why he and his father are so anxious for this marriage. Evidently his father got involved in some bad business deals with bad people. Mob, Syd. That's why Rod's father wants this marriage. He figures with you in the family, he can keep them off his back."

"Still, if he can help us find Duke—"

Sam shook his head. "I won't put you in that position. You are not a piece of property he can own. You are no one's price."

Warmth coursed through her. He was right, of course. But to hear the words and see the fierce look of possession on his face made her think he might be able to forgive her. Perhaps their love had a chance.

She yawned. "I'm so sleepy."

"I know, baby. I'm gonna get out of here and let you rest."

Her body quivered. Being alone scared the hell out of her. "Please don't. I mean, please stay with me."

"Syd..."

"I won't come on to you. I promise. You can sleep in the other bed if you want. I just can't be alone."

He nodded. "I don't relish being alone tonight ether, truth be told." He stalked toward her. "And I don't relish sleeping in the other bed."

* * * *

Sydney woke in Sam's arms. They hadn't made love, just held each other, and it had been perfect.

Or it would have been, if not for everything else going on.

Her cell phone vibrated on the nightstand and she picked it up. Her neighbors from the adjacent ranch.

"Sydney," Marcia Tucker said, "Jay went over early this morning. No one's home. The foreman hasn't heard from your parents. He hadn't checked his cell yet, so that's why he hasn't called you back."

"Thanks, Marsh. I'm sorry I bothered you."

"Not a problem. Is everything okay?"

"I'm not sure yet. I'll keep you posted."

Sydney ended the call as Sam began to stir next to her.

"That was my neighbor," she told him. "Mom and Dad aren't home, and the foreman hasn't seen them or heard from them."

"I'm not surprised." He held his arms open and she snuggled into them. "We'll find them, sweetheart. I promise."

"Where do we start? It'll be like looking for a needle in a haystack."

"I know. We need to look for clues. They must have left something behind."

"The only clue we have is the bank account in the Caymans," Sydney said.

"That'll be our starting point. Of course they can have the money wired anywhere. We need a good hacker."

"And a PI."

"Chad knows a great one. I'll give him a call and get his number. He knows his way around computers too. He got into Dusty's medical records a while back."

"What? That's illegal."

"That's my point. The guy can do pretty much anything. He's probably a good place to start. In the meantime"—he ogled her—"I need a shower. How about you?"

"I could use one," she said, "but I'm not in the mood to…you know."

"I understand. You want to go first?"

"You go ahead. I want to lie here for a few minutes."

Sam gave her a quick kiss on the cheek and traipsed to the shower.

Sydney closed her eyes as the whoosh of the water met her ears. Sam in the shower. Naked. Warm water pulsating on his amazing body, soothing his fatigued muscles. He was so beautiful. So masculine.

So perfect in every way.

She so didn't deserve him.

Her eyes misted. She was tired of crying. If only she had told Sam the truth when she was pregnant, none of this would have happened. Maybe he would have wanted her and the baby. Maybe they would have fallen in love then.

Maybe, maybe, maybe…

She needed him. Needed his body close to hers, needed the comfort of his loving touch.

She got up and went into the bathroom. "It's me," she said.

"You okay, baby?"

"Yeah, I just—" She sighed. "You want some company?"

He pulled the shower curtain back. His sandy hair was wet and matted down, his golden body covered in gleaming water. She wanted more than company. She wanted him inside her.

"If you come in here all naked and wet, I may not be able to keep my hands to myself."

"I'm sorta counting on that."

She pulled off her robe and entered. Mmm, the warm water soothed her tired body. Sam pulled her close to him for a kiss.

It was a sweet kiss, a comforting kiss, just what Sydney needed.

As they kissed, he lifted her and eased her open with his hard cock.

She was tight, and her channel offered resistance at first. Sam didn't force it. Just held her in his strong arms and eased her down gently until she took all of him.

How good it felt. How right.

He lifted her up and down, oh so gently and so slowly, his groans music to her ears.

"Yes, Sam, yes. That's so nice. So good."

He moaned in response.

His strength was more of a comfort than a turn-on at the moment. His presence a salve, a healing ointment.

She didn't plan to climax, didn't even want to, so when the explosion sneaked up on her, it was a welcome surprise.

He continued his slow movements as she spasmed against him, and when she finished, he pulled her down hard on his erect cock.

"Yeah, baby. God, you feel good."

When he went limp and slacked against the wall of the shower stall, she slid down his body until her feet hit the wet floor. She leaned against him, fearing her legs would wobble. After a few minutes, she had her footing and she pushed backward to look into his warm brown eyes.

"Thank you," she said.

He smiled, his own eyes glazed over. "It was wonderful. You are wonderful."

"We are wonderful. Together."

Disappointment crept into her when he didn't respond, but she refused to let it spoil the beauty of what had just occurred between them.

They were right together. He would see that eventually.

I will hold onto that belief. She had to. She wasn't sure she could go on if she didn't.

Sam was done washing so he left the stall, leaving Sydney to finish her shower alone.

When she finished, toweled off, and went into to bedroom, Sam was already dressed.

"Your cell rang," he said.

"It was probably Blake. Why didn't you answer it?"

"Not my place." He tossed it to her.

"Hmm, not Blake after all. In fact, not a number or an area code I recognize. Looks like whoever it was left a voicemail." She quickly dialed voicemail.

Sydney, it's Dad. Your mother's in the hospital in Branson. I'm catching a flight and bringing Duke home to you.

Chapter Twenty

"I'm sorry, Sam," Doug Cartwright, the county sheriff, said. "I can't arrest the man when he gets off the plane. He took his own son away. That's not a crime."

Sam took a sip of his coffee. He and Sydney sat with Doug at Rena's Coffee Shop. Sam had called Doug after Sydney had told him about Roy's voicemail.

Now what? Sam drummed his fingers on the table until a jolt went through him. "Hey, stealing's a crime around here."

"Sure is," Doug said.

"He took Sydney's purse money from her barrel race."

"That's a horse of a different color," Doug said. "Tell me more."

Sydney's hand touched his arm. "No, Sam."

"No, what?"

"I'm sorry. I can't have my father arrested and thrown in jail. I won't press charges for the money."

Is she serious? Smoke threatened to come right out his ears. "Are you kidding, Syd? That's all we've got."

Tears welled in Sydney's eyes. "He's my father. And he's bringing Duke back."

"Jesus H. Christ."

"He'll have an explanation, I'm sure of it. My mother's in the hospital. I don't even know what's wrong with her. I'm worried."

"Worried? After what they did?"

"They're still my parents."

"Sydney, they've been lying to you your whole life."

"I know, I know." She sniffed. "And I'm sure they thought they had a good reason."

"Fuck their good reasons. Did they have a good reason for taking your son away? For stealing your money?"

"I'm sure they thought they did."

Doug's police radio buzzed. "Excuse me," he said and headed to another table.

Sam said nothing, just stared at the beautiful woman who'd stolen his heart—and his son. How could he reconcile any of this? And now she was turning a blind eye to her father's theft. How could she? After all her parents had done? All the lies? How could she get past all that?

How could anyone get past that?

Sam shook his head slowly. How could he get past Sydney's lies?

As if reading his mind, she said, "I never actually lied to you, Sam."

Well, she had him there. She didn't lie. She just didn't tell him, first about the child five years ago, and then about her engagement to Rod Kyle.

Nope, she wasn't getting away with that one. "Omission is betrayal. Case closed." He stood.

Doug walked back toward the table. "I have to get going. Are we done here?"

Sam looked down at Sydney. "You're not pressing charges?"

Sydney shook her head.

"Then, yes, we're done here." Sam walked out the door, his own words ringing in his ears. They had so many meanings.

He wanted to look back, see Sydney's face. Would she come after him? He didn't know. His car wasn't far. His walk turned into a jog and then a sprint. He got into his car and shut the door.

He didn't look to see if Sydney was behind him. Nope, he looked only ahead.

Ahead to Denver. He'd go to the airport, wait for all the flights from Branson, and he'd have it out with Roy Buchanan once and for all.

Driving to Denver was usually relaxing, full of natural scenic beauty. He hardly ever saw another vehicle on the country roads. Normally Sam loved driving through the canyons, loved the fresh aroma of pine. Today he appreciated none of that. His nerves were on edge. He wasn't sure what he'd do to Roy when he saw him. His fists itched to pummel the bastard, but he'd have the boy with him. Sam had to think about Duke.

Duke.

His son.

His and Sydney's son.

If only things had been different. If Sydney had told him. Perhaps they could have started their life together five years ago, and today Duke would be their son. Maybe they'd have had another.

Who knows?

He'd never know.

He loved Sydney. She touched a part of him that no other woman had. Making love to her was like a beautiful symphony. It was perfection.

But they could never be together.

Love without trust was nothing.

Nothing at all.

The semitruck came out of nowhere. To avoid collision, Sam, at eighty miles per hour, drove off the two lane road into the ditch. His windshield shattered, and a loose board from the fence he hit broke through it, scattering shards of glass all over him. Barbed wire from the cattle fence poked through and gouged his face and eyes.

Searing pain shot through him.
Move. I've got to move.
Then nothing.

* * * *

"Sam! Oh my God, Sam!"

The country road was dead. Sydney had been driving to Denver to find Sam. Where else would he have gone? To the airport to find Roy and Duke.

Fear had overwhelmed her when she saw the white sedan in the ditch on the empty road halfway to the city.

It's not Sam. It can't be Sam.

But the white sedan was none other than Sam's rental car.

He was pinned in the driver's seat. A pool of shattered glass surrounded him. One of his eyes was lacerated and bleeding.

Sydney gulped back nausea. *God, he can't lose his eye.*

The rest of his face and arms were covered with lacerations from the glass and barbed wire. She checked the pulse on his neck.

Weak, but there.

Thank God. He's alive. I have to help him. I have to. Please, Sam, don't die.

Quickly she grabbed her cell phone to call 9-1-1.

No service. *Goddamnit!* She threw the phone into the road. Then, realizing she'd need the phone, she ran into the road and retrieved it.

Thank God it was still working. *Now what? Now what? Now what?*

She had to get help. Had to help Sam.

She touched his bloody cheek. "Sam? Sam, can you hear me?"

His lips twitched.

"It's Sydney, Sam."

More twitching, a soft grunt.

"Can you hear me?"

"Sssss."

Yes! He was trying to reach her. She knew it.

"Sam, listen to me. I'm going to get help. I promise you."

"Sydee," he whispered.

"I'm going to take care of you. I have to leave to get help. My cell phone doesn't have any service. But I will get you to a hospital. I promise. Hold onto that. Please."

"Ssss."

"I love you, Sam O'Donovan, and I promise you, I'm not going to let you die."

She summoned all the strength and courage within her. Leaving him felt all wrong, but she had to.

"I love you," she said again. A tear dropped onto his cheek. Oh no! It probably stung him.

She eased backward, leaving him as still as possible. Then she raced to her car and gunned the engine. She kept going on the route to Denver, checking her cell every thirty seconds for service. When she finally got one bar, she quickly typed in 9-1-1.

Damnit! The call didn't go through.

She tried again.

"9-1-1," the operator said.

"Yes, hello," she said breathlessly. "There's a man on Route 5, about twenty miles outside Bakersville in route to Denver. His car went into a ditch. He's hurt badly. He needs help now!"

"Can you describe the vehicle, ma'am?"

"A white sedan. Might be a Honda. Shit, I don't know. Just get out there!"

"Your name, ma'am?"

"Sydney Buchanan. The man's name is Sam O'Donovan. Please! Now!"

"We'll send an ambulance."

"No! Damnit, not an ambulance. You won't make it in time."

"Ma'am, we need to—"

"The helicopter. Or something better. I'd get him there myself but I can't move him!"

"Ma'am, try to calm down."

"I can't fucking calm down! I love this man! Please help him. God, he can't die. I promised him I wouldn't let him die. Please!"

A few moments elapsed. "Helicopter has been dispatched."

"Thank God. How long?"

"As soon as humanly possible, ma'am. No longer than a half hour."

Damn, too long! But she didn't have a choice. She couldn't do anything else.

She thanked the operator but had a hard time hanging up. The call was her lifeline. Sam's lifeline.

She drove back to Sam. *God, please let him still be alive.*

The sedan shone innocently in the sun, as if it didn't know it held a life in peril. Fear gripped Sydney as she ran toward the car.

Sam sat in the same position she'd left him.

She gulped back her tears. "I'm back, Sam. Help is coming."

No response.

She touched his cheek again. "Sam?"

Still no response.

She took a deep breath and pressed her shaky fingers to his pulse point.

Nothing.

Chapter Twenty-one

Oh my God!
"Sam, no! No, no, no!"
This time she couldn't hold back the tears. Why? Why hadn't there been cell service here? Why hadn't she run after him when he left Rena's? Why hadn't she told him about Duke in the first place?
Why?
Why?
Why?
She laid her head in his lap and sobbed. *Please don't leave me, Sam. Please don't leave me.*
She'd promised she wouldn't let him die.
She'd promised.
How would he ever trust her again?
But it didn't matter anymore.
The whipping blades of a helicopter whooshed through the air.
Too late.
Too fucking late.
Sydney didn't move, so lost in Sam she was.
"Get out of the way, ma'am," a voice said.
No. I'm not leaving him.
"Ma'am, move, or I'll move you."
Not leaving him.
Strong hands jerked her from her love.
"No!" she screamed.
Emergency technicians crowded around Sam.
"He's still with us," one said.
Sydney's heart leaped in her chest. Did that mean…?

"Let's get him out of here," another said.

In a few minutes, Sam was on a stretcher with an oxygen mask covering his face.

"Is…is he alive?" she asked.

"Yes, ma'am, but barely." They loaded him on the helicopter.

"Can I come with you? Please?"

"You a relative?"

"Not exactly."

"Then I'm sorry. You can't. We're taking him to Denver General. Meet us there."

Damn! Why hadn't she said yes?

She gunned it all the way to Denver. She had no idea where Denver General was, so she stopped at a convenience store for directions.

And realized she hadn't called Dusty.

She looked at her cell phone. Her fingers had stopped working. How could she call Dusty now? And tell her what? That her parents had taken Duke and Sam had gone half mad? And now he was barely holding onto life and might not make it?

She couldn't formulate the thought herself, let alone tell someone else.

She'd wait. Wait until she got to the hospital and found out how things were. There wasn't anything Dusty could do now anyway.

She found the hospital and went straight to the emergency room. "Sam O'Donovan?"

The nurse receptionist rustled some papers. "He's in surgery. You a family member?"

"Yes," she said this time. "I'm his fiancée. Sydney Buchanan." *Would that work?* "Can you tell me how he is?"

"I'm sorry, ma'am. I don't know anything. Please have a seat and I'll find you when I have any information."

Sydney sat down in an empty chair. A few chairs down, a young woman held a crying infant. On her other side, an elderly man stared into space. Was he wondering if he should call someone too?

She couldn't put it off any longer. She had to call Dusty.

"Hi, Sydney," Dusty said.

Sydney cleared her throat. "Hi, Dusty. I'm not sure how to tell you this. I'm at Denver General with Sam. He was in a car accident."

"Oh my God! Is he okay?"

"He's in surgery right now. I won't lie to you. It looks pretty bad."

"Oh my God. I'll come right over."

"I don't know how long he'll be in surgery."

"It's okay. I have to be there. He was always there for me."

"Whatever you think is best," Sydney said, though she didn't want company. She wanted to sit alone and pray for Sam.

Sam had to make it.

He had to.

I promise I'll leave him. I won't put him through any more torment. If you spare him, I'll let him go. Clearly I'm not what he needs. I've caused him only pain. But he's innocent in all of this. None of this is his fault. Please let him have his life, and I'll leave. I promise.

Tears fell onto her blouse and she wiped her nose. So she'd live without him. She could do it. It couldn't be that hard to live when your heart was with someone else. She owed it to him. And she'd do it.

The waiting dragged. She leafed through magazine after magazine, not even glancing at the pages.

In an hour, Dusty arrived and gave her a hug. Luckily, after she described what had happened, Dusty wasn't in a talkative mood either. They sat in silence.

And waited.

Sydney lost track of time. Five hours later—six? seven?—a surgeon appeared.

"Miss Buchanan?"

"Yes, that's me." Sydney stood.

"Mr. O'Donovan is in recovery. He's going to make it."

Sydney threw her arms around Dusty. "Oh, thank God! How is he?"

"He had some internal bleeding that we were able to stop. That was the major concern. After that we turned to his eye."

"Oh God," Sydney said.

"Luckily the optic nerve was not severed, but the bleeding was causing quick damage. If we had been even ten minutes later, he would have lost his vision in the right eye."

"Thank God you called when you did, Sydney," Dusty said. "You really came through for him."

Sydney's body froze. She couldn't move, couldn't speak.

"Is there anything else, Doctor?" Dusty asked. "I'm his sister."

"Multiple lacerations on his face and neck, but only a few of them required stitches. All in all, he was very lucky."

"Thank God," Dusty said.

"Do either of you know what happened? How he ended up in that ditch?"

Dusty shook her head. "Sydney found him."

Sydney tried to speak, but her vocal cords didn't cooperate. She cleared her throat. "I don't know. I found him en route to Denver."

"It's lucky you were on that road when you were," the doctor said.

She nodded. She couldn't speak past the lump in her throat.

"You saved his life."

"Yes, you did," Dusty agreed. "Thank you so much."

Sydney swallowed. She couldn't accept their thanks, their accolades. Their words hung in the air around her, jeering at her.

For the truth of the matter was, had she told Sam the truth about Duke in the first place, he would not have been on that road to Denver, driving to the airport to find her father.

She had been the catalyst for this whole situation. There was no way around it.

It was all her fault.

* * * *

Twenty-four hours later, Sam was moved out of ICU. He was still heavily sedated. After sitting with him for several hours, Sydney realized she had to contact her father and find out what was going on with her mother and with Duke.

Her cell phone had long since died, and she hadn't been back to her hotel room to charge it. How to get in touch with her father? She could use a hospital phone, of course, but her father's cell phone number had been disconnected. She tried the hotel.

Yes, Mr. Buchanan was registered, but he was not answering at this time. Sydney was bewildered. After all, her parents had prepaid and hadn't bothered checking out, so the clerk on duty could have been referring to their previous reservation. Probably not, though, since security had been notified. Sydney vowed to be optimistic. Roy and Duke had returned to the hotel. They were no doubt wondering where *she* was.

After checking with the reception desk in the waiting area, she found a recharger not in use that fit her phone. Thank goodness. In an hour or so she'd be able to make the calls and find out what was going on.

In the meantime she sat with Sam, holding his hand, hoping her presence soothed him. She couldn't stay with him long-term, but for now, she needed to be with him. Needed to see him through this horrible situation she had caused.

When he was okay again, she would leave.

He was still unresponsive when she left to get her cell phone.

Yes! Two calls had come in from her father. After listening to the voicemails, she learned he had returned to the hotel and he and Duke were in a different room. He left a new cell phone number. Quickly she dialed.

"Sydney," Roy Buchanan said, "where have you been?"

"I'll get to that," she said, "but first, I think it's you who owe me the explanations."

Her father's sigh whooshed into her ear. "Yes, I suppose you're right about that. Where do I start?"

"How about stealing my purse money and taking Duke away?"

"Your purse money? What are you talking about?"

"Did you or did you not steal my twenty grand out of the safe in my room?"

"Sydney, I didn't. I swear to God."

"Then Mom did."

"How could she...? Oh." His voice clouded. "She did leave for a few minutes before we left the hotel. Did she have access to your room?"

"Of course. I gave her a key."

"Oh no."

"So what's going on? Where is she? You're saying you didn't take my money?"

"I did not take your money, Sydney. But why didn't you put it in the safe?"

"I did."

"Then how...? What was your combination?"

"Duke's birthday."

Roy was silent for a moment. Then, "Easy for your mother to guess. She's ill, Sydney. If I wasn't sure before, I sure as hell am now, knowing she stole her daughter's money."

"What happened, Dad? Why did you leave?"

"Your mother was scared that Sam would take us to court and drag Duke through a big mess. I tried to tell her Sam was a nice man, that we'd work something out."

"Sam had decided to talk to you about that, Dad. He also wants what's best for Duke. But honestly, I don't know what he'll do now. There are other circumstances as well. He was—"

"Sydney," Roy interrupted, "please let me explain about Duke and your mother. I need you to know what's going on. Then you can tell me what's going on at your end."

"All right. Go ahead."

"As I said, your mother was scared about Sam trying to take Duke. She insisted we run. She was adamant. I figured I'd go along with it and head for home. No harm done, right?"

"Well, not exactly."

"Yeah, I know what you mean. After we got on the road, she canceled our cell phones and started to talk about... I don't know how to tell you this."

"Tell me what?"

"About our families, your mother's and mine."

"Don't worry about it. I've talked to Blake. I know everything."

Silence again. Then, "How is your brother?"

"He's had some rough times, but he's doing okay now from what I can tell. He was very willing to help Sam and me find you."

"I'm sure he was. Anyway, if he told you about your mother and me being children of rival crime families in Chicago, he was telling the truth."

"Yes, that's what he told us."

Her father's sigh cut into her ear. "I'm sure you have a lot of questions about that, and I promise I will take the time to tell you everything you want to know, but right now, let me get back to your mother.

"We were taking turns driving. When it was her turn I dozed off for several hours. When I woke up, she had changed our route. She said we were going to Florida to get the money from our Cayman Island account. I assume Blake told you about that?"

"He did."

"Okay. I can only imagine what you must think of us."

"Please, Dad, just go on."

"All these years, I have refused to touch that dirty money. And now, all of a sudden, she wants to get it. She admitted she'd been withdrawing money from the account for years for one reason or another. She also admitted she'd been in contact with her father and taken additional money from him. I was shocked. She knew how I felt about that money.

"She said we were taking Duke out of the country where no one could find us. I told her she was being paranoid, that we'd work it out, but she was determined. Still, I thought she was just stressed out. Until—"

"Until what?"

"She said she was going to call her father and have him take care of Sam."

"Take care of what?"

"That's mob speak. 'Take care of' means have someone killed."

Sydney's heart nearly stopped. "My mother wants to kill Sam?"

"No." Roy cleared his throat. "What I mean is, she's no longer in her right mind."

"Oh my." Sydney didn't know what else to say.

"We were near Branson, so I drove to the nearest hospital and had her committed. After only a few minutes of arguing, she relented. So at least part of her knew it was for the best."

"And you left her in Branson?"

"Not for long. I'm going back. We're going to find the best possible treatment for her. But for now, I need you to take care of Duke. I can't be the single parent to him that he deserves and take care of your mother at the same time. Can you do this for me? For your mother? Can you take care of your son for us?"

Your son. Her father had referred to Duke as *her* son, not his own.

But right now, she had to take care of Sam. "Of course I'll take care of Duke. But I can't take him for a day or two, or maybe more. I have to take care of Sam right now. He's been in a bad car accident."

"What? Oh my God. Is he all right?"

"Yes, he'll be all right." She explained what had happened. "He's lucky he didn't lose the vision in his right eye."

"It sounds like that's because of you."

She sighed. "Maybe. But this whole thing is because of me. If I'd told him about Duke in the first place, none of this would have happened. He and I might be living happily together. Now I can never be with him."

"Why not?"

"Don't you see? I've caused all this. All his pain is because of me."

"But you saved his life."

"If I hadn't kept Duke from him in the first place, he wouldn't have been rushing to the airport to find you. He wouldn't have been in the accident."

"Sydney—" Her father's voice was stern. "This is not your fault. What if I had told your mother 'no' when she wanted to leave? I wanted to, but I didn't. If I had, Sam would also not be in this situation. And neither would you. And neither would Duke. Don't talk to me about guilt. I'm harboring a ton of it. What do you say we both let it go?"

A tear fell from her eye and rolled down her cheek. "I can't."

"Sydney, you're my daughter and I love you. Please don't let the past dictate the future. We've all made mistakes, but we need to live as things are today. Would I rather your mother not be in the hospital? Of course. But there she will get the help she needs. She is not well, and I'm afraid she hasn't been for some time. I should have seen it.

"Would I rather keep Duke with me? Absolutely. I love that child. He is my son. But I can't give him the life he deserves while I'm trying to take care of his mother.

Lucky for me, my daughter, who I know loves him as much as I do, is available to see his life isn't disrupted too much."

"Not disrupted? Don't you think he'll miss you two?"

"Of course he will, but he'll be home with his big sister who adores him and can care for him as well as anyone. He won't be with his distracted father who's trying to do right by him and his mother at the same time."

Sydney sniffed. "I'll just get attached, and when Mom's better, she'll want him back."

"We'll deal with that when the time comes."

"I suppose so. I just—"

"Miss Buchanan?" a nurse interrupted.

"Excuse me, Dad." She turned to the nurse. "Yes?"

"Mr. O'Donovan is awake. He's asking for you."

Chapter Twenty-two

"I hear I have you to thank," Sam choked out.

Sydney spoke through tears. "Thank God you're okay. I'm so sorry for all of this, Sam. This is all my fault."

"You promised me you wouldn't let me die."

"You heard that?"

"I heard you. I knew you were there. I wanted to tell you so much, but I couldn't."

"I know. How are you? Are you in much pain?"

"I can't see out of my right eye."

Sydney smiled. "There's a patch on it."

His lips twitched. "Oh."

"But you didn't lose your sight, Sam. You were really lucky."

"Lucky because you got help in time. Like you promised. Thank you."

"Please, don't thank me."

"I—" He choked, and his words came out in a gurgle.

Sydney touched his parched lips with her fingers. "Don't try to talk anymore. Just rest."

"Will you stay?"

"Of course."

Sam dozed off again. Sydney booked a room at a nearby hotel and called her father with the information.

"What have you told Duke about Mom?" she asked.

"Just that she's sick and has to be at the hospital for a while. He misses her, but he's doing okay. The virus is completely out of his system now and he's eating like a horse."

Sydney smiled. "I'm glad to hear it. Would you…would you consider bringing him to Denver to see Sam? I know it would mean a lot to him."

"Absolutely. There's no reason for us to stay in Bakersville any longer. The rodeo's nearly over."

"Great. You can stay in my room. I have two queen beds."

"We'll be there as soon as we can."

She hung up and called Dusty.

"Should I come up?" Dusty asked.

"No, he's going to be fine. I know you can't miss Harper and Amber's wedding tomorrow."

"I'm sure they would understand."

"Of course they would, but there's no reason for you not to be there. Harper is your sister-in-law's brother. You should be there."

"All right," Dusty relented. "Just take good care of him, okay?"

"Absolutely."

She'd take the best care possible of him.

Before she left.

* * * *

"Well, hello there," Sydney said to Duke. "I've missed you."

"I missed you too, Sassy." The little boy gave her a big hug.

"I hear you and Daddy had quite an adventure."

"Yes. Mama's sick."

"I know. But she'll be better soon."

"And Sam is sick too?"

"Yes, he is. But seeing you will make him feel a lot better."

"Daddy said he had a accident in the car."

"Yes, he was hurt pretty bad. But the doctors fixed him right up."

"Will the doctors fix up Mama too?"

Sydney melted. Duke's big brown eyes shone with love and trust. "Yes, Duke. The doctors will fix Mama." She hoped she wasn't lying to the little boy. "Let's go say hi to Sam, okay?"

A few days had made a big difference in Sam. The lacerations on his face looked much better, though he still wore the eye patch. The doctors said he'd be able to leave in a few more days. He finally felt he looked okay enough to let the little boy visit.

"Look who came to visit," Sydney said, holding Duke's hand as they entered Sam's room.

Sam and Sydney had asked that any machines, other than his IV, be removed before Duke came. The nurses had smiled and said Sam no longer required the other machines, he was doing so well. Now he lay in bed, his lips curved into a smile at the sight of Duke.

"How are you doing, buddy?"

"Fine. I'm sorry you got hurt."

"That's nice of you, but I'm going to be fine."

"Good, I'm glad. My mommy's in the hospital too."

"Yes, I heard. I'm sorry about that, but they're taking really good care of her."

"Yeah, that's what Daddy says."

Sam paused for a moment. "Daddy's right."

Sydney knew immediately the reason for the pause. It was hard for Sam to say "daddy." He thought of himself as Duke's daddy.

They'd agreed Duke wouldn't stay long. They didn't want him to get upset at the sight of Sam.

"We should get going," Sydney said.

"Thanks for coming to see me," Sam said.

"You're welcome. We'll come back soon, won't we, Duke?"

"Sure. We'll come back soon." Duke smiled.

Sydney relinquished Duke into her father's care and went back to Sam.

"Thanks for bringing him," Sam said.

"No need to thank me."

"That's not true. I need to thank you for so many things."

The long fingers of guilt threatened to choke her. "No, you don't."

"Sydney, please. Let me do this."

She sighed and looked around the hospital room. So sterile. So empty. Thank goodness Sam would be leaving soon. He'd have to wear the eye patch for a few weeks, but other than that, he'd get along fine.

"Okay, Sam. Say what you need to say."

"Look at me."

She turned.

His expression glowed with seriousness.

"I love you."

She closed her eyes for a moment. A pang of remorse shot through her. She loved him too, but it didn't matter. She was leaving. She'd made up her mind.

"I love you too."

"Sydney, I'd be dead if it weren't for you."

"I did what anyone would have done."

"You promised you wouldn't let me die, and you didn't. And you promised you wouldn't leave me here alone, and you didn't."

"Sam, I—"

"Please, let me finish. I love you. Yes, I still wish you'd told me about Duke from the beginning, but I forgive you, Sydney. I forgive you."

Tears welled in her eyes. She didn't deserve his forgiveness. She didn't deserve him.

"And I trust you, Sydney. I trust you with my life."

"Sam, please."

"I want to be a part of your life. I want to be a part of Duke's life. I won't disrupt his life. I'll settle for being his brother-in-law."

Sydney dropped her jaw open. "What?"

"I want to marry you, Sydney." He squeezed her hand. "You are what I've been waiting for all these years. Please. Marry me. You'll make me the happiest man in the world."

Her heart nearly leaped out of her chest. "Sam, are you sure? After all I've done? The lies?"

"I've never been more sure of anything. I love you."

Joy bubbled through her. Could it be true? "Sam, I love you too. I love you so much."

"Then you'll marry me?"

Her mouth trembled as she brushed her lips over his. "Yes, Sam. I'll marry you."

Epilogue

"We catched seven Rocky Mountain trouts!" Duke beamed as he held up the fish.

"I catched one and Duke catched two," Sean announced. "Daddy and Uncle Sam catched the rest."

"They're both born fishermen," Zach said. "It's enough for dinner, if you ladies are up to it. The boys can share one, and that leaves one each for you two and two each for Sam and me."

"Ugh, trout?" Sydney rubbed her belly. At ten weeks into her pregnancy, morning sickness—rather, all-day sickness—was at its peak. The thought of putting anything fishy in her mouth made her want to retch.

"Make that two for you then, darlin'," Zach said to Dusty. "Saltines for Sydney, I assume?"

"Sassy eats so many crackers," Duke said. "That's all she eats!"

"You'd rather have crackers than trout?" Sean shook his head.

"Leave Auntie Sydney alone," Dusty said. "When there's a baby inside you, sometimes certain foods make you feel icky."

"Did you feel like that when I was inside you?" Sean asked.

"Goodness yes," Dusty said. "I couldn't eat beef. It darn near killed your daddy that I wouldn't eat his genuine McCray beef."

They all erupted in laughter.

Duke had been living with Sam and Sydney on the McCray ranch for nearly a year. He missed his parents, but

Roy had taken Duke to the hospital twice to visit with Carrie. Sam and Sydney had gone along. Carrie was improving, but it was slow going.

Roy had sold the ranch in Carson City for a decent price and now lived on the McCray ranch as a ranch hand. It was the best way to stay near Duke and be able to see to Carrie's needs. None of them wanted to disrupt the little boy's life.

"Will your mother be able to come home soon?" Dusty asked after the boys had run outside to play.

"Yes, Daddy thinks so. She's chosen to stay longer and get further treatment. She feels terrible about everything and wants to make sure she won't relapse."

"What's going to happen with Duke?"

"We've talked about it. Sam and I are willing to do whatever's best for him. He can stay here with us, or he can move in with Mom and Daddy. Either way, we'll see him often. He's right here on the same ranch."

"Will you ever tell him the truth?"

"Someday, when he's older."

After a dinner of saltines, eaten with a clothespin on her nose to avoid the fish stench, Sydney tucked Duke into bed and joined Sam in their own bedroom.

"I'm beat," Sam said. "A day with those two critters can take it out of a man."

"Hmm, that's too bad." Sydney smiled. "Those crackers settled my tummy, and now I'm feeling"—she reached over for his erection—"a little frisky."

"Oh yeah?" He rolled toward her. "I think I can accommodate you."

Sydney turned, reached into her nightstand drawer, and pulled out two bandanas.

Sam's eyebrows shot up. "I didn't think you wanted to try that again."

She winked at him. "That's what you get for thinking."

Dear Reader,

Thank you for reading *Cowboy Passion*. If you want to find out about my current backlist and future releases, please like my Facebook page:

https://www.facebook.com/HelenHardt.

I often do giveaways, as well.

If you enjoyed the story, please take the time to leave a review on a site like Amazon or Goodreads. I welcome all feedback.

I wish you all the best!

Helen

Helen Hardt's Bakersville Saga

Cowboy Heat—Volume One

Ivy League Cowboy—the story of Zach and Dusty
A Cowboy and a Gentleman—the story of Dallas and Annie

Cowboy Lust—Volume Two

Rodeo Queen—the story of Chad and Catie
Taming Angelina—the story of Rafe and Angie

Cowboy Passion—Volume Three

Treasuring Amber—the story of Harper and Amber
Trusting Sydney—the story of Sam and Sydney

Also by Helen Hardt:

Daughters of the Prairie:
The Outlaw's Angel
Lessons of the Heart
Song of the Raven

Sex and the Season:
Lily and the Duke
Rose in Bloom
Lady Alexandra's Lover (coming soon)
Sophie's Voice (coming soon)

Snow Creek Series:
Craving (coming soon)
Obsession (coming soon)
Possession (coming soon)

Non-Fiction:
got style?

Discussion Questions

1. The theme of a story is its central idea or ideas. To put it simply, it's what the story *means*. How would you characterize the theme of *Treasuring Amber?* Of *Trusting Sydney?*

2. Amber clearly had a rough childhood. What do you think her daily life was like as a child living with Karen? After Karen threw her out when she was sixteen? Did she make the right choice to become an exotic dancer for the money? Obviously, not, but without hindsight, what would you have done in her shoes? Consider her self-esteem. How might her life had differed if her father had known about her?

3. Harper and Amber seem an unlikely couple at first, but they fall in love. What kind of marriage do you think they will have?

4. Discuss the character of Thunder Morgan. What do you see in his future? Will he marry? Why or why not? Do you see a future for him and Karen?

5. What do you think of Sydney's choice not to tell Sam about Duke? Though he forgives her in the end, do you see this affecting their relationship in the future? How? When do you think would be the best time for them to tell Duke the truth?

6. What kind of childhood you think Sydney and Blake had growing up with Roy and Carrie? Contrast that with the childhoods Roy and Carrie might have had growing up in mafia families.

7. What type of mental illness do you think Carrie suffers from? Do you see her recovering? Will she have a part in Duke's life? Why or why not?

8. We first met Sam in *Ivy League Cowboy*, as Dusty's big brother. What kind of a man is he? What are his strengths and weaknesses? Will he be a good husband and father? Why or why not?

9. What do you think of Sydney's decision not to file charges against her parents for theft? What would you have done?

10. Of all the characters in the Bakersville saga, whose story would you like to see next? Why?

Acknowledgements

Cowboy Passion is the third installment in my Bakersville Saga, which consists of six (so far) category length romance novels. The third two in the series—*Treasuring Amber* and *Trusting Sydney*—make up *Cowboy Passion*.

Special shout outs and hugs to Jeanne De Vita for your friendship and for being my sounding board for this project, to Kelly Shorten for the beautiful cover art, to Celina Summers for editing the original versions, and to Michele Hamner Moore for your eagle eyes during line editing.

And to all my readers—thank you!

About the Author

Helen Hardt is an attorney and stay-at-home mom turned award-winning romance author and freelance fiction editor. She writes contemporary, historical, paranormal, and erotic romance from her home in Colorado. She's a mother, a black belt in Taekwondo, a grammar geek, and a lover of Ben and Jerry's ice cream. Visit Helen at:

http://www.helenhardt.com
http://www.helenhardt.blogspot.com

Made in the USA
Charleston, SC
15 October 2015